If Memory Serves

Other Books by Vanessa Davis Griggs

Blessed Trinity

Strongholds

Practicing What You Preach

Goodness and Mercy

Published by Dafina Books

If Memory Serves

VANESSA
DAVIS GRIGGS

Kensington Publishing Corp.
http://www.kensingtonbooks.com

DAFINA BOOKS are published by

Kensington Publishing Corp.
119 West 40th Street
New York, NY 10018

ISBN-13: 978-0-7582-5296-8
ISBN-10: 0-7582-5296-X

First trade paperback printing: October 2008
First mass market printing: May 2010

10 9 8 7 6 5 4 3 2 1

Printed in the United States of America

Dedicated to my children Jeffery, Jeremy, and
Johnathan Griggs;
in loving memory of Joshua and Jarrod Andre Griggs
(one of whom I was able to hold in my arms for a few
precious minutes;
both of whom I will forever hold in my heart);
and all who know and understand what
loving someone is truly all about.

Acknowledgments

I can never begin this process without first acknowledging and giving thanks to my Heavenly Father who loves me and shows it with every breath I take. To my mother Mrs. Josephine Davis and my father Mr. James Davis Jr.: I am more than blessed and greatly honored to call you *my* parents.

I truly have a remarkable family. To my husband Jeffery; children Jeffery Marques, Jeremy Dewayne, and Jonathan LeDavis Griggs; grandchildren Asia and Ashlynn; sisters Danette Dial and Arlinda Davis, sister-in-law Cameron; brothers Terence Davis and Emmanuel Davis: I love and thank you all for blessing my life in so many ways. We've been together through thick and thin, and we're still standing.

To my cousin Mark Davis and a host of fantastic friends (too many to name) but especially Rosetta Moore, Vanessa L. Rice, Zelda Oliver-Miles, Linda H. Jones, Bonita Chaney, and Ella Wells: I thank you for all that you bring to my life. To Stephanie Perry Moore: It's been such a pleasure having you as a fellow author as well as being a special friend. I know God has some awesome things in store for you. I'll always be in your corner, enthusiastically cheering you on. To the members of The WBRT Society book club, GAME book club, and the many other book clubs that choose or have chosen my book(s): Thank you so much. To the members of Delta Sigma Theta Sorority Birmingham Alumnae Chapter: You do so much for so many and I humbly appreciate the way you've embraced, supported, encouraged, and shown me so much love.

To my editor Rakia A. Clark: Thank you for who you are and all that you do. I appreciate you. Thanks also to the wonderful staff of Kensington/Dafina for the awesome work all of you do from my gorgeous covers to the distribution of all our books.

To those of you who are choosing to read *If Memory Serves*, I thank you so much! I don't now and never will take you for granted. When I write, please know that I'm thinking of you, desiring with every stroke of the keyboard and my pen that I give you my very best. I consider this a deal of sorts that you and I have entered into together, and I want more than anything to always uphold my end of this deal. With this book (as you take this reading journey along with me), I ask that you resist any and all urges to turn to the end of the book. And yes, there will be times when I believe it might be difficult and you may feel you can't take knowing (or not knowing) any longer. I only ask that you trust me and trust this experience I've worked so hard to bring to you.

I love hearing from you. I'd also like to thank you for helping me spread the word about my books. May you walk in God's exceedingly, abundantly, above-all-you-can-ever-ask-or-think blessings!

Vanessa Davis Griggs
www.VanessaDavisGriggs.com

Chapter 1

For I was hungry, and ye gave Me meat: I was thirsty, and ye gave Me drink: I was a stranger, and ye took Me in. . . .

Matthew 25:35

Memory, who was going by the name of Elaine Robertson and had asked Johnnie Mae Landris to just call her Elaine instead of Ms. Robertson, sat on the bed in the room Johnnie Mae said would be hers for as long as she stayed. Certain that she was alone, she picked up the phone and dialed. "Hi, Sam," she said with a grin. "It's me—Memory."

Johnnie Mae had just finished showing her two bedrooms, in both of which the beds were low and close to the floor. The first room had a queen-size sleigh bed with stone-top nightstands set on each side.

"What's the name of this collection?" Memory had asked, attempting to show she was *somewhat* knowledgeable about life's finer things. Fine furniture always had a name.

"The Amherst collection—it's English inspired," Johnnie Mae said with a smile. No one had ever asked her that before. She was impressed Memory had, but even more impressed that she'd recalled the collection's name to be able to answer her.

"They certainly crafted some exquisite pieces," Memory said, leisurely strolling around the room, touching and tracing various intricate details lightly with her fingers for an up-close-and-personal feel. Fully aware Johnnie Mae had another bedroom she wanted her to see, Memory wasn't trying to be snooty or picky. She'd just never been this close to a setup so nice and was determined she would experience this on her own terms without rushing or glossing over it in order to appear even more refined.

Memory touched the antique brass hardware, felt the smoothness of the cherry-finished wood . . . the coolness of the stone-topped nightstand. She marveled at the overlaid carving on the bed's head- and footboard and the doors of the large, three-drawer armoire. Yet nothing she'd seen rivaled the swirling, hand-carved pilasters that topped the nine-drawer dresser's mirror and the armoire that stood catercornered between two walls.

Easing down gingerly on the cushioned bench at the foot of the bed, she looked around again, taking a visual inventory of the entire room. "This is lovely," she said. "So lovely. It's warm and engaging. Feels like . . . home." She nodded. "Yes, like home."

"Thank you," Johnnie Mae said as she quickly glanced around the guest bedroom. It was a place she rarely came into and—with the exception of having to periodically dust the furniture and hardwood floor covered largely by a maroon Oriental rug—really had no reason to. "Before you get *too* comfortable," she said, "don't forget there's one other bedroom I want you to see. Then you can decide which of the two you prefer."

Memory stood up. "This one's fine. In fact, it's *better* than fine. I keep trying to tell you that I'm not sure I'll even be here long enough to need a place to lay my head."

"Look, Elaine, you can at least stay the night," Johnnie Mae said. She hadn't had a chance to call Sarah Fleming yet, so she wasn't sure what the plan for Memory would be. She just knew she needed to keep her close until she could relay her suspicions to Sarah and find out how she wanted to proceed from here.

Memory strolled toward the doorway and looked back at the room as she and Johnnie Mae stepped into the all-white carpeted hallway. They walked two doors down, passing the opened door of a large bathroom accentuated with gold fixtures and faucets.

Johnnie Mae opened the door to another bedroom. This was the room her mother usually stayed in whenever she came over (which had only been a total of three times since they'd moved into their newly built house back in August 2004).

"Oh my goodness," Memory said, gasping aloud as she scanned the bedroom with one quick swoop. "This is breathtaking . . . absolutely breathtaking! Whose collection is *this*? Not that I'd ever be able to afford anything this grand, but, still, I can certainly brag about having seen it."

"It's called the Royale collection," Johnnie Mae said, then leaned over and whispered, "and it's really not *that* expensive." She flashed Memory a warm smile.

Memory began to walk around the room. "It has a sort of architectural feel to it."

Johnnie Mae was slightly taken aback. "That's exactly what the woman at the furniture store said when we were looking at it." Each piece had elements found in medallions, crown moldings, and various ceiling tiles (often used throughout Europe) embedded in it. "You're really quite good at this," Johnnie Mae said, again impressed.

Memory noted the low poster bed with its smoky cherry tone. She sat down on the mattress, bounced on it, then stood up—just to see how easy it would be to get in and out of it. That was one thing, at almost seventy, she and people her age cared more about these days: whether they could get in and out of bed without having to climb up or slide down. This bed was perfect, as was the one in the other room. She walked toward the dresser that proudly boasted twelve drawers: three small ones across the top, nine large dovetailed ones below. Her attention darted from the dresser to the armoire to yet another piece of furniture in the room that was too large to be a nightstand yet too small to be any type of dresser.

"What's this called?" Memory asked as she glided her worn, wrinkled fingers across the furniture's gold-painted shells, leaf moldings, and scrolls while noting how the details on it were identical to the other pieces in the collection.

"Oh, this? It's called a demilune. It has shelves inside," Johnnie Mae said, opening its door to show Memory the three shelves now filled with various books.

"A demilune?" she repeated with a look that indicated more information was needed.

"Yes, demilune—for the crescent or half-moon shape of the furniture's top."

"Oh," Memory said, tapping its top with her fingers. She walked back to the dresser, fascinated by how much the design resembled the cherrywood tiles she'd seen on the ceilings of expensive homes in a magazine she'd thumbed through just the other day. The medallions on it—as well as the ones on the armoire, mirror, and dresser—favored floral rosettes. The furniture was visibly solid. A baby blue chaise longue in front of a white-mantelled fireplace seemed to commandeer attention to the large sitting area.

"We can put my things in here," Memory said, deciding on the Royale room. "But again, I want to make it perfectly clear that I don't wish to impose on you or your family. Of all the things I intended today, believe me, this was *not* one of them."

Johnnie Mae nodded. "Oh, I know. But as I've told you already, you won't be imposing. You can clearly see for yourself, we have more than enough room here."

Memory smiled. "I do thank you for this time to, at least, regroup. I still need to decide where I should go and what I should do next." Memory looked at the French-style telephone on the nightstand. "Would it be okay if I use your phone? I have a calling card, so the long-distance charges won't be charged back to you."

"Of course it's okay. Please make yourself at home. And we have unlimited long distance, so save your calling-card minutes for another time. Feel free to talk as long as you need, to whomever you need." Johnnie Mae headed toward the door. She stopped and turned around. "Can I get you anything? Something to eat or drink, maybe?"

"No, thank you. I'm good for now. Perhaps after I'm finished here, though."

"As soon as Pastor Landris gets home, I'll have him bring up your luggage."

"Oh, I can get them," Memory said as she eased down onto the bed. "With four suitcases, it'll take a few trips, but I'm used to it. I've been dragging those bags around for a while. But I really don't see a reason to bring them up, especially when we're just going to end up having to take them right back to the car, most likely, later tonight."

"Nonsense," Johnnie Mae said. "Pastor Landris will get them. And whether you stay a few hours, a night, or a week, I'm sure there are things in your suitcase you need."

"*Whether* I stay or for how *long* . . . Well, we'll just have to see about that. But please know that I appreciate you." She looked around the room once more. "Truly, I do."

"Again, feel free to call as many people as you need to and talk for as long as you like. When you're finished, you can come back downstairs to the den. Now, there's a private bathroom right there," Johnnie Mae said, pointing to a closed door.

"I was thinking how I might need a map just to find my way around this place."

Johnnie Mae smiled. "You'll be fine. I'll see you downstairs. I'm going to close the door"—she grabbed the door handle—"so you can have your privacy." She stepped out, shut the door quietly, leaned against it, then released a long, slow sigh.

Johnnie Mae couldn't help but think this might be a good time to call Sarah. Only she wasn't sure how much time she'd have before Memory came looking for her. She decided it was best to just wait for Landris to come home. That way, he could keep Memory occupied while she took the time needed to explain everything that was going on to Sarah and whomever else she might have to. Almost two weeks shy of being seven months pregnant, Johnnie Mae waddled slightly as she walked down the winding staircase.

Memory picked up the phone. She'd been quietly listening to make sure Johnnie Mae had indeed gone back downstairs. Johnnie Mae had told her it was okay to use their long-distance service, but Memory figured that would likely leave some type of paper trail. She pulled her calling card out from the purse she'd kept securely underneath her arm, pressed the toll-free number to connect her, keyed in her calling-card number, then the number of the person she was dialing, and waited patiently as it began to ring.

"Hi, Sam," she said with a grin when the familiar voice answered the phone. "It's me—Memory."

"Well, it's about time I finally hear from you," a deep, scratchy voice replied. "I've been worried sick about you. What's going on? Where are you? Are you all right?"

"Everything's fine and going according to plan." Memory glanced around the room. "Well, truthfully, it's going *better* than planned. Would you believe I'm at Pastor and Mrs. Landris's house? That's if it's proper to call a mansion a house."

"You're kidding," Sam said.

"Nope. And get this. I had my choice of two of the most gorgeous bedrooms I've ever laid eyes on. Of course, you know me. I ended up going with the Royale room. It's a gorgeous blue. Johnnie Mae says I can stay for as long as I want. Can you believe this?"

"You're lying, Memory. Stop lying."

Memory lightly brushed her hand over the baby blue, jacquard satin comforter (half of the bed was covered up with baby blue and dark blue shams as well as geometrically shaped designer pillows). "You know I wouldn't lie about something like this. I didn't plan for it to work out this way, but you know what they say about God."

"Memory, now, I done told you—don't be playing with God or His name."

"I ain't playing. I'm just telling it like it is. God really *does* work in mysterious ways. Don't forget, you were the one who reminded me that I'd visited Pastor Landris's church back in Georgia when I stayed with my daughter and granddaughter that time," Memory said. "That *had* to be God. You know how it is when you think you know someone from somewhere but you can't recall when or where it was or whether it's just your mind playing tricks on you? Well, that's how it was when I saw Pastor Landris here. It was you who ended up helping me pinpoint where I'd most likely seen him before."

"Then I guess you should be thankful for me," Sam said in between a hard cough.

"Now, you know I appreciate you." Memory stopped for a second. "And what are you doing for that cold or whatever that is you have? You sound terrible."

"Oh, I'll be fine. You're the one who needs to take care and watch your back."

"I'm doing that. After that no-good Christopher Harris double-crossed me . . ."

"Memory, don't go getting your blood pressure all worked up over him again. God is going to take care of that situation one of these days. And you can believe *that*."

"Yeah . . . Well, God takes a little too long for me. You of all people know how impatient I can be when it comes to having to wait."

"So, what happened with that woman you were staying with last we talked?"

Memory got up and walked toward the closet. The phone wasn't cordless, but the cord was long enough to reach it. She opened the double doors and walked in. The closet was huge. "Arletha was threatening to tell that private detective fellow who's been following me everywhere that I was at her house. I had to get up out of there in a hurry."

"Does she know where you are now?"

Memory came out of the closet and closed the doors. "No. Nobody knows, except for you and the Landrises. And they only know me as Elaine Robertson."

"Well, my lips are zipped. You plan on staying there a little while or what?"

"I don't know what I'm planning to do at this point. As I said, I wasn't expecting any of this to happen this way. But now that this opportunity has practically fallen in my lap, maybe I'll just ride it out and see where it takes me. I just need to think about this a little more, I suppose."

"Memory, I know I don't have to tell you this again,

but I'm going to say it anyway. You *really* need to be careful. Take care of yourself. My friend Mabel died the other night. And you know what they say about death—it always comes in threes."

"Well, don't you worry none about me. I'll be careful. Just because I got saved here recently for real, it doesn't mean I got stupid."

"You just keep me abreast of what's going on," Sam said. "Check in every chance you get, 'cause you know I worry about you when I don't hear from you every few days."

"I know. I'm going to get off the phone now. I'll call you again later and let you know what's happening on my end. 'Bye, dear." Memory placed the receiver on its hook, sat down, then grinned as she looked around the room once more. As she relaxed on the stack of pillows behind her, Memory's grin quickly began to swell into a low, soft chuckle.

Chapter 2

Hope deferred maketh the heart sick, but when the desire cometh, it is a tree of life.

Proverbs 13:12

Landris had come home earlier than was normal for him. In fact, he'd been caught off guard by just how blinding the June sun could be if you happened to be facing west between four and five o'clock in the afternoon. As soon as he walked in the house, Johnnie Mae asked him to get Memory's luggage out of the car and take it to the bedroom her mother generally used. Johnnie Mae, Memory, and Johnnie Mae's daughter, Princess Rose, were all laughing and talking in the den next to the kitchen when Landris came and joined them.

After Johnnie Mae felt certain Landris had Memory's full attention, she excused herself and hurried upstairs to her bedroom to call Sarah.

"Don't be giving me hypotheticals. Bring my child home to me," Sarah said after Johnnie Mae explained the situation as she perceived it. "Catch a plane first thing in the morning, or if you must drive up, then drive. Just bring my child home to me."

"Okay, Sarah. But I need to know how much you want me to tell her about who you really are," Johnnie Mae said.

Going by the name Elaine Robertson, Memory didn't have a clue Johnnie Mae suspected whom she really was.

Then again, Memory didn't know that most of what she believed to be true regarding her own life was, in fact, not the whole truth. If she was truly the Memory Patterson they were seeking, the world as Memory knew it was about to quickly go from flat to round. Johnnie Mae wasn't sure she should be the one telling Memory any of this or whether this was truly the best place for it to be done.

"Tell her whatever you need to tell her to convince her to come. Everything, if you have to," Sarah said.

Johnnie Mae hung up the phone and made her way back downstairs. She walked into the den just as Landris was telling Memory one of his favorite jokes.

"There was a feud between the pastor and the choir director of this church," Landris said, smiling just a tad. "Now, the first hint of trouble seems to have come when the pastor preached on 'Dedicating Yourselves to Service' and the choir director decided the choir should sing 'I Shall Not Be Moved.' Of course, the pastor believed the song had merely been a coincidence, so he put it behind him and didn't think any more about it. The next Sunday, the pastor preached on 'Giving.' After that sermon, the choir members squirmed as the choir director led them into the hymn 'Jesus Paid It All.' By this time, the good pastor was starting to get a bit upset." Landris chuckled a little.

"Sunday morning service attendance was beginning to grow as the tension increased between the pastor and the choir director," Landris continued. "One of the largest crowds the church ever had showed up the next week to hear the sermon, which just happened to be 'The Sin of Gossiping.' True to form, the choir director selected 'I Love to Tell the Story.' Well, it was on—there was no turning back. The next Sunday, the pastor told the congregation that unless something changed, he was considering resigning. The congregation collectively gasped when the choir director led the choir into 'Why Not Tonight?' " Landris struggled to maintain a serious face. He continued.

"Well, of course no one was surprised when the pastor resigned a week later. He explained to the congregation that Jesus had led him there, and Jesus was leading him away. The choir looked at the choir director, who just couldn't resist. Jumping to his feet, he joyfully led the congregation into the hymn 'What a Friend We Have in Jesus.' "

Memory started laughing and couldn't stop. "I've never heard that before," she said, trying to compose herself. "You're really funny. I didn't know preachers were allowed to have a sense of humor."

"Oh, you didn't?" Landris asked. "Well, the Bible says, 'A merry heart doeth good like a medicine.' " Landris looked at Johnnie Mae, who stood by the couch, beaming.

"Pastor Landris can be quite the funnyman when he wants to be," Johnnie Mae said. "He's not stuffy like some preachers can tend to be."

"So I see," Memory said. She looked from Johnnie Mae to Pastor Landris and instantly picked up on an unspoken communication between them. "Miss Princess Rose," Memory began, "you're in school, huh?"

Princess Rose stood up and began to hop on one foot. "Yes, ma'am," she said, then hopped on the other foot. "Today was our last day."

"What grade are you in?"

Johnnie Mae touched Princess Rose to make her stand still. Princess Rose stopped hopping and began to twist her upper body from side to side, causing her two long pigtails to swing the way she loved for them to do. "I'll be in the *first* grade, Miss Elaine," she said, emphasizing the word "first," "when school starts back."

"Oh, you will?" Memory said, glancing at Johnnie

Mae with a smile, then back over to Princess Rose. "How old does that make you? Five? Six?"

Princess Rose held up one hand, showing all five fingers, and the index finger of her other hand.

"Talk, Princess Rose. You know how to talk," Johnnie Mae said, looking sternly but lovingly at her daughter.

"Six and a half," Princess Rose said.

"Then why aren't you going to the second grade when school starts?" Memory asked.

"Her birthday comes late. She was born in December," Johnnie Mae said, answering the question for her daughter. "I considered putting her in private school for a few years so she could be in her right-age grade, but I decided against it."

"Well, I bet you're really, really smart," Memory said, looking at Princess Rose.

Princess Rose started to nod, then stopped when she looked at her mother. "Yes, ma'am. I *really*, *really* am," she said with a contagious giggle. "*Everybody* says so!"

They all laughed.

"M . . . Ms. Elaine," Johnnie Mae said, having almost slipped and called her Memory, "would you mind if I borrow Pastor Landris for just a few minutes?"

"Of course not," Memory said, immediately taking a swallow of her iced tea.

"I'm sure you're past ready for supper," Johnnie Mae said.

"Oh, no, I'm fine for now. That snack you gave me earlier really did the trick."

"We'll only be a few minutes," Johnnie Mae said with a smile. "I promise." Landris stood up and they went upstairs to their bedroom.

"Okay. What's up?" Landris asked as soon as Johnnie Mae closed the door.

"I spoke with Sarah."

"And—"

"And . . . she wants me to bring Memory to Asheville, North Carolina, tomorrow morning."

He shook his head. "I don't know about that, Johnnie Mae. You're pregnant. I don't think you need to even be considering anything like that." Landris stared firmly into her brown eyes. "Just put her on a plane. It'll be faster that way, anyway."

"Landris, you know how important this is to Sarah. I'm pretty sure that's Memory downstairs. What if she decides to run away again?"

"That's, of course, *if* the woman downstairs really is her. Has she admitted to you that she is, in fact, Memory?"

Johnnie Mae glanced at the floor for a brief second, then back up. "Well, no."

"Then you really can't be certain she's Memory. And you just may have gotten Sarah's hopes up for nothing."

Johnnie Mae looked lovingly into her husband's hazel-brown eyes as she spoke softly. "I know it's her, Landris. I can feel it. So can you. I plan on talking with her and finding out once and for all, though."

"When?"

"As soon as I go back downstairs. I wanted to talk with you first." Johnnie Mae walked toward the door. "I didn't want to do anything before talking with you about it. If my suspicions are correct, then Sarah's long-lost daughter is downstairs in our den at this very moment. Sarah's been searching everywhere for her. You know this. I can't take the chance of losing her before the two of them can meet. And if that means I have to drive her to Asheville, North Carolina, myself, then that's exactly what I'm prepared to do."

Landris came over and pulled Johnnie Mae into his arms. "Now, you know I'm not going to let you go up to Asheville by yourself. You know that. But first things first. You need to be certain the woman downstairs is really Memory Patterson. So tell me. How are you planning on accomplishing that little feat?"

"Now, that much I'm not so sure about yet. She was telling me things at the church earlier today. I don't know whether I should see if she'll tell me on her own who she is, and then I tell her what I know, or whether I should just tell her what I know, and we move on from there. I just don't know."

"And precisely how much are you planning on telling her?"

Johnnie Mae grabbed the door handle. "Landris, I truly don't know. Just pray for me while I do this, okay? Honestly, I haven't a clue what my plans are from here on out. All I know is that something has to be done. And now is the time. I'm just trusting God."

"Do you want me there while you talk to her?"

Johnnie Mae released the door handle, tilted her head, and smiled before rising up on the tips of her toes, caressing his face with both hands, then giving him a quick peck on his lips. "No. But if you could keep Princess Rose occupied for me, that would be such a tremendous help. Princess Rose appears to be somewhat smitten with 'Ms. Elaine,' and I don't want any interruptions when she and I begin our talk."

"Are you sure?" Landris asked. "We both know this is some heavy stuff here."

"I'm sure. It's going to be okay," Johnnie Mae said as she smiled at him.

It was Landris this time who planted a soft kiss on her lips. "Well, whatever you need"—he planted yet another kiss on her lips—"you know I'm here for you."

She nodded, opened the door, and they walked back downstairs hand in hand.

"Princess Rose, how about you and I go to the game

room and watch a little TV on the wide-screen," Landris said as soon as he and Johnnie Mae entered the room. "Or maybe we can play a game. If memory serves, I believe you and I are due for an air-hockey rematch." Straightaway, he noticed how Johnnie Mae's eyes widened right after the word "memory" came out of his mouth. He touched her hand to put her back at ease.

"I'm just going to beat you again, Daddy Landris," Princess Rose said, getting up off the couch and skipping toward him. "I don't know when you're going to ever learn."

"Yeah, well, we'll just have to see about that then, missy, now won't we?" Landris said with a sly grin. Princess Rose grabbed his hand and started pulling him toward the hallway that led to the downstairs game room.

After the room was quiet, Johnnie Mae went and sat down across from where Memory was sitting at the end section of the U-shaped sectional sofa.

"I suppose you want to finish what you and I were talking about at the church," Memory said, releasing a deep sigh. "I did say some things that could cause you to be a bit leery of me right now. Especially considering you've so graciously opened up your home to me—a perfect stranger, in actuality."

Johnnie Mae was still unsure of which direction she should take. Should she let Memory tell her the rest of what she had begun at the church and see whether or not she would tell her the whole truth? Or should she admit to Memory up front what she suspected and tell her the things she knew?

Namely that Memory Elaine Patterson, the daughter of Mamie and Willie B. Patterson, was neither Mamie nor Willie B.'s child, but in fact, the daughter of one prominent and extremely wealthy Sarah Elaine Fleming. Johnnie Mae prayed silently.

Chapter 3

He that answereth a matter before he heareth it, it is folly and shame unto him.

Proverbs 18:13

"Elaine, back at the church," Johnnie Mae began, "you were telling me about your family and how you were feeling bad about some things that had happened in your life."

"Yeah. And you probably think I'm a real jerk or something now."

"No. No, really I don't. We just didn't get to finish the conversation, and there appeared to be more you wanted to tell me."

Memory looked at her and frowned. "Yeah. There was more. It's just, now I don't know if I feel so great about telling you like I did earlier."

Johnnie Mae pursed her lips, then nodded one time. "And why is that?"

Memory looked around the rather large area. The kitchen and the den were like one big room since nothing divided the two except for their identifying furnishings. In the den was a fireplace, sectional sofa, and glass-top tables (one with tropical fish swimming inside of it), while the kitchen featured a work island, glass-top table, cushioned bench and chairs alongside normal kitchen appliances like the double oven, steel stove, and refrigerator. A sixty-inch, flat-screen television was mounted on the wall in the den that could easily be viewed from practically anywhere a person might happen to be in either of the two areas.

"Look at all this," Memory said. "You invited me to come and stay in your home. What if something I tell you causes you to believe I'm some horrible person you can't trust? What then?"

"So you're considering my offer to stay a while?"

"Let's just say I'm thinking about at least staying the night. But what if I were to tell you the rest of my story and you decide you want me out of here? Then what do I do?"

"Is that what you think? Is what you've done that awful?"

Memory shrugged. "I took something from my own family when they trusted me to do the right thing. What's to keep you from believing I wouldn't do something like that to you, too?"

"Elaine, please. Whatever it is you wanted to tell me earlier, I'd really like to hear it now. You need to trust someone other than yourself."

Memory stood up and began to walk around the room. "Yeah . . . right." She stopped in front of a painted portrait that hung over the fireplace. She nodded her approval. "Nice painting of you."

Johnnie Mae glanced at it. "Thanks. Pastor Landris painted that some years ago."

"He's a talented man, I see."

"Yes, he is," Johnnie Mae said. "But you're avoiding the subject. Elaine, there are things I need to talk with you about, but first—I need you to come totally clean with me."

Memory turned around and looked in Johnnie Mae's eyes. She released a half grin before walking back and sitting down on the sofa.

"You know, don't you?"

"Know what?"

"Who I am," Memory said.

"And who might that be?" Johnnie Mae asked.

Memory released another sigh as she shook her head. "Look, I'm tired of running. I'm tired of all the deceit and lies. My name is Memory." She looked at Johnnie Mae and started to chuckle. "Just what I thought. You're not the least bit surprised hearing that."

"No."

"So who told you, and how much time do I have before they show up to take me away?"

"Memory, I don't know who you're talking about is coming to take you away."

"Some private detective. He's been looking for me for years, although for the life of me I can't understand why he's still following me. He's definitely relentless. So what was it? Did Arletha Brown call and tell you, and you decided to turn me in, or what?"

"Memory, I don't know an Arletha, and I've not spoken to any private detective."

Memory laughed and shook her head again. "And I'm supposed to believe that?"

"I'm telling you the truth. Listen, there's something I need to tell you. I've not been totally straight with you myself. I figured out who you were because of things you said to me earlier today during your counseling session."

"Things *I* said?" Memory asked, obviously confused.

"Yes. It's a bit complicated. In fact, if I wasn't so involved, I'm not sure I would believe it myself," Johnnie Mae said. She placed her hand on her stomach. Her baby had begun to move what felt to be a bent elbow across her stomach.

Memory's eyes followed Johnnie Mae's hand as she rubbed the georgette top that covered her stomach. She sat back against the sofa. "I'm all ears."

Johnnie Mae readjusted and sat forward. “The truth is, I’ve met your daughter, Lena Patterson, as well as your granddaughter, Theresa Jordan. It was back in 2001.”

“Oh. So you just *happen* to know Lena and Theresa? From a church in Georgia?”

“Kind of. I don’t know them that well, although we did travel together to Asheville, North Carolina, in October of that same year.”

“Asheville, North Carolina—seems to be a popular town these days. In fact, that’s the place the private detective throws around whenever he leaves a message for me.” Memory reached down and picked up her glass of tea. She swirled the remaining amount around. “I’m sure you want me to believe you’re not working with this man now. But what if you’re merely stalling . . . trying to keep me here until he shows up?”

“Memory, trust me; if I was up to something like that, I sure wouldn’t be having this conversation with you now. We could have continued on with our little charade, and no one would have been the wiser. But there’s more to this story—so much more.”

“Then say what you have to say and be done. I’m a big girl. I can handle it.”

“It’s not whether or not you can handle it. It’s whether or not I should be the one telling it.”

“Look, Johnnie Mae, I appreciate you for having listened to me earlier today. And I especially appreciate you for having opened up your home to me like you did. But realistically, if you know Lena and Theresa and you were hanging out with them back in October of 2001, then I’m sure you know they consider me a thief.” Memory grabbed her purse and stood up. “So if you don’t mind, I think I’ll get my things and be on my way.”

Johnnie Mae struggled to get up off the couch. “Memory, I do know about the Alexandrite necklace, but I can’t let you leave yet.”

"You can't keep me here against my will." Memory started out of the room. "I'm going up those stairs, getting my suitcases, and getting out of here while the getting is good."

"Memory, I'm not trying to keep you here. There's something I need to tell you."

Memory continued to walk hurriedly out of the room and toward the staircase.

Johnnie Mae walked as quickly as she could after her. "Memory, wait! There's something I need to tell you! It's important."

Memory trotted up the stairs. Johnnie Mae turned around and looked back in the other direction. Landris was downstairs in the game room. She knew she could make her way to the intercom to call him, but it would take a few minutes for him to get upstairs. As Johnnie Mae started to go back in the den, Memory appeared at the top of the stairs with two pieces of her luggage. She set them down, turned around, and went back, returning shortly with the other two.

"Memory, please don't try carrying those on your own. You might hurt yourself." Johnnie Mae started up the stairs.

"You're pregnant, Johnnie Mae." She started down the steps with one of the suitcases. "Don't do anything that might endanger you or your baby. Just let me pass, and I promise I'll leave your home peaceably. All I want is to get out of here—that's all. I'm not trying to cause you any trouble, and I would appreciate it if you'd extend me the same courtesy."

"Where are you trying to go? You don't even know where you are, so what are you planning to do if you leave here? Wander the streets?"

Memory struggled as she carried the heaviest piece of luggage down first. She huffed and puffed, her body wobbling with each step taken. "Is that why you brought me here? So I could become a prisoner in your home? Did you think I wouldn't be paying attention enough not to know where I was?" She now stood face to face with Johnnie Mae. "Please let me pass. I don't want you or your baby to get hurt, okay?"

"I'm not going to let you hurt either of us," Johnnie Mae said as she moved closer to the side of the wall to be sure she was totally out of Memory's way.

Memory reached the foyer, set the suitcase down near the door, and hurried back up the stairs to get another one. "In case you want to know," she said, lifting up the second suitcase, "I do know the address here. You don't honestly believe I've been doing this for this long and don't know how to take care of myself any better than that, now, do you?" She set it down. "I know what street we're on, and, yes, I noted the house's address when you drove in." Back up the stairs, she picked up the last two suitcases and took them down.

"Memory, please stop. If you'll just allow me to finish what I'm trying to tell you, this will all make sense. After I finish, if you still want to leave, I'll drive you wherever you're trying to go myself. I promise."

Memory laughed as she once again walked past Johnnie Mae, who had now made her way to the marbled-floor foyer and was standing next to Memory's other two suitcases. "Yeah, I just bet you will."

"Why won't you trust anyone?" Johnnie Mae asked.

Memory set the two suitcases down, twisted her pocketbook from being pushed to her back, straightened up, then shoved her fists into her sides and said, "Because people somehow always manage to let me down, that's why."

Johnnie Mae reached out to touch her hand. "Please, I'm begging you. Give me five minutes and let me tell you what's really going on. Five minutes. Can we please go back in the den and talk?" Johnnie Mae began pressing her hand against her stomach.

"You in pain?" Memory asked.

"No, just feeling a bit uncomfortable at the moment. But I *really* do need to sit down. I'm certain this will pass, but it's important that I tell you something." Johnnie Mae became tired . . . out of breath almost, as she spoke.

Outside, a horn honked twice.

"That's my ride," Memory said as she turned and opened the door. "They got here a lot faster than I thought they would. I guess they must have had one already in the vicinity." A yellow taxi sat in the circular driveway. She beckoned for the driver to come up and help her as she pulled two of the suitcases outside using their rollers.

Johnnie Mae didn't know what to do at this point. She looked around as though she was searching for something to stop Memory. Spinning back toward Memory, she quickly blurted out, "Mamie Patterson wasn't your real mother!"

Memory stopped, turned around slowly, and began to frown at Johnnie Mae. "What did you just say?"

Johnnie Mae let out a sigh. "Mamie Patterson wasn't your biological mother," she said in a much calmer tone.

The taxi driver took the suitcases and headed for his cab.

"Sir, wait!" Memory called out to him. "Give me a minute, please." She then looked hard into Johnnie Mae's now-pleading eyes. "Okay," Memory said to Johnnie Mae. "Start talking."

Chapter 4

Rise up, ye women that are at ease; hear My voice, ye careless daughters; give ear unto My speech.

Isaiah 32:9

"Well? Does the cat have your tongue?" Memory asked as she patted her foot. "If you have something you want to say, then say it."

"Memory, I really need to sit down. Honestly, I'm not feeling so well."

"Maybe you should let Pastor Landris know so he can see about you," Memory said, clutching her purse strap. "Look, the meter's running. Tell you what. See ya."

Johnnie Mae stood straighter. "Mamie Patterson is the woman you grew up believing was your mother. She wasn't. There's more to this story, but I can't tell it standing here like this. I really need to sit down. Why don't you come inside, and we can go to the den and talk about this in private?"

Memory turned to the taxi driver and told him she wouldn't need him after all. He set the luggage back in the foyer. She paid him what she owed and came back inside.

Johnnie Mae contemplated, as she closed the door, whether she *should* go get Landris to come and help her tell Memory. Things were not going as she'd hoped at all.

Memory walked toward the den. "You want to come

on so you can start explaining this nonsense you're spouting off about Mamie not being my real mother?"

"Sure," Johnnie Mae said, catching up. "Would you care for some more tea first?"

"From what you're alleging, I'm not sure tea will be strong enough." Memory walked in and sat down. She held up her glass for Johnnie Mae to refill.

Johnnie Mae went to the kitchen and put crushed ice in both her and Memory's empty glasses. She then pulled two cans out of the refrigerator and went back into the den area. "Here you go," she said, handing Memory her glass of ice and one of the cans.

"What's this?" Memory asked, looking at the yellow can with maroon letters.

"You said you may need something stronger. That's Buffalo Rock. It's a type of ginger ale, great for relieving stomach ailments and motion sickness. Personally, I enjoy its stronger-than-normal ginger taste. You have to be careful though; it really is strong."

"So you believe I'm going to need something for motion sickness, huh? You suspecting it might get a bit turbulent around here?" Memory popped the tin on the cap, then poured the dark-colored liquid into her glass. She took a huge swallow in spite of Johnnie Mae's previous warning. "Whoa!" she said, shaking her head a few times. "Oh, this ought to do the trick. It has a kick to it, that's for sure!" She only sipped it this time.

Johnnie Mae rubbed her stomach as she poured the can of Buffalo Rock ginger ale into her glass. Taking only a sip, she shook her head as though she too was attempting to dislodge something inside of it. "Is it okay if I call you Memory?"

"It hasn't stopped you so far. Memory . . . Elaine . . . Whatever suits you is fine with me. I'd just like for you to get on with it, though. Time's a-ticking." Memory pointed at the digital clock on the mantel.

Johnnie Mae took another sip before setting her glass down. "I'd rather this had been handled a different way. Let me begin by admitting that I don't know everything—"

"Just tell me what you *do* know," Memory said with a bit of agitation in her voice.

Johnnie Mae looked seriously at her. "It all started when I met this elderly woman in a nursing home back in 2000. She was living in Selma, Alabama, at the time, but she told me she had originated from Asheville, North Carolina."

"That's where I grew up."

"Yes." Johnnie Mae nodded as she rocked a little. "I know. Anyway, this woman ended up telling me a tale about how her family had been hiding her away for decades, which was why she happened to be in Alabama. She then asked for my help."

"And let me guess. She told you she would tell you something important if you would only agree to help her escape that place?"

"Not exactly. She told me about a baby . . . her baby. How she believed her baby hadn't died as she'd been told when the baby was born. It seems a few villainous members of her family were trying to make her out to be crazy, when, clearly, she was not." Johnnie Mae leaned forward. "Memory, the woman's name was Sarah Fleming."

"I don't know anybody by the name of Sarah Fleming. In fact, I don't know anyone with the last name of Fleming at all."

"Sarah Fleming had a friend named Mamie Patterson."

"My mother. So she knew Mamie. So what? This Sarah woman knew my mother, and now she's trying to say my mother wasn't really my mother just so she can break out of some nursing home. And you fell for *that*?"

"Memory, Sarah Fleming really is your mother."

Memory's body began to shake as she started to laugh. "Yeah, okay. Mamie Patterson, who happened to have had twins, mind you—me and my brother—was not really my mother because some woman you met in an old folks' home, crazy, but not really crazy according to her own diagnosis, says so." Memory stood up. "Okay. I've given you more than five minutes here. You've said your piece. I heard you out. Now, if you don't mind, I'd like for you or Pastor Landris to take me to the nearest bus station so I can get out of here before I end up going crazy." She turned and started walking away.

"Memory, that Alexandrite necklace you took from Lena and Theresa. The one that was in the safe-deposit box at the bank—"

Memory stopped, spun around slowly, and stared at Johnnie Mae. She grinned. "Okay. So now we're finally getting to the real reason that I'm here. There's no Sarah Fleming. That's just something you made up to get me confused and disoriented while you try to find out what happened to that necklace." Feeling a little lightheaded, Memory sat down and began to rub her head. "All right. Let's just do this and get it over with."

"Memory, I'm only bringing up the necklace because I want you to see that it's tied to the truth about your biological mother."

"Right. And that would be Sarah Fleming."

"Please, just listen. The necklace was in a box . . . a box with wings etched on it. In fact, the woman who brought it to Mamie . . . when you were younger, the box that housed the contents you believed belonged to you, that was Sarah's mother—Grace."

"Man, that private detective is good! So, what else did he tell you?"

"Memory, I haven't spoken with a private detective. Your mother, Sarah Fleming, has been looking for you since she first learned for sure you were still alive in 2001."

"Yeah? Let's see. I'm almost seventy, and that would make her about . . . how old now?"

"I believe she turns ninety this year."

"And this woman, this Sarah Fleming, who claims to be my mother, is still living?"

"Yes. In fact, I spoke with her a little while ago. She really wants to meet you."

Memory stood up and walked around. "Sarah Fleming, you say, who is actually my mother, a mother I didn't even know existed, wants to meet me?"

"I know this is hard, and it's a lot to spring on you. Believe me, I really didn't want to do it this way." Johnnie Mae readjusted her body so it would be easier for her to keep up with Memory's wanderings.

"And how exactly were you planning on telling me all of this if you hadn't been forced to do it this way?"

Johnnie Mae relaxed a bit more. "Honestly, I wasn't sure. I wish I could have just taken you to Asheville and let Sarah and Lena tell you everything."

She stopped walking. "Lena knows?"

"Yes."

"And she's met this Sarah Fleming woman? What am I asking? Of course she's met her."

"We all went to Asheville together. That's another story, but, yes, Lena and Theresa both have met Sarah. In fact, had you been there that day, it would have been five generations together in one place, along with your great-granddaughter."

Memory came and sat down. "My great-granddaughter." She smiled as she rubbed her sagging face with her hand. "And this Sarah lady is back in Asheville now? Not Selma?"

"Yes. She's back in Asheville."

"And you say you talked with her today?"

Johnnie Mae sat back against the sofa. “I called her this evening to let her know that I suspected you might be her daughter. I needed to know what she wanted me to do in case my suspicions turned out to be correct.”

Memory nodded. “Is she in a nursing home in Asheville?”

“No. She lives in her own house there. I’ve not seen her since 2001, but she’s a remarkable woman, Memory.” Johnnie Mae smiled as she tilted her head. “The two of you have the same gray eyes.” Johnnie Mae took a swallow of ginger ale. “I told her I’d bring you to see her tomorrow. We can drive up. It’s about a six-hour trip from here.”

Memory smiled. “And do I have any say-so about whether I meet her or not?”

“I’m sorry. Forgive me. Of course you do. You’re not a prisoner here. We’re not trying to keep you in order to turn you over to anybody. I would think, though, after learning this news, you’d want to meet the woman who gave birth to you. She certainly has been praying and waiting a long time to meet you.”

Memory took a swig of drink directly from the can this time. “Almost seventy years, according to my calculations. Well, I’ll have to think about this. Obviously, she’s had more time to get used to the idea than I have. But you say I’m not a prisoner here? And I can leave if I want to? So if I get up and walk out right now . . .”

“I’ll not physically try and stop you. I only thought it fair that you know the truth. If you decide to leave or that you don’t want to meet your biological mother, that’s your choice. I just can’t imagine you not wanting to at least meet her,” Johnnie Mae said.

“What if I’d prefer calling her first? Talk to her over the phone before we meet?”

“That would be great! I can give you her phone number.”

"I think I'd like to have it, if you don't mind. I'm not sure I'll call her, but if you would give me her phone number, I would appreciate it."

Johnnie Mae nodded. "It's upstairs." She stood up. "I'll get it for you."

Johnnie Mae went and retrieved the number. She wrote it down, came back, and handed it to Memory. "I do wish you would call her. I know she'd love hearing your voice. You can talk to her tonight, and tomorrow, if you want, we can go up there so the two of you can meet. I realize I can't force you to call or to meet her. But Memory, she's an old woman and as sweet as she can be. She doesn't have a lot of time left on this earth. I would think you'd want to spend as much of that time with her as possible, now that you know the truth. I know there's so much more about all of this she can tell you."

Memory took the number. "Yeah. There's a lot I still don't know or understand. I think I'd like to call her now. Is it possible for me to have some time here alone?"

Johnnie Mae touched her hand. "Of course. I'll go down and see what Landris and Princess Rose are up to. What do you think? Twenty . . . thirty minutes?"

"Twenty's enough. I don't mean to put you out. And I'm still not sure what I'm going to do. If I call her, what do I say? But I do think calling is what I should do first."

"It's no problem. And you're not putting me out. The phone's right there." Johnnie Mae pointed at the cordless phone. "Sarah will be ecstatic to hear from you." Johnnie Mae smiled, then left Memory in the room alone.

Memory looked at the number, picked up the phone, dialed, then quickly hung up before it could connect. Opening her purse, she put the paper with the number inside of it. After a few minutes, she opened up her purse again, took out the paper, stared at the number, dialed, then waited—practically holding her breath—as the phone began to ring.

Chapter 5

For Jacob My servant's sake, and Israel Mine elect, I have even called thee by thy name: I have surnamed thee, though thou hast not known Me.

Isaiah 45:4

Johnnie Mae went downstairs to the game room. Landris rushed over to her as soon as she walked in. "How did it go?" he asked.

"I'm giving her some time to process what I've just told her. I think she's going to give Sarah a call."

"Daddy Landris, are you gonna play or what?" Princess Rose asked as she placed the hockey puck on the table and stood in position to slam it to her stepfather's side.

"Honey, why don't you go and play the arcade machine while Daddy Landris and I talk for a little while?"

"Okay, I'll go play Ms. Pac-Man or something," Princess Rose said, shaking her head. She dragged over to the arcade machine, climbed up on the bar stool, and pressed the button to start the game. As the familiar music blasted, Princess Rose began moving the joystick.

Landris and Johnnie Mae went and sat down at the table that also doubled as a checker- and chessboard.

"So, what happened?" Landris asked, leaning in close.

"She admitted she's Memory. She thought I was working with a private investigator. At first, she didn't believe me when I told her I wasn't, nor was I trying to trap her," Johnnie Mae said.

"She didn't believe you were being on the up-and-up with her?"

"Not at first. I think she believes me now. I told her a little about Sarah, and we touched momentarily on the Alexandrite necklace."

Landris retrieved the checkers from inside the drawer of the table and placed them on the surface. "Did she happen to mention what became of the necklace?"

"No," Johnnie Mae said, pulling out all the black checkers and lining them up on her side of the board.

"Did you even ask her?"

"No."

Landris stopped and looked at her. "No?"

She widened her eyes and smiled. "No."

He looked at the checkers on her side. "Why do you always get to have the black checkers first every time we play?"

"Who said we were playing?"

He pointed at her side. "You have your checkers lined up like we are."

Johnnie Mae leaned in. "I was busying my hands. Is that all right with you?"

Landris set up the red checkers on his side. "Fine. I was merely asking." After his checkers were in place, he signaled for her to make the first move. "And why are we all down here instead of up there with Memory right now?"

"I'm giving her time to think about what she wants to do, and hopefully to call Sarah. I told her I'd be about twenty minutes, in case she did decide to call and verify what I've told her so far."

"And you told her that Sarah was her real mother?"

"I had to." Johnnie Mae moved another checker piece after Landris moved. "She was trying to leave, so I had to do something fast. She had a taxi here and had managed to drag her luggage down the stairs."

"She lugged those bags down the stairs by herself?" Landris jumped her checker and removed it off the board. "She's pretty tough for an older woman."

"Yeah. She had to make three trips to do it, unlike you, with your strong muscles, who was able to take the four pieces up in two. I started to come and get you, but I didn't want to chance her leaving before I was able to tell her about Sarah. I told her enough to get her attention. She knows Mamie wasn't her biological mother and that Sarah is. She's aware that we know all about the Alexandrite necklace. I figure when she arrives in Asheville, Sarah will fill her in on whatever else she needs or may want to know." Johnnie Mae triple jumped his checkers and removed them.

"You've been down here for about twenty minutes now. Don't you want to go back up and check on her?"

"I don't want her to think we don't trust her," Johnnie Mae said. "Let's give her another five to ten more minutes."

Landris made a double jump. "Crown me," he said with a grin.

Johnnie Mae added a checker on top of the checker that was now in the king spot. She glanced at the Wurlitzer jukebox. Landris noticed she was looking at it. He stood, pulled her up next to him, and with his arms wrapped around her, walked her over to it. Locating the song he was searching for, he pressed the corresponding buttons.

"Unwritten," a song by Natasha Bedingfield, began to play. Princess Rose immediately stopped what she was doing and hopped down off the black swerving bar stool. She began singing the words to the song—a song that was definitely a hit in their house. The entire family loved it. Landris began to twirl both mother and daughter around ever so gently during certain parts of the song. He started "Walking the Floor" with Johnnie Mae, a dance that could be crowned the black waltz. Princess Rose continued to sing her heart out.

When the song ended, all three of them laughed, clapped, and cheered.

Princess Rose jumped up and down. "Play it again, Daddy Landris! Play it again! That's my song!" She began to sing "I am unwritten" without the music, then said, "I love that song! Oh, please, play it again!"

Johnnie Mae smiled, leaned down, and kissed her daughter on the top of her head. "Another time, sweetheart. We have company upstairs. We don't want to be rude and leave her alone too long, now, do we?"

Princess Rose lifted her head high and opened her arms in a dramatic fashion. "Then let's invite Ms. Elaine down here so she can have some fun with the song, too!"

"It's suppertime. Maybe Ms. Elaine will come down afterward and enjoy the song with us. We'll see how things go." Johnnie Mae tapped Princess Rose on her nose and then planted a kiss on it. "All right, let's go." She pointed toward the stairs. "March."

Princess Rose began to step hard in a military-type fashion as instructed, Johnnie Mae followed her, and Landris pulled up the rear.

When they reached the top of the stairs, Johnnie Mae noticed how quiet it was. There was no sign of Memory in the den.

"Where is she?" Princess Rose asked. "Ms. Elaine!" Princess Rose yelled. "Ms. Elaine!"

"Princess Rose, don't yell like that. She's probably upstairs. She may be on the phone up there."

"You want me to run upstairs and get her?" Princess Rose asked, purposely swinging her two plaits from side to side.

"No. You and Daddy Landris go wash up and set the table. I'll go check on her."

Landris reached out and caught Johnnie Mae's hand before she could walk away. He gave her a quick kiss on her cheek.

Johnnie Mae smiled, then continued on. When she reached the bedroom where Memory was staying, she knocked on the closed door. No answer. She knocked again. Still no answer. "Memory . . . ?" Johnnie Mae said, knocking louder. "Are you okay?"

Nothing but silence answered her. She opened the door slowly. Still no sign of Memory. Walking over to the bathroom door, she knocked on it. "Memory? Are you in there?" She wasn't in there, either. Johnnie Mae quickly made her way back downstairs.

"We set the table in the nook area so it would feel a little cozier," Landris said. He stopped and looked at Johnnie Mae. "What's wrong? Is everything all right?"

"She's gone."

"Gone?"

"Yes. Gone. The bedroom's empty. She's not upstairs."

"Maybe she just stepped outside for some fresh air," Landris said.

Johnnie Mae thought for a second, then hurriedly walked back into the foyer. Landris followed her. "Why didn't I see that before?" she said. "Her suitcases are gone. They were right by the door. They're not upstairs. She's gone, Landris." She sighed hard.

"Before you get upset, let's see whether she left a note or something."

Searching in the den where Memory was last, neither one of them found a thing.

"I don't believe this," Johnnie Mae said, disappointed. "How could she just leave like that without saying a word? What am I going to tell Sarah now?" Johnnie Mae shook her head as she started walking out of the den area.

Landris grabbed her by her shoulders. "Johnnie Mae, it's not your responsibility. Sarah hired the best people out there to find her, and look—you came closer to getting her to Sarah than any of them have been able to do so far. You did your best. Now, don't go beating yourself up about it. She may contact us later or just come back on her own."

Johnnie Mae shook her head again emphatically. "She's not coming back." She pulled away from his grasp and continued out of the room.

"What are you going to do?" Landris asked.

"Call Sarah and let her know Memory's gone. I'm sure this is going to devastate her. We were so close, and I allowed her to slip through my fingers."

Johnnie Mae walked up the stairs to her room to get Sarah's number. She sat on her bed then dialed the number.

"Sarah, this is Johnnie Mae. Yes, I know you're excited about the possibility of finding Memory. Well, I did find her. Memory was here at my house when I spoke with you earlier. But something happened since then. I'm sorry, Sarah. I told her the truth about you, but she must not have believed me, because she left. I am *so* sorry, Sarah. So very, very sorry. We were so close, and it looks like I ended up letting her get away."

Chapter 6

He giveth power to the faint; and to them that have no might He increaseth strength.

Isaiah 40:29

Lena was at Sarah's house. She and her husband, Richard, had gotten in their car and driven up to Asheville almost immediately following Sarah's call late that evening.

"I believe Johnnie Mae's found Memory," Sarah had said to Lena over the phone after she hung up with Johnnie Mae. "She was talking hypothetically, but I know better. If it turns out it's her," Sarah said, "Johnnie Mae's going to bring her to me tomorrow."

If this ended up being the case, Lena didn't want Memory arriving at Sarah's without someone present who truly knew Memory. So she and Richard had quickly thrown a few things in a single suitcase and made the four-hour drive in record time from Atlanta to Asheville, arriving a little after eleven o'clock that night. That was when Lena learned Johnnie Mae had called back and confirmed it was, indeed, Memory.

Lying in bed, dabbing her eyes as tears rolled out, it was evident Sarah was tired. Almost ninety years old, her body seemed determined to remind her of that. "There's a problem though," Sarah said, her chest slowly rising, her breathing noisily shallow.

"What?" Lena asked. "Memory's insisting on flying first-class instead of coach?"

"No. When Johnnie Mae called back, she called to say Memory's gone."

"What? Gone? You mean she left to come up here without Johnnie Mae?"

"No. It appears she left because she didn't want to come here at all." Sarah relaxed more into the pillows stacked behind her.

"I don't understand. Didn't Johnnie Mae tell Memory about you?"

Sarah took a deep breath and released it. It was almost becoming work for her to breathe these days. "She told her." Sarah closed her eyes for a second, then opened them and forced a smile. "She told her pretty much everything. That I was her mother, that you and Theresa met me." Sarah then told her everything that Johnnie Mae had relayed to her.

"So, what was it? She didn't believe Johnnie Mae? Did Johnnie Mae not tell her that you're not well?"

"Johnnie Mae doesn't know the status of my health." She smiled, this time genuinely. "I'm old, Lena. When you get to be my age, things start to break down and wear out. This heart"—she patted her chest softly—"has ticked quite a few beats during its time. Yes, I'm a little worn for wear, but I'm still here. Still trusting and believing God."

"I'm sorry. I know how much seeing Memory means to you."

Sarah motioned for the glass of water on the nightstand. She took a sip and handed it back to Lena. "And I am not oblivious to how you feel. You've made yourself more than clear regarding your thoughts about Memory, my dear. But she's still my child. My flesh . . . and . . . blood." Sarah closed her eyes and became eerily silent.

Lena looked down at the elderly woman, her hair completely gray and willowy. She looked so peaceful lying there. Lena could see her chest rising and falling under the blinding white duvet cover. She leaned down and kissed her grandmother on the forehead. Stepping out of the room, she closed the door gently behind her and slowly walked down the stairs to the parlor.

"Is she asleep?" Gayle asked. A slim woman in her early forties with caramel brown skin, Gayle was the nursemaid the family had hired to stay with Sarah. Faithful to Sarah and the family, she'd been a true blessing for the past three and a half years. Gayle didn't look at what she did as a job; it was more of a calling—her ministry.

"Yes," Lena said. "She's asleep. She told me what happened with Memory."

Gayle began to nod her head. "Well, it's good she finally went to sleep," she said. "She was so excited when she thought at long last she was going to get to meet her daughter. She'd picked out what she was going to wear, even down to the jewelry. It appeared for certain it would happen this time. I hate it's turned out the way it has."

"What happened with Memory?" Richard asked, looking over at Lena. "Did that person end up not being Memory after all?"

High school sweethearts, now a cute elderly couple, Richard Jordan and Lena Patterson had married June 22, 2002, as part of a double-wedding ceremony. Their daughter, Theresa, and Maurice Greene had been the other couple who took their vows alongside them. That had definitely been a special day. Lena and Theresa had been the most beautiful brides, and the grooms hadn't been too shabby, either. They married in the church where Bishop Jordan had retired as the pastor years earlier.

"No, turns out it was Memory, all right," Lena said.

"But she did what she's famous for doing—left without letting anyone know she was going or without bothering to say good-bye." Lena was trying, albeit unsuccessfully, not to sound too bitter.

"I'll go check on Miss Fleming while you two talk. Do you need anything before I go?" Gayle asked. At five feet eleven, she towered over Lena, even wearing her signature flat, fuchsia tennis-like shoes.

"We're fine. Thanks, though," Lena said.

"You know where everything is. If I don't see you before you turn in, have a good night."

"Thanks, Gayle. We probably will turn in," Lena said as she yawned. "We're not as young as we used to be. That drive seems to drain Richard and me every time."

"Speak for yourself, Lena girl. I'm ready to go dancing if you want to," Richard said.

Lena fanned her hand at him. "Don't start nothing, Richard." She then turned back to Gayle. "How do you think my grandmother is holding up through all of this?"

"I think she's doing okay. I will admit, though, she was almost a different person when she got that call today. She even called Minnie, the housekeeper, to come back and give the house a once-over again to ensure everything was perfect, just in case company did show up tomorrow. I sure hate she had the rug yanked out from under her yet again."

Lena smiled and nodded without speaking another word. After Gayle left, she turned to Richard. "You ready to go upstairs and turn in?"

"Truthfully, just thinking of those stairs tires me out. I'm almost considering staying down here and sleeping on this fine pink and white couch."

"We could stay in the bedroom down here if you'd prefer. It's not as large as the one we usually stay in upstairs, but if you really don't feel like going up, I can bring some of our things back down here," Lena said.

"You'll do no such of a thing. I'll make it all right. I still have some fire left inside of me."

Lena rubbed his bald head. "Yeah," she said with a smile. "I know."

He stood. "Let's get going." He held out his arm. "Madam, may I have this dance?"

Lena laughed and took his arm. "So now we're going to dance?"

"Yeah," he said. He started walking with her holding onto his arm. "I think they call this the two-step. One-two," he said as he shuffled his feet forward. "One-two."

Lena shook her head. "You're too much."

"And while we're on our way up, you might want to tell me what you're really thinking about Memory."

"Honestly, except for breaking Grandmother's heart, I can't say I'm surprised or sorry she disappeared. I know I'm supposed to forgive her, but, Richard, I don't know if I can. You know the kind of money and wealth Grandmother possesses. I don't know what Memory will do when she finds out about that."

"So Johnnie Mae didn't tell her that part?"

"No. According to Grandmother, Johnnie Mae didn't tell her she was well-off. She only told her that Sarah Fleming was her mother. And you see what she did after she learned that much. Memory—the same old mother I've grown to know."

"I don't know, Lena girl. I just have a feeling, down deep in my bones, something's about to happen around this place. I'm just glad you're here to see about Sarah."

Lena stopped when they reached the top of the stairs and looked directly at him. "And I'm just glad you're here with me to love on me the way you always do."

Richard smiled as he caressed the left side of her face. "Lena girl, there's no other place I'd want to be *except* wherever you are. No other place."

Chapter 7

Remember ye not the former things,
neither consider the things of old.
Isaiah 43:18

Lena was up early. She had helped Sarah get ready. Sarah still liked to dress nicely even if she was only planning to sit around the house all day. The past few days, Lena had been thinking of things she could do to possibly cheer Sarah up and keep her mind off Memory as much as possible. The Saturday started off a beautiful sunny one.

Richard had gone early to play golf with a group of men he'd formed a friendship with from earlier visits to Asheville. They preferred hitting the golf course in the early morning hours, especially during the summer months, when midday could be rather hot. All of the men were in their late fifties and early sixties. Lena and Sarah were sitting out on the terrace about to eat breakfast when the doorbell rang.

"Will you get that, Lena?" Sarah asked. "It's probably my friend Polly checking up on me. Like clockwork, she stops by early every Saturday morning."

Polly Swindle was a woman in her mid-fifties Sarah had met at church when she came back to Asheville to live. Polly made it a point to stop by frequently. And when she didn't come, she'd call to check on her friend. Sarah had left Polly a message telling her she didn't have to worry about her this week since Lena and Richard were there. Sarah figured either Polly didn't get the message or she just wanted to come by anyway.

Lena hurried to the door. She saw a woman with her back to the door. Lena, smiling, opened the door. The woman faced her; Lena's smile dropped. "*You,*" she said.

"Lena?" the woman said, her head held high. "You look wonderful. I mean, look at you. You got your face fixed and everything!" She smiled as she shook her head. "My, my, no one would ever be able to tell you were once badly scarred in a fire."

Lena's voice was soft as she tried to control her emotions. "What are you doing here? Why don't you just leave now and save everybody a lot of heartache later?"

"Now, why on earth would I want to do a thing like that? I've come to see Sarah Fleming." She turned and beckoned for the cab driver before continuing. "Would you be so kind as to let Sarah know I'm here?" Her voice was soft and nonthreatening.

"Lena, who's that at the door?" Sarah called out as she slowly shuffled into the foyer toward the entranceway. "Polly, dearest, is that you? Your timing is impeccable."

Lena turned around to Sarah as she tried to keep the person at the door out of Sarah's vision. "No, it's not Polly. Why don't you go back out on the terrace?"

"Well, if it's not Polly, then who is it?" Sarah asked as she continued to get closer, attempting to get a better look at the visitor standing in the doorway.

The woman stepped inside the house, politely pushing her way past Lena.

Sarah, now almost face to face with the stranger, stopped and looked at her. "Oh, I'm sorry. I thought you were some—" She began to look closer. "Do I know you?"

"Sarah Fleming?" The woman extended her hand. "My name is Memory."

Sarah placed both hands on her heart. "Memory?" she said. She appeared to be struggling for her next breath. "*My* Memory?" She reached out to her. "Is it really you?" Just then, her right hand clutched her chest as her body crumpled to the floor.

Chapter 8

In those days was Hezekiah sick unto death. And Isaiah the prophet the son of Amoz came unto him, and said unto him, Thus saith the Lord, Set thine house in order: for thou shalt die, and not live.

Isaiah 38:1

Johnnie Mae sat in the window seat in the kitchen nook enjoying the sun early Saturday morning. She was deep in thought. In just two more weeks, she would be entering her seventh month of pregnancy. Her mother was still holding her own, although lately it appeared she was having more bad days than good ones. It was June 4th, four days since Memory had disappeared without a word. Johnnie Mae felt awful having been so close to reuniting Sarah with Memory, only to have it blow away in what amounted to mere minutes.

Sarah had insisted when she and Johnnie Mae spoke four days ago that Johnnie Mae not beat herself up about it. "It wasn't your responsibility, and it's not truly your problem," Sarah had said. "If it's for me and my daughter to meet, it will happen. In God's good time, I have to believe, it will happen. You told her, and either she didn't believe you or she didn't care. Either way, it's not on you. And I don't want you to feel bad about it, do you hear me?"

But Johnnie Mae couldn't help but feel bad. Maybe she hadn't gone far enough with the truth. Maybe she hadn't been convincing enough. Maybe she shouldn't have let

Memory out of her sight until she'd personally delivered her to Sarah's door.

The phone rang, causing Johnnie Mae to jump. She got up and looked at the caller ID. The number was unfamiliar to her.

"Hello?"

"Yes. I'm sorry to bother you so early on a Saturday morning like this, but is Pastor Landris available, please?" The older woman's voice shook as she spoke.

"Hold on, let me check," Johnnie Mae said as pleasantly as she could muster. She wasn't sure if Landris was awake yet or not. She pressed the button to place the line on hold and walked up the stairs to their bedroom.

"Landris?" she said when she walked inside and didn't find him still in bed.

He stuck his head out of the bathroom. "Morning, baby."

"Good morning. The phone's for you. Line one."

"Do you know who it is?" he asked as he walked out of the master bath.

"No. I wasn't sure if you were up yet, so I didn't ask. She's been holding a few minutes." That was his cue to not keep the person waiting any longer than necessary.

Landris walked over to the phone on the nightstand and pressed the button. Johnnie Mae left and headed back downstairs. Now that she knew Landris was awake, she decided to fix him some pancakes and fresh fruit for breakfast. He still liked his cup of coffee every morning, even on weekends, so she started a fresh pot of coffee. She wasn't a big coffee drinker before she got pregnant. Now that she was, she had cut down on her caffeine intake of all kinds to as little as possible.

Landris came into the kitchen just as she was finishing up. He walked up behind her, wrapped his arms around her, and kissed her twice on the cheek. "You didn't have to fix me breakfast this morning," he said.

Johnnie Mae handed him his plate. "Oh, but I enjoy doing things for you," she said. "So, who was that calling so early, if you don't mind me asking?"

Landris bit down on his bottom lip as he went and sat at the table. "That was Reverend Knight's wife. He had asked her to call me. But she was also calling to tell me that the doctors weren't giving him much time left. In fact, they're not expecting him to make it through the day. She didn't want him hearing what the doctors were saying, so she called me from her cell phone."

"Are you going over there now?"

"Yeah. I wanted to get there as soon as possible. But first I'm going to eat this wonderful breakfast"—he waved his hand over his plate—"you so lovingly made me."

She set a cup of coffee down next to him and brushed his dreadlocks with her hand a few times. "You don't have to eat this, if you want to go on over to the hospital now. It's okay. I know how close you've grown to Reverend Knight over this year."

"Yeah." He bowed his head and prayed, then looked back up and started eating some pineapples. "I still need to eat. Who knows how long I'll be, once I get there?"

"Do you want me to come with you?" She sat down across from him.

He took a bite of pancake. "No. I know you're still trying to get over what happened with Memory. Besides, didn't you say your blood pressure was up when you went to the doctor on Thursday, and that your hands and feet were swelling yesterday?"

"Yes. But right now I feel fine."

"Well, I don't want you overdoing it. I don't want to take any chances with you or our baby. So you just rest like Dr. Baker told you. And please quit worrying about Sarah and Memory. I know you, Johnnie Mae. But this battle is not yours; it's the Lord's."

She sighed. "I'm not worrying. I just feel bad about how things turned out."

"Then you need to quit feeling bad. Do you understand me?"

"I know. But we were so close there, and then—"

He took his fork, speared a piece of fresh strawberry, and held it up to Johnnie Mae's mouth—effectively halting her from saying another word as he put the fruit into her mouth. "And then it didn't happen," he said. "So don't worry yourself about what you can't change. You did your best. In fact, you did more than most folks I know would have even attempted to do. You brought Memory to our home. You were going to let her stay here." He shoved some more pancake into his mouth and gulped down his coffee.

"I know, Landris. It's just hard when you come as close as we did and you end up letting it slip through your fingers. But you're right—I can't change what's already passed. We'll just have to keep praying and believing that God is working it all out."

Landris finished the last of his fruit and coffee. "Not *is* working—*has* worked it out. In the spirit realm, it's already done. We just have to walk it out down here. God's will will be done on earth as it already is in Heaven." He grabbed a paper napkin out of the holder on the table and briskly wiped his mouth. Standing up, he then kissed her with a quick peck on her lips. "Get some rest today, okay? If you're going to pray, then stop worrying about it. Just thank God that—"

"It's already done," Johnnie Mae said, finishing the familiar saying. She looked at him and smiled as he put the dirty dishes in the dishwasher. "Give Reverend Knight my love, and tell Mrs. Knight that if she needs anything to not hesitate to let me know."

"I'll tell her. But I'm telling you, I'm not going to let you overdo it. For now, your job is to take care of yourself and our baby." He put his hand on her stomach and grinned.

Landris hurried to Brookwood Hospital. He prayed for his friend as he drove, reflecting back to the first time they'd met in that old rundown building he was looking to lease or buy to begin his ministry in Birmingham. He hadn't been sure whether or not he could really trust Poppa Knight, as the older man preferred being called. But in time, they had become close. By then, Reverend Knight had been diagnosed with lung cancer. Reverend Knight managed to attend their first service in the new sanctuary of Followers of Jesus Faith Worship Center even though he was sicker than he was letting anyone know.

When Landris arrived at the Critical Intensive Care Unit, or CICU, Mrs. Knight greeted him at the entrance of Reverend Knight's room.

"Pastor Landris, thank you so much for coming so quickly," she whispered.

"Who's that?" Reverend Knight asked, his voice muffled by an oxygen mask.

Mrs. Knight nodded and smiled at Landris as she turned back toward her husband. "It's Pastor Landris. He's here to see you. I'll leave you two alone for a few minutes."

"How are you feeling this morning, Poppa Knight?" Landris asked as soon as he was next to the bed. Seeing his mouth covered, he wasn't actually expecting him to talk.

Reverend Knight took the oxygen mask off and tried hard to smile. "Hanging in here," he said, hardly able to speak as he held up his hand to show the IV tubes attached.

"I can't stay long. They're making an exception for

me to visit with you outside of normal visiting hours. But you know I had to come by this morning and see you," Landris said.

Reverend Knight closed his eyes and swallowed. "How long?" he whispered.

"Well, the nurses are pretty strict about these minutes," Landris said.

Reverend Knight opened his eyes wider and shook his head. "No. To live. Doc, the truth." Doc was what Reverend Knight called Landris from time to time.

Landris touched his hand. "Reverend—"

"Don't, Pastor Landris. Please don't. Don't do me like everyone else. Tell me—how long are they saying I have left?" His voice was barely a decent whisper.

Landris moved in a little closer. "Not very long. But you know man doesn't have the final say-so. You recall in the book of Isaiah?"

"Hezekiah," Reverend Knight said, nodding. "He was dying. Isaiah told him the Lord said for him to set his house in order because he was going to die and not live."

"Yes, Hezekiah. Only I was thinking more about the part where Hezekiah turned his face toward the wall and prayed unto the Lord. And God told Isaiah He had heard Hezekiah's prayer and had seen his tears."

"And God added fifteen more years to his life," Reverend Knight said, smiling.

Landris squeezed his hand. "Yeah—that part."

Reverend Knight struggled to speak. "I've already turned and prayed once. And God has given me more time than the doctors originally gave me. I've made my peace; I'm ready to go home to be with the Lord. I just wanted to see you and to thank you while I still could."

"Thank me for what?"

"For helping me to see the error of my ways and getting things straight with so many people before I leave this earthly tabernacle. The relationship I've had with my wife this past year"—he began to gasp for air—"has been such a blessing. I only regret I didn't change sooner so she and I could have experienced this much earlier. All that wonderful time lost because of my arrogance and pride." He touched Landris's hand. "Keep doing what you're doing, Doc. No matter what people say about you—no matter who may try to stop you." He wheezed. "You're making a tremendous difference for the Kingdom. I'm a living example of that."

"Reverend Knight, I feel your heart. Save your strength, okay?"

"Save my strength?" He grimaced. "For what? No, I have to encourage you to keep pressing toward the mark. Still, you need to watch your back and pray. Watch and pray." He closed his eyes. "Will you do one other thing for me?" He opened his eyes. "Will you check on my wife from time to time to ensure she's all right after I'm gone?"

"I'll do that. I promise."

Mrs. Knight came back into the room. Landris looked at her as she stood on the other side of her husband's bed.

Reverend Knight turned to her. "Joyce, I want Pastor Landris to preach my eulogy," he said.

She put her hand on his hand. "Paul, let's not talk about this right now—"

"If not now, then when? I want Pastor Landris to preach my funeral when I'm gone." He took hold of her hand. "Please." He looked at them both.

"Sure, Paul. If that's what you want. But what about Marshall?" she asked, referring to Reverend Marshall Walker. "He's always believed he would be the one who would preach your eulogy if you went before him."

"Call Marshall again for me and ask him one more time to come and see me," Reverend Knight said to her.

The nurse came in. "I'm sorry, but I'm going to have to ask you to leave now," she said, her attention directed at Landris. "We don't want Reverend Knight to overexert himself."

"Of course," Landris said. He turned to Reverend Knight. "I'll be back to see you later, okay?"

Reverend Knight nodded. "Thank you for coming."

Landris patted his hand. "Sure thing, Poppa Knight." He smiled. "Sure thing."

Reverend Knight closed his eyes as though he was trying to hold back tears. He nodded as the nurse placed his oxygen mask back on.

Landris went home.

Later that afternoon, the phone rang. Johnnie Mae answered it. She quickly made her way to the exercise room, where Landris was. "I just got a call," Johnnie Mae said, breathing hard.

"Mrs. Knight?" Landris asked as he continued pumping the bar with its round weights attached to each end into the air. "Has Poppa Knight taken a turn for the worse?"

"No, it wasn't about Poppa Knight. It was Lena Patterson."

"Lena?" He held the bar with the weights high and steady in the air.

"Yeah. She's still at Sarah's house. Memory showed up there this morning!"

Landris set the weights back on the bench holder and sat up. "Memory showed up at Sarah's house? But how? How did she know where to find her?"

"I'm not sure of all the details. But apparently the shock of finally seeing Memory was too much for Sarah. They put her to bed and had to bring her doctor in."

Landris grabbed his towel and wiped some of the

sweat off his muscled body. "Is she going to be all right?"

"They're not sure. But she is conscious. Lena wanted to know what we thought about Memory, since we spent time with her. She asked if I felt Memory could be trusted."

"What did you say?"

Johnnie Mae handed him his bottle of water. "That she seemed to be on the up-and-up with us as far as we could tell. Even her leaving the way she did—she never promised she'd stay or that she would go meet Sarah. I don't know, Landris. I told her she has to pray about it and go with how *she* feels she's being led."

The phone rang. Johnnie Mae jumped. "I'll get it," Landris said as he walked over to the phone on the wall. He spoke for a few minutes, then hung up. "That was Mrs. Knight. Reverend Knight just lapsed into a coma. I'm going to go over to the hospital to make sure she's okay."

"Yes, of course. Do you want me to come with you this time?"

He took her hands and looked at them. They were still swollen. "What I want is for you to go back up those stairs and get off your feet. I'm going to shower and change. I'll bring you and Princess Rose something for lunch when I come back." He kissed her and began walking with his arm around her expanded waist as they made their way up the stairs together.

Johnnie Mae leaned in closer to him. "You're soaking wet," she said.

"Yeah. It's called sweat. That's why I'm taking a shower." He hugged her tighter. "Oops. I guess that makes you wet now."

She pushed him away from her in a playful manner. He stopped walking, leaned down, and gave her yet another kiss.

Chapter 9

Put Me in remembrance: let us plead together: declare thou, that thou mayest be justified.

Isaiah 43:26

Thirty-five-year-old Theresa Jordan married forty-three-year-old Maurice Greene on June 22, 2002. It had been quite sentimental, with her and her mother, Lena, marrying on the same day in a double-wedding ceremony. Mauricia, Theresa and Maurice's baby girl, had been born on September 11, 2001. Almost a year after they wed, Theresa learned she was pregnant again. A healthy, seven-pound-six-ounce baby boy was born to the two of them on February 16, 2004. She and Maurice had disagreed from the start what his name would be. Maurice wanted him to be a junior or the second, and Theresa didn't think that was such a great idea in the least.

"Then we'd have Mauricia and Maurice. People might mistake them for being twins or something," Theresa had argued.

"So," was all Maurice had said in defense of it. "Who cares what other people think? This is my son, and I'd like him to be named after me. Who knows when we'll have another boy," he said as his counterargument.

"Oh, I can tell you. This is *it* for me. I'm getting too old to be running around behind children," Theresa said.

So the baby was named Maurice Gilead Greene the Second.

Now the sixteen-month-old toddler, whom they most times called M-double-G or MGG, was being hurriedly placed in his car seat as Theresa rushed to leave for Asheville, North Carolina. Theresa had asked Maurice to come with her, but he couldn't get Monday off from work. If he went with Theresa, they would have to return on Sunday night. Theresa wasn't certain of all that was awaiting her at Sarah's house, so she didn't want to be obligated to come home that quickly in case there was a need for her to remain longer.

"Didn't you tell me your parents are there?" Maurice asked.

"Yes," she said, wringing her hands.

"Look at you, Theresa. You're a nervous wreck," Maurice said. "I really don't want you driving to Asheville alone, not when you're like this. So here's what we'll do. I'll drive you up there, and if you decide you need to stay longer than Sunday night, I'll leave you there. You can either ride back with your parents, or I can come back and get you next weekend. Flexibility—yet another advantage to being a stay-at-home mom."

"You'd do that, Maurice? Because I really don't want to go up there alone. I honestly don't know how I'll react to seeing Memory again."

"I know. I saw you almost falling apart when you hung up from talking with your mother after she told you Memory was there."

"I don't understand how she could just show up without warning like she did."

"Well, Theresa . . . now, your great-grandmother *has* been searching for her. This is what Sarah's been praying a long time to happen."

"Yeah, but Memory could have called and prepared her by letting her know she was coming instead of just showing up on her doorstep the way that she did. All I know is that if Memory serves to hurt either her or my mother again . . . I just don't understand what motivates Memory to do what she does. That's all. I just don't understand."

Maurice threw enough things in a duffle bag to last the weekend, and off they went to Asheville. They arrived late Saturday afternoon.

"Hi, Mama," Theresa said to Lena as the two of them hugged at the door. "How are you holding up?"

Lena shook her head. "Let's not ruin this moment just yet." She hugged Mauricia and made a fuss over her before reaching for the baby to come to her. "Look at both of you! You've both grown just in the past few weeks since I saw you last," she said.

Maurice Senior kissed his mother-in-law on the cheek, then carried their things upstairs to their usual bedroom.

Lena and Theresa exchanged pleasantries, and Lena got to spend a little more time fussing over her grandchildren as they sat in the parlor. Maurice came downstairs and sat next to his wife. M-double-G toddled over to his father and scrambled up into his lap.

"Do you want to go up and speak to your great-grandmother now?" Lena asked Theresa. "She's awake."

"How is she doing?" Theresa asked.

"The doctor says she's much better. It wasn't bad enough for him to have to put her in the hospital. She just got a little too excited, I guess. It put a strain on her heart and the rest of her system. He wants her to take it easy and not overdo it. They're closely monitoring her blood pressure, as well as other things. She's getting top-of-the-line care."

"And Memory?" Theresa asked, looking as though she'd eaten something nasty.

"She's upstairs . . . with Sarah."

"Of course. And you left Great-grandmother alone with her?"

"Yes," Lena said. "It's what Sarah wants."

Theresa began shaking her head. "I just don't believe this."

Lena touched Theresa's knee. "It's not like we weren't expecting one day for this to happen. Sarah has paid tons of money to find Memory. This day was inevitable."

"Yeah, I know. But I guess, deep down, I was hoping . . ."

"What? That Memory would never show up?" Lena asked as she smiled and cocked her head to the side.

Theresa rolled her eyes and sighed. "No. I wanted Great-grandmother to get to meet her. I'm sorry, Mama, but I just don't trust Memory. Okay, there—I said it. I don't want Great-grandmother to end up hurt."

"You mean like you and I ended up hurt?"

Theresa leaned her head back and placed her hands on her face. "Yes, like you and I ended up hurt." She looked at Lena. "Mama, we put ourselves as well as our hearts out there for Memory, and look what she did to us. Look what she did to you, her own child. She left you when you were a child. And when you needed her most, she came back after your grandmother died . . . or should I say Mamie—"

"As far as I'm concerned, Mamie was and always will be considered a grandmother to me. I'm not disrespecting Sarah in any way by saying that. Mamie raised me. People say that blood is thicker than water, but love is thicker than them both. Big Mama loved me. She loved Memory, too, in spite of all the awful things Memory did."

"I still can't believe how they pulled that off," Maurice said, chiming in. "Sarah having a baby on the same day Mamie Patterson had hers. In order to save Sarah's baby from Sarah's half-brother, Heath, Sarah's mother,

Grace, got Mamie, a stranger, to pretend she'd given birth to twins, a boy and a girl, and then raise Sarah's child as her own. Truth can definitely be stranger than fiction."

"And that's the point here we must remember. Memory is Sarah's child," Lena said. "There's no denying it. My goodness, you can look at the two of them and see that."

"Great-grandmother has gone through so much during her lifetime," Theresa said as she picked up MGG, who was standing before her with his arms raised high. "I just can't sit back and allow somebody like we know Memory to be to come in and possibly do the exact same thing to her that Sarah's family did all of these years."

"Memory claims she's changed," Lena said.

"Yeah? Now where have we heard that before? Oh, that's right. At my house. Right before she *lied* and *stole* the Alexandrite necklace right out of our safe-deposit box from a bank *vault*, no less! I can't possibly fathom why we wouldn't believe her now."

"Theresa, there's no need in you getting all upset about it. Sarah is fully aware of what Memory did and how we feel about her for that. But the bottom line is that Memory is her daughter . . . her only child . . . her flesh and blood. And we know how a mother can be when it comes to her own."

"Oh, yes. Tee, of all people, should identify with how motherhood changes you," Maurice said, using the name he sometimes still called her. "She lets our two darlings get away with all sorts of things."

"I do not," Theresa said as she continued to turn her face away from the hard pats MGG was inflicting on it simultaneously with both his little hands.

"M-double-G, stop that," Maurice said sternly. Maurice the Second turned, looked over at his father, and started laughing as he unexpectedly reared backward. "See what I mean?" Maurice said, pointing at Theresa. "There's no way Theresa would have *ever* stood for something like that before she had Mauricia and Maurice. No way." He laughed.

Theresa put MGG on the floor. He ran over to Mauricia and started trying to take away a toy she was playing with. "I suppose I really need to go speak to Great-grandmother," Theresa said. "But honestly, I don't feel like seeing Memory just yet."

"Well, hello, Theresa," a voice said softly from the arched entranceway.

Theresa looked in that direction. "Memory," she said, acknowledging her grandmother with barely an audible word and a nod.

"It's good to see you," Memory said as she came closer. "And *these* two beauties *must* be my great-grandbabies." She headed more in the direction of the children. "They are beautiful!" Memory said, smiling at them. She glanced over at Theresa.

Theresa found herself just staring at Memory. The closer she was getting to her and her children, the more Theresa's jaw had tightened. The rage she thought she'd gotten under control was rapidly beginning to make its way to the surface. Theresa turned away from Memory and looked at Lena, who, she quickly discovered, was watching *her*.

It was all but apparent to Theresa: being around Memory, in the same room with her, in the same house with her, in the same city with her, in the same state, was going to be a lot harder than she ever thought. A *lot* harder!

Chapter 10

Can a woman forget her sucking child, that she should not have compassion on the son of her womb? Yea, they may forget, yet will I not forget thee.

Isaiah 49:15

Theresa stood up, leaned down, and kissed Lena. She picked up little Maurice, grabbed Mauricia by the hand, then walked toward Memory. When she reached her, she turned back to look at Lena and Maurice. "We're going up to see Great-grandmother now."

"Theresa," Memory said as she reached out and touched her arm.

Theresa looked at Memory's hand. "Please don't ever do that again," Theresa said.

Memory removed her hand. "I'm sorry. Theresa, I'm sorry about everything."

Theresa laughed and shook her head. "Yes. I'm sure you are." She then left and went upstairs.

When Theresa reached the top of the stairs, she let out a long sigh. She took her hand and wiped away the tears that, despite her best efforts to keep them at bay, had somehow managed to squeeze out and down her cheeks. She took a deep breath, knocked softly on the door, and walked in with all smiles, into Sarah's bedroom.

"Well, well. Look who's here," Sarah said. "Gayle told me you all were here. I was wondering how long it would be before you would come up to see me. Come give Grammy-grand a kiss," Sarah said with a smile. Grammy-grand was what her great-great-grandchildren called her.

Mauricia didn't talk much. She was shy and, most times, had to be coaxed into interacting with others. "Mauricia, give Grammy-grand a hug and a kiss," Theresa said, giving her daughter a little push toward the bed.

"Hi, Grammy-grand," Mauricia said as she gave Sarah a halfhearted hug and a carefully placed kiss on the cheek.

Theresa leaned MGG down so he could kiss Sarah. "Mmmm-mmmh!" MGG said as he kissed her.

"Wow! That was some good sugar," Sarah said. "I have a present for you two."

"You do?" Mauricia said, her face lighting up now. "What is it? Where is it, Grammy-grand?"

Sarah laughed. "Oh, so you're only as quiet as you want folks to believe you to be, I see," Sarah said to Mauricia. "Miss Gayle, will you take them down to the playroom and give them their presents from me?" Sarah said to her nursemaid.

"Sure thing, Miss Fleming. Come on, kids. Let's go see what Grammy-grand got for you," Gayle said, knowing Sarah was really trying to garner some alone-time with Theresa.

After the room was cleared out, Sarah motioned for Theresa to sit down in the chair next to the bed. "Why so much sadness? Why the down face?" Sarah asked.

"I'm sorry. I must be tired from the ride. I didn't realize I appeared down."

"Oh, you don't. In fact, you're doing a terrific job faking that smile to show just how peachy keen things are. You forget though . . . I have a gift to see beyond all of that. So tell me. What's wrong?"

"Nothing really."

"Theresa, I know you're not happy about Memory being here. I know Lena isn't, either. I'm sorry about that. You both brought your cases against her to me from the very beginning. And believe me, it's not that I'm being insensitive to your and Lena's feelings or discounting what she did to you both. But she's *still* my child—my only child."

"Great-grandmother, please don't let the way I or my mother feels affect you and your happiness. We truly don't mean to dampen this joyous occasion for you."

Sarah smiled. "I'm well aware you don't trust Memory any farther than you can throw her. But Theresa, in loving Memory I must move past the things she may have done in her past. For this to work, I have to give her a fair shake now. I want to know her for however much time I have left on this earth. I have to do all I can to make every second of our time together count for something good. Do you understand?"

Theresa took her great-grandmother's hand. "I understand, and I won't ruin this for you. But will you do just one thing for me?"

"What's that?"

"Be careful. Memory may be trying to convince everyone that she's changed, but I don't want her to hurt you. That's all. In loving Memory, I don't want *you* to get hurt."

Sarah squeezed Theresa's hand slightly. "Theresa, what can Memory do to hurt me? Honestly? What do I have that she can take that's not already hers? I know I just met her today, but she's the true heir to all of this," Sarah said, making a sweeping gesture with her hand. "She doesn't have to take what's already hers. All I want is her heart and to give her mine. That to me is more important than these temporary material things."

Theresa relaxed in the chair and sighed. "You know,

you are *so* wise. You almost make me feel bad about being angry with her about a *thing*."

"Be angry, but sin not. Theresa, you know you weren't really angry at her about that Alexandrite necklace. The necklace was a mere symbol, that's all it was. Both you and your mother were hurt because she took your heart and your love, and to you, she stomped all over it without any regard to what she was doing. She made you feel your love was nothing to her. That's the thing you and Lena will have to find your way back from. You trusted Memory with your heart, and she didn't take care of it the way you thought she should have. You gave her your love, and it appeared she didn't return that love or respect back to you." Sarah began coughing uncontrollably.

Theresa immediately jumped up and poured water into her glass. She handed it to Sarah and helped her hold it as she drank. "Do I need to get Gayle for you?" she asked.

Sarah sipped the water and released a sigh, then a smile. "I'm okay. Maybe a little tired now. It's been a long day, to say the least. A good one, but a long one nevertheless."

Theresa took the half-empty glass and set it back on the nightstand. "Do you need me to get you anything else?"

"Would you mind sending Memory back up here for me?" Sarah said as she closed her eyes. "I'd like to see her again."

"Of course, Great-grandmother." Theresa leaned down and planted a kiss on the matriarch's forehead. She appeared in such perfect peace. "Of course," Theresa whispered so as not to wake her.

Chapter 11

I will go before thee, and make the crooked places straight: I will break in pieces the gates of brass, and cut in sunder the bars of iron. . . .

Isaiah 45:2

Memory had gone in and sat in the light pink wing-back chair near Lena. She looked at her, then smiled. "So, you had plastic surgery done on your face?" she asked.

Lena looked at her, shook her head, and smiled. She still found it hard to believe just how insensitive her mother really could be. "Yes, I had plastic surgery. But not for the reason you may think."

"How could you possibly know what I'm thinking?" Memory asked. She could see the tightness in Lena's demeanor. "I think you might be a wee bit too sensitive still."

Lena laughed. "See there, the same old Memory."

"I'm not the same, Lena. I told you that. At least I've tried to tell you that, but you refuse to spend any time in the same room with me long enough to hear me out." Memory leaned forward. "I'm not the same person I was the last time you saw me."

"Yeah. Well, I find it interesting how pleased you seem to be about my face."

"I'm pleased because you're so beautiful."

Lena began to nod her head and prim her mouth even

more. "And I suppose I wasn't *so beautiful* when you saw me last."

"Look, Lena. I'm sure you still have a lot of mental issues about your face. But I haven't done anything to merit your attacking me like this. Frankly, I didn't care what you looked like the last time I saw you."

Lena shook her head slowly and smiled. "That's right. You didn't care what anybody looked like the last time we were together. You were only interested in getting your hands on that Alexandrite necklace. Well, I hope it was worth it." She looked right in Memory's face. "And for your information, I had the plastic surgery not because I cared so much about how I look, although I'm sure you have a problem with that statement. I had it done because of medical problems it was causing with my eye and that side of my face. It was for health reasons, not vanity."

"Lena, I was merely pointing out how good you look. It was meant to be a compliment. And as for the comment you just made about the necklace, let me say it here. No, Lena, it was not worth it."

Just then the doorbell rang. Lena looked at her watch. "That's probably Richard finally getting back from his outing. Excuse me," she said as she made her way toward the door.

Richard stepped in the foyer. "Sorry I'm so late getting back. After we finished playing golf, we decided to have lunch at the club. We got to talking . . ." He looked at his wife. "Lena, what's wrong?"

"Memory's here."

"Here as in this house?"

"In the parlor," she said as she took a few steps away. Richard set his golf clubs out of the way and followed Lena. They walked into the parlor together.

Memory looked up, saw Richard when he entered,

and smiled. "Well, well. It's good to see you together. I guess this means the two of you finally got hitched?"

"We're married, if that's what you're asking," Richard said with a puzzled look. He could tell he'd walked in on something; what that something was, wasn't quite clear.

"Memory was just about to tell me how taking the Alexandrite necklace like she did hadn't been worth it. Come in, Richard. Have a seat." Lena led him to the sofa, and they sat down practically in sync. "Please, Memory. Do continue."

Memory shook her head. "Lena, I'm sorry for what I did that ended up hurting you and has caused you to distrust me so right now."

"Who said anything about distrusting you now? Did you, Maurice?" Lena glanced over at Maurice and flashed a smile. "You, Richard?" She touched his hand. "Oh, that's right. You just got here, so it couldn't have possibly been *you*. I suppose that leaves . . . me." She looked at Memory as her smile dropped. "No, I don't suppose I do trust you."

"You don't, and I can't say I blame you for being skeptical. But I'm a different person now. You see, there was this church I was attending in Birmingham, Alabama—"

"That's where you were hiding out," Lena said.

"Birmingham is one of the cities I stayed in, but I've graced a few places over these past years. I'm certain you're aware of that fact since I'm sure Sarah kept you informed of the times she'd just missed me. Sarah thinks the world of you, dear."

"And I think the world of her. She's a good woman," Lena said. "A real good woman. A strong woman who has survived a lot. And I'm telling you here and now—I won't allow you to come in and hurt her." She shook her head slowly. "I won't."

"You mean . . . the way that I hurt you?" Memory asked.

"What makes you think you hurt me? I knew what was up with you when you showed up on Theresa's doorstep in Atlanta that day. All you did was prove me right."

"Okay, so I lived down to your expectation, which wasn't that high to begin with."

"O-kay, ladies," Richard said, holding up his hand as though he was directing traffic. "I'm sure you're both pretty hot with emotions right now. What say we grab something to eat and table this discussion until cooler heads prevail?"

"We're not emotional," Lena said. "Memory's my mother. She's Sarah's daughter. Sarah's been actively looking for her since October of 2001. And today . . . today Sarah's prayers were answered. As we can all see, Memory's here now. This is a joyous occasion. Memory says she's here with the right heart and with the right spirit. Granted, all we have is her word, but her word should be enough." She looked at Memory, scarcely blinking as she spoke. "Right, Memory?"

Maurice got up and left out of the room.

"I never claimed when I was in Atlanta that I wasn't there to get back what I believed was rightfully mine. That Alexandrite necklace belonged to me, Lena. I heard that woman, Grace, who—as it turns out—was actually my grandmother . . . my *grandmother*." Memory began a nervous laugh. "My goodness, the more I think of what's happened . . . how out of control this all got . . ." Memory placed her hand to her face and sucked in a long, deep breath before noisily exhaling it.

Lena looked at Memory and couldn't help but feel a little sorry for her. She seemed sincere enough. Lena realized this part truly had to have shocked Memory's system. Learning, after all these years, that Mamie wasn't her real mother. Hearing from strangers that her biological mother was alive and had been searching for her for years now. Then to show up at a mansion and discover your mother is not just light-skinned as she probably assumed upon seeing her, but white and quite financially well-off. All of this had to be difficult for her to process in such a short amount of time.

"Richard's right," Lena said, getting to her feet. "Why don't we go in the kitchen and get something to eat? Sarah had all this food brought in, and nobody's eaten much of it." She looked at Maurice, who was just walking back into the room with a plateful of food. "Well, almost nobody."

Maurice sat down and took a big bite of his shredded barbecue pork sandwich. The sauce oozed out onto his finger as he bit. He licked the sauce off and bit again. "Mama, I'm still a growing man," he said, talking with his mouth full. "Besides, I didn't have time to eat anything before we left. I'm starving!"

"Yeah, you're still growing all right—out. I think it's safe to say that your vertical growing days are long behind you." Lena patted his stomach, then started out of the room. "The kitchen's this way," she said to Memory, who hadn't ventured much farther than the upstairs area, mostly in Sarah's bedroom after they managed to get her up there and in the bed. "Later, I'll show you the rest of the house if you like. Grandmother asked if I would take you on a tour. . . . When you're ready, of course."

"It's quite *impressive* just from what I've seen so far," Memory said, looking around from where she remained.

Lena stared at her. The way Memory emphasized the word "impressive" caused Lena to be even more determined than ever to keep an eye on her.

Just to be on the safe side.

Chapter 12

Like as a woman with child, that draweth near the time of her delivery, is in pain, and crieth out in her pangs; so have we been in Thy sight, O Lord.

Isaiah 26:17

Seeing his wife twisting and turning on top of the bed, Landris walked hurriedly to her and leaned down. "Johnnie Mae, what's wrong?" he asked, immediately noting that her hands and feet seemed to have swollen even more.

"I'm not sure. All of a sudden, I started feeling sick," Johnnie Mae said, rubbing her head with one hand while her other hand rested on her basketball-looking stomach.

"Are you in any pain?"

"My head hurts a little. But babywise, I'm not hurting . . . just feeling really uncomfortable for some reason. It came down on me all of a sudden."

He stood up. "I'm calling your doctor. Where's her phone number?"

"In my purse. . . . It's over there on the coffee table by the chaise longue." She pointed toward the sitting area.

Landris brought her purse to her. She took out a business card and handed it to him. Landris called the number, which was immediately routed to the doctor's answering service. Ten minutes later, Dr. Brenda Baker called him back.

"Take Johnnie Mae to the hospital," Dr. Baker said. "I'll meet you there."

Landris did as he was told.

Dr. Baker examined Johnnie Mae soon after she arrived.

"I'm going to have to admit you," she said in her calm, soft-spoken voice.

Johnnie Mae swallowed hard. "Is the baby okay?"

"For now, the baby's fine. But your blood pressure is dangerously high. Dangerously high. You've developed what we call preeclampsia."

"Is that the same as toxemia?" Johnnie Mae asked, clarifying the terminology to ensure they were talking about the same thing.

"Yes, toxemia. Johnnie Mae, I'm not going to sugarcoat this. Preeclampsia or toxemia can put both you and your baby at risk."

"What risks?" Landris asked.

"For the mother, the most serious is brain damage," Dr. Baker said. "There's also the possibility of blindness, kidney failure, and liver rupture. The baby is at risk of premature birth, which, as you're both aware, can carry its own complications."

"Then what do we do to fix this?" Landris asked as he looked from Johnnie Mae to Dr. Baker.

"We're going to put her on bed rest here and monitor both her and the baby. Our first course of action is to get her blood pressure down." She then looked at Johnnie Mae. "Where it is right now, you're at risk of having a seizure or, worse, a stroke. Of course, even doing this, we still have to be careful. Lowering your blood pressure can decrease the amount of blood that gets to the baby. If that happens, the baby could end up deprived of oxygen, which can cause brain damage as well as other things." Dr. Baker began alternating her attention between Johnnie Mae and Landris as she continued. "But if we can't get your blood pressure under control and keep it that way, you could progress to true eclampsia. And should that happen, we'll have no other choice except to take the baby."

"I'm not yet seven months. If you put me in labor or take the baby this early, that will really put our baby at risk." Johnnie Mae looked directly at Landris. "I don't want to do anything that will harm or cause us to lose this baby. I don't."

Dr. Baker touched Johnnie Mae's hand. "For now, we're going to see if we can't get you stabilized using medication. If we're successful, none of this will be an issue. But Johnnie Mae, as your doctor, my first responsibility is to ensure *your* well-being."

"And my baby's," Johnnie Mae said, her voice pleading as she said it.

"We're going to do all we can to ensure the well-being of you both. But Johnnie Mae, I want you to know. Should it come down to saving your life or allowing this pregnancy to continue for the sake of the baby, as your doctor, I'm going to do what's necessary to save you." She looked intensely, seriously, and directly at Johnnie Mae.

"Dr. Baker, I understand what you're saying, but we have to make sure this baby is all right." Johnnie Mae caressed her stomach. "I'll stay here at the hospital for as long as you like. I'll do whatever you tell me to do, exactly as you tell me to. But if it comes down to me or this baby, we've got to give this baby a fair chance. We just have to."

Dr. Baker glanced at Landris, then back at Johnnie Mae. She managed a comforting smile. "Let's not give so much attention to the negative at this point," she said, her voice even softer than usual. "What say we just concentrate our attention on getting you better? That will be the best for all concerned. Okay?"

Johnnie Mae nodded slightly as she looked down at her now-clasped hands.

Dr. Baker glanced at the two nurses who had just entered the room. "The nurses need to do a few things to get you settled in. They're also going to move you to a permanent room," Dr. Baker said to Johnnie Mae, patting her hand twice. "Pastor Landris, will you walk out with me while they do what they need to?" She picked up Johnnie Mae's chart and headed to exit the room.

Johnnie Mae looked first at Dr. Baker, who was waiting to leave, then at the slightly worried expression in Landris's hazel-brown eyes.

Landris leaned down and kissed her softly on her forehead. "I'll be back as soon as they're finished. Okay?" He looked lovingly at her and smiled. She smiled back, giving him a nod of confidence.

When Dr. Baker and Landris were far enough away, Dr. Baker stopped and turned to him. "Pastor Landris, I know this is hard. I've seen this happen more times in my eighteen years of practice than I care to think about—a mother insisting on sacrificing herself for the life of her baby should it come to that. I'm certain this would be the case with Johnnie Mae. I assure you, I plan to do all I can to help this pregnancy reach full-term. It's a known fact that the longer a mother carries a baby inside the womb toward the forty weeks, the better. But please make no mistake about this. What's happening here is not something we want to play around with. For now, Johnnie Mae's condition is preeclampsia. That's for now. If her condition turns into eclampsia, that's almost always fatal. This is as direct and honest as I can put it for you. With all the advances in medicine we have today, a premature baby has a higher rate of survival than ever before. We have a terrific neonatal unit and staff here. Be assured that your baby would receive top-notch care. I need you to understand everything that's going on because, honestly, if we have to move, we'll need to move quickly and without hesitation. We can't allow time and indecision to become our enemy."

Landris looked at her with a puzzled stare. "So what you're saying is that it really could come down to a question of doing something that will save Johnnie Mae's life, yet put our baby's life in danger, or losing Johnnie Mae in order to save the baby? You're telling me it's possible I may have to choose between my wife and our unborn child?"

"I hope and pray it doesn't come to that. But I need you to know, at this point, there's a strong possibility this could well be the case," Dr. Baker said. "For now, though, it's imperative that we keep Johnnie Mae as calm and experiencing as little stress as humanly possible. That can make a world of difference. Couple that with the medication I'm prescribing for her, and I'm optimistic this just may do the trick and put us all back on track for a normal, healthy, full-term-delivery scenario."

Landris shook his head, mostly in disbelief. "In essence, what you're really telling me is this is spiritual warfare, and I need to be doing some serious, fervent praying *before* this battle gets an even greater foothold."

She looked back at him, and, without any hesitation whatsoever, she said, "Yes, Pastor Landris. I suppose that's *exactly* what I'm telling you."

Chapter 13

But now, O Lord, Thou art our father;
we are the clay, and Thou our potter;
and we all are the work of Thy hand.
Isaiah 64:8

Johnnie Mae heard a knock on the half-closed hospital door. "Come in," she said. A smile came across her face. "Charity!" she said when Charity Morrell walked in.

Charity came and gave her a hug. "How are you?" she asked, almost gushing.

Johnnie Mae repositioned her body. "I'm feeling much better, thank you. But how did you know I was here?"

"They announced you were in the hospital in church on Sunday. It's also posted on the church's Web site." Charity sat down in the chair next to the bed. "I still keep up."

"I am *so* happy to see you. Look at you! You look absolutely wonderful!"

"That's what everybody keeps telling me," Charity said. "Things are going well. But what's going on with you? No one's saying what's happening with you, just that you're in the hospital and that you'll likely be here for the remainder of your pregnancy."

Johnnie Mae smiled through the thought of her rather distressing prognosis. "The doctor calls it preeclampsia, but you may have heard it called toxemia."

Charity glanced at the monitor that displayed various readings. She was familiar with some medical readouts. "Your blood pressure's up quite a lot," she said.

"Yeah, but it's better than it was when I came in on Saturday, thank the Lord."

"Well, the entire church is praying for you." Charity sat back against the chair. "I'm glad I got to see you. I was afraid they wouldn't let me in. Pastor Landris requested that we pray for you but for us not to come by or call because you need lots of rest."

"But you came anyway," Johnnie Mae said with a grin.

"Yes. I hope you don't mind. I don't intend to stay long. I just had to come see you. I know how much it meant to me when you would come by and see me."

"Of course I don't mind. I'm glad you came." Johnnie Mae pushed her body up straighter. "Tell me, how are things with you? Really."

Charity smiled. "I'm really doing well. Really, I am. I'm back in my own house again. Both Dr. Holden and Sapphire say it looks like I'm conquering my disorder. In fact, neither Faith nor Hope has made an appearance of any kind in months now. We're *all* encouraged by that."

"Does that mean you're completely cured?" Johnnie Mae asked.

"I don't know if we can go *that* far yet. As a matter of fact, I have an appointment with Dr. Holden at one PM. But I *can* say I've unearthed a lot about myself. I still can't recall what happened that caused me to split my personalities the way I did in the first place. And now that Faith appears to be gone for good, I'm not sure if I'll ever know."

Johnnie Mae readjusted her body yet again. It was hard for her to get comfortable.

"Do you need me to get something for you?" Charity asked, rising to her feet.

"No, I'm fine. It just gets tiring lying in a bed all day and night, being in one position all the time. I try and make a point to move myself around and reposition my body to keep my blood circulating. Please go on; I didn't mean to interrupt you."

Charity sat back down and continued. "Faith refuses to come back and cooperate with either Sapphire or Dr. Holden. For reasons I can't explain, Faith seemed to prefer Dr. Holden. She just didn't care to talk to Sapphire. That's why I've been seeing both of them. I see Sapphire only weekly now, and Dr. Holden once a month. I did ask Dr. Holden about possible hypnosis, but he's not too keen on doing that. He and Sapphire both prefer the route we're taking. So I'm meeting Dr. Holden today to see what else, if anything, we might discover about my life and/or 'Trinity' "—Charity crooked her fingers and pumped them to quote the word "Trinity"—"that hasn't been uncovered already."

Johnnie Mae smiled. "Still calling the three Trinity, huh?"

"Sometimes I do. It just makes it easier than saying or trying to explain Faith, Hope, and me." Charity sneaked a quick glance at her watch. Timewise, she was doing okay. "How's your mother?" Charity asked.

Johnnie Mae's countenance quickly changed. "Physically Mama is fine; her mind, *not* as sharp. Still in and out of real time. With me being here now, I don't know what's going to happen. And I told you my oldest sister, Rachel, moved; then, just as quickly as she left, she ended up moving back."

"When she moved, where did she go?" Charity asked.

"Columbus, Georgia. She was only there for about two weeks, though. My baby brother, Christian, is in the military. He just returned from Iraq. He and his family will be stationed there for the next year. They just bought a big new house, which is why Rachel went there. But with this Iraq war still going on, he may have to go *back* to Iraq again."

"That doesn't seem fair. Why does he have to go back if he's been there once?"

"It has something to do with the commitment of tour they make. They may only stay a year, but they signed up for two. So when they come back to the States, they can be sent back to finish out the rest of the tour they didn't serve already," Johnnie Mae said.

Charity let out a sigh. "You know, I miss your mother. I wish I could see her."

"I know. Mama really enjoys your company. You have such a way with her. But with me being in here for who knows how long . . ."

"Oh, you don't have to explain. I'm aware that the rest of your family is not too enthusiastic about me being anywhere near her," Charity said. "They've all made that abundantly clear."

"Well, I know you'd never do anything to harm her. Those are my siblings, though. Who can say what will happen now that I'm temporarily out of commission?"

Charity could tell this conversation was bringing Johnnie Mae's spirits down. Looking at her watch again, she stood up. "I guess I should get going. I don't want to be late for my appointment. I'll continue to pray for all of you, just like y'all prayed for me."

"Please do."

Charity stepped up closer to the bed. "If it's okay, I'd like to come back and see you again. I can sit over there in the corner and not talk if my talking bothers you. But I really care about you, and I care what happens to you and your family."

"I'd like that—you coming by. And I love talking to you, Charity, so you can forget about that sitting-in-some-corner-and-being-quiet nonsense. I'll let Landris and the hospital staff know that you're welcome to visit me anytime you want."

Charity smiled. "Well, you get some rest and make sure you do what your doctor tells you." She headed toward the door, then turned back around. "Johnnie Mae, would it be okay if you and I have a word of prayer before I leave?"

Johnnie Mae smiled. "I would like that." She reached her hand out to Charity.

Charity came back over and grabbed her hand, holding it as they prayed for healing and health for them, as well as for the health of the baby Johnnie Mae was carrying.

Chapter 14

And it shall come to pass, that before they call, I will answer; and while they are yet speaking, I will hear.

Isaiah 65:24

Dr. Holden was in his office. Charity was his first appointment of the afternoon, although he wasn't sure whether there was anything more he could do to help her. She'd made tremendous strides in her recovery over the past few months. He thought back to when they seemed closest to getting into the mind of one of her personalities . . . back when Faith wanted to talk to him and only him.

Faith had been something else that day. She'd tried her best to get to him—going as far as turning the tables on him . . . pretending to write things in a notebook, evaluating him the way he was supposedly evaluating her. He thought about that notebook. He'd originally placed it in his desk drawer. Later he had looked at it, only to find the pages she'd written were childish doodling—scribbles, just as he'd suspected.

Inspired to find the notebook to see what, if anything, Faith may have hidden that he might have originally missed, Dr. Holden opened his desk drawer and rummaged through it. Locating the notebook, he looked at the doodles. Nothing. Flipping past those pages confirmed only blank pages. Determined to check every page all the way to the end, he continued to turn. And that's when he saw it—a page where Faith had actually written words. He began reading, engrossed by what were five pages of actual words.

The intercom buzzed, interrupting him. "Dr. Holden, your one o'clock is here," his secretary announced.

"Would you ask her to wait a few more minutes, please," Dr. Holden said. He finished reading Faith's words, then closed the notebook. Picking up the phone, he pressed the speed-dial number to Sapphire's private line.

"Sapphire, this is Dr. Holden. I know this is short notice, but is there *any* way possible you can get away for about ten minutes and meet with me in my office?"

"I'm really swamped today. What about in the morning?" Sapphire countered.

"It's about Charity Morrell's case. I've discovered something, and I'd like you in on it. She's here for her appointment now, but I was hoping to let you see this first."

There was a moment of silence. "I can't possibly come now. My next patient is already here and waiting. Is it something you can tell me over the phone?"

He flipped back to the pages of words. "I'd prefer not to," Dr. Holden said.

"Are you planning on sharing this with Charity today?" Sapphire asked.

"I believe this is going to help her. So, yes, I definitely plan on showing it to her. If you like, I can see about rescheduling her for a time when you *can* be here."

"Dr. Holden, I realize you're being polite wanting me in on this. But please feel free to do what you believe is best to help Charity. You can fill me in later."

Dr. Holden glanced at the first page of writings once again. "I think I'll go on and move on this. I'll let you know what happens." He closed the notebook, said good-bye, and hung up. Pressing the intercom button, he told his secretary to send Charity in.

A minute later, Charity walked cheerfully into his office. "It's good to see you again, Dr. Holden." She shook his hand. "So . . . you ready to get this show on the road?"

He gestured for her to sit as he picked up the notebook. "Charity, do you recall some months ago when you were here in my office and Faith made an appearance?"

Charity looked in Dr. Holden's face, trying to figure out where he was going with this. "You mean the one and only time, and, as far as I know, the last time anyone has seen or heard from her?" Her eyes widened. "Unless you know something I don't."

"As far as we can tell, it was. But I started thinking back to that day and how Faith had written some things in a notebook. This notebook." He held up the steno pad.

"Do you remember it?" he asked. She nodded. "Well, I decided to pull it out a little while ago. Originally, I thought Faith had written things about me since that's what she claimed she was doing. I believe she was trying to distract me during that session. Upon my examination of the notebook, I saw she'd been doodling, which only confirmed my initial suspicion. The rest of the notebook appeared to be blank, which is why I didn't even bother to place it in your file. As it turns out, I was mistaken." He leaned forward.

"Charity, Faith wrote things in here I believe will be the key to helping you. To see what she wrote, you'll have to flip closer to the back of the notebook. She was quite sneaky yet clever in doing that. That's why I missed it." He held the notebook out to her.

Charity stared at it as though it were a poisonous snake.

Dr. Holden studied her, making note of her hesitance. "What is it? Tell me."

She shook her head slightly. "I'm just not sure I want to see it," Charity said as she slowly took the notebook. "You know what it says, and you believe I'll be okay?"

"Yes. Trust me. If I felt you couldn't handle it, I wouldn't be doing this. I did call Sapphire before you came in to see if she might be available to come over while you and I were in session this afternoon, but she had a patient and couldn't come today."

Charity flipped open the notebook, saw what was all-too-familiar childish doodles and scribbles, and just as quickly closed it. "I can't," she said. "Not now."

"Yes, you can. Charity, you can do this. It's time for you to face those demons of the past that have been haunting you for so long. You need to move forward in a positive way in your life. I believe what's written in there will push you toward the place you truly need to go. I'm here for you; so is Sapphire. We'll help you through this."

"I'm sorry, Dr. Holden, but I just can't do this right now." She rubbed her head. "All of a sudden, I'm not feeling so well." Charity reached down, picked up her purse off the floor, and stood up, rubbing her head once more. "I think I'm going to cut my session short and go home and lie down." She turned and hurriedly walked toward the door.

"Are you experiencing one of your headaches?" he asked. She shook her head slowly without turning around. "Charity, I'd really prefer you read that here. In fact, I insist. It will make me feel better knowing that you're not alone when you see it."

She turned around and faced him. "Dr. Holden, I'm never alone. And trust me, before I read this, I'll have prayed mightily to ensure the Holy Spirit . . . my Comforter is there with me *to* comfort and guide me. You see, for the first time in my life, I truly do believe I can do all things through Christ who strengthens me. This is something I need to do on my own . . . without any crutches. I know I'll be all right." She smiled.

"Will you at least call me and let me know how you're doing after you read it? No matter how you're feeling—good or bad? And if you need to see Sapphire or me, I don't care when or what time, you'll let us know no matter how booked or busy we might be?"

"I will. I promise. But Dr. Holden, there are just some things we have to do ourselves," Charity said. "You understand." She then opened the door and walked out.

Chapter 15

Woe unto them that call evil good, and good evil; that put darkness for light, and light for darkness; that put bitter for sweet, and sweet for bitter!

Isaiah 5:20

Montgomery Powell the Second stood as she entered the room. "Thank you so much for agreeing to see me," he said, extending his hand to her.

"You made it sound like it would be worth my while," Memory said as she shook the hand of the dirty-blond-and-gray-haired white man who looked to be in his sixties.

He gestured for her to have a seat on the green brocade, French-styled couch. "As I told you over the phone, I believe this could be a win-win situation for us all."

Memory sat down. "You said this concerns the welfare of my family. In your letter, you said the least I could do is talk to you." Memory was referring to a letter he'd written and sent to Sam's house a few years back when she was once hiding out there. Memory didn't know why she'd kept that letter in her purse, but she had. His phone number was on it. She'd called him from Sarah's shortly after Theresa went back home.

"I was starting to believe I'd never hear from you. It's been some time since I sent that letter," Montgomery said. "I'm thankful you got in touch with me when you did."

"Mr. Powell, if you don't mind, I'd like to get to the point of why I'm here," Memory said. "In your letter, you mentioned you have something I might be interested in getting back. When I received this letter, I'd never heard of you and couldn't imagine anything you might have of mine I'd want, let alone want back. But since I just happen to be visiting your fair city, curiosity has gotten the best of me. So tell me, Mr. Powell the Second, what on God's green earth could you and I possibly have to do with each other?"

He turned over a clean glass and began pouring brandy into it. "Memory." He glanced at her as he poured. "Is it okay if I call you Memory?" He was prim and proper.

"Memory's fine."

"And you can call me Montgomery." He held up the crystal decanter filled with brandy. "Care for something to drink?"

"No, thanks. It's a bit too early to be drinking."

He took his glass in his hand, swirled the brown liquid around, sniffed, exhaled loud and slow, then sat in the solid, hunter green wingback chair next to the couch. "Trust me, my dear, it's never too early for good brandy." He took a sip, then exhaled again. "So tell me. How much do you know about Sarah Fleming?"

"Not much. In fact, I just met her for the first time in my life a week ago."

He nodded slowly while gazing at her. "It's quite astounding how much you two actually look alike. There's no disputing you're her child. Well, Memory, when I first heard she had a child, of course, I didn't believe it."

"Excuse me, but I suppose I'm missing something somewhere. Now, how exactly is it you happen to know my mother?"

"Sarah's family. Her half-brother, Heath, was my father, making her my aunt."

"Forgive me," Memory said, cutting him off yet again. "But I'm still a bit confused. Your last name's Powell—hers is Fleming. She never married to change hers."

"Allow me to clarify. My father's mother was married to another man when she conceived him. Reportedly, it was common knowledge that she and Victor Fleming had a deep love for one another that lasted for many years. Forgive me for not divulging all the details. Rumor also has it that my grandfather was quite the ladies' man. I'm sure you can relate. Things weren't as easy for people like my grandmother as they can be today."

"Okay, so what you're saying is your grandmother was fooling around on her husband while still married *to* and living *with* him, ended up knocked-up—excuse me, I meant with child by another man—and, let me guess, probably passed the baby off as his?"

He turned up his nose, then forced a smile. "My grandmother was trapped. She did what she had to. When my father was born, yes, she was still married to her husband, thereby my father's name, Montgomery Heath Powell. Everybody called him Heath. However, six months after my father's birth, her husband died. A month later, she married Victor Fleming. Tragically, she died days after giving birth to her second son, Victor Fleming Jr. My father's name was never legally changed to Fleming, I suppose due to my grandmother's own untimely death, after which Grandfather married Grace, and they had Sarah. My father died twelve years ago, two years after Uncle Vic. I, being the next male in line, was appointed in my father's will to take over and manage the family's home and all family affairs in Aunt Sarah's stead, while she was . . . away."

"And why exactly was she 'away?' " She placed emphasis on the word "away."

He rubbed his temple. "Oh dear. No one's told you?"

He began to stroke his chin. "You know, I was afraid of that. Let's just say Aunt Sarah has had serious challenges for many, many years now, and we'll leave it at that."

"Oh, you're dying to tell me. So, do . . . tell. What kind of *challenges*?"

"I see you don't know how to leave well enough alone." He drained his glass dry, then stood up and poured himself another. "Aunt Sarah hasn't always been stable, mentally that is. She's a dear, sweet woman, and we as a family unit have done as much as we could to get her the help she needs. I must say that I'm impressed with how well she's held up while searching for you. You are a slippery one. At her age and in her fragile state, it's a wonder the two of you *ever* got to meet."

"But as somehow you already knew before I arrived here, we did," Memory said.

"Yes, and I don't know if anyone, other than Aunt Sarah, is happier about that than I. But I'm also astutely aware of the riff caused, shall we say, by a certain piece of Russian jewelry." He walked over and opened the drawer to the sofa table. Taking out a flat black velvet box, he handed it to Memory as he took a sip from his glass. "Open it," he said.

Memory took the box and did as instructed. She looked up at him with a frown. "Where did you get this?"

"I bought it. But, of course, you should know that. It's the Alexandrite necklace you sold, for a handsome price I might add, about four years ago. It's a shame, too. I mean a shame that I had to buy it back, considering it already belonged to our family to begin with." He sat back down, glass in hand as he swirled it, while staring into her eyes.

"That necklace was given to my mother. . . ."

"You mean Mamie Patterson?"

"Yes . . . Mamie."

"That's something, isn't it? The way everybody was deceived. Aunt Sarah made to believe her child—you—had died all of those years ago. It's no wonder she stepped off the deep end. That was all Grace's doing. Personally, I believe she wanted to drive her own daughter crazy to keep her from the inheritance." He took another swallow as he peered over the glass rim before setting it on the coffee table. "You know Grace—again, that was Sarah's mother in case no one besides myself has told you that—was in on the whole baby-deceiving scheme from the start. I suspect she didn't want a half"—he paused, then continued—"black child in the family. You understand. She was also the one who took that necklace. We concluded it was merely a payoff to keep Mamie Patterson's mouth shut. Anyway, that's how the necklace came to leave our family in the first place."

"I wouldn't say it *left* our family," Memory said as she relaxed against the sofa.

"That's right. You ended up taking it back. I think that was quite brilliant—the way you tracked it down and all. I'd almost resigned myself to the fact that it was lost to our family forever." Montgomery crossed his leg. "Then all of a sudden, I get a call, out of the blue, in September of 2001—that the necklace had been located and was on its way via a special courier. I paid two million dollars to get that little jewel back. But as you can see, it's worth every penny." His eyes appeared to twinkle as he spoke.

Memory recalled how the reward paid had been a million dollars. *So, he'd paid two to get it back?* "What makes you think I was the reason it came back to you?"

"Memory, please, let's not play games. We're both too old to play games. You're here now, and you're learning the truth. The truth that who you thought was your mother all those years really wasn't. . . . That

Sarah Fleming was and is the woman who gave birth to you." He stopped briefly and grinned. "Now *that* must have been a true shocker. Lies and deception from your own family. But from all indications, now it appears you have a credibility problem because of that magnificent piece of jewelry you hold in your hands."

"And how would you happen to know about my issues?" Memory asked.

"Oh, I have my ways. Aunt Sarah, bless her heart, believes in you because she loves you. But your daughter . . . it's Lena, isn't it? And your granddaughter, sweet little Theresa, both find it hard to trust you. Or at least I would imagine they do. But you know what they say. 'Oh, what a tangled web we weave.' " He smirked again. "Well, you know the rest. Now, who could have predicted things would turn out the way that they have?" He reached forward and retrieved the necklace from her. "Stunning piece of work, don't you think?"

Memory's eyes began to bore a hole in him as she stared him down. "Let's just cut to it, okay? What do you want?"

"Me? Why, I just want you and your family to get along better. I want to work something out so you can give your daughter this necklace back, and the two, or I should say three, of you can mend your fences and become a happy family again. This should be a joyous time for all of you. There should be no strife or animosity between mothers and daughters . . . or granddaughters, for that fact." He smiled. "Family unity. Forgiveness. That's what I want. For y'all to be one big, happy family—what Sarah wants most."

"And why don't I believe you?"

He set the box with the necklace down on the coffee table in front of her. "Maybe because we tend to see our own selves in others. Meaning you can't trust yourself, so you can't possibly trust others for seeing who *you* are, and not who *they* really are." He sat back against the chair. "I'm offering you a way to make up for what you did to your own flesh and blood. Consider it as my early seventieth birthday present to you. And as I'm sure you've already learned, that necklace was technically yours anyway. In truth, you had a right to take it back and sell it, which, we can see, you clearly did." He pointed at it. "I had a right to buy it, which, as we can also see, I did. Now I'd like to figure out a way to return this necklace to its rightful owner—you."

"What makes you so sure that necklace ever belonged to me? And who said I received any money from the sale of it?"

He began to swing the crossed leg that rested on top. "According to family legend, that necklace was your inheritance anyway. It was designated to go to the first-born grandchild. That's you. Grace made sure no one messed with that when she gave the necklace to Mamie to hold for you. Unfortunately, others decided to take matters into their own hands, namely, Lena, and keep what was rightfully yours." He grinned slightly, then sucked his bottom lip. "At least, that's the story I was told. How am I doing so far?"

Memory rolled her hand in a circular fashion, indicating he should continue.

"As for how I know you received the money from the sale, I know the money was paid to your friend . . . what was his name . . . ?" He tapped his right temple several times with his index and middle fingers. "What was his name?" He got up, walked over to the sofa table again, opened the drawer, took out a folder and opened it, then closed the drawer. "Ah, yes! Christopher Harris," he said, returning his attention to Memory.

"Well, since you think you know so much, do you know that Christopher Harris double-crossed me? That the little weasel left me high and dry?" Memory's tone was harsh and slightly laced with anger. "Left me with nothing except a slew of folks looking for me. Which now I can see, apparently, you were one of them."

"Hmmm, it is a shame, isn't it? How there's just no honor among thieves these days. Which is why I have a legally enforceable business proposition I think you'll be most interested in." He sat down and handed her a sheet of paper from the folder. "I'm willing to let you have that Alexandrite necklace, and all you have to do is agree to sell me the house my aunt Sarah lives in after she passes on."

Memory almost laughed out loud. "Sell you the house?"

"Yes. I have it on good authority that you're going to inherit the house upon her death. I'm sure you don't care anything about that old place. I'm not asking you to give it to me; I intend to pay you its fair-market value. You're not going to get gypped in the deal." He leaned in closer to her. "All it will take is your signature on that agreement"—he pointed at the paper she held—"witnessed by a notary public or a lawyer, which—believe it or not—my lawyer just *happens* to be here, waiting in another room. If you sign that piece of paper today, you can have the Alexandrite necklace . . . free and clear today."

She snickered. "I can have it? And it won't cost me one red cent, you say?"

"Not one red cent," he said, practically mocking her.

"And the only thing I have to do is sign this paper stating I'll sell you the house once my mother dies, should I inherit it—which neither one of us can be certain will end up being the case," Memory said. "Looks to me you're taking quite a risk here."

"Trust me—you're the main heir to my aunt's vast fortune." Montgomery began to stare off into the distance. Returning his eyes to her, he said, "And there's quite a fortune to be had. I should know. I was the one managing things. That's until Aunt Sarah came back four years ago and commandeered almost everything I and my family have worked so hard to keep and acquire completely away from me." There was a twinge of anger in his voice this time. He suddenly began to chuckle quietly to himself.

"And how do I know for certain you have the funds to purchase her house, *should* I inherit it and decide to sell it to you as you're asking *here*?" She shook the paper.

"I assure you, I still have plenty of money." He took out a pen and laid it on the table. "However, the agreement states I'll purchase the house at fair-market value, and if I can't, then I don't get it. It's as cut and dry as that. This won't cost you a thing. The way I see it, you're not going to want to keep that old house anyway. This makes it easy for you to take the money, a quite substantial amount of cold, hard cash, in fact, and do whatever you want. See the world, share the money with your family . . . buy yourself a nice home wherever you'd really like to settle down—whatever you want to do. All I want is the house and all of its contents. When the time comes, you sell it, take the money, and walk away . . . free and clear. In the meantime, your having the necklace makes things right with your family. A win-win situation for everyone. So, shall I call my lawyer in now?"

"And why do you want that house and its contents so badly?"

"Pure and simple—sentimental value. That house and all the things inside of it have been in our family for generations now."

"Oh, just say it. You believe you'd appreciate and take much better care of it than I ever would." Memory brought the paper closer as she began to slowly scan over it.

"Honestly? Yes."

"Seeing as you say we treat people according to how we see ourselves, I'm sure you'll appreciate my wanting to read this agreement thoroughly before signing it."

"Fine. But I would like to make one request, if I may," Montgomery said.

She laid the paper down on her lap and stared at him. "And that would be?"

"That we keep this between the two of us. I'd prefer you not mention any of this to Aunt Sarah or anyone else for that matter."

Memory looked hard at him. "Why . . ." She nodded, then smiled. "Of course."

Chapter 16

And the mean man shall be brought down, and the mighty man shall be humbled, and the eyes of the lofty shall be humbled. . . .

Isaiah 5:15

Reverend Marshall Walker walked into his old friend's hospital room. Occasional whirling, hissing, sucking, and pumping sounds from the various medical machines filled the air. Poppa Knight's wife had called him Saturday morning at her husband's request. She'd also informed Reverend Walker that Poppa Knight's imminent departure was at hand. For whatever reason, Reverend Walker didn't come Saturday. It was now Tuesday.

"Hey, Poppa Knight, can you hear me?" Reverend Walker said in his slightly bass voice. "It's me—Marshall." He was standing next to the bed. Poppa Knight had been in a coma since Saturday afternoon and was now on a ventilator.

"If only you had come Saturday when I called," Mrs. Knight said. "I told you how dire things were. If you'd have made it before Saturday afternoon, you might have—"

"I'm sorry. You know I wanted to, Sister Knight. It just couldn't be helped," Reverend Walker said. "Duties. You understand?" His face softened as he looked at her.

In truth, he could have come Saturday. *But then, who would have been in charge of the ministers' meeting?* There was much to discuss—namely, his upcoming pastor's appreciation. In a few weeks, top folks would be coming into town from all around the country. He didn't really need the other ministers' input. Although secretly, he did enjoy watching the awe shown whenever he mentioned certain bigwigs' names he knew personally and those taking part in his celebration. If anyone would understand why he couldn't make it Saturday, he knew Poppa Knight would. Sundays were always full with two worship services and afternoon preaching engagements. Mondays were his off-days. So Tuesday was really the first day he could come. How was he supposed to know before he could get there Poppa Knight would slip into a coma? After he heard about it, he knew Poppa Knight wouldn't know he was there no matter what day he came now.

The light-skinned, medium-size-framed Mrs. Knight excused herself and left the room to give the two of them some alone-time together.

"Well, old friend, it looks like you're trying to give up on us," Reverend Walker said to Poppa Knight. "Believe me, I understand. I suppose this just got to be too much for you. We've seen a lot in life, that's for sure. But don't you worry. . . . I promise, I plan to preach a heart-wrenching, powerful sermon at your funeral—one folks won't soon forget. I owe you that much. You absolutely deserve it. Not that I'm trying to hurry you along or anything. You know I have nothing but love for you. Together, we've been through much, my friend—you and I. So much that even today, you're the only person on earth who holds my deepest, darkest secret . . . our secret, really. That alone proves how close we are and have remained." He slowly lowered himself into the chair next to Poppa Knight's bed and leaned in closer, placing his hand on the rail of the bed as he continued.

"I suppose when you do leave us, you'll be taking all those secrets with you. I'm going to miss you, there's no question about that. You've been a good friend and a loyal confidant. Although I admit you did change somewhat on me this past year. You even went as far as visiting Pastor Landris's church, more than once from what I hear. But I'm not mad at you. Oh, no. And don't you worry about good old Pastor Landris, either. I'm going to make sure he's well taken care of after you're gone."

He looked up and watched as Mrs. Knight dragged herself back into the room. "It's hard seeing him like this," Reverend Walker said to her. He stood up and wiped away a nonexistent tear.

"Yes. The doctor feels we should take him off life support. At this point, I'm just not sure what I should do." She forced a smile. "What if he really could get better later? What if I tell them to do it, but if I'd merely waited another day or another week . . . ?"

Reverend Walker went to her. "Sister Knight, there are times when we need to learn to just let go and let God. The way I see it is, if God wants our dear brother to remain with us, He'll keep him here long after that man-made machine is turned off." He pointed at the ventilator. "If God wants him to come on home to glory to be with Him, then who are we to stand in God's way?"

Mrs. Knight broke down and began to cry. "I know what you're saying is right. But it's so hard. In spite of our ups and downs, Paul and I had a pretty good marriage. Not perfect by any stretch of the imagination. But for the most part, it worked for us. We loved each other. And this past year, oh"—she clapped her hands and shook her head as she blushed—"has been positively wonderful! Even with him being sick and all, it's been almost like I was married to a totally different man." She yanked out four paper tissues.

Reverend Walker embraced her. "I must apologize. I was so busy; I wasn't there much for either of you. I'm sure this *has* been a challenging time for you both."

She looked up at him, wiped her tears with the fistful of tissues, and smiled as she nodded. "Yes, it has. I know how busy life can be and especially life in the ministry. But others have filled in where you couldn't. His friends have visited regularly, doing whatever they could here and there . . . giving words of encouragement just when we needed a word the most. Theodore, and especially . . . especially Reverend Grant."

Reverend Walker nodded. "Reverend Simpson certainly is a good man," he said, commenting on Reverend Theodore Simpson only. Reverend Grant had become distant with him lately. He was changing . . . like Poppa Knight had. So Reverend Walker wasn't sure what was going on with him, nor did he care to talk about Perry Grant right now. He continued to console Mrs. Knight.

"And then there's Pastor Landris. He has been a true godsend," she said. "I truly, truly thank God for him."

Reverend Walker pushed her away gently and looked at her. "Pastor Landris?"

"Yes," she said, dabbing at her eyes with her tissue as though that would stop the flow. "In fact, he came by early Saturday morning and again Saturday afternoon after Paul went into this coma." She looked down and smiled at her husband. "That morning, Paul asked him to preach his funeral."

Reverend Walker fought to maintain his composure. "He did? Well, now, you do know Poppa Knight has always said if he ever went before me, he wanted me to preach his funeral. You don't really believe you can take seriously what he said on Saturday . . . seeing that he was most likely too heavily medicated to even know *what* he was saying, do you?"

"He was pretty lucid. That's why I suppose he wanted to see you on Saturday. He wanted to say his good-byes himself and make sure some of his last wishes were known. Maybe he wanted to relay to you his desire regarding his funeral and Pastor Landris. I can't honestly say what all he wanted; he didn't tell me before he lapsed into this coma."

Reverend Walker pulled her back close to him again. "Well, let's not talk on such things right now. I believe Poppa Knight's going to pull through, and all this talk about a funeral will be for nothing. At least for now, anyway. We all have to leave here someday; this is not our home. We're just pilgrims traveling through this unfriendly land. But we know that God is still in the healing business. Who's to say what our Father in Heaven is up to when it comes to our brother in the Lord?" He released her and planted a kiss on her cheek as he patted her on the back.

He then looked at his Rolex watch so that there would be no mistaking he was checking it. "Look at the time. So much to do. I really must be going now. You, of all people, know that a pastor's work is never done." He had a look of true sincerity. "Are you going to be all right here alone?"

She took a deep breath as she nodded. "I'm not alone. There are others here with me in the waiting room." She exhaled as she carefully and tenderly took hold of her husband's limp hand and placed it against the side of her face.

Reverend Walker hugged her once more, then started out of the room. Right before he completely walked out, he turned around and looked back at his long time friend . . . one more time, and nodded.

Chapter 17

Until I come and take you away to a land like your own land, a land of corn and wine, a land of bread and vineyards.

Isaiah 36:17

Memory came back after having met with Montgomery Powell the Second. Sarah had given her a key so she could come and go as she pleased. She'd been there a week now. Theresa had gone home Saturday, shortly after noon when Maurice came back and got her and the children. Lena and Richard were still there. Other than "Hello" and "Good night," Lena and Theresa had barely exchanged twenty words with Memory after that first day.

Lena knew how much Sarah wanted everyone to get along and become a true family. She only wished she could trust Memory's motives enough to do that. She and Memory hadn't had a real chance to sit down alone together and talk. Memory had told Sarah earlier that day that she was going out to see a little more of Asheville. The last time Memory was in Asheville, she'd been in her midteens.

Lena looked out the window when Memory was leaving that afternoon and saw her get into a black Lincoln Town Car. Curious, she watched as it drove away. Lena couldn't help but wonder who Memory could possibly know well enough that they would send a car for her. That same car brought her home a few hours later.

"When you get time, I'd like to talk with you," Lena said as soon as Memory stepped foot back into the house.

Holding tight her purse's strap, Memory said, "I have some time right now."

"Can we go up to my room? I have something I need to show you," Lena said.

They went to the bedroom Lena and Richard stayed in whenever they visited.

Lena closed the door and motioned for Memory to have a seat on the couch.

"Lena," Memory said as she sat down while reaching into her tourist-bag-size purse. "I have something I want to give you first before we begin." She pulled out a black velvet box and held it out to her daughter.

"What is it?"

"Take it and see for yourself," Memory said. Noting Lena's hesitation she said, "Please" in a not-so-pleading voice.

Lena took the box and opened it as Memory had instructed. She looked at Memory as her knees began to buckle, causing her to sit beside her. "The Alexandrite necklace. But I thought . . . Didn't you sell this for a reward? How did you get it back?"

Memory released a sigh. "Lena. I made a mistake, and that mistake cost me dearly. It cost me the love and trust of my family. You and Theresa mean so much to me—you have no idea how much. Yet both of you have barely been able to force yourselves to look at me except with a look of contempt and disdain this whole week we've been here."

Lena shook her head reflectively as she took out the necklace and touched it lovingly and gently with her fingers. So many memories came flooding back as she gazed down at this spectacular piece of jewelry. Tears welled up in her eyes—she couldn't help but think of Big Mama and those last days spent together. "I'm sorry. I'm confused. Does this mean you really *didn't* sell it?" She buttoned her lips tight, then relaxed them.

"Can we not talk about that part of our past right now? I admit I was wrong, and I'm apologizing. I never should have taken that necklace the way I did. But I'm trying to make things right. I'm asking you to forgive me. Please." Her eyes were now pleading.

Lena looked at her. Again, she shook her head as she slowly held the necklace out to Memory. "Here you go."

"What? You don't want it? You can't find it in your heart to forgive me? What?"

Lena began a nervous laugh. "No. That's not it at all. This necklace has always belonged to you. I didn't know that when Big Mama told me to keep it safe. But I've learned this much to be a fact after all that's transpired." She grabbed Memory's hand; holding it, she let the necklace drop. It appeared as though it was being poured into Memory's palm.

Memory put the necklace back in its box and back in her purse. "Okay, I'm lost now. If you didn't want the necklace, then what has all this silent treatment been about?"

"You don't get it. It's been about love and trust and the breaking of that love and trust. I opened up my heart to you, and again you stomped on it like it was nothing. Only it wasn't just *my* heart you trashed this last time around. When you left in 2001, you trampled Theresa's heart as well. Let's move on." Lena stood, walked over to the dresser, and opened the bottom drawer. Taking out a wooden box, she walked back with it.

Instantly, Memory recognized it. "That's the box the Alexandrite necklace was in when that woman, Grace, gave it to Mama . . . to Mamie," Memory said, stuttering slightly as she hurriedly spoke. "But it was empty when I found it, and I threw it away. I distinctively remember throwing it away. How did you happen to find it?"

Lena stood next to Memory. "It's not exactly the same box. There were three of these made. Big Mama had one—that's the box that held the necklace and other things given to her by Grace. Sarah had one she gave to a woman named Pearl Black for safekeeping here in Asheville right before she was sent away all those many years ago. And then . . . there was this one. The one Grace left to me and you in her will."

Memory took the exquisite box and examined it more closely. "I love the workmanship."

"Your father made it. Your biological father, that is," Lena said as she continued to stand there. "A man named Ransom Perdue."

Memory's face suddenly drained of all color and expression as she looked at Lena. "My father?" She tried to compose herself. "Ransom Perdue? I hadn't even thought about that. I've only known Willie B. as being my father. I'm sorry, but I need a moment to digest this. That kind of caught me off guard." She stood up, purse on her shoulder, and held the box against her chest. Pacing, she mindlessly ran her hand over the box.

"Memory, Grace left that box with instructions for you and me to open it together. She also left a video she recorded."

Memory turned and shot her an evil look. "I've been here for a week. Why are you just now telling me this?" She backed away from Lena until she bumped into the bed and could go no farther. "Have you seen what's inside this box already?" she asked.

Lena shook her head. "No, I haven't. And the reason I'm just now telling you this . . . Quite honestly, I'm aware of how much Sarah loves you. But you have hurt and disappointed so many people so many times, Memory, I found it difficult to even be in the same room with you. I've tried hard to understand how or why you do the things that you do. And do you know what's so bad? It doesn't seem to bother you. It's whatever serves you at the time. It's never the other way around."

Memory looked at her. "Lena, when I took that necklace, believe me, it bothered me. And do you know why? Because of you and Theresa. For the first time in a long time, I actually felt like I had and was part of a real family. But after I did that, I knew that was the end of all of that. I knew neither of you would ever forgive me. And judging from the look on your face even after everything now, I see I was right."

"I just don't understand why you do what you do."

Memory sat down on the bed. She set the box down next to her. "The thought of all that money made me greedy to the point where I didn't care about anybody else other than myself. That's why I came to Atlanta in the first place. But something changed while I was there. I changed. And if only you knew how horrible I felt leaving Theresa the way I did that day, that horrible day that only seemed to have gotten worse as the day went along. And then knowing that I had a brand-new great-grandbaby that I'd likely never be able to see or hold . . . Oh, that tore me up something awful inside."

"I'm sorry. But I still don't understand why you did it."

"Sometimes we get ourselves into things pride won't let us walk away from. I never knew how much I was going to love you or Theresa . . . or that baby even, which, incidentally, I only got to see this past week. But I'd already made a deal with the devil, so to speak, and there was no way of getting out of it. I'm trying to prove to everybody that I *have* changed. This necklace"—she took the necklace out of her purse and out of the box—"should say how much." Memory sighed. "So . . . what do we do about *this* box?"

"We break the seal. We take this special key"—Lena poured an unusual-looking key out of a small manila envelope and held it up, then went and sat on the bed next to Memory—"and we open it. We go wherever the contents of that box happen to take us."

Memory set the necklace on the bed, picked up the box, and started to break the seal, when she stopped. She handed the box to Lena. "Why don't *you* do the honor?"

Lena took the box and looked at Memory. This was the first time in all of her life she could ever remember her mother putting someone else before herself. She looked at Memory, nodded, then smiled.

Lena broke the wax seal off the box. She placed the key inside the lock and turned it. Slowly opening the lid, she and Memory began exchanging looks between them.

The door to the bedroom flew open. "I'm sorry," Gayle said, practically out of breath. "But you need to come quick! It's Ms. Fleming. Something's wrong. She's asking for you both."

Lena closed the lid quickly and set the box down on the bed right next to the necklace. "What's wrong with her?"

"Her breathing's not stable. Her blood pressure has shot up. I called her doctor, and he said we had to get her to the hospital as quickly as possible. The ambulance is already on its way, but Ms. Fleming insists you both need to come right now," Gayle said.

Lena and Memory were already out of the door while Gayle was still speaking.

"Grandmother, what's wrong?" Lena asked as she

hastily took hold of her grandmother's now cool and clammy hand.

Sarah looked at Lena and frowned. "Memory? Where's my Memory?"

Memory stepped over and up where she could be seen better. "I'm right here."

Sarah smiled, reached her other hand over to Memory, and closed her eyes. "That's good. That's good." She fought to speak and breathe. "You're both here . . . together. That's good. . . ." She suddenly became quiet as she appeared to merely drift off to sleep.

Chapter 18

Seeing many things, but thou observest not; opening the ears, but he heareth not.

Isaiah 42:20

Sapphire had spoken with Dr. Holden and had become concerned when she learned that Charity had taken the notebook and left the safety of Dr. Holden's office to read what was inside it.

"Why did you just let her leave?" Sapphire respectfully asked Dr. Holden over the phone.

"Now, you know I can't force anyone to stay here, no more than I could have forced her to read it while she was in my presence, nor taken it back when she refused to read it while she was here," Dr. Holden said. "Besides, I didn't see anything, at least from what I read, that would be too much for her to handle."

"Well, I've been calling her for the past hour, and she's not answering either her home or her cell phone. I'm going over to her house to make sure she's all right."

Standing outside Charity's house, Sapphire rang the doorbell. No answer. She knocked. She called from her cell phone. She called out "Hello" as she knocked. But no matter which route she took, there was no answer. Pressing the doorbell repeatedly, Sapphire prayed Charity would come to the door and relieve her increasing concern. Beginning the cycle again, she rang the doorbell, called from her phone, called out to "Anyone in there," and knocked. For whatever reason, there was no answer.

Sapphire knocked on the door a few more times. After ten minutes of no response, she walked around the house and peeped through any of the windows she was able to see into. The house was eerily quiet, but she knew that didn't mean Charity wasn't in there.

Knowing it was past his work time, Sapphire called Dr. Holden on his cell phone.

"Dr. Holden, I'm at Charity's house, and she's not answering the door, either." Sapphire pressed the doorbell while speaking as though she were trying to show him.

"Sounds to me like she's just not home."

"Yes. Or maybe she read the notebook and everything came flooding back to her. Who can say what might have happened?"

"I'm telling you, I didn't see anything in there that would send Charity over the edge. Sapphire, you know if I had, I wouldn't have given it to her the way that I did."

"But you did say it shed at least *some* light on what may have happened."

"A hint. But in my opinion, it wasn't some conclusive, damaging revelation."

"Respectfully, Dr. Holden, but you know what may not be damaging for one can be devastating for another," Sapphire said. "What if there was coded information in it that holds the key to some unwritten message only Charity could decipher?"

"I believe Charity has made tremendous progress these past months. So even if that's the case, I trust that she'll come through this just fine," Dr. Holden said.

"I pray that's so." Sapphire looked at her watch. She had asked Pastor Landris earlier if it was okay for her to visit Johnnie Mae. He thought seeing Sapphire would be good for her. "I'm going now. I want to stop by and see Johnnie Mae before it gets late."

"I thought they asked people not to visit her right now," Dr. Holden said.

"I cleared it with Pastor Landris. Besides, I wasn't planning on staying long."

"Please give her all of our best."

"I will."

"And Sapphire?"

"Yes?"

"Don't worry about Charity. She's a lot stronger than you give her credit for."

"Yeah. Well, I'm going to leave a note on her door to let her know I was here."

Sapphire went to the hospital and located Johnnie Mae's room. She stopped as soon as she stepped inside. "Charity?" she said with a smile and a huge sigh of relief.

Charity smiled back. "Hi, Sapphire."

"Well, hello there, Sapphire," Johnnie Mae said with a grin. "Now, how awesome is this? Two of my favorite people here at the same time."

Sapphire walked over and kissed Johnnie Mae on the cheek. "How are you?"

Johnnie Mae nodded as she quickly glanced at her stomach. "We're doing okay."

Sapphire sat down in the other chair in the room. "I just left your house," Sapphire said, addressing her attention to Charity.

"My house?" Charity asked. "What were you doing at my house?"

"Checking up on you. . . . Making sure you're okay."

Charity smiled. "As you can tell, I'm fine."

Sapphire nodded. "So I see."

Johnnie Mae quickly picked up on some tension in the room. She wasn't sure where it was coming from or why, but it was definitely thick enough to dip a spoon in.

A nurse came in, pushing a small cart. "I don't mean to put you two out, but I have a few things I need to do. It shouldn't take but ten or fifteen minutes," she said.

"Why don't you both go down to the cafeteria and get a cup of coffee or a bite to eat? By the time you get back, I'm sure we'll be done," Johnnie Mae said, looking from Sapphire to Charity as she spoke.

"I realize we're supposed to be staying out of the way," Charity said. "Besides, I've been here once already today. Why don't I just come back another time?"

"Now you're going to make me feel bad," Johnnie Mae said. "I really want to see you both; I love the company. Go get something or do something and come back in about fifteen minutes." She lowered her head, raised it, wrinkled her nose, then said, "Please."

Sapphire looked at Johnnie Mae, then Charity. "You know, I think that's a great idea. I haven't eaten anything since lunch, and this will give you and me some time to talk, Charity. You can catch me up on what's going on with you these days."

"See now, this is going to work out for everybody," Johnnie Mae said. "The nurse can do what she needs, you two can visit with each other for a little bit, then the both of you can come back and visit with me a while longer."

Sapphire and Charity left the room and caught the elevator to the cafeteria. Getting something to eat, they exchanged looks as they set their trays down on the table.

Sapphire began. "Johnnie Mae must have somehow known we needed to talk."

"So it appears," Charity said. "Would you say grace?"

She bowed her head, as did Sapphire, who prayed a short prayer of thanks for the food they were about to receive. "Okay," Charity said as she picked up a chunk of chicken salad with her fork, "what exactly do you feel we need to talk about?"

Sapphire concentrated her full attention on Charity's face as she tried to read her. "I know we had a session last week, but how are you? I mean *today*, how are you?"

"I'm doing very well. My life feels normal for a change, and I like it. There haven't been any blackouts or unaccounted-for time as far as I can tell. It seems there's only me and my life to deal with these days. That was our goal when we began, right?"

"The goal was to get your personalities integrated . . . to make you whole again. But also to ensure you stay all right. Listen, Charity, Dr. Holden told me about the notebook. He said he gave it to you today during your session. Have you read it yet?"

Charity looked down as she began to play with her food. "No."

Sapphire used a quiet, nonthreatening voice. "May I ask you why not?"

Charity looked up at her. Sapphire's eyes were piercing, but in a good way. She felt like Sapphire honestly cared. "I'm afraid of what it might unleash. Sapphire, I'm doing really well now. We thought I needed to face what happened all those years ago in order for me to reach a good place. Well, we can see I'm there already without it. What if the words in that notebook send me back to a divided place again? What if I can't handle it the way you and Dr. Holden believe I can?"

"But you need to face it, Charity. That's how strongholds are brought down." Sapphire leaned in closer. "Why didn't you read it while you were in Dr. Holden's office?"

"Because then I would have *had* to read it. He would

have sat there waiting for me to do it, saying things to urge me to do it, and I wasn't ready." She took a sip of her cola. "I just wasn't ready. To be honest, I'm not sure when or even *if* I'll ever be ready. Maybe it's best we leave the past in the past. Besides, if Faith wrote it, maybe she was merely setting me up so she could do her worst damage and rid herself of me once and for all."

"The Faith personality knows you have support now." Sapphire sat back. "I think she may have written that because she knew you were stronger, and that she truly wasn't needed, separately from you, anymore. She wanted to leave you with the truth so you could be whole again. Faith is still inside of you. . . . She's a part of the real you—the strong part you've always possessed."

Charity bit down on her bottom lip, then placed her hand over her mouth to keep from crying.

Sapphire leaned in again and touched the back of Charity's left hand that now rested on the table. "Charity, what are you thinking right now? What's getting you so upset? Dr. Holden would never have given you that notebook if he thought it would damage the progress you've made. This much I'm certain of. Dr. Holden's one of the best."

"But what if you and Dr. Holden are wrong? What if those words mean something to me that you or he has no way of knowing? Do I really want to take that chance? Do *you* want to, after all the work and efforts you've put into helping me finally get to this great place in my life? You, wrestling with the conflict-of-interest question when it came to Faith being part of me and whether or not you should even treat me?"

Sapphire fell back against her chair as though she were letting go of something she'd been tightly holding on to. "Why didn't you just read it with him there with you?"

Charity speared a grape tomato with her fork and stuck it in her mouth. Chewing it up and swallowing it, she said, "Because I don't know if I ever really want to know the truth. Whatever it was, it can't be good. It caused me to develop split personalities."

Sapphire reached over and touched the back of Charity's hand that held her fork. "Charity, you were a child then. A child. You're not a child anymore. What you might not have been able to handle then, you're a different person now." She removed her hand. "Would you like for me to read it, or at least be there with you when you do?"

Charity's body visibly relaxed; she looked up and smiled. "Yes. I really would like you to be there."

"Okay," Sapphire said as she released a quiet sigh. "When would you like to do that? We can go to your house, my place, or to my office—wherever you feel more comfortable. Whenever and whatever you feel will work best for you."

"I have the notebook in my car. Can we go to my house after we finish visiting with Johnnie Mae? That's if you don't already have plans."

Sapphire smiled. "Sure." Sapphire could see the tenseness come back in Charity's face. "Relax. . . . Everything's going to be all right. You and I, with the help of the Lord, are going to get through this together."

Charity forced a smile in return. She nodded. "Yeah," she said, trying to maintain a smile that, despite her best efforts, continued to fall. "Yeah."

Chapter 19

Now will I sing to my well-beloved a song of my beloved touching his vineyard. My well-beloved hath a vineyard in a very fruitful hill. . . .

Isaiah 5:1

Pastor Landris had just finished powering down his computer. Johnnie Mae was in the hospital, and he was doing his best to effectively juggle church work, home life, and family obligations while making sure he spent as much time with her as possible. His main priority was to keep his wife calm during this touchy and stressful time. Dr. Baker had laid the entire situation out to him. She'd held nothing back. They were maintaining close checks on both Johnnie Mae and the baby. So far, things appeared to be stabilizing.

Brent Underwood had become Pastor Landris's trusted right-hand man. Angela Gabriel was Johnnie Mae's executive assistant for the things dealing with her books and speaking engagements and her work at church. Brent and Angela became engaged on Valentine's Day, with the wedding, to be held at the church, set for mid-October. They'd secured a new golf-course clubhouse facility called Ross Bridge for the reception. Angel, as most called her, had been extremely busy managing and rearranging Johnnie Mae's calendar as needed, while continuing to work diligently on her own wedding plans.

Pastor Landris looked up as Brent rapped his knuckle on his opened door.

"You're getting ready to go?" Brent asked, seeing Pastor Landris shutting down and putting things away for the day. He stepped inside, closing the door behind him.

"Yeah."

Dressed in a white shirt that didn't require a tie in order for him to look as though he was dressed up, Brent was a businessman from his heart. "May I speak with you a minute before you go?" Brent asked. "I promise I'll be brief."

"Sure, Brent. No problem." Pastor Landris pointed at the chair in front of his mahogany desk and sat down.

Brent sat and began to smile. Pastor Landris smiled back as he patiently waited. He had a feeling, from the grin plastered on Brent's face, where this conversation was most likely headed.

"You know I love Angel, right?"

"Yeah, I kind of picked up on that." Pastor Landris continued to return Brent's smile. "Your being engaged and set to be married soon was a dead giveaway," Pastor Landris said seriously but jokingly.

"Well, we're running into a small problem. Let me see. How do I say this?" He darted his head in and out a few times as he made various facial expressions.

"Why not just come right out and say it?" Pastor Landris said, smiling.

"Yeah. Well . . . you see . . . things have been getting a bit intense with us here lately—Angel and I." He looked at Pastor Landris, trying to gauge his reaction. "I'm talking sexually. . . . I don't mean sexually, but I mean when we're together. It's like sparks and electricity and sweating, with increased heart rates, which is not good with that much electricity flying about. Angel walks in a room, and I light up like a Christmas tree. I mean, literally. I can't help it. I find myself smiling just thinking about her."

"Oh, you mean like now?"

Brent started laughing and shaking his head. "Yeah, like now. It's hard to keep my mind on anything because it somehow manages to wander back to thoughts of her. I don't know what happened. I've been with other women, but I've never felt anywhere *near* anything like this with anyone else before. I'm Brent Underwood. And it's not lust."

"So, are you two still . . . ?"

Brent sat up straight and quickly dropped his smile. "Oh, we're still keeping things holy. But Pastor Landris, I have to be honest with you—it's hard. I never knew anything could be so hard. Maybe it's because I've never made a true commitment like this with a woman *and* with God. I suppose what I'm trying to say is, Pastor Landris, I don't think Angel and I can make it to October fifteenth."

Pastor Landris tried to maintain a straight face. "What if you two spent less time alone together until then? You know, only do things with other people. Talk on the phone instead of in person, those sorts of things."

"Pastor Landris, I sit in my office working hard, and all day long, I'm thinking about her. I walk around with this silly grin on my face throughout the day. No matter who I'm talking to, somehow, my thoughts end up drifting to thoughts of Angel. Sitting here . . . right now . . . talking to you, my pastor, who I know has plenty of troubles of your own, and the thought of her is right here with us. I want to be with Angel now. Four months feels like an eternity to me. Sure, my head knows I can hold out until then, but my heart has gone off on a tangent all its own."

Pastor Landris nodded. "I feel you. Believe me, I feel you. And don't think for a minute that I'm so religious I don't understand what you're saying. Tell me. How does Angela feel about this?"

"The same way I do. We can be sitting innocently on the opposite ends of the couch watching a television program together, and it's there. Just last night, she was handing me the remote control, my hand touched hers, and she pulled back like I had burnt her or something. The next thing I know, she was on her feet saying 'You have to go!' and she put me out of her apartment. We can't even kiss anymore, quite frankly, because we're afraid where that may lead us. I'm just being honest with you."

Pastor Landris sat back and started swiveling his chair. "If you two can manage to keep focused and keep yourselves until October, I assure you, you're going to have some kind of a special honeymoon."

Brent stood to his feet. "That's the problem. Angel and I talked extensively on the phone last night and earlier today at lunch, and we both decided we can't wait. We were wondering if it's possible for you to marry us in the next two weeks." He stuck his hand in his pocket. "I know you have a lot going on. I promise you, she and I discussed this from all angles. We really don't want to get married in the courthouse—that's just too impersonal. I know we could ask another minister to perform the ceremony, but . . ."

Pastor Landris stood and walked in front of Brent. "There's nothing that would bring me more joy than to marry the two of you. But are you sure about this? You guys were planning a pretty elaborate wedding ceremony."

"Here's what we were thinking. We could have a secret ceremony, just a few people knowing about it. That way we'd be legally married and fully permitted to be a married couple in every sense of the word. We could still have the ceremony in October, which would be for everybody else's benefit," Brent said. "I don't want to take Angel's dream wedding away from her. I know how much it means to her. She's so sentimental about everything. But Pastor Landris, the truth of the matter is, we can't wait to become one. There's no need in us trying to fool ourselves and continuing to play with fire."

"If you want to have a private ceremony, we can do that. I admire you both for your resolve to keep yourselves pure until marriage. Many couples would have just acted on their feelings, with *only* four months left to go." He gently slapped Brent on his back. "But I'm proud of you both." He smiled. "It takes a *real* man, a *real* woman, to stand like you two are choosing to do. *Anybody* can cave in."

"So, if you can look at your calendar and see what will work for you, we'd like to have it on a Friday or Saturday, if that's possible. I know you have your hands full already."

"What about a Sunday evening?" Pastor Landris asked.

"That would be fine. I just thought you might not want to do it on a Sunday. That's why I didn't suggest it."

Pastor Landris hunched his shoulders. "A Sunday evening is fine with me. Just let me know what date and time you and Angela desire, and we'll go from there." He walked back around to his desk and wrote himself a note.

"I'm going to let you finish up so you can get on out of here." Brent reached his hand across the desk to shake Pastor Landris's hand. "Sorry for holding you. Thanks again for hearing me out."

Pastor Landris pumped his hand once with a firm handshake then sandwiched his hand with his other hand prior to releasing it. "No problem. It's been my pleasure. As I said, you're a good man, Brent Underwood. And I'm proud to know you."

Brent shook his head and smiled. He looked like a little boy who had just been commended for having helped a person in need cross the street. "It's funny. You often tell me how proud you are of me. You rarely ever hear that come from one man to another. I've certainly never heard it from my own father."

"That's a 'man thing' we need to get out of," Pastor Landris said as he went and took his suit coat off the back of the closet door in his office and put it on. "It's particularly important we as men tell our children how we feel—both sons and daughters. Let your father know what you need from him. Help him to help you become the man God is calling the men of your generation—the Joshua generation, the *'Well able to take the land'* generation—to step up and be. He just may not know hearing something like that is important to you. Tell him how you feel." Pastor Landris placed his hand on Brent's shoulder and shook him gently. "Communication is the key to *any* successful relationship—both the vertical and the horizontal ones. Remember that."

Brent nodded and smiled as he turned and walked away. He placed his hand on the door handle, then turned back to Pastor Landris. "Yeah," he said, smiling even more. He pointed his index finger at Pastor Landris to show his appreciation once again, then left.

Chapter 20

And even to your old age I am He; and even to hoar hairs will I carry you: I have made, and I will bear; even I will carry, and will deliver you.

Isaiah 46:4

Sarah opened her eyes and looked up.

Memory smiled at her. "Welcome back," she said.

Sarah turned to survey her surroundings. "What happened? Where am I?"

"You're in the hospital," Memory said. "Lena's here." Lena moved closer to the forefront, where it would be easier for Sarah to see her.

"How are you feeling?" Lena asked as she took hold of Sarah's hand.

Sarah shook her head. "I was at home. What happened?"

"You had a slight stroke, but the doctor says you're doing much better," Lena said.

Sarah slowly raised her left hand and, just as slowly, let it back down.

"It didn't appear to have caused any major damage," Memory said, realizing that must be what she was looking to see. "At least, not from what they can tell so far."

"When can I go home?" Sarah asked Memory.

"They want to keep you here for a few days—mainly, to check you out some more and for observation purposes. Just making sure you're really okay."

Sarah looked at Lena. "I feel just fine. I'd like to go home now. I really don't care to be here. Didn't y'all tell them I have my own nurse at home? Gayle? Where's Gayle? She can monitor me from my house." She looked around the hospital room slowly. "I just don't want to be here."

Lena brushed back the stray graying hair that had made its way out of the pulled-up bun Sarah was wearing. "Gayle's talking with your doctor now. You'll be able to go home soon. Everybody just wants to be sure you're okay. This is for your own good."

Sarah turned her focus more toward Memory. "Please get me out of here. I don't want to be here. I've lost too much time being confined as it is already. Always for my own good. I feel fine, truly I do. Will you please tell them I'd prefer being at home?" The more she spoke, the more agitated she was becoming. She reached out her hand to Memory.

Memory took her hand. "We'll see what we can do. But we want you to be okay first and foremost. A few days in here won't be that bad. And Lena and I will be here with you every step of the way." She looked at Lena and smiled. "Won't we?"

Sarah squeezed Memory's hand. "You promise?"

Memory smiled. "I promise." She looked at Lena again. "Don't we?"

Lena smiled down at Sarah. "You know we're not going to leave you here all alone. You don't ever have to worry about being alone again. We promise. One of us will be somewhere close by as long as you're here."

Sarah smiled, then closed her eyes. "Never alone," she started mumbling again and again. "Jesus promised never to leave me," she said, then quietly started drifting off to sleep again. "Never to leave me alone . . ."

Lena and Memory walked out of the room. "Richard will be here shortly. He was going to take us back to the house, but one of us should be here when she wakes up again," Lena said.

"I was thinking the same thing. Why don't you go back to the house tonight, and I'll stay. Then I'll go in the morning while you stay," Memory said.

"Are you sure? I know you're probably tired now, too. You were out earlier visiting the city before this happened. I don't mind if you go home while I stay."

"I'll be fine. I'll just make myself comfortable in that reclining chair. . . . Stretch it out—you know the routine. When I get tired enough, I'll simply close my eyes and catch me some shut-eye. I've learned how to pretty much sleep anywhere with no problems."

"Okay, I'll go home and do what I need to, get some rest, and be back here first thing in the morning." Just then, Lena spotted Richard and a middle-aged white woman walking toward them. "Here's Richard now," she said.

When Richard and the woman reached Memory and Lena, Richard hugged Lena.

"How is she?" he asked.

"She was awake and talking earlier. She's asleep right now." Lena looked at the woman, impeccably dressed in a flower-print, form-fitting dress, standing beside Richard. "I'm Lena Jordan—Richard's wife . . . Sarah's granddaughter. And you are?"

"Oh, I'm sorry. This is Polly . . ." Richard looked at her for help in recalling her last name.

"Swindle. *Mrs.* Polly Swindle. I'm a good friend of Sarah's." She shook Lena's hand, then Memory's. Her speech was proper, clearly London English mixed with a kiss of some Southern influence.

Lena smiled slightly. "Oh, yes. Polly. My grandmother has mentioned you quite often. Thank you for looking in on her the way that you do."

"Oh, I adore Sarah Fleming."

Lena turned to Memory. "And this is my mother—Memory."

"So this is Memory," Polly said. "I finally get to meet you. Sarah has waited so long for this, and when she told me you were here, I wanted to come over right then and there to give you a great big Asheville, North Carolina, welcome-home hug."

"So why didn't you?" Memory asked with a smile.

Lena gave Memory a "behave yourself" look.

Polly continued without missing a beat. "Sarah asked me to give you some time alone. So you could get better acquainted. I believe she was planning on a dinner party or something of the sort so we could all meet. And now, this happened. . . ." She looked toward the door where Sarah was. "Tell me. Is she going to be all right?"

"She's holding her own," Memory said. "You know with her age and all, it complicates things a little more. We're hoping to be able to take her home in a day or two, though."

Polly clapped her hands. "That is *great* news!"

"So, Polly, how is it you happen to be here with Richard?" Memory asked, her face not showing any hint of friendliness.

Polly looked at Richard as though she thought he would tell how they ended up together. When he didn't offer the explanation, Polly smiled and turned to Memory and Lena. "I just happened by the house. Quite frankly, even though Sarah had asked me to give you all some time, I just *had* to come by to see how she was doing. I don't know if you're aware of this"—she looked from Memory to Lena—"but I generally stop by every Saturday morning to chat with Sarah. Of course, last week she called because she was expecting you, Memory. Then she learned you weren't coming, but she left me a message that Lena and Richard were here so there was no need for me to come by as I normally do. When I did speak with her, she told me you had indeed made it and that you all were getting to know one another famously. I didn't come this morning out of respect for her previous request. But I suppose we must have some sort of connection, because for some reason I felt compelled to come by tonight, wishes or not. That's when I learned what had happened."

"Polly was there when you and I were on the phone," Richard said to Lena. "It was just when I would have been trying to figure out how to find the hospital. I would have had to call one of my golfing buddies—"

"And that's when I volunteered to bring him myself. I know how difficult it can be for folks from out of town to find certain places and the like. Since I was coming here anyway, it didn't make sense for us to drive separate vehicles. Plus, this way was easier on him."

"Well, we thank you for that," Lena said. "Memory's going to stay here with Grandmother tonight while I go home and rest up. Then I'll come back and relieve her in the morning."

"I'm going to peep in on her. If she's awake, I'll speak for a few minutes just to let her know I was here," Polly said. "I imagine you all must be exhausted and anxious to get home. I won't be long."

"Take your time," Memory said as she watched Polly sashay inside.

After she was in Sarah's room, Lena turned to Memory. "Well, now, she seems nice enough."

"Yes, she does," Richard said, nodding his head in agreement.

Memory stared at the door without making a comment one way or the other. "Uh-huh," she finally said as she continued to stare at the closed door. "Yeah. Right."

Chapter 21

Say ye to the righteous, that it shall be well with Him: for they shall eat the fruit of their doings.

Isaiah 3:10

Driving her own car, Sapphire followed Charity home. After they were inside and sitting on the couch in the den, Charity reached in her purse and pulled out the stenographer's notebook. She stared at it. Holding her head up, she looked at Sapphire.

"Will you read it first, and if you believe, as Dr. Holden did, that I'll be all right when I read it, then I will." Charity held the notebook out to Sapphire.

"Sure," Sapphire said as she reached over and took it out of Charity's hand. Sapphire opened it up and instantly saw all the doodling and scribbles.

"You have to go more toward the back to find where actual words are written," Charity said. "At least, that's what Dr. Holden told me."

Sapphire turned a lot of pages before reaching a page that had readable writing. After she read it, she held her breath for a few seconds, then exhaled slowly as she looked over at Charity. "I'm not going to lie to you. There may be a few troubling things here; I can't know for certain. But I do agree with Dr. Holden. I don't believe it will hurt the progress you've made. And there's no denying you have made tremendous progress."

"I guess you're right if you call Hope and Faith leaving me as separate personalities progress. I just know I don't ever want to revert back to where I was before. It's been nice living life without having to wonder what might have taken place during missing clumps of time. That's all gone now. Or at least it seems that way."

Sapphire moved a little closer to Charity. She handed her the opened notebook. "I'm here, and however you deal with this when you read it, I promise I'll be right here for as long as you need me to help you work through this."

Charity glanced at Sapphire. "Well, here goes nothing."

She began to read. As she turned the pages, tears began to flow down her face. Sapphire looked for some tissue. She got up in search of the bathroom. When she returned, she handed Charity a box of pink tissues. Charity pulled out a few and began gently dabbing her tears as she looked at Sapphire.

"It was my fault," Charity said, almost whispering it. "It was all my fault."

"What was?" Sapphire asked. *What am I missing?* She'd read what was there.

Motherphelia was outside working in her flower garden. Outside of family, flowers and working in her garden was her only other passion. She'd come into the house when Charity ran outside to get her. Motherphelia had thrown down her hoe and came rushing in. She'd heard the urgency in Charity's voice. Yelling at Mr. Lucious, she told him to leave. Demanded he leave. Everyone called the elderly man Mr. Lucious, including Motherphelia. Mother begged Motherphelia not to do it . . . to give him just one more chance. Where would he go? He had no place else; he had no one but us. Still, Motherphelia did it. She told him he had to go, and he would—one way or another. "No more chances. Three strikes and you're out!" she said. "The nerve of you! I want you out of this house now!"

Mr. Lucious stumbled as he made his way to the door. Then he stopped. Turning around, he raised his shirt and pulled out a gun tucked in the band of his pants. He threatened everybody, talking all out of his head. But Motherphelia meant business. She didn't back down. Coming closer, she told him to leave before he'd really be sorry. "And don't you ever step foot back inside this house again! I mean it, Lucious," she said.

After that day, he never did.

Motherphelia loved him, that much I'm sure. Who could resist his smile and infectious laugh? But nothing could rival with her love for Charity. And that day, she proved there was nothing she wouldn't do when it came to her greatest love—Charity.

"Charity, is there something you're remembering that's not written there?" Sapphire swiftly kneeled down on the floor in front of Charity and grabbed both of her hands in hers. "Charity, talk to me. Do you recall what happened that day?"

Charity slowly began to nod. "The gun. I'd forgotten about the gun. Mr. Lucious pulled it out and started waving it around, pointing it at everyone. He was so drunk. He shouldn't have been drinking. Mother told him as much. Motherphelia claimed that demon juice made a perfectly good man smack crazy. He wasn't supposed to drink at all—that was the agreement. He didn't mean to. I guess he just couldn't help himself."

"Charity, who was Mr. Lucious?"

"Mother and Motherphelia called him Mr. Lucious,

with the exception of that day Motherphelia lost it and merely called him Lucious. That's what they taught me to call him. Oh God!" Charity began to cry out as she bent forward and gently rocked. "Please help me. I can't do this. I can't handle this. Faith can. I thought I could, but I can't."

"Charity, stay with me now. We're getting there. I want you to take a deep breath and tell me what you remember that's not written here." She continued holding on to one of Charity's hands as she raised the notebook up with her other one. "What's not in here?"

Charity pulled her hand out of Sapphire's and fell back against the couch as she continued to cry. "Mr. Lucious had visited before in the past. But he showed up at our door one day, and against Motherphelia's objection, Mother allowed him to move into a makeshift bedroom. He'd lived there for months now, but on this day, he got real drunk. 'Drunker than a skunk,' Motherphelia said. The agreement was, he could stay as long as he didn't drink. He was normally quiet and reserved, but alcohol seemed to unleash demons in him."

Charity sat up straight. "I would overhear my mother remind him of that when she smelled liquor on his breath. Whispering it at times . . . taking him off to a private area to talk, she'd tell him he had to stop before he got caught. Mother tried her best to keep it hidden from Motherphelia. She made him drink lots of coffee and use mouthwash to mask the smell. Still, I'd see him, several times, sneak swallows from a bottle he kept under the couch that remained full no matter how much he drained it. The way that bottle kept mysteriously refilling itself made me believe it was a magic bottle or something."

Charity slowly closed her eyes, then opened them. "But Mr. Lucious was so nice to me, even when he drank. He would tickle me or do something to make me laugh. Every day, without fail, he played this one record he absolutely loved. 'The Dock of the Bay,' by Otis Redding. And every day, he would give me either a silver- or half-dollar. When my mother discovered he was secretly giving me money, she told me those coins might be worth a lot later, so I should give them to her for safekeeping."

"Charity, why was he giving you money every day?"

Charity looked at her and started shaking her head as the tears rolled down her face. She bowed her head, and the tears began to fall into her lap, plummeting on her folded hands like drops of rain hitting dirt-dry ground before finally being soaked up.

"Charity . . . Did Mr. Lucious sexually molest you?" She waited a few seconds. "Charity, talk to me. Did Mr. Lucious molest you? Look at me. Charity, look at me."

Charity forced herself to look at Sapphire.

Sapphire spoke deliberately and forcefully. "Did Mr. Lucious sexually molest you?"

"No. He did not," Charity said as she began to make successive heaving sounds.

"Then I don't understand. What happened that affected you the way it did? What happened that caused you to need separate personalities? What created Faith and Hope?"

Charity began to cry out loud. "Don't you get it, Sapphire? I loved Mr. Lucious. I . . . loved him! Mr. Lucious was Motherphelia's husband—my father's father. Mr. Lucious was my grandfather, and I *adored* him! Motherphelia never would have come in the house right then had I not gone outside and gotten her. My mother told me to go to my room and play. But instead, I ran as fast as I could and got her. I made her come inside. Had I not, then maybe, just maybe, nobody would have gotten hurt and things would be different today."

She looked at Sapphire as she tilted her head. "You see? It was my fault. All of it. A chain of horrible events happened because of things I did. Me."

Sapphire sat on the couch and put her arm around Charity to stop her now-incessant shaking. "You're doing fine, Charity. It's okay. I'm here." Sapphire looked toward Heaven. "God, please help her," she whispered. "Please, Jesus. We need You."

Sapphire was painfully aware that this was surely only the beginning of even more revelations to come.

Chapter 22

For thus saith the Lord, Ye have sold yourselves for nought; and ye shall be redeemed without money.

Isaiah 52:3

"Charity, take your time and tell me everything you remember. It's going to be okay. You're doing fine," Sapphire said.

Charity stood and started pacing around the room. "From all I can recall, I'd never met my grandfather before that year when I was seven. That's when he started coming to the house. I gathered he'd left my grandmother a few years into their marriage. But after this tall, white-haired man showed up, my world as I'd known it flipped. Up was down, and down was up. Motherphelia wasn't her usual jovial self. In the beginning, the two of them argued violently, so naturally I didn't care for him much. Before he came, I'd never even heard Motherphelia raise her voice, let alone lose her temper. She was mild-mannered . . . queenly. After he moved in, there was Motherphelia singing, dancing, smiling, and cooking for him like they'd never exchanged a cross word between them."

Charity looked at the palm of her hand as though it was her first time ever seeing it. She went and sat back down. "When he wasn't drinking, he was all you'd imagine a grandfather to be. He'd let me climb up in his lap, and he would make up some silly song while bouncing me on his knee. He loved to tickle me, although Motherphelia didn't like him doing that. In fact, if she saw him starting up, she'd shut him down. There were times when he would drink, and you could smell it on his breath. If Motherphelia felt he'd taken only a few swigs, and I was anywhere in the vicinity, she would make me go to my room. I was sent to my room a lot following his arrival. When she'd give the okay for me to come back out, he'd either be gone or locked away in his room."

Sapphire sat quietly, patiently allowing Charity to tell her story at her own pace. Occasionally, she'd nod or smile, but she kept her eyes completely fixed on Charity.

"Then there was that fateful day—the day he got so drunk, he continued to drink right there in the den without even bothering to hide it. He patted his leg, his signal for me to come and sit in his lap. Trying not to be disrespectful or rude, I shook my head. He got up and started to chase after me. When he caught me, he commenced with his normal tickling ritual. I don't know if he did it on purpose or if it was because he was drunk, but he put his hand in the wrong place a few times. My mother came over and began talking nice to him. Smacking his lips, he looked at her the way he looked at smothered pork chops. He turned on 'The Dock of the Bay,' grinned, then tried dancing with her."

Charity rubbed her forehead a few times. "My mother was trying to keep things hushed. Telling him he needed to 'Go sleep it off' before Motherphelia came in and caught him. At one point, he pushed her up against the wall and started trying to kiss her as he groped her. Remaining calm, my mother told him he didn't really want to do that. That he would be put out of the house for sure if he didn't stop all his drunkard nonsense. But he kept on." Hands in a prayerlike position, Charity pressed them up against her lips.

"I then heard the trembling . . . the fear in her voice. That's when I ran outside to get Motherphelia despite my mother's demand that I go to my room now. Motherphelia would make him stop. She was working in her flower garden, flowery garden gloves on, a garden hoe in hand. I told Motherphelia that Mr. Lucious was hurting my mother. As soon as she heard, she threw down that hoe and made her way to the house, peeling off her gloves as she hurried inside. I now fully understand how she must have felt walking inside and finding her husband all over my mother. He was so drunk, it looked like he'd fallen asleep standing there against her. My mother was struggling to push him off of her, but he was too large. Motherphelia, who was nearly as big, yanked him by his shirt and flung him off, causing him to stumble and fall. He laughed. That's when she told him he had to leave. She didn't put up with his mess when they were together years ago, and no matter how much she still loved him, she wasn't about to put up with it now. And she did love him; you could see it in her eyes. Sober, he was charming and irresistible. Mother pleaded with Motherphelia not to put him out on the streets again. He wasn't well. He was too old to be out there fending alone. 'Phelia, regardless, he's still family,' Mother said."

Charity stood. She took her hands and pulled her hair back taut, then let it go. "My mother assured my grandmother that he would quit drinking. Now that he was seeing the consequences of his actions, he would surely straighten up this time. 'Just give him one more chance,' Mother begged. Motherphelia said it wasn't so much his drinking she couldn't stomach, but who he became when he drank. She called it a stronghold and told my grandfather he'd have to find Jesus to be delivered. He laughed and said if Jesus was lost, how was

He possibly going to be able to help him even if he did find Him?

"Well, that infuriated Motherphelia. She yelled for him to get out. He told her he needed to get a few of his things . . . that he'd come back later for the rest. Walking to his room, he came back in minutes, empty handed. He walked to the front door, then turned around. That's when he pulled out the gun and started waving it and pointing it in a drunken stupor. Motherphelia looked at me and softly told me to go to my room. For some reason, I just stood there like she hadn't said a word to me. Motherphelia and Mr. Lucious continued. He grabbed me, and that was it." Charity began to sob out loud.

"He placed the side of the gun against my face. I should have gone to my room like Motherphelia told me, but I hadn't. I just *had* to see what was going on. I wanted to tell him good-bye. He'd given me half-dollars and silver dollars. He'd played endlessly with me during those six months he'd been there. Truthfully, I didn't want him to leave. I didn't. My daddy was gone, and he'd made me feel like I was a little princess or someone equally as special." Charity grabbed more tissues and gently dabbed at her tears.

"What happened next, Charity?" Sapphire stood and touched Charity's hand. No more just her therapist, she was now a caring friend.

"He staggered as he held his arm around my neck, warning us not to do anything stupid. He said he didn't have anywhere else to go, and he had no plans to leave anytime soon. My mother started crying, but Motherphelia kept her cool. She continued talking to him while calmly telling him to let me go. She reached out for me. He started to push me forward, then quickly snatched me back. I don't know why, but that's when I decided to fight him—a seven-year-old attempting to fight a grown man. I wanted him to let me go. Motherphelia yelled for me to stop and to just be still, but I was determined to get away. I bit his hand. He yelled out as he released his grip. I ran in the direction of Motherphelia. He cursed, and the next thing I knew Motherphelia was shoving me hard to the floor just as I heard a firecracker-like noise. Motherphelia fell." Charity let out a pained cry. "I thought she'd slipped when she shoved me. But, she was so still . . . lying there . . . her hand pressed against her stomach. She wasn't moving."

Sapphire hugged her. "You're doing great, Charity. It's okay. It's okay."

Charity gently pushed her away. "No, it's not! It's not okay! There was blood . . . soaking through her top. Don't you see, Sapphire? Motherphelia got shot because of me!" Charity wiped her nose. "Me! I flipped when I saw the blood. Mother screamed out her name. Motherphelia tried to move. She started mumbling that everything was going to be all right. My grandfather must have sobered up enough to realize what had just happened, because he dropped the gun and rushed over to her. 'Phil,' he said, short for Ophelia. 'I'm sorry.' Then he panicked. It appeared he was debating whether or not he should try and pick her up. 'Get away from her,' I yelled. 'Leave her alone!' Motherphelia tried to take control of the situation, but she was so weak." Charity paused and stared into space.

"I saw him glance over at the gun," Charity said, continuing. "I wasn't sure what he was planning to do next. He must have seen me look at it. Something suddenly rose up in me. We raced for it. I got there first. I was only trying to protect Motherphelia. There was a struggle as he tried to wrestle it away from me. I really was no match for him, even in his drunken state. The gun fired. My mother screamed. He fell to the floor."

Charity shook her head. "I made my way back to

Motherphelia. That's when she made me promise I wouldn't tell a soul what happened. It would be our secret until she told me otherwise. She was going to fix everything, but she needed me to be a big girl and do exactly as I was told. I was to go to my room and not come out until my mother came and got me. But I refused to leave her side. Later, I heard sirens and then a loud pounding on our front door. Someone identified himself as the police and demanded that we open up. 'Go now,' she whispered. 'Quickly.' I froze. 'Now!' she yelled, still barely above a whisper. 'And don't forget, not a word to anyone.' She smiled, then looked at my mother, who then grabbed my hand and dragged me to my room. I was crying more than ever now. I didn't want to leave Motherphelia there like that. She needed me. My mother shook me and told me to stop it and to be quiet. For Motherphelia, I did as I was told."

Sapphire held Charity in her arms. There were no more tears now. It was as though Charity had successfully depleted her reservoir.

Sapphire moved strands of hair out of Charity's face and brushed them back in place. She looked in Charity's eyes. "It was an accident, Charity. An accident."

Charity shook her head. "Yeah, an accident. Only, he died, Sapphire. My grandfather died because of me. And I never told a soul what happened that day. I've never talked about it with anyone, including my mother. I suppose, in part, because I didn't remember. Faith and Hope made certain of that. And that secret became the tri-fold cord that bound us together."

Sapphire pulled Charity down on the couch by her shoulders as she herself sat down. "Charity, what happened with your grandmother?"

Charity's eyes began to glaze over. "They took her to the hospital. Not long after that, Mother told me she'd died." Charity looked intensely at Sapphire as her lips began to quiver. "I never got to see her again. They didn't even let me go to her funeral. Motherphelia went to be with Jesus. She left me, and it was all my doing."

"Charity, you rarely talk about your mother. What happened with her?"

Charity shook her head slowly. "After my grandmother died, my mother became what people in the neighborhood called 'a certified alcoholic.' Ironic, huh? But I suppose, just as I had done, she found her own way to forget. And I don't have to tell you this, but life as we'd known it was never the same again."

Chapter 23

Every valley shall be exalted, and every mountain and hill shall be made low: and the crooked shall be made straight, and the rough places plain. . . .

Isaiah 40:4

"How are you feeling now?" Sapphire asked Charity.

"Drained, but okay. I just wish I could understand how I could have blocked something like this completely out of my mind all these years. It makes no sense."

"To your mind it made sense. May I make a suggestion?"

"By all means," Charity said.

"Don't dwell on it now. What's important is that you *have* remembered and that you're coping wonderfully, from everything I'm seeing now, anyway," Sapphire said.

"Sapphire, why do you think my mother allowed me to go all of these years and never talked about this with me? I was a child. I needed her."

Sapphire took her by both hands. "Your mother probably never knew how much it affected you. She may not have realized anything was even wrong with you. And since you never mentioned what happened, she likely concluded you were fine and it was best not to stir up the bees, so to speak. Plus, it sounds to me like she started self-medicating with alcohol. I'm curious, though. When she found out about your Dissociative Identity Disorder diagnosis this year and that you were being treated, what did she say?"

Charity stood and rubbed her hands slowly together. "To be honest, I haven't told her about my disorder and what's going on with me. I figured she had her hands full without all of my burdens. She drinks excessively, and she's married to this man who, I'm convinced, beats her, although she works hard to hide it. When I relocated to Birmingham back in 2001, I was looking for a fresh start. I tried to get her to come with me, but my mother is never going to leave New Orleans. It's her home. It's all she's ever known, and she's not the type to move out of her comfort zone."

Sapphire nodded. "Which is why she stays with someone who abuses her. Though painful, it's familiar to her. In her mind, at least she feels she knows what to expect."

"Yeah. She gets drunk, passes out, and claims she doesn't remember much of what happened before or after that. Me, I developed Dissociative Identity Disorder, a.k.a. multiple personalities, with my manifested personalities being Faith and Hope. I allowed them to deal with things I didn't want to deal with. But honestly, I didn't want to dump my troubles on my mother. That's why she didn't come when I was in that facility. She knew I was having some problems and was getting help, but she didn't know the severity of what was going on. I suppose it's about time I come clean and tell her everything."

Subtly, Sapphire glanced down at her watch. It had been almost three hours since she'd first arrived. "How do you think you'll tell her?"

Charity pursed her lips, then bit down on her bottom lip. "I'm not sure. But I know I need to go home and talk to her face to face. Maybe discussing what came about that day will release her from her own torture as well. I would also like to find out what occurred after the police came inside the house, and what they were told took place, as well as what happened with Motherphelia. I don't know any of these things."

"Since no one seems to have been charged," Sapphire said, "it was likely ruled either self-defense or an accidental shooting."

"Well, I think I'll be visiting New Orleans in August. My mother usually takes her vacation then. I can go spend the week with her since I can't get her to come visit me," Charity said. "She and I can catch up, and maybe I can do a little investigation into the parts of this story I don't know, now that I recall what actually took place." Charity looked at the digital clock on the mantel. "My goodness, look at the time. Sapphire, you've gone above and beyond the call of duty. My bill this time is going to be a whopper."

Sapphire grabbed her purse and stood up. "I do have to go. But we've accomplished so much tonight, thanks in part to Faith and that message she wrote. Faith must have known what would click for you. Now valleys in your life have been exalted. Mountains and hills have been made low."

Charity smiled. "And the crooked places have been made straight. Or at least, we're working on them."

Sapphire walked to the door. She stopped and turned around. "I would like to know what exactly it was that made things click for you."

"The gun, which I'd forgotten about, and recalling 'Mr. Lucious' in the context of how things were. . . . How much Motherphelia loved him. That last paragraph Faith wrote, for some reason, brought back a flood of memories I'd gone to much trouble to forget."

Motherphelia loved him, that much I'm sure.
Who could resist his smile and infectious laugh?
But nothing could rival with her love for Charity.

And that day, she proved there was nothing she wouldn't do when it came to her greatest love—Charity.

A little after Sapphire left, Charity picked up the phone and dialed.

"Hello," a woman's voice on the other end said.

"Mother, it's me—Charity."

"Charity, baby! It's been a while since I've heard from you. I'm so happy you called."

Charity was relieved her mother sounded sober. "Mother, there are some things I believe you and I need to talk about. I'd like to come home when you take vacation if you don't have any major plans. I really need to see you. I want to talk to you about *that* day."

"What day, baby?"

"That day Motherphelia and Mr. Lucious, my grandfather, got shot and died."

There was suddenly an eerie silence.

"Mother, I remember everything. Everything. And you and I need to talk. There are things that have happened over these years . . . things I'm positive you can't possibly know concerning me. Things I've dealt with because of what took place that day."

Charity could hear her mother as she began to cry. "You remember? Everything? You remember *everything*, Charity? All of it?"

"Yes, everything—all of it. Everything except what transpired after you took me to my room."

Her mother seemed to quickly compose herself. Her voice became strong and commanding. "I tell you what. You come home to New Orleans the last week in August. Come, and I'll tell you whatever you want to know. It's past time we finally lay this to rest. I think Motherphelia would want that. Yeah, I *know* she'd want this now."

Chapter 24

And the Lord said unto Satan, Hast thou considered My servant Job, that there is none like him in the earth, a perfect and an upright man, one that feareth God, and escheweth evil?

Job 1:8

It was Tuesday, and Johnnie Mae had been in the hospital for a little over a week now. Charity had visited her at the hospital several times. On her last visit, she told Johnnie Mae all she'd learned about what had caused her to split into multiple personalities. Johnnie Mae was both enthralled and amazed at how the mind could find a way to protect a person the way it had done with Charity. She hated what Charity had gone through, but it was evident by her bubbly attitude, coupled with her now-more-balanced personality, that she was going to be all right. Johnnie Mae could see traits of Hope and Faith alongside the Charity she had known and grown to love dearly over these past months. With God's touch, Charity was completely being made whole.

Landris was in his office at church. He made it a point to go by the hospital and see Johnnie Mae in the morning hours before he went in to work. In the afternoon, he would pick up Princess Rose from the summer day-camp program she was attending and take her with him to see her mother. He'd been off all day on Monday, so he was able to spend more time with both Johnnie Mae and Princess Rose. Tuesdays, no matter what was going on, were always hectic for him, but this Tuesday had been unusually so.

"Pastor Landris, Angel Gabriel is here to see you," his executive assistant announced over the intercom.

"Thanks, Sherry. Please send her in." Landris hit several keys on his computer just as Angel walked in.

"Thank you, Pastor Landris, for seeing me at the last minute. I know how super busy you are and that you're trying to get out of here so you can get to the hospital."

Landris pointed to the burgundy leather chair as he smiled. "Have a seat. It's fine. All a part of the life I've chosen. You said it was important."

"It is. I'll get right to it." She opened up a red folder. "You know I'm handling all of Johnnie Mae's personal, book-related, and church business for her while she's out. Well, several things have surfaced that need to be addressed immediately, but I realized I probably shouldn't show them to Johnnie Mae at this time. Especially since the whole idea is to keep her as stress-free as possible while she's in the hospital."

"And please know I appreciate everything that you're doing toward that end."

Angel pulled out a letter. "This was delivered today." She handed it to Landris. "It's from a lawyer. It appears Johnnie Mae's mother has rescinded the power of attorney from Johnnie Mae and granted it to Johnnie Mae's oldest sister, Rachel."

Landris read the letter, then released it. It floated like a feather, then dropped like a rock to his desk. "I don't believe it," he said, shaking his head while twisting his mouth.

"Those were my sentiments as well."

Landris picked up the letter and leaned back then forward as he bit down on his bottom lip. "The nerve of them to claim Johnnie Mae is not in a position to carry out her duties in executing their mother's affairs while she's in a delicate state herself." He shook the letter. "Johnnie Mae doesn't need to have to deal with something like this. Rachel knows she's in no position to fight her; she's fighting for our baby. That's why Rachel chose now to do it. I *knew* she was being too nice. It figures she was up to something."

"It is disheartening when family members do things like this."

"Well, don't you worry. I'll handle this one." He put the letter back down on his desk.

Angel sat back in her chair. "But if her mother's condition *is* getting worse—"

"Her condition doesn't appear to be any worse now than it was six months ago. In fact, her medication seems to have stabilized her. Rachel just believes this is an ideal time to take over. She's counting on Johnnie Mae not being able to fight her, that's all."

"At this stage, would Johnnie Mae's mother even be considered competent enough, by the legal system, to sign a legally binding document to change anything?"

"I'll admit Mrs. Gates has stretches where her mind is present and very lucid. It's possible she was fully aware of what she was doing when she signed this. Then again, it's also possible Rachel took advantage of her during one of her confused states. I'm going to speak with my sister-in-law myself, although I don't know what good it will do."

"Well, while you're talking to her about that, you may want to discuss this document with her as well." She handed him a thick packet of stapled pages. "Rachel is also having the house changed out of her mother's name into her own."

Landris took it and started reading. He couldn't do anything except shake his head and laugh out of frustration. "I *do* not believe this. Yet, there it is . . . POA, Rachel Turner. And according to this, with the exception of Johnnie Mae and their baby brother, Christian, who remain to agree not to contest it, all of the other siblings have signed off on it," Landris said. He threw the packet on top of the other paper. "Goodness. What next?"

Angel pulled out yet another piece of paper with an envelope clipped to its back. "Well, I hate being the bearer of more bad news, but Johnnie Mae received this certified letter from Jean Cannon, one of Princess Rose's aunts on her father's side." Angel handed him the letter. "She says she's called and left several messages for Johnnie Mae to call her. Since Johnnie Mae hasn't done so as yet, she's sending that certified."

"Jean wants Princess Rose to come and stay with her while Johnnie Mae is in the hospital," Landris said without bothering to read what the letter said. "I haven't even mentioned her calls to Johnnie Mae. Johnnie Mae will never go for that. There's no way she wants Princess Rose all the way up in Chicago while she's here in the hospital. No way. I told Jean that when she and I spoke last week. I thought that was the end of it."

"According to that"—she nodded toward the letter—"it's not. She obviously has a problem with you keeping her niece. She believes Princess Rose should be with family. And since no one in her family is presently in a position to take Princess Rose for the weeks or months that may be needed while Johnnie Mae is in the hospital, she feels the only option is for Princess Rose to come to Chicago and stay with her."

Landris looked at the letter and began to read it. When he finished, he tossed it on top of the ever-increasing stack. "I'm not going to lay this on Johnnie Mae. I'm not. So I'll call Jean and talk to her again. Princess Rose is fine where she is. She's happy in her own home. Princess Rose doesn't even know this aunt, and it's not because Johnnie Mae hasn't tried to get them to spend time with her. But after Solomon died and she married me, his entire family cut off communication with both Johnnie Mae and Princess Rose. Of course she would choose *now* to want Princess Rose to visit her. But I can't do something like that to Johnnie Mae. It's just not a good time. Jean *must* know this."

Angel placed the empty folder on the corner of the desk and sat up straight. "What if you ask Johnnie Mae . . . just to be sure? She really might not mind her staying with this aunt while she concentrates on her health and the health of this baby," Angel said.

"When Princess Rose walks in that hospital room, Johnnie Mae's face literally lights up. I know her. If I tell her what Jean wants, it'll cause nothing but more stress. She'll be trying to figure out if that would be the best thing to do, knowing that Princess Rose may be distressed about going, knowing that she doesn't want Princess Rose to go or to feel abandoned during all of this. Things are hard enough right now on both of them as it is. Besides, Princess Rose has Johnnie Mae's family around. And she's used to them."

"Still, why not let Johnnie Mae know what's going on and see what she thinks about it? Then you'll know how she'd like you to proceed. Johnnie Mae is strong."

He hunched his shoulders. "I just wish I knew what Jean's *really* up to."

"Well, on a more positive note, Johnnie Mae has gotten another stack of mail from fans of her books. The word must be circulating that she's in the hospital. I literally have a bucket full of cards, letters, and e-mails to carry to her. Johnnie Mae insists I bring them to her even though she's supposed to be resting. I see how much they cheer her up. There are definitely a slew of folks who care about your wife, no denying that."

"Yeah, I know. We've had to funnel many of the flowers she's been receiving out of her room. It was so many, the nurses said they were sucking up all the oxygen." He chuckled. "I thought they were joking; I quickly learned they weren't. Now when she receives flowers and fruit baskets, she takes off the card to see who sent them, then gets a nurse to carry them to some elderly or other patient who may not have received much, if anything, in the way of gifts or visitors. It works out all around."

Angel retrieved the folder off the corner of the desk and stood up. "Do you want to keep all of those?" she asked, pointing to the papers on his desk.

"Yeah, I'll handle them. And thanks for screening things and not just passing them on to Johnnie Mae. I'll have to pray about these," he said, placing his hand on top of the stack. "Johnnie Mae has a right to know what's going on, but I don't want to do anything that will upset her or put her or our baby at more risk right now. I just don't."

"I understand. I only wish those folks did," she said, pointing once again to the stack. She placed the papers back inside the folder. "Changing the subject, Brent and I want to thank you again for agreeing to perform our marriage ceremony and keeping it quiet. I sort of felt bad even asking you, with all that you have going on these days."

"Like I told Brent, it will be my pleasure. Truthfully, I admire the two of you for taking a vow to keep yourselves until marriage. And when you saw you possibly weren't going to be able to honor that commitment, instead of giving in to the temptation, you decided to take steps to still do things God's way. Now, that's real integrity there."

"Even if it means having a secret ceremony," Angel said, nodding, "before the big one?" She smiled. "Brent is *so* sweet. This was his idea. He knows how much work I've put into planning our wedding. And having a reception at Ross Bridge is neither easy nor cheap. We have already invited a lot of people, and they're so excited about attending our wedding. We didn't want to cancel the whole thing and end up disappointing everybody."

"Oh, I understand," Landris said. "You don't have to explain things. Believe me, it's an honor to do this. You and Brent are special to both me and Johnnie Mae. I just hate that Johnnie Mae won't be able to attend the actual ceremony. But she will be able to come to the ceremony in October, along with our *new* baby." Saying that caused him to grin.

Angel said good-bye and left. Landris opened up the folder, picked up the papers, and scanned each piece again. Picking up the phone, he touch-toned a phone number.

"Jean? This is Pastor Landris. If you have a few minutes, I'd like to talk to you about this letter you sent certified to Johnnie Mae. You and I spoke briefly last week, but perhaps I failed to make clear the situation we're dealing with down here."

"Pastor Landris, you've stated your case perfectly. Nevertheless, our family would prefer our late brother's daughter be with someone in *his* family, since it appears Johnnie Mae won't be capable of taking care of her for a while."

"I assure you, Princess Rose is being well taken care of, even with Johnnie Mae in the hospital. I take her to see her mother every day, and both of them look forward to that. As I told you before, Johnnie Mae doesn't need stress right now. She's in a rather fragile state at a critical point in her pregnancy." He sighed audibly. "May I be frank with you?"

"By all means," Jean said.

"I really would prefer not to dump any of this in Johnnie Mae's lap right now. I understand you'd like to see your niece, and I'm sure once we're past this crucial point and the baby is here, something can be arranged." He picked up his Mont Blanc pen and began to twirl it between his fingers like it was a miniature baton. "You understand?"

"Well, Pastor Landris. Let me be frank with you. I have another sister who is not as nice or considerate as I am attempting to be. She lives there in Birmingham, and she doesn't have a problem with going to that hospital and laying it all out on the table for Johnnie Mae. Honestly, this sister can't take care of Princess Rose, which is why I stepped up. But Pastor Landris, this is our niece we're talking about—my brother's only child. Frankly, she's not your biological daughter. And although I'm sure you're a decent man, none of us are comfortable knowing our brother's child is being left totally alone in a house with just you, while Johnnie Mae is in the hospital for who knows how long."

Landris had a scowl on his face. "Excuse me, but what exactly are you trying to imply?"

"I'm not trying to imply anything. All I'm saying is Johnnie Mae could be in the hospital for—what? Another two . . . three months? We don't want any mess. Our family just believes it will be best for all concerned if Princess Rose is staying with someone else other than alone with a man who is not her real father but merely a stepfather."

"Step or not, I *am* a real father to her. So are you saying that if one of Johnnie Mae's sisters took Princess Rose while she's in the hospital, you'd not be pursuing this?"

"I don't know if we can trust that, either. Let me level with you. Even though I have the means to take Princess Rose, I'm really not that excited about having to care for a child, any child, at this point in my life. I have a very active career and social life. But someone has to protect that child. It looks like I'll have to sacrifice and be the one."

She paused and then continued. "Now, either you can let Johnnie Mae know what I'm proposing, at a great sacrifice to myself, mind you, or we'll figure out another way to let her know. And Pastor Landris, I assure you we're not trying to add stress to anyone, but our family is willing to take this as far as we have to. If you think about it, this could actually be a blessing in disguise. If I have Princess Rose, then that gives you more time to concentrate on your wife and the baby you both are fighting so desperately for. So my deal to you is this. I'll give you until tomorrow evening to get back with me with your and Johnnie Mae's decision. After that, I take the next step. Good-bye." She hung up.

Landris stared at the phone, then hung it up. Closing his eyes, he began to pray.

Chapter 25

While he was yet speaking, there came also another, and said, The fire of God is fallen from heaven, and hath burned up the sheep, and the servants, and consumed them; and I only am escaped alone to tell thee.

Job 1:16

"Pastor Landris," Sherry said as she stuck her head into his office. "I have a surprise for you." She opened the mahogany wooden door wide.

A golden-haired woman dressed in a royal blue pantsuit waltzed in. "Well, hello there, darling."

"Mom, what are you doing here?" Landris asked. He stood and hurried to greet her.

"I came to see about you . . . all of you," Virginia LeBoeuf said. She hugged her son tight as he kissed her cheek. "How is Johnnie Mae?" she asked. "And the baby?"

"So far, so good. Our confession is all is well. But why didn't you tell me you were flying in today? I could have picked you up from the airport."

She waved him away with her hand and gracefully sat in the chair that faced his desk. "Nonsense. You didn't need to. You have enough on your plate as it is."

He sat in the chair next to her. "How did you get here? Did Thomas bring you?"

She cocked her head and raised an eyebrow. Patting his hand, she smiled. "No, Thomas didn't bring me. But I did stop by to see him at the halfway house on my way here. I can only assume, with all that's going on with you, you haven't seen him lately."

"No, I haven't seen him in a couple of weeks. But I did call him just yesterday. It was a brief conversation. I quickly picked up that he wasn't in the mood to talk. Or maybe it would be more accurate to say he wasn't in the mood to talk to me. So what prompted you to make that statement? Am I missing something?"

She set her Louis Vuitton purse on his desk. "Your brother has completely quit taking his medication."

"What makes you think that?"

"A mother knows. Besides, I asked him point-blank, and he admitted it. He claims he's doing so much better now, he feels it's unnecessary for him to keep having to take it. I tried to explain to him that his medicine is not a cure by any means, but a tool to help him manage his bipolar disorder." She placed her hand on her chest as she let out a deep sigh. "Well, you of all people know how unreasonably hardheaded your brother can be when he's normal. Unfortunately, all of us also know how bad things can get with him when he's not taking that medication." She started glancing around his office.

"What are you looking for?" Landris asked. "What do you need?"

"Some water. You used to keep a pitcher of water in here. Talking about medicine made me remember I need to take my *own*. Can you get me some water, please?"

"Sure," he said as he went to the mini-refrigerator, grabbed a bottle of water, then handed it to her. "What's your doctor saying these days?" He knew this was a touchy subject with her, one—over the past months—she generally found a way to skirt around.

"Oh, you know them—forever wanting to do this test or another. I suppose that's why people call what they do 'a practice.'" She twisted the cap off the medicine bottle first and shook two round blue pills into her hand, then twisted the top off the bottled water. Carefully placing one pill in her mouth, she took a swallow of water, snapped her head back, then repeated the process. "I *despise* having to take pills," she said as she screwed the childproof cap back on the medicine bottle and put it back in her purse. "That's probably where your brother gets it from."

Landris continued eyeing her without saying a word.

"What?" she said after a minute of him staring silently at her. "You don't like my new golden hair color?" She began to pat her hair. "What?!" she snapped.

"Mom, are you even supposed to be here right now?"

She set her purse back on the corner of his desk. "Well, I'm here, aren't I? So I guess that means I'm *supposed* to be here."

"That doesn't answer my question. But allow me to rephrase. Does your doctor know you're here, and did he say it was okay for you to come?"

She smiled and touched his hand. "I don't need a doctor's permission to come see about my children. I'm sure you understand that, especially now that you have Princess Rose in your life. And you're *really* going to appreciate it once this new baby gets here." She took another sip of water. "What time are you going to the hospital to see Johnnie Mae today?" she asked, attempting to change the subject.

He looked at his watch as he walked back behind his desk and sat down. "I usually have to pick up Princess Rose from summer day-camp by five. I'll take you to the house and get you settled in. By the way, where is your luggage?"

"Oh, Sherry has it out there with her. Some nice-looking gentleman was kind enough to bring them in for me. It's only two pieces. I'm only staying a few days."

He smiled. "Traveling light this trip, huh?"

She gave him one of her infamous "behave yourself" looks.

"Sorry," he said, laughing. "It was a joke, Mom. A joke."

Landris hurried to finish up despite his mother's insistence she was fine and he could take his time. Legs stretched out, head laid back on the arm of the couch, Virginia had made herself comfortable with her pledge to him that if something important came up he needed to handle in private, she would step out swiftly so as not to hinder him.

Landris was working away when out of nowhere she suddenly said, "The doctor says I need to have triple-bypass heart surgery."

Landris stopped and glanced over at her with a puzzled look. "What?" He began to frown even more. "When? I mean, when does he want you to have it?"

"As soon as possible," she said, sitting up completely and setting the *Oprah Magazine* she was reading down on the coffee table. "'Yesterday' was his exact word."

"Then why are you here, Mom?"

She moved closer to the edge of the couch. "Because you and Thomas need me."

"But Mom . . ."

She smiled. "Continue what you were doing. You need to get finished. I don't want you getting behind because of me. Everything's going to be all right."

"Mom—"

"George Edward Landris," she said with a look only a mother can give her child, "we walk by faith and not by sight! The just shall live by faith. I'll tolerate no negativity or undue concern, especially not from you. We will keep our eyes on Jesus, the author and the finisher of our faith. I've prayed about this already. And I refuse to live my life in fear. I just won't do it. Not ever again. Not now that I know the truth. What's that scripture that speaks on fear?"

Landris picked up a tattered and worn handwritten index card from off his desk and walked it over to her. He handed it to his mother, and as she read it silently, he began to quote it out loud. "Second Timothy, first and seven. 'For God hath not given us the spirit of fear; but of power, and of love, and of a sound mind.'"

She smiled as she looked from the card to her son. "Yes." She nodded. "But if you'll permit me, I'd prefer to say it this way. God has given us the Spirit of Power, the Spirit of Love, and the Spirit of a Sound Mind. And no matter what happens to us in *this* life, we win. The children of the Most High God, whose salvation has been secured through Jesus Christ—in the end, no matter what—we still win." She pressed the card against her heart and closed her eyes as she lifted her face toward Heaven and smiled.

Chapter 26

While he was yet speaking, there came also another, and said, The Chaldeans made out three bands, and fell upon the camels, and have carried them away, yea, and slain the servants with the edge of the sword; and I only am escaped alone to tell thee.

Job 1:17

Sherry knocked on the door and came inside after Pastor Landris said, "Come in."

"I'm sorry to interrupt again, Pastor Landris"—Sherry nodded to both Landris and his mother—"but Mrs. Knight is on the phone. She sounds really upset and said she would only be a minute."

Landris told her it was fine; he would get it. Sherry left.

"Excuse me, Mom, while I take this," Landris said.

"Do you need me to step out?" she asked as she quickly scooted forward on the couch to get up to leave.

"No," he said, raising his hand for her to stay where she was. "You're okay."

Landris picked up the phone and, after a few minutes of conversation, softly placed it back in its cradle.

"Bad news?" his mother asked as she looked intensely at his face.

"Reverend Knight just died. His wife is having a hard time, even though everyone—including her—was expecting it to happen at any time."

"I'm sorry. I know you two had become close, especially during this past year. Death is never easy on those left behind, even though we know—as sure as we live—it's coming to each of us. If the rapture doesn't take us first, death is the corridor we all must go through. But for those of us in Christ, Jesus is our door. I'll pray for the family's loss."

"Yes, it's natural we miss our loved ones physically. But in loving memory, they forever remain in our hearts. I often think of my sister, killed in that church parking lot by that speeding driver when she was only twelve, and my father, who died shortly after her. I know and can now rejoice that—at least for those who die in Christ—to be absent from the body is to be present with the Lord. Our loss is their gain. That's why I'm so committed to what I do. I pray that none should perish . . . that all would come to accept Jesus as their Savior and be saved. That's the reason it's important I preach the Word in season and out—that Jesus died on the cross and God raised Him from the dead." Landris turned the pages of the calendar he kept on his desk in spite of all the electronic gadgets that duplicated the schedules of his time and quickly wrote on one of those pages.

"Mrs. Knight wants to have his funeral this Saturday at twelve o'clock," he said. "There's just so much going on in my life." He shook his head. "I tell you what."

"I'm certain she'll understand your not being able to make it," Virginia said.

"A few weeks ago, Reverend Knight asked me to preach his funeral. It was one of the last requests he asked of me before he went into a coma. That's what his wife was calling to find out—whether I was in a position to preach his eulogy still. I told her I would do it, so I'll just have to find a way to manage. I'm not confessing this, but honestly, it feels like before I get past one thing good, here comes something else."

"You know what the French say: *c'est la vie*—that's life," his mother said.

He looked at his mother, then at the digital clock on

his desk. "I know you're ready to get to the house and get out of your traveling clothes. I'm going to send Sherry a note to put the funeral on my main calendar, finish up a few more things, and then we can go." He turned back to his computer.

After about ten minutes of tapping keys, he put away the things that were on his desk and stood up. "All done," he said. "Now let's go get Princess Rose." He went and got his suit coat and quickly put it on. "We'll go to the house, and if you feel up to going to the hospital today, we can all visit Johnnie Mae. I know she's going to be surprised to see you." Towering over her by about eight inches, he hugged his mother again, this time longer than usual. "I'm so glad you're here, Mom," he said. "I really am."

She looked up at him and smiled. "Me, too." She nodded. "Me, too. What was that song Bob Marley used to sing?" She began singing the words, "Everything's going to be all right." She smiled again. "God said He would never leave us nor forsake us. Because He tells us that, we can rest in the fact that everything really *is* going to be all right."

"No matter what we may be going through, God knows, and He promised He'd be right there with us through it all," Landris said, walking beside her, his arm around her shoulders. "*Through* it all. I know God is going to bring us through. And we can count on what God promises us because He is not a man that He should lie."

Virginia smiled. "God knows, and He cares. It's like I've heard you say so many times since you made Jesus the Lord of your life. It's good to be saved."

"Oh, I know that's right!" Landris said as he opened the door. "It *is* good to be saved!"

Chapter 27

While he was yet speaking, there came also another, and said, Thy sons and thy daughters were eating and drinking wine in their eldest brother's house. . . .

Job 1:18

Landris, his mother, and Princess Rose went in the house. Preparing to go see Johnnie Mae, Virginia and Princess Rose were upstairs changing. Virginia had bought Princess Rose a sundress identical to the one she was changing into. Landris had just come from carrying his mother's luggage upstairs to her room, when the phone rang.

"George, thank goodness I found you," Thomas said. "I called the church and they said you'd left already. I tried calling your cell phone, but you must have been out of range or something, because it went straight to your voice mail."

"Hey, man. Mom tells me you're not taking your medicine. Is that true?"

"Aw, man, she told you that? You know how Mom can be."

"So are you taking your medicine or not?" Landris untied his baby blue necktie and slid it from around his neck. "You promised you were going to do right."

"See, that's why I'm calling. Mom must have also told someone here I wasn't taking my medicine. The director said she was going to call you to come talk to me and her," Thomas said. "You know how they are with their rules. Dotting every i; crossing every t. I told her she didn't have to call, that you were already planning to come by."

"Well, I was getting ready to go to the hospital to see Johnnie Mae right now. Can it wait until tomorrow morning?"

Thomas sighed. "I suppose it could, but they're claiming I'm not acting rational. She insists she has to see you today, if it's at all possible. If you ask me, I'd say they all just need to get a life. George, those pills were starting to do things to me I didn't like." He lowered his voice. "And between me, you, and the couch, I believe these folks are really out to get me. I don't trust anything they give me these days to eat or drink. That's why I have my own stash here in my room. I think they're trying to slip me something."

Landris looked at his watch as his mother walked into the room with Princess Rose's hand gently tucked inside of hers. Landris couldn't help but admire how cute they looked dressed alike. "Thomas, no one's out to get you. You were doing so well. They were about to sign off on your release. Why would you just stop taking your medicine?"

"Because I saw a commercial on TV about the drug I happen to be taking, and the lawyers were saying if you've taken this medicine that you may have a case against the makers of it. I believe the pharmaceutical companies are just using us as guinea pigs. You remember the Tuskegee experiment, don't you? Well, I refuse to let these folks continue experimenting on me and messing me up. Fixing one thing but making something else go wrong. Then you need to take another pill just to fix the new problem you didn't have prior to your being treated for the previous thing. Something's wrong with that! Can you just please come by and tell this lady you and I talked, and you agree I don't need to take this medicine anymore? Better yet, why don't I just check out and come help you out?"

Landris looked at his mother and stepdaughter and smiled. "Thomas, look. I'll be by there to see you before we go to the hospital. But I can't stay long, now." He was trying to cover, not wanting his mother to suspect anything major was going on. He'd visit Thomas and see for himself how he was really doing, then proceed from there.

Arriving at the facility, he talked to the director briefly, then went to Thomas's room. Landris could tell immediately there was a problem. Thomas wasn't in bad shape, but it was obvious he was spiraling headfirst in that direction. His eyes showed signs of little sleep. He couldn't manage to be still for more than a few minutes at a time. As soon as they came inside, he had jumped up and poured them a glass of apple cider, even though Landris told him they weren't staying long and didn't want anything to drink.

"Thomas, listen to me," Landris said. "I know you think you're fine, but, man, you're not. You need to start back taking your medicine. All right?"

Thomas looked at his mother, then Princess Rose. "Hey there, little beauty," he said to Princess Rose. "Uncle Thomas has something for you." He walked over to the cabinet and took out a bag of Gummi Bears. Walking back, he held out the bag to her. "I know you love these. It's okay. You can take it. I bought the whole bag for you."

Princess Rose looked at Landris, who nodded it was okay. She reached up slowly and took it. "Thank you," she whispered, then grinned—her two bottom teeth visibly missing.

"I know that's your favorite kind of candy," Thomas said. He briskly brushed his face as though he were trying to brush crumbs or something from around his mouth. "I bought those just for you. I know you've been having a hard time with your mother being in the hospital and all. Uncle Thomas just wants you to know he's thinking about you."

Landris looked at his watch. It was six-thirty. He needed to hurry if he wanted to visit with Johnnie Mae for any real amount of time. *Where does time go?* he wondered.

"Thomas, you're in this facility so you can be on your own while still being monitored and treated medically," Landris said. "And you were doing great while you were taking your medicine. You were starting to act more like your normal self again."

"Man, I'm still cool. See, the way I figure it is the medicine has fixed the problem, so there's no reason to keep taking it. I believe I'm healed, in the name of Jesus"—he raised his hands in praise—"so I'm acting like I believe. Isn't that what you preach all the time? That we should act like we believe the Word of God is true?"

Landris glanced over at his mother, who had a look of pain on her face as she watched her oldest son. "What I preach, when it comes to areas like this, is that God also gave us sense, and He still intends for us to use wisdom. I'm not going to tell you that God can't completely heal you from your disorder, Thomas. But in your case, until it's fully manifested, you need to continue taking your medicine."

"But see now, even the logic behind *that* statement is whack. How are we going to ever know that I'm healed if I keep taking the medicine? See, the only way for us to know that I'm healed is for me to stop taking the medication for sight. You get it?"

"Thomas, stop talking foolishness," his mother said. "Your brother teaches that healing can, in some cases, be assisted through doctors. The word 'doctor' means healer. Your doctor prescribed medication that has helped you tremendously. I told you earlier today it's not a cure, but it helps you manage your thoughts and actions better."

"So are you saying that God can't heal me from this?" Thomas asked Landris, seemingly ignoring his mother's statements. He cocked his head to the side. "Are you saying that I shouldn't stand in faith because it's not possible for God to be able to do something like this for me? Are you saying my situation is too *hard*, even for God?"

"No, Thomas. I'm not saying God can't heal you," Landris said.

"Then what are you saying? That God *can* heal me, but He really can't, or should we say *won't*, because you don't think I have enough faith?"

Landris ran his hand over his face. "It's not that." He let out a sigh. "Thomas, please . . . just take your medicine. Okay? Because if you don't take it, you're just going to continue deteriorating and end up right back where you started from, if not worse."

"See, now that's not the kind of faith or support I need," Thomas said. He picked up the untouched glasses of cider and began pouring them back into the bottle. "I'm here believing God for my healing, and you're here speaking all this negative junk! It's like you're a hypocrite or something. You preach one thing, but obviously you don't really believe it." He looked at Landris as he screwed the top back on the bottle. "So, do you believe in healing or don't you?" He stopped what he was doing completely and waited.

"Yes, Thomas. I believe in healing."

"Then why can't you believe with me for mine?!" His voice cracked as he spoke.

"Thomas!" Virginia stood up and walked over to him. "Thomas, baby. Look at me." She reached up and touched his face with both hands. "Look . . . at . . . me." He looked at her. "You need to take your medicine," she said lovingly. "Do you know what a blessing from God it is to even have medication that can help you?" She went over to her purse and took out her bottle of blue pills. "Do you see these? Well, I've had to take them every day for a few months now," she said, shaking the bottle in his face. "And if I hadn't, I can't promise you I'd be standing here even now. If I can take my medicine while believing God for *my* total healing, then what is the problem with you doing the same?"

"Mom, it's different in your case."

She frowned. "How so? What if I was going around spouting off the same thing you're doing? I could decide against taking my medicine, but my not taking it means my heart might stop. What would *you* be telling *me*? What would you be saying to me?"

Thomas shook his head. "Mom, I'm telling you your situation is different. You don't need to be playing with your life that way."

Virginia touched his hand. "And you don't need to be playing with your life this way, either. Do you know how bad you can get if you don't take your medicine? Do you? We've seen it, Thomas. And believe me, it's not a pretty sight. You're putting your life in danger. Your judgment is off. You don't see it, but we do. Can you just trust me and your brother along with the people here? Trust that we see what you don't? Baby, you can't see right now that you're really not doing as well as you think without your medicine."

Landris stood. "Thomas, please. I have a lot happening now. I don't want you back in bad shape, because then I'll have to be worried about you, too."

"Where is your medicine?" Virginia asked.

Thomas let his head drop in defeat. "All right. All right. I'll take it."

"Then go get it right now and take it while I'm here," Virginia said. "I want to see you take it. And I want to see the medicine bottle for myself so I can be certain it's really your pill and not just an aspirin or something." She crossed her arms and waited.

Thomas got his medicine and gave it to his mother, who examined it then shook a pill into his hand. He took it, opening his mouth wide to show her it was indeed gone.

Landris's cell phone began to ring. He looked at the caller ID. "Pastor Landris."

"Pastor Landris, this is Dr. Baker. We need you to get to the hospital right away. Right away. I'm here already. We'll talk as soon as you get here. Just please hurry."

Chapter 28

And the Lord said unto Satan, Behold, all that he hath is in thy power; only upon himself put not forth thine hand. So Satan went forth from the presence of the Lord.

Job 1:12

Princess Rose and Landris's mother went with him to the hospital. As soon as Landris arrived, he stopped by the nurses' station and had Dr. Baker paged. She came quickly and led him off to another area to speak privately.

Virginia and Princess Rose went in the waiting room and sat down. Virginia could see the sadness on Princess Rose's face. She called her over to her and let her climb up on her lap. "I imagine it's been hard having your mommy away, huh?" Virginia said as she looked at Princess Rose and smiled.

Princess Rose nodded, then relaxed into Virginia's loving embrace.

"Well, I'm here. And you know we all love you, right? All of us."

"Yes," Princess Rose said as she blinked several times. "But I miss my grandma, too. I'm talking about my mommy's mama."

"Oh, so you haven't seen your grandma lately?"

"I saw her a little before Mommy went in the hospital. But I haven't seen her since then. Am I still going to get to see Mommy today like Daddy Landris said I would?"

Virginia hugged her. "Honestly, honey, I'm not sure right now. But I think so." She looked away then ran her hand slowly over Princess Rose's hair. "Oh, look," she said, pointing to the now-open door. "There's Daddy Landris."

Princess Rose jumped down and ran into Landris's open arms. He picked her up and swung her gently while hugging her tight. Virginia stood up as he came closer to her. She didn't say anything but tried to gauge his facial and body expressions to get some insight into what might be happening. His uptight demeanor told her things must be pretty intense.

"Sweetheart, I'm sure you're hungry. How about you and Nana go down to the cafeteria, and you can get whatever you want to eat." He set her back down on the floor.

"Hamburger and French fries?" Princess Rose asked with a grin.

"Whatever you want," Landris said, grinning back.

"Are you coming too?" Princess Rose asked Landris as she twisted back and forth.

"No. I need to see about Mommy and the new baby."

"Is the new baby here already?" Princess Rose asked as she smiled and began to jump up and down.

"Not yet." Landris looked at his mother, his eyes pleading for a little assistance.

"Come on, Princess Rose," Virginia said, reaching down and taking her hand. "Let's go see what they have in the cafeteria. I'll even break down and have dessert with you. Your choice."

They walked out of the waiting room together. Virginia and Princess Rose headed for the elevator—Princess Rose skipping the whole way. Landris watched them get on the elevator, then started toward Johnnie Mae's room.

He knocked on the door, then stuck his head inside.

Johnnie Mae was sitting up, the television was off, and she was twiddling her thumbs.

"Hey," he said as he walked in. He leaned down and kissed her softly on her lips.

"You've spoken with Dr. Baker?" Johnnie Mae asked as she stared at him.

"Yeah. She called and told me I needed to hurry. J. M., listen," he said, calling her by the name, years ago, she once had insisted everyone call her. Now, he used it only during very special times.

She turned her head away. "I don't want to hear it, Landris."

"Johnnie Mae, you have to let them take the baby now."

She looked at him. "It's too early. Just a few days longer and at least I would be seven months then. A few more days, and the baby's chances of survival will increase drastically."

"Johnnie Mae, you don't have a few more days. According to Dr. Baker, you really don't have a few more hours. Dr. Baker insists she has to take the baby now."

Johnnie Mae reached out for Landris. He held her close. "Landris, please don't do this. Please. Let's just pray. Okay? Right now . . . me and you. We just need to pray, that's all. The prayers of the righteous availeth much." She began to cry. "Please, Landris. We can't do this now."

He held her even tighter. "Johnnie Mae, I *have* been praying. Constantly, I've been praying. We've all been praying. And I believe God has answered us. The baby has a great chance of being all right at this stage. Dr. Baker is an outstanding physician. The neonatal unit will be there ready and waiting. These days, premature babies grow up perfectly fine without any lasting effects or problems. It's almost becoming routine."

Johnnie Mae pulled away from him. "But Landris, I

feel like I'm going to be all right. Honest, I do. In my heart . . . down in my spirit, I feel it. We don't have to put the baby through this. Why won't you trust me on this? I'm going to be fine." Her eyes were pleading with him. "Give our baby a little longer. Help give our baby a fighting chance."

He smiled at her. "Baby, I trust you, but I'm not willing to take this chance with your life in the balance. Dr. Baker is going to perform a C-section on you. She's getting things prepared as we speak."

"You told her it was okay to do it?" She had a frown on her face now.

"Yes."

"Why, Landris? Why? Why would you do that before you came and talked with me about it first? I told her I didn't want to do that. This is still my body. I should be the one who ultimately gets to decide."

He tried to take her hand; she quickly moved it away. "I can't believe you told her she could do it. I told you what I wanted when I first came here. I told you from the start. You could have at least come in and talked to me about it before you told her it was okay." She reached over and quickly took his hand in hers. "Go find her and tell her you've changed your mind. Tell her you and I talked . . . that we prayed about it and that we've decided we're going to totally trust God with this."

He kissed her. "Johnnie Mae, I trust God more than anyone will ever know. And I trust that God is going to bring both you and our baby through this. Johnnie Mae, I know Dr. Baker told you everything. That even taking the baby now, we still have a fight for your life on our hands. You'd better believe I'm praying right this second like you'll never know. I don't need you mad with me or upset with me about this decision. I'm not the enemy."

He released a long sigh. "I'm here for you, Johnnie Mae. And I don't ever want you to doubt my love for you. You're going to have the C-section. Then you, me, Princess Rose, and this new baby are going to go on and live our lives to the fullest. When this is all said and done, we're going to have a testimony like nobody's business and be able to tell people just how God brought us through."

She held onto his hand even tighter now. "Where is Princess Rose?"

"With my mother."

"Virginia's here?" she asked with a lift in her voice. "Did you know she was coming?"

"No. She surprised me. We were on our way here to see you when Thomas called, so we stopped by to see him." Landris didn't want her to know that there was a problem with Thomas, so he left that part out. "Thomas gave Princess Rose a bag of Gummi Bears. While we were at his place, Dr. Baker called and said I needed to get here in a hurry. Mom and Princess Rose went to the cafeteria so you and I could talk alone."

Johnnie Mae began to smile nervously. "I'm really not being fair, am I?"

"Honestly, you're just doing what you think is right. Johnnie Mae, I have to believe our baby is going to be all right even being born this early. Dr. Baker explained everything to me—the best- and worst-case scenario for both you and the baby. So I know that if you don't have the baby within the next few hours, there's a good chance you're not going to make it through tomorrow. I'm not going to sugarcoat this situation at this point. And that possibility, Johnnie Mae, is not fair to Princess Rose . . . or to this baby or . . ." His voice started to trail off. He wiped one of his eyes.

She touched his face as she tilted her head. "Or to you," she whispered, finishing a statement she knew he probably wouldn't. "I'm not being fair to you, either."

He looked at her. "I love you, Johnnie Mae. I want to

spend the rest of my life with you. A long, healthy life. I want your children to know and hear you, and not hear *about* you from other people. Both children. And personally, Johnnie Mae, I'm not willing to put your life on the line when there's another way we can do this that can possibly save both you and the baby. I prayed about this before I ever opened my mouth to tell Dr. Baker it was all right to do it. It's still all in God's hands."

"Landris, I know. I know this has to be hard on you, too. I just can't help but wonder, by doing this now, does this mean we don't trust that God will take care of it?"

"Johnnie Mae, I believe this is God's way of taking care of it. God still has to guide Dr. Baker and that medical team's hands. We're not doubting God any less going this route. In fact, I believe we have to trust Him that much more. We must trust God to go in that operating room and do what man has no control over. We still have to have faith—the working kind of faith . . . unwavering faith."

Johnnie Mae smiled and caressed his face. "Are you going to be there with me?"

He hugged her. "We're one. That means where one goes, the other must follow. We're in this together. Yes, I'm going to be right there by your side, holding your hand."

"Is it possible for me to see Princess Rose before I do this?"

He smiled and stood up straight. "Sure. I'll go get her."

"Landris . . . will you call my mother for me? I can't talk to her right now." Her voice was breaking up as she spoke. "Will you call her for me, and if it seems like she's okay, and if she feels up to it, will you see if someone will bring her here for me?" She glanced down at her now-clasped hands.

"Of course. I'll call her," he said, then pulled out his cell phone and pressed the number to speed-dial.

Chapter 29

For He put on righteousness as a breastplate, and a helmet of salvation upon His head; and He put on the garments of vengeance for clothing, and was clad with zeal as a cloak.

Isaiah 59:17

Sarah was now resting at home. She'd stayed in the hospital for two days. Memory and Lena had stayed with her during those days. Sometimes taking turns, sometimes there at the same time.

"You know what I'd like for us to do," Sarah said to Memory and Lena. "I'd like to celebrate Christmas . . . here . . . together."

Lena smiled. "I'm sure we can do that. Christmas is some six months away. We can have a grand Christmas celebration."

"Sounds like a lot of fun to me," Memory said.

Sarah began to shake her head. "No, I don't mean wait until December. I mean, I want to celebrate Christmas now."

"Now? But it's June," Memory said.

"I know it's June," Sarah said with a sheepish grin. "But who says we can only celebrate Christmas in December? What about we celebrate it this month? Lena, didn't you and Richard get married in June?"

Lena nodded. "Yeah. Both Theresa and I will be celebrating our anniversary on June twenty-second."

"Then would you like to have a Christmas-like celebration on your anniversary, or would it be best not to mix them?" Sarah asked as she brushed a strand of hair out of her face.

"I think it would be best not to mix them," Memory said, although the question wasn't addressed to her. "Lena and Theresa may want to spend that special time with their husbands," she quickly added.

"Oh dear," Sarah said. "I suppose that is selfish of me to wish to impose on their anniversary date with my own desire."

"No, I think it's a great idea. I can run it by Richard to be sure it's okay with him, and, of course, Theresa and Maurice, since we're looking for this to be a family affair. But if you want to have Christmas in June, and you'd like to include our anniversary, it's fine with me," Lena said.

Memory got up and looked at the calendar pinned on Sarah's bedroom wall. "Did you know June twenty-fifth is a Saturday?"

"Really?" Sarah said. "Well, that would be even better! We would be celebrating Christmas exactly six months ahead of time if we go with that date. Let's do it then. Let's shoot to celebrate our own special Christmas celebration June twenty-fifth."

Lena took Sarah's hand and patted it. "If that's what you want, Grandmother."

"I'll let Minnie know so she can get the place changed around. Oh, and can one of you call Polly and ask her to get in touch with the people she usually gets to come in and decorate the house for Christmas for me? Polly's number is in my address book in this nightstand drawer." She patted the nightstand, then clapped her hands as she began to laugh. "Oh, I just believe this is going to be the best Christmas ever! Ever!"

Memory smiled at Sarah. "I can't wait," she said.

When Memory and Lena left Sarah's room, they stopped when they were farther down the hallway.

"What do you really think?" Memory asked Lena. "Why do you think she wants to do this now?"

"I don't know."

"Do you think she's getting ready to leave us or something?" Memory asked.

Lena looked at her mother and shook her head. "Honestly, I don't know. But if this is what she wants to do, there's no downside to doing it. I say, let's do all we can to make this the best Christmas celebration ever."

Chapter 30

And the loftiness of man shall be bowed down, and the haughtiness of men shall be made low: and the Lord alone shall be exalted in that day.

Isaiah 2:17

"Richard, what did you do with that box?" Lena asked.

"What box?"

She pushed both fists into her waistline. "The Wings of Grace box. You know, it was on the bed. I left it on the bed when all the commotion was going on to get Sarah to the hospital a few days ago. When I came home, it was gone. I figured you put it up."

He shook his head. "It wasn't me. I haven't seen it since you showed it to me that one time. I didn't even know you brought it here with you."

"Are you *sure* you didn't move it? It was right there on the bed."

"Lena, I might be getting old, but I'd remember if I'd seen that box and put it somewhere."

Lena looked in the drawer where she had originally placed it, then other drawers throughout the bedroom. She looked in the closet and under the bed.

"Are you sure you had it in here last?" Richard asked as he began searching the uncluttered room.

Lena stopped and stared at him. "I'm sure. It was right there on that bed. Memory and I were in here talking. In fact . . ." She suddenly stopped talking, went to the bed, dropped to her knees once more, and began looking under the bed.

"Why are you looking under the bed again?" Richard asked. "It's not that small of a box you wouldn't have seen it the first time you looked."

She stood up. "I was looking for the Alexandrite necklace," she said.

"The Alexandrite necklace? Okay, now I'm really confused."

"The Alexandrite necklace." Lena walked over to him. "Memory gave it back to me. The same day I showed her the Wings of Grace box. Gayle came in while we were talking and told us Sarah was sick and needed us to come quickly. Memory and I jumped up and left everything right where it was. The Alexandrite necklace . . . the box . . ."

"All right, come sit down," Richard said, grabbing her by the hand and pulling her down on the bed with him. "Now, did you come back here after you left to go see about Sarah? You know, to get your purse when you got ready to go to the hospital that night?"

Lena thought for a second. "I didn't need a purse because we rode to the hospital with Gayle. I had about thirty dollars in my pocket from when you gave me back my change after you went to the store for me," Lena said, "so I didn't have to come in here."

"All right. So you didn't come back in the room at all after you left until . . ."

"Until you and I came home later that night." Lena began to shake her head slowly. "When we got home, it was late. I was tired, and I pretty much crashed. I didn't think about them because I guess I thought you had put them away or something." She shrugged her shoulders, then shook her head even more. "I don't believe this. I just don't believe it. She did it to me again."

"Who did what to you again?"

"Memory. If you didn't move the box and the necklace, then that can only mean she must have sneaked back in here at some point and took them both."

"But when would Memory have had a chance to do that? If you both were in here together, you both went to see about Sarah, you went to the hospital together, and you came home before she did that night," Richard said, "when could she have done it?"

Lena turned more to face him. "I don't know when she did it. Maybe while I was watching them put Sarah in the ambulance. I can't remember if Memory was there with me during those fifteen to twenty minutes or not."

He took her hand and held it. "Tell me what you were saying about the necklace."

Lena started talking, moving her hand up and down as she spoke. "Memory and I came in here to talk. I was going to tell her about the box her grandmother, Grace, left for us to open together—that third Wings of Grace box. But before I could do that, Memory pulled out the Alexandrite necklace and handed it to me."

"But how? I thought she turned that necklace in for the million-dollar reward."

"I don't know how she did it, and I didn't get a chance to find out. All I know is that she said she wanted to give it back to me," Lena said. "She claimed she wanted to make things right between us. All of us. I gave it back to her. She laid it on the bed."

"If that's the case, then why would *she* take it? Lena, that doesn't make sense."

Lena had a smirk on her face. "Because she's trying to convince me she has changed when she really hasn't, that's why. And to think I almost believed her, too."

"Lena, listen. I don't think you should jump to any immediate conclusions about Memory, the necklace, or that box. I'm sure there's some kind of a logical explanation."

"Like?"

"Like maybe someone else saw them and put them up for you. But you should ask Memory before you get all worked up about it. She may have just put them up to keep them safe, and in the commotion—like you forgot—maybe she forgot to tell you."

Lena stood and started toward the door.

"Where are you going?" Richard asked.

"To ask her. I'm going to settle this once and for all."

Lena went to Memory's closed door. Standing and about to knock, she could hear Memory talking to someone. Detecting only one voice, she concluded Memory was on the phone. She started to walk away, when suddenly she stopped in her tracks.

"Sam, I told you. I'm sorry I just got a chance to call. It's been crazy around here. But guess what? I got it back," Memory said in a slightly muffled but audible voice. "It took some doing, but I got the Alexandrite necklace back. More than that: an early July ninth birthday present to *me.* Only thing is, I think I may be in a slight pickle. You know, a bit of a jam. All right, in plain English . . . in trouble."

Having heard enough, Lena turned around and rushed back to her room.

"That was quick," Richard said. "What happened? Was she busy? Not there?"

Lena fell into his arms. "Just hold me, please. Hold me, okay?"

"What happened? Did you get to talk to Memory and ask if she took them?"

Lena pulled herself away from his embrace. "I didn't have to. I was standing outside her door about to knock. I heard her on the phone. She was telling someone named Sam that she'd gotten the necklace back." Lena laid her head back on Richard's shoulder. "If she took the necklace, Richard, then she took the box as well."

Richard rubbed her back as she cried. "I'm sorry, Lena girl. I'm *so* sorry."

Chapter 31

So shall they fear the name of the Lord from the west, and His glory from the rising of the sun. When the enemy shall come in like a flood, the Spirit of the Lord shall lift up a standard against him.

Isaiah 59:19

"Lena, would you like to tell me what's bothering you?" Sarah asked as she sat propped up in her bed.

"Nothing," Lena said.

"Listen, dear. I've been around a long while. I can tell when someone has something on their mind. Now, if you just don't want to share it with me, that's one thing. But to tell me it's nothing is just not true, and you and I both know that."

Lena forced a smile. "I really don't want to talk about it."

"Well, all right then. But if you're worried about me, I'm feeling so much better. It was a blessing having you and Memory here with me throughout this ordeal." Sarah pushed her body up to sit more erect. "Every time I opened my eyes in that hospital room, one or both of you were there. I had to remind myself it was real . . . that I wasn't dreaming."

Lena leaned over and patted her on her hand. "I'm glad, Grandmother."

Sarah looked toward the window. "It's a beautiful day today. I'd really love to go outside." She turned back and smiled at Lena. "Do you think we could all eat out on the terrace for lunch today? Just us girls—me, you, and Memory. I'm not trying to cut Richard out, I'd just like it to be only us three."

"If you want to do that, I don't see why we can't. The doctor said that the more you get up and move around, the better it will be for you." Lena stood up. "And you know Richard practically lives on the golf course these days, so he's already up and gone. But I'll let Monica know," she said, referring to the cook. "Is there anything special you'd like her to fix for lunch?"

Sarah shook her head. "No. But before you leave, sit back down and let's talk."

Lena came back and sat down.

Sarah reached over and grabbed her hand once more. "Lena, I know you and Memory have had your seasons of being angry."

Lena tried, but couldn't help it. She turned away just from the mention of Memory's name.

"Lena, look at me. I don't know what has happened recently, but you can't keep letting things fester between you and your mother." She patted Lena's hand twice, then released it. "A few days ago you and Memory seemed to be really connecting. What has happened, seemingly in one day, that changed things?"

Lena stood up again. She didn't want to be close enough for Sarah to look in her eyes. "Nothing, Grandmother. Now, I really need to go let Memory and Monica know about our lunch plans. I'll ask Monica to fix some of your favorite dishes."

"Lena, I love you," Sarah said as she stared at her. "But I love Memory, too. Yes, she's done some pretty horrible things. Yes, she's disappointed a lot of people. Yes, she's hurt people I care deeply about. But Lena, in loving Memory I have to let all those things go. In loving Memory, I have to learn to forgive. In loving Memory, I have to give her a chance to prove that she's really changed, and I have to do that without holding back any of myself or my heart. If I don't, I may miss out on things and moments I can never get back." Sarah reached her hand out to Lena. "I've missed too much already. I don't want to live out the remainder of whatever time I have distrusting or guarding my heart. Because in doing that, I limit the joy I could experience. I want to feel it all. And if that means having to take the good with the bad, then so be it. If in loving Memory it means I may be hurt, then I'll just have to take that chance."

Lena squeezed her hand. "I'm glad you can do that," Lena said.

"Talk to her," Sarah said sternly. "Tell her what you think. Tell her how you feel. Give her a chance. Fight for what's right. We must stop letting the devil win."

"Has Memory said something to you?" Lena asked out of curiosity.

"No. But I can feel the difference in you both. I asked her about you last night, and she became instantly sad. Her whole countenance changed. When I asked her what had happened between you two, she told me she didn't know . . . that you had abruptly shut down on her, and she was at a loss as to what had occurred to cause it."

"Is that what she told you?"

"Lena, I don't believe she's the same woman anymore that *you* believe her to be."

Lena took her hand back. "How do you know that, Grandmother? You've only known her for less than two weeks. You don't know how manipulative she can be. You don't know how she can make you think she really cares about you only to stab you in the back when you least expect it." Lena saw the shocked look come over Sarah's face. "I'm sorry. I'm sorry. I don't mean to upset you. You don't need this now. I apologize."

"It's okay. I'm strong enough to hear this. But will you trust me on this? At least tell Memory what's bothering you in regards to her. You may discover this is all some big misunderstanding. If you talk about it, you won't lose precious time that honestly can never be gotten back. Confrontation is not always a bad thing. I learned that when I had to go against Montgomery and the others to take back what was rightfully mine. It would have been easy to just walk away. Sometimes we have to meet a thing head-on."

Lena leaned down and kissed Sarah on the cheek. "I hear you."

Sarah grabbed Lena's wrist and held her before she could stand back up straight. "Do more than just hear me. I want the two of you to resolve whatever is going on between you. If you can't do it for yourselves, then please, can you do it for me?" She released her grip.

Lena stood up and straightened her top by pulling it down. She nodded.

"Oh, and Lena? Just in case you're wondering, I had this same conversation with Memory a little while ago. Sometimes you have to wash off all the junk to see the true treasures in life. I don't know what happened, but I know you need to put whatever it is out there and get to the bottom of it so you can experience all God has for you. Deal with it before it ferments that much more."

Lena leaned down and kissed her again. "For you, Grandmother, I'll do it."

"Not just for me; do it for yourself as well. Do it for your own child and for her children." Sarah nodded, then looked back toward the sunlight that streamed like a beam through her window. "What a beautiful day, Lord. You've given me one more day. This *is* the day that the Lord has made, and I *will* rejoice and be glad in it. I will! Thank You, Lord. I thank You for one more day."

Chapter 32

Thy sun shall no more go down; neither shall thy moon withdraw itself: for the Lord shall be thine everlasting light, and the days of thy mourning shall be ended.

Isaiah 60:20

"All right, Lena. Let's talk," Memory said as soon as Lena entered the kitchen.

"I need to tell Monica—"

"That Sarah wants to have lunch out on the terrace," Memory said, completing the sentence for her. "I've already told her. So . . ." She held her hand out toward the terrace. "Shall we go talk?"

"Sure," Lena said with an attitude that showed in her body language.

Lena stepped out the door first and sat down at the patio table. Memory sat directly across from her.

"So tell me—what did I do?" Memory asked.

Lena let out a small huff. "Like you don't know."

"Lena, I don't know. We seemed to have been making progress that evening we were talking in your room. We pulled together to take care of Sarah while she was in the hospital. When Sarah came home, you were fine. Then, in the last twenty-four hours or so, it's like someone left the freezer door wide open, and it's causing a deep freeze to go throughout the entire house."

Lena shook her head. "Just stop. Why don't you just stop?" She looked at Memory, her eyes visibly sad.

"Stop what?" Memory asked, clearly annoyed. "Stop

trying to make up for my past mistakes? Stop trying to do the right thing by you and by Sarah and Theresa if I get the chance? Stop what?"

"Stop lying. Stop pretending that you care about other people when you don't," Lena said in a controlled but stern voice. "The only one you really care about is yourself."

"Lena, what are you talking about? Why don't you just come out and say what you have to say and quit leaving breadcrumb trails, expecting me to follow you? Just say it and get it over with."

Lena sat back in the chair and made a long sucking sound with her teeth, then buttoned up her lips before relaxing them. "Okay. Let's play another game. Let's play Tell the Truth No Matter What for a change."

"Fine. If it will help you get past whatever this is you're going through at the moment, then bring it on," Memory said.

Lena sat forward. "This is how we're going to do this. We'll tell the truth no matter what the truth really is, and no matter whose feelings may get hurt in the process. It's just you and me. All right?"

"Go ahead. Ask away," Memory said as she leaned in toward Lena.

"Did you or did you not take the Wings of Grace box?" Lena asked.

Memory began to laugh. "Oh, so it's that again. Yes, Lena. I took it. You know I took it."

Lena looked a little shocked. "You took it, and you're admitting it?"

"Yes, I took it," Memory said. "That's old news. So you're telling me that you've been walking around mad all day yesterday because of something I took back when you were young? Something you didn't even know existed until you were older?"

Lena sat back against the chair. "Okay." She nodded

her head swiftly. "Okay. Okay, so now you're back to playing games again."

"You asked me if I took that box. I'm telling you the truth. Yes, I took it."

"I'm talking about the box that was in my room the other day. You remember . . . the one Grace left in her will for me and you to open together. We were in my room when Gayle came in, and I left it on the bed. *That* Wings of Grace box."

Memory folded her hands together. "I didn't take that box, Lena."

Lena began to smile a phony smile. "Of course you didn't."

"Lena." Memory leaned in closer. "I'm telling you the truth. I didn't take that box. Look into my eyes, Lena. I promise you, I didn't take it."

Lena looked at her. "What about the Alexandrite necklace? It just so happens to be missing as well. I suppose you're telling me you didn't take it back, either?"

Memory reached over and grabbed both of Lena's hands. "Lena, why would I give that necklace back to you, then turn around and take it? That makes no sense."

Lena removed her hands from Memory's. "I don't know. That's what frustrates me about you. I never know why you do anything. All I know is it hurts like you'll never, ever understand." Lena stood and walked to the limestone banister. "I want you to really love me. I've always wanted you to want me." She turned and looked at Memory as tears ran down her face. "But you never seemed able to. And every time I decide to give you one more chance, it's obvious you don't really care. Because you manage to stomp on my heart all over again like it's some kind of a sport to you."

Memory stood up and went to her daughter. "Lena, I am sorry for all the hurt I've caused you. I sincerely am. I thought giving you back that necklace would make up things to you . . . that it would let you know how much I really do love you . . . how sincere I really am about us being closer."

Lena began to cry. "Then why take it back like that? I said you could keep it."

Memory pulled her close and held her tight. "I'm sorry I hurt you. I'm sorry you don't feel you can trust me. But Lena, I've been on the up-and-up with you since I've been here. I didn't take them. I'm trying to make amends here. Lord knows, I'm trying. I really am."

"And why is that?" Lena asked, pulling away from her mother's embrace. "Why now? Is it because you see a bigger payday with Sarah? Are you just biding your time, trying to pretend to be a changed woman who loves the Lord now, all of a sudden?"

"Don't discount my love for God. He changed me, Lena. Whether you believe that or not, that's the truth. The old Memory would definitely be looking at all of this trying to see how she could score big and get out fast. But God took out that old, stony heart"—she put her hand over her heart area—"and gave me a brand-new, clean heart. And now, I just want to serve Him and do right by people."

Lena walked back over to the table and stood by the chair she had just occupied. "Memory, if you've changed, then what about that phone conversation you had the other night?"

"What phone conversation?" Memory walked over toward the table. "Oh, you heard me talking on the phone? So what are you doing? Spying on me now?"

Lena sat down and folded her arms across her chest. "I heard you the other night on the phone, but I wasn't spying on you. I was coming to ask if you might have put the Wings of Grace box up along with the necklace. I was looking for them, thinking originally that

Richard had put them up during all the commotion with Grandmother going to the hospital. Night before last, I asked him. He didn't move them, so we thought you might have put them up . . . you know, for safekeeping."

"So you came to my room and heard me on the phone?" Memory asked as she sat down.

"Yes." Lena started rocking her body a little. "You were talking to someone named Sam."

Memory tilted her head slightly. "So, what all did you hear me say to Sam?"

"Why don't you tell me what you said? That way I can see how truthful, how much on the up-and-up, you really are these days," Lena said.

"Okay, Lena. I'm going to tell you everything. I'm going to tell you about Sam and about Montgomery Powell the Second—"

"Montgomery Powell the Second? You know Montgomery?"

"Yes. I met him that Saturday when I told you I was going out to visit Asheville. You remember, the night I came home and gave you back the Alexandrite necklace."

Monica came outside with a tray. "I thought you two might like some fresh lemonade," she said, setting the tray with a glass pitcher and two glasses filled with crushed ice on the table.

After Monica left, Lena poured Memory a glass of lemonade, then herself. Taking a sip, Lena set her glass down. "All right. I'm all ears," Lena said as she sat back, relaxed.

Chapter 33

Truth shall spring out of the earth; and righteousness shall look down from heaven.

Psalms 85:11

"First off, when you came to my room the other night and heard me on the phone, I was indeed talking to Sam," Memory said.

"And I suppose Sam is another one of your con-artist buddies like that phony lawyer friend you had come to Theresa's house that day," Lena said with a slight smirk.

"Sam is my closest and dearest friend. Her name is Samantha McCoy, and she really has been the only person who's tried to show me the error of my ways." Memory took a drink of her lemonade. She held the glass up in the air and looked at it. "Ahhhh! Now that's *real* lemonade," she said, then set the glass back down.

"So I guess I'm supposed to believe Sam is a woman?"

Memory hunched her shoulders. "I'm not trying to make you believe anything. You say you want the whole truth. I said I'd tell you the truth. You'll either believe what I'm saying or you won't, but it's not going to be on me. Anyway, Sam was like me at one time—always trying to find a way to get over on somebody. Actually, we viewed it more like trying to figure out a way to get ahead."

"Okay, let's say Sam really is a woman named Samantha. What were you talking about the other night?"

Memory looked down, then back up. "I was telling Sam that I'd managed to get the Alexandrite necklace back."

Lena started nodding her head and smiling in a sarcastic way. "Exactly. At least you're telling the truth about that."

Memory leaned in. "I was telling her I'd gotten the necklace back from the person who had ended up with it . . . after I took it out of the safe-deposit box and turned it over to Christopher Harris, a.k.a. Christopher Phelps of Phelps & Phelps."

"So you're admitting you did steal the necklace?"

"Lena, you already know that. I was wrong, and right after I did it and found myself sitting there waiting for Christopher to pick me up, I wanted so badly to turn around and somehow put everything back the way it was. But I couldn't," Memory said. "I'd already deceived Theresa, and she was on her way to the hospital to have my great-granddaughter. Christopher picked me up shortly after Richard dropped me off at the bus stop."

"You still could have taken the necklace back and returned it to the safe-deposit box," Lena said as she exchanged looks with her mother. "We could have gotten past all of this."

"Oh, yeah. I can see *that* working out. Anyway, it was too late to turn back. Christopher took the necklace and put it up for safekeeping while he made arrangements to get the reward money for it." She took another swallow of lemonade. "We were supposed to split the million dollars sixty-forty, my favor. Instead, that snake decided to double-cross me." She looked up and smiled. "I suppose you can say the con got conned."

"So you're telling me you didn't get anything from the necklace?"

"Oh, Christopher was not heartless. He came by and left twenty thousand dollars for me with Samantha.

That's how she and I ended up close. Sam is diabetic, and she's lost both her legs because of it. She was living in a ground-level apartment. Christopher and I had an apartment two floors above hers. We would see Sam on occasion and speak. After Christopher turned in the necklace, he told me we would have to wait a few days for them to verify that the necklace was genuine and not just some fake."

"And you believed him," Lena said.

"Why wouldn't I? That was a million dollars they were giving up. Everybody knows they weren't going to give up that much money without checking out the merchandise first. Christopher was the one who knew the guy who was paying the reward." Memory let out a hard sigh.

"Anyway, Christopher left and never came back. I was worried something bad had happened to him. One day I was on my way out a few weeks after not hearing from him. Sam stopped me. She didn't know my phone number, and she couldn't get up the stairs to come find me. That's when she gave me a package she said Christopher had left with her to give to me. She didn't understand why he didn't just bring it up to me himself. I opened it, and there was cash money inside with a note thanking me for everything."

"Wow," Lena said.

"Sam saw me break down. She opened up her door for me to come in. We talked, and I told her everything. I don't know why it's easier sometimes to tell a stranger things like that, but it was for me. That's when Sam explained to me the truth regarding the law of sowing and reaping." Memory primped her lips in a snooty way, then laughed.

"Oh, I'm sure you wanted to hear that," Lena said sarcastically. She drank the last of her lemonade. Reaching over and picking up the pitcher, she offered Memory a refill. Memory held her glass up as Lena poured.

"Actually, Sam was just what I needed at the time," Memory said as Lena filled her glass. "I didn't need to stay in an apartment under my own name, so I took her up on her offer to move in with her. She needed someone there to help out, and I needed to keep a low profile until I was sure things had blown over." Memory swirled the liquid in her glass slightly before putting the glass up to her lips and taking a sip. "To be honest, I was also hoping Christopher might have a change of heart and come back for me. I knew if he did, he would come to Sam's apartment to see if she knew where I was."

"Did he ever come back?" Lena asked.

"Nope. But a lot of other people started showing up asking for me," Memory said. "Sam was great, never letting anyone know my whereabouts, even after I left her place. We've always kept in touch. She got saved and started telling me how she was praying for me. I'd go back and stay with her on occasion, but it seemed best for me to keep moving since I couldn't seem to shake those private detectives that had nothing better to do, it seemed, than track me down."

"So how did you get the Alexandrite necklace back?" Lena asked.

"I believe it was the summer of 2002 that I received a letter at Sam's place. It was from some man in Asheville, North Carolina, who said he was sure he had something I'd like to have back. His name was Montgomery Powell the Second, which meant nothing to me except possibly some clever trick to smoke me out."

"Montgomery, the one you went to see the Saturday Grandmother got sick?"

Memory nodded, using her whole body in a rocking motion. "Yes. Anyway, until Johnnie Mae Landris told me the truth about my real mother a few weeks ago, none of this had made sense or, truthfully, any difference. When Johnnie Mae told me everything, including the fact that Sarah was in Asheville, I started to call Sarah that night. But I just couldn't manage to bring myself to hear the truth, at least not then." Memory laughed. "It's funny. It was like as long as I didn't come face to face with it, it was merely a thought . . . a remote possibility . . . words spoken by some woman I barely knew, who could be wrong. I knew I had become a different person, but what if this knowledge sent me back to being the person I thought I'd buried when I gave my life to Christ?"

"So you're sincere about the Lord?" Lena asked with a quizzical look. "It's not just a con you're using to get over?"

"Lena, it's the most incredible feeling and experience I've ever had," Memory said, touching Lena's arm. "It's hard to describe, but to actually put someone else first, instead of yourself, that's just something I can't honestly say I'd ever done before in my entire life. Not until Jesus came into my heart. He changed me."

"So you didn't want to see Sarah that day Johnnie Mae told you everything because you were afraid you really hadn't changed?"

"I suppose I was afraid I might hurt her the way I had hurt you and Theresa," Memory said, removing her hand from Lena's arm. "I didn't want to take the chance of finding out that maybe I really *hadn't* changed. That the old Memory was just waiting for the chance to rise up . . . to be resurrected. My intentions had been to leave the Landrises' house and disappear quietly into the night."

"What made you change your mind?"

"Sam did," Memory said with a nod. "That's what . . . or should we say who. I called Sam, and she prayed with me that night. She told me she'd seen a change in me, and that the right thing for me to do was go and meet my mother. Also, that if I ever got the chance to make things right with you and Theresa, I should do it . . . *whatever* I had to do to make it right. So I called the number Johnnie Mae gave me for Sarah, told the person who answered the phone that I had a special delivery for Sarah Fleming, but I couldn't make out the address as written and needed to verify it. Whoever answered the phone gave me the address. I got on a bus, and here I am."

Lena stared deep into her eyes as Memory held her head up high. "You're telling the truth," Lena said.

"Yes."

Lena released a sigh. "So tell me. How does Montgomery fit in all of this?"

Memory raised an eyebrow and smiled. "Are you sure you want to hear this part right now?"

Lena looked at her watch. It was nearing noontime. Sarah would be down shortly. She nodded. "Yes. I want to know everything. But it will be lunchtime in about twenty minutes," Lena said. "So you need to hurry up."

Chapter 34

Fill their faces with shame; that they may seek Thy name, O Lord.

Psalm 83:16

"As I was saying, Montgomery sent certified letters to Sam's place for me. Samantha signed for them because she didn't know whether or not they were something important since no one, other than possibly Christopher, would know I was there unless I had told them." Memory sat back against the chair.

"So it appears Montgomery not only knew *who* you were but *where* you were," Lena said. "And how long ago did you say this was?"

Memory frowned and twisted her mouth as she bit down on her thumbnail. "The first letter came about three years ago, around June of 2002." She began to nod. "A couple more letters came over the years."

"Grandmother began searching for you October of 2001, as soon as she learned you were still alive. So Montgomery must have learned of your whereabouts some months after that." Lena shook her head. "But why? Why would he want to make contact with you? What is he up to?"

"I take it Montgomery must really be bad news?" Memory popped her lips and scrunched her mouth as she spoke.

"Yeah. I've had a taste firsthand. He's definitely someone to steer clear of."

"Then what I've done may not have been a good thing," Memory said. She leaned her head back and exhaled loudly. Sitting up straight, she began to shake her head once more.

Lena leaned her body in closer. "What did you do?"

"I was the one who called Montgomery. It was a few days after I arrived. If you recall, you and Theresa weren't too happy to see me when I showed up in your lives again. I was curious as to how he might possibly fit in this ever-evolving puzzle. For some strange reason, I'd kept his three letters in my pocketbook. I knew he lived here in Asheville. I'd been mysteriously summoned back to Asheville after having left here when I was fourteen. So I decided to give him a call and see what he had to say. He turned out to be quite a little charmer over the phone, and, surprisingly, he seemed genuinely excited to hear from me."

Memory sat back against the chair and situated her body more comfortably as she continued. "I didn't want him able to see where I was calling from in case he had caller ID. I have a calling card I generally use for long-distance calls, so I decided to use it to call him, even though I knew it was a local call. We talked, and eventually I admitted to him I was in the city. He insisted that we meet, again enticing me by saying he had something he was certain I wanted back while being adamant that he couldn't tell me anything more than that over the phone. He also informed me that he knew I was here at Sarah's house. That kind of bothered me a little."

"That is interesting."

"He didn't want me to mention anything to anyone here about him or the call. If I did, he said he would somehow know, and that the sweet deal he was planning for me would immediately be taken off the table before I ever even got to know what it was."

Lena crossed her legs at her ankles. "Oh, yeah . . . a real charmer, that Montgomery Powell the Second. So you felt safe enough to go off alone and meet with a stranger, in reality, without letting anyone know?"

Memory smiled. "Lena, you know I haven't lived a charmed life all these years. I've hung out with some rough folks, to put it mildly. I learned a long time ago how to take care of myself."

"But you're older now. It was dangerous when you were young, but even more dangerous now that you're almost seventy," Lena said, crossing her arms.

"I know. That's why I told Sam everything. I gave her the phone number here and told her that if I didn't call her back before the night was over, she was to call you and tell you everything she knew about Montgomery and my seeing him. In all that happened Saturday night, I almost forgot to call her and let her know I had made it back okay. I ended up having to call her from the hospital. We spoke long enough for me to let her know I was all right, with a promise that I'd call her again later when I could talk."

Lena unfolded her arms and looked toward the doorway. "Grandmother likely will be down soon."

"I know; I'll hurry." Memory took a deep breath and released it. "Montgomery had the Alexandrite necklace."

"What?" Lena said, shocked.

"And somehow, he knew that you and Theresa were upset with me about my having taken it. He said he wanted to give it back to me—"

Lena started shaking her head. "He wanted to *give* it back? The man paid two million dollars to get it, and you're telling me he was going to just give it back to you out of the goodness of his heart?" She shook her head even faster and turned up her nose as though she had suddenly caught whiff of something that had been dead and hidden away for weeks. “I don’t think so.”

“He mentioned he’d paid two million dollars for that necklace,” Memory said, still showing her shock. “Two million dollars.”

“Yes. And according to Pastor Landris who knows all about this, your *boyfriend* got one million of those dollars, minus your twenty thousand. Frankly, I don’t have time to tell everything I know right now,” Lena said. She started rotating her index finger in a circular motion, indicating to Memory she needed to finish up her story. “Please hurry.”

“I asked him how he knew Sarah, and he told me about his father being Sarah’s half-brother,” Memory said.

“Yeah, I know all about that. Get back to you, him, and the necklace.”

“As you already know now, Montgomery ended up giving it to me.”

“For what reason? What did you have to give him or promise him in return in order for you to get the necklace? That’s what I want to know.”

Memory stood up and walked over to the door and looked inside. It was quiet, but she could smell the various cooking aromas that were slipping through the cracks, making their way outside to the terrace from the kitchen.

Lena got up, walked over to the door, and practically dragged Memory away from it. “Tell me what you did in order to get the Alexandrite necklace.”

Memory walked away from Lena over to the limestone banister and looked out at the rolling blue hills. “I don’t believe I did this.”

Lena came over and stood next to her. “What . . . did . . . you . . . do?”

Memory looked at her. "I signed a document stating that I would sell him this house, at a fair and marketable price, of course, should I be the one to inherit it upon my mother's death. That's what."

Lena stared at her. "How could you?" Lena started walking away.

Memory ran and grabbed her arm. "Lena, I did it because I love my family. I love you, and I love Theresa, and I love my great-grandbabies. I wanted to make things right with us. I figured if I had the necklace and gave it back, you and Theresa might forgive me for having taken it in the first place. You might have thought I'd kept it all this time. You know—no harm, no foul."

Lena wriggled her arm out of Memory's grip. "But how could you agree to sell this house like that? I thought you said you'd changed? You haven't changed! This is exactly what you did when I was sixteen years old. You took the house that Big Mama left me, and you sold it without any regard for anyone else other than yourself. It was about what you wanted. It's always about you . . . always what's best for you." Lena stared at her, then plodded away. She turned and looked at her before opening the door. "How could you do that to your own mother?" she asked. "How could you?"

Memory walked swiftly to catch up with her. "Lena," she yelled. "Lena!"

Lena opened the door and went inside the house, quickly making her way up the stairs to her room. Closing her door, she locked it, then fell to her knees as she began to quietly cry.

Chapter 35

Thus saith the Lord, thy Redeemer, the Holy One of Israel; I am the Lord thy God which teacheth thee to profit, which leadeth thee by the way that thou shouldest go.

Isaiah 48:17

Lena sat on her bed. Looking at her watch and seeing it was close to noon, she got up and wiped the tears from her eyes and face with a wet washcloth. Knowing she had to pull herself together, she went to Sarah's room with a big smile on her face. Sarah was holding onto Gayle's arm with one hand while holding a walking cane with the other.

"Grandmother, are you ready for lunch?" Lena asked cheerfully.

"I absolutely am," Sarah said. She walked up to Lena and looked into her eyes. Lena looked away. "Is Memory already downstairs?"

Lena nodded. "Yes, she's on the terrace waiting."

"Good," Sarah said as she removed her arm from Gayle's arm and wrapped it around Lena's. "Thanks, Gayle. Lena will see me downstairs. You can run on and take care of that errand you said you needed to handle."

Gayle nodded. "Thank you. I'll be back in a few hours. Y'all have fun, now."

As Sarah and Lena slowly made their way down the stairs, Sarah stopped on the landing area before starting down the last set of stairs. "Give me a second,"

Sarah said. “This is more than a notion. Definitely a lot more work than I first thought,” she said.

“It’s fine. Take your time. We don’t have any reason to rush.”

Sarah stood there. “So . . . did you and Memory talk?”

Lena nodded.

“Is that why you’re upset?” Sarah asked, looking up at Lena from her slightly bent position. “Did things not go well with you two?”

Lena looked at her and smiled. “It went okay. We didn’t get to finish our conversation, but we covered a lot of ground.”

Sarah grabbed Lena’s arm tighter. “Well, I won’t pressure you about it. If you want to talk, I hope you know I’m here.”

“I know,” Lena said as she started moving along with Sarah’s pace.

They stepped out on the terrace, and Sarah immediately shielded her eyes with her hand. “What a *lovely* day!” Sarah said, grinning.

Memory got up and met Sarah and Lena. She helped Sarah to the chair underneath the oversized patio umbrella. “You look so pretty in your flowery dress,” Memory said as she held on to Sarah, who was lowering her body slowly into the chair.

“I’ve always loved flowers. Chocolate and flowers. I thought I’d brighten my day even more by wearing this dress.”

Lena and Memory sat down. Monica rolled out the serving table and began setting the table. It didn’t take her long to finish. “If you need anything else, let me know,” Monica said.

“Food fit for queens,” Sarah said as she lifted the sterling-silver domes and began putting various items on her plate. “This looks more like a Sunday dinner than a Thursday lunch on the terrace. Will you look a’ here.

There are collard greens with okra, grilled chicken, and squash casserole. Oh, I simply love Monica's squash casserole! Nobody can touch Monica's squash casserole. As an old friend of mine in Selma, Alabama, Ms. Azile, used to say when we ate something that was absolutely delicious, 'That woman know she can put her foot in it.'"

"We told her to fix all your favorites," Lena said, smiling.

"So I see," Sarah said. She looked at Memory. "Will you please say grace?"

Memory looked at Lena, then Sarah. "Of course." They bowed their heads as Memory prayed a short prayer. "Amen," she said.

They began eating in silence except for occasional comments about a certain dish.

Sarah set her fork down. "Okay, so who wants to tell me what's going on here?" She looked from Lena to Memory. "Memory? Lena?"

"Nothing, Grandmother. Just enjoying the food and the company," Lena said.

Sarah looked at Memory again. "Will *someone* please tell me the truth for a change and stop all of this foolishness of trying to protect me?"

Memory looked at Lena. "It's all my fault," she said to Sarah. "I'm ruining your beautiful day. Lena's upset with me, and, truthfully, she has every reason and right to be."

"Don't do it," Lena said to Memory. "I'm not upset. I just have a lot on my mind. Richard's becoming quite a little golfer these days. I was thinking he would be bored, and it looks like he's more active here than when he's at home." Lena put a forkful of food in her mouth. "You're right, Grandmother. This squash casserole is divine! Monica definitely put her foot in this. Don't you think so?" Lena asked, now addressing Memory.

"Yes," Memory said, taking a bite of squash casserole. "It's delicious."

Sarah didn't say a word. She just sat there and watched as Lena continued on with a few minutes more of frivolous chitchat about nothing really.

"Lena, I should have brought my straw hat down with me," Sarah said. "Would you be a dear and run up to my room and get it?"

Lena smiled as she looked at Sarah, then Memory.

"I'll get it for you," Memory said, pushing her chair back as she started to stand.

"If you don't mind, I'd like Lena to get it for me," Sarah said, touching Memory's hand. She looked at Lena. "She's the youngest between us. That's if you don't mind?"

Lena smiled and got up. "Of course I don't mind." She wiped her mouth and placed the crisp, white linen napkin down next to her plate. "I'll be right back."

"It's in the chifforobe," Sarah yelled as Lena opened the French door.

After Lena left, Sarah dabbed her mouth, being extra careful not to wipe off her ruby red lipstick she'd so artfully put on. She set her full attention to Memory. "Now, would you like to tell me what's going on?"

Memory wiped her mouth and took a few swallows of lemonade. "Nothing," she finally said.

"Memory, please don't insult my intelligence or my sanity. Something is going on, and I want to know what it is." Sarah stopped eating and folded her arms across her chest.

Memory looked up at the sky, then at Sarah as she let out a loud sigh. "Okay. Okay. I'll tell you. For one thing, I met with Montgomery Powell this past Saturday. It was the same day you got sick. The day you went to the hospital."

Sarah nodded. "Is that all?"

Memory shook her head. "I got the Alexandrite necklace back. The one I'm sure you're aware that I took from Lena and Theresa a few years back."

Sarah nodded again slowly. "Let me know when you're finished," Sarah said.

Memory sat back against her chair. "I gave Lena the necklace. She gave it back. Lena showed me the Wings of Grace box your mother left for me and her to open together." Memory cocked her head to the side. "We left them on Lena's bed, and now both the box and the necklace have mysteriously disappeared out of her room."

"Would you care to tell me how you managed to get that necklace back?"

"I made a deal with Montgomery. He had it." Memory stopped and readjusted her body in the chair. "I signed an agreement that says if I should inherit this house, I'll sell it to him."

Sarah nodded, her demeanor remaining the same. "So, I see."

"Now that the necklace and the box are both missing, Lena thinks I'm probably behind their disappearance." Memory waited for Sarah to say something. "But I didn't take them."

Sarah picked up her knife and fork, cut off a piece of her grilled chicken, placed it in her mouth, and proceeded to chew slowly.

Lena walked back outside, handed Sarah the hat, and sat down. "It wasn't in the chifforobe," Lena said. "It was in your closet, on the top shelf."

"Oh, I suppose someone must have moved it then." Sarah ate one of the peas in a pod.

Lena looked at Sarah, trying to figure out what may have happened while she was gone.

Sarah pointed her fork at Lena's plate. "You need to eat, dear."

Lena smiled at Sarah, then looked over at Memory,

whose demeanor had completely changed since she'd gone to get Sarah's hat.

Memory looked back at Lena. "I told her everything," Memory finally said to Lena.

Lena narrowed her eyes somewhat, her eyebrows furrowing as she frowned. "Told her what?"

"I told her about Montgomery and our meeting, about the necklace, and how the necklace and the box are both missing now," Memory said.

"Why?"

"Because I asked her to," Sarah said. "And I needed to know." Sarah ate some more of the squash casserole. "Let me ask you something. The Wings of Grace box—did you get a chance to see what was inside of it before it went missing?"

"No," Memory said. "Gayle came to Lena's room just after we unlocked it."

"And I never opened it before that day, so I don't know what was in there," Lena said.

Sarah set her fork down in her plate. "Lena, you believe Memory took the box and the necklace, correct?"

Lena tried to smile and play it off. "Why are you ruining this perfect day with talk about things like this, Grandmother?"

"Because something is going on here, and we need to get to the bottom of it. I believe it's Hosea four-six that says, 'My people are destroyed for lack of knowledge.' I don't care for our family to be destroyed. I've waited too long to get here, and I don't intend to tiptoe around issues any longer because no one wishes to upset the apple cart. Let's get to it so we can figure out what's going on and know exactly what we're dealing with here. Knowledge is always power. Always. I will not allow our family to be destroyed. So let's do what needs to be done, however painful it might be."

"Do you think I took that box and the necklace?" Memory asked Lena.

Lena looked at Sarah. Sarah's look was stern.

"I think it's a strong possibility you may have," Lena said. "You went to see Montgomery, and you weren't planning on ever telling us that. Do you have any idea the agonies and heartaches those people have put Grandmother through all these years, going all the way back to his father and uncle?"

"I really don't," Memory said. "All I know is he had the necklace, and I felt that getting it back was one way I might have a chance of you and Theresa not being angry with me anymore."

Sarah touched Lena's arm. "What Montgomery and my half-brothers did is my battle." She looked at Memory. "They were the reason I was locked away all those years from my home until Johnnie Mae Taylor, now Landris, with the help of the Lord, aided me to set things straight. Montgomery lived here in this house until I had him removed in October of 2001. So, please, tell me everything you know about him wanting this house."

"He wants to buy it from me should I inherit it from you. But I didn't believe you were really intending to leave me the house, so I didn't see any harm in signing that paper he had me sign in order for me to get the necklace back."

Sarah nodded. "Well, he is correct regarding my intentions for this house. My will does state you'll inherit this place upon my death."

"How did he know that?" Lena asked.

"Obviously, someone is leaking my confidential information to him," Sarah said.

"Do you think it's your lawyer?" Memory asked.

"No. My lawyer, Lance Seymour, is a trusted and loyal friend. He wouldn't do something like that."

"What about someone in his office? Maybe Montgomery has someone on his payroll in there or paid them for your information," Memory said.

"The Wings of Grace box and the necklace," Sarah began. "Tell me from the start what happened there."

"I gave Lena the necklace. She took out the Wings of Grace box. We broke the seal and unlocked it with its special key," Memory said, looking at Lena for agreement.

"Then Gayle came in and told us you were sick and needed us. We got up and left everything on my bed," Lena said. "I came home later that night from the hospital and, honestly, I wasn't thinking about the box, the necklace, or anything else except getting some rest. I suppose I thought Richard had put them away when he came home. I asked him about them the day before yesterday, and he said he hadn't seen them at all."

"So naturally she thought I took them," Memory said. "With my track record, I can't say I blame her. But I promise you both, it wasn't me."

"Lena, do you believe Memory now?" Sarah asked.

Lena looked at Memory. "It's like I want to. But Memory and I have a history. I just don't know. I can't think of anyone else who may have moved them or would have taken them except her. Not in that time frame. The timing is suspicious."

"Well, I don't think Memory took them," Sarah said. "There's something else going on around here, and I think we need to put our heads together and get to the bottom of it. We must pull together, because the Bible tells us that a house divided cannot stand."

"But Grandmother, how can you be so sure it wasn't Memory who took it?" Lena asked as she looked at Sarah intensely. "I've seen what she's capable of doing."

Sarah looked at Memory. "I know because somehow a mother knows when her children are lying. They may not always want to admit that they know . . . but they know." She took a deep breath and released it. "So let's see what we can figure out."

"You need to change your will and leave this house to Lena or Theresa," Memory said. "Anybody except me. I may have signed that paper, but I'll not be a part of Montgomery's plans to hurt you. I won't."

Sarah placed her hand on Memory's. "You let me take care of this my way. I may be old, but I still have my wits about me. I still have a few tricks up my sleeve. There's more than one way to crack open an egg. We need to find that Wings of Grace box, though. I have a feeling my mother had something important in there. That's why she wanted the two of you to open it together."

"But what if whoever has the box has already removed its contents?" Memory asked.

"We'll just have to pray that's not the case. Let's not think negatively." Sarah reached over and took Lena's hand, then grabbed hold of Memory's hand. "Let's pray."

"Yes," Lena said. "The Bible says one can put a thousand angels to flight, and two can put ten thousand. There are three of us here. Ecclesiastes says that a three-corded strand is not easily broken. We *must* stand strong."

"Lena and Memory, I want you to take one another's hand," Sarah said as she bowed her head. "Dear Father in Heaven," Sarah began. "We come to You asking for guidance and Your help. Please Jesus, order our steps in the way we should go. Keep us strong as a family that we may be pleasing in Your sight. Heal any hurt that still lingers among us. Remove all fear and replace it with love. For we know that love covers a multitude of faults . . . a multitude of sins. Father, we acknowledge that we have all sinned and come short of Your glory. Forgive us. Heal us. Direct us. These things we ask in the name of Jesus, Amen."

"Amen," Lena and Memory said in unison. Memory squeezed Lena's hand. Lena squeezed back.

"Let's do this," Memory said. "Let's find out what's going on around this place."

Sarah smiled. "I don't know where Monica is with our dessert. Could you go tell Monica we're about ready for dessert now?" Sarah asked Lena.

Lena got up and went inside.

"Thank you," Memory said to her mother.

"For what?"

"For loving me," Memory said.

Sarah nodded. "I can't help it. It's as natural to me as breathing. Don't you worry now; we're going to fix this. And you and Lena . . . in the end, you're both going to be all right. I feel it in my heart."

"I hope so."

"Hope is always a good start, but don't ever stop with hope. Always . . . always move on to faith. And not just any kind of faith, I mean the working, love kind of faith."

Chapter 36

For since the beginning of the world men have not heard, nor perceived by the ear, neither hath the eye seen, O God, beside Thee, what He hath prepared for him that waiteth for Him.

Isaiah 64:4

When Gayle returned from her errand, Sarah was in the foyer about to go back upstairs to lie down.

"How was lunch, Miss Fleming?" Gayle asked as she closed the front door.

"Divine," Sarah said. "Monica outdid herself. Then we had this rich chocolate cake for dessert. You know, I've *always* been partial to chocolate."

"Yes, you've told me. And I told you that you need to be careful that you don't indulge too excessively, especially when it comes to sweets."

Sarah waved her hand. "I'll be ninety years old on October first. I think I'm allowed *some* indulgence at my age. I don't want to get to Heaven and wish I'd eaten just one more slice of chocolate cake that I happened to have turned down because somebody felt it was bad for my health." Sarah looked at Lena. "Gayle can take me up from here."

Lena started to protest, then decided against it. She nodded and went back in the kitchen to find Memory, who had insisted on helping Monica clear the dishes.

Memory was, in reality, working to find out what Monica knew about the missing items from Lena's room. She'd remembered that Monica was still at the house when Gayle came in the room to let them know Sarah was ill. The best way to determine who might have taken the things was by hard questioning and the process of elimination.

When Lena walked in, Monica was closing the dishwasher and turning it on. The quiet rumblings of the dishpan-hand-saving appliance began.

Monica smiled at Lena, appearing almost relieved to see her walk in. She finished wiping off the kitchen countertop. "That's pretty near all I can tell you," Monica said to Memory in her own brand of Southern drawl. "I'm sorry I can't be more help."

"What you told me was good," Memory said. She stood up. "I suppose I'll get out of your way," she said as she walked past Lena and nodded that she was finished with Monica.

"Is there any more lemonade left?" Lena asked.

"Yes," Monica said. "In fact, I just finished making a fresh batch and put it in the refrigerator. It's not cold yet, though."

Lena walked over, opened the cabinet, and took down a glass. She pushed the empty glass against the button that produced crushed ice. Opening the refrigerator door, she grabbed the gallon glass pitcher of lemonade by its handle and poured—turning the pitcher sideways when her glass was half full to ensure a slice or two of lemon would flow into her glass. Taking a sip, she let out a deliberate sigh to indicate her satisfaction.

"I tell you, Monica. You make the best lemonade," Lena said. "Not too sweet, not too tart. It's always just right."

"You sound like Goldilocks in *Goldilocks and the Three Bears*," Monica said with a chuckle. "Just right." She mocked the way Goldilocks said it in the story.

"I want to thank you for that fabulous lunch. It was perfect. Absolutely perfect!"

Monica rinsed out the dishrag, folded, and draped it across the divider in the sink for later use. "I'm just glad to have Miss Fleming home safe. She really gave us a scare."

"I suppose I'll go see what I can get done," Lena said as she made a show of leaving.

"Lena?" Monica called out to stop her from leaving just yet.

Lena stopped and turned back toward her. "Yes?"

"Memory was asking about some things that were in your room that appear to have come up missing. I just want to let you know, I had nothing to do with it. I would never do anything like that. I told that to Memory, but if you don't mind me saying this, and I know I don't know her all that well, but you can't always tell what Memory's up to or thinking," Monica said. "She's not the most tactful. With her, what comes up usually comes out. No sugar or artificial sweetener added."

"I know." Lena took another sip of lemonade. "So, what did you tell her?"

"Just that about ten minutes after y'all left for the hospital, I locked up and left."

"And no one came by before you left?"

Monica shook her head. "Not while I was still here. And I didn't go upstairs."

Lena smiled and nodded. "Thanks. And for the record, I didn't think you did it. The best I would have hoped for with you is that you moved them, you know, put them up for me, and just maybe forgot to mention it with all that's been going on around here."

"Miss Fleming's been too good to me. I would never do anything to cause her or anyone in her family discomfort or stress. And I don't steal. I just don't do that."

Lena went to Memory's bedroom. When she walked in, she sat in the wingback chair. They exchanged looks.

"I believe we can eliminate Monica from our list of suspects," Memory said.

Lena sat back in the chair and relaxed. "Yeah, she told me what you were talking about before I walked in."

"I'm *pretty* sure it wasn't her," Memory said. "Monica's too much of a scaredy-cat. If she'd done it, I believe she would've broken down or confessed when I questioned her. So let's go back over everything." Memory crossed her legs as she sat. "We were in your room. We'd broken the seal and unlocked the box. Gayle rushed in and said Sarah needed us. We got up to go see about her. Did Gayle come to Sarah's room with us?"

"Honestly I don't remember. I just remember running to Grandmother's room."

"I don't remember, either," Memory said. "Did you come back to your room after you went in to see Sarah?"

"No. I had money on me, so I didn't need my purse." Lena brushed a speck off the chair's arm. "Gayle drove us to the hospital in her car, so I didn't need anything else."

"Okay, so let's scratch Monica's name off with a tiny question mark beside it. I mean, she could be lying, but my gut feeling says she's not. And Richard said he didn't move them?"

"No, Richard didn't see them, and he came home after we'd gone to the hospital."

"So it looks like whatever happened, happened between the timeline of you and I leaving the room and before Richard came home from playing golf." Memory stood up.

"Where are you going?" Lena asked.

"To talk to Gayle. I'd like to know what she knows, if anything, about this."

Lena got up. "You don't really think she moved them, do you?"

"Somebody took those things. And I want to know who and what we're dealing with here," Memory said. "One way or the other, we're getting to the bottom of this!"

Chapter 37

Blow the trumpet in Zion, sanctify a fast, call a solemn assembly. . . .

Joel 2:15

Landris pushed open the door and held it for Johnnie Mae's mother as she walked into the hospital room.

"Mama," Johnnie Mae said, holding out her arms to her mother. Mrs. Gates hurriedly went and embraced her middle child.

"Hey, baby," Mrs. Gates said. She rubbed Johnnie Mae's hair as she stood above her. "I hear you're not doing so good right now. Well, it's going to be all right. God is still on the throne."

Johnnie Mae looked up at her mother. "You know me?"

"Now, what kind of a crazy question is that? Of course I know you," Mrs. Gates said. "You're my baby girl—Johnnie Mae."

Johnnie Mae looked down at her hands. "They have to take the baby early."

"Yes. Landris told me." She glanced over at him. "But I don't want you to worry none. Just keep on trusting and believing God. He hasn't failed us yet, has He?"

Johnnie Mae couldn't help but smile. Her mother was her normal self again, at least for now. That in itself was a miracle and even that much more special, since it was happening during a time when she really needed her.

Two nurses came in. "We're ready to take you in," one of the nurses said to Johnnie Mae.

Mrs. Gates took Johnnie Mae's hand and squeezed it. "It's going to be okay. Jesus will be there with you. And I'm going to be in the waiting room, waiting on you when you come out—you and my brand-new grandbaby." She squeezed Johnnie Mae's hand again, leaned down, and softly planted a kiss on Johnnie Mae's forehead. Nodding her approval, she stepped back to allow Landris an opportunity to get to her.

Landris came and took Johnnie Mae's hand. "Your sisters are here, and Donald. They're all in the waiting room with my mother and Princess Rose."

"Thank you for bringing Princess Rose in to see me so quickly. Your mom and Princess Rose looked so cute dressed alike. Princess Rose is being such a big girl." Johnnie Mae smiled nervously. "You're going in there with me, right?" she asked.

"Of course."

She looked at her mother. "Mama, you know you can come in with us if you like. They'll let you come in," Johnnie Mae said, looking at the nurses for their concurrence.

"Oh, no, baby. I'm going to let you and Pastor Landris have this special moment to yourselves. But rest assured, I'll be out here praying, waiting, and cheering you two—well, actually, three—on. You can count on that." She came back over and patted Johnnie Mae's hand. "I'm going to go now. Okay?" She leaned down and gave Johnnie Mae another kiss on her forehead, this time allowing her lips to linger. She brushed her hair with her hand one more time. "Stay strong," she said as she walked to the door, then left.

Johnnie Mae grinned before letting out a joyful laugh.

"She's doing so well today," she said. "Thank God." She looked up. "Thank You, Lord."

"Yes, she is," Landris said.

He stepped back as the nurses got Johnnie Mae ready. As they began wheeling her out of the room, she reached her hand out for his. She could see from the look on his face, although he was working hard to hide it, he was concerned. She watched his face and could see his lips were moving ever so slightly. She knew at that moment he was praying. She closed her eyes as she too said a prayer for herself and their baby. And she said a special prayer for Landris, her husband, who was standing by her side.

"You know we're going to be all right," Johnnie Mae whispered to Landris as he stood next to her in his blue hospital cap and gown in the operating room, waiting as various hospital personnel were doing the things that needed to be done.

"I know," Landris said as he smiled. "I know."

Chapter 38

This people have I formed for Myself;
they shall show forth My praise.

Isaiah 43:21

Johnnie Mae was in the operating room having a C-section while various members of her family congregated in the waiting room. An hour and a half had passed, and they hadn't heard anything.

Donald glanced at his watch. "How long does something like this usually take?" he asked, never one good at waiting.

"I thought they would have been out by now, too," Marie said.

Rachel, who had stood minutes earlier and was pacing somewhat while wringing her hands, said, "Unless there were complications."

"Let's try not to think negatively," Landris's mother said. "We must continue believing that everything is fine."

Mrs. Gates hugged Princess Rose, who was sitting on her lap, then reached over and patted Virginia's hand. "Thank you. You took the words right out of my mouth."

Rachel sat back down. "Well, you'd think somebody would have come out here and told us *something* by now. Something. But I suppose no news is good news."

"You know what we need to do?" Marie asked. "Pray. We need to pray."

Rachel looked at her. "Well, what exactly do you think we've been doing all this time?"

"No, I mean pray as a family," Marie said. "As a whole. We need to touch and agree as we pray together."

Rachel looked around at other people sitting in the area. "I don't believe any of these people here care to hear us pray out loud," she said.

"Excuse me," Marie said to the other four people in the waiting room. "Would y'all mind if we prayed in here?"

The man sitting at the far end shook his head. Two women sitting next to each other on the right-hand side smiled and said they didn't mind.

Marie looked at the woman nearest them. The red-headed woman smiled. "I'd really rather not hear your prayers myself. But I think they have a conference room you can go in if you really want to pray in that manner."

Donald looked at the woman. "So you're telling me this is a free country, but if I want to pray, I can't pray unless you say it's okay?"

"Donald, don't," Marie said as she got up and walked over to him. She knew her brother. "It's okay. We can go to the conference room. Really, it's not that big of a deal."

"No, I want to pray right here," Donald said, getting to his feet.

"Donald, it's not like you're such a religious person that you need to make a scene about this," Marie said. "It's okay. We'll go find a conference room and pray."

"I don't want to go find a conference room to pray. I want to pray right here, right now, right where I am. And if that bothers anybody in here, then they can just close their ears or leave," Donald said as he stood flat-footed in a stance of pure defiance.

"Listen, you asked if I mind if you prayed out loud

in here," the woman said. "I told you I did. Personally, I don't think your right to pray trumps my right not to hear you pray," she said.

"Well, quite frankly, I don't think your right to *not* hear me pray trumps my right to pray if I want to talk to *my* God. This is America. We have certain guaranteed rights, certain freedoms here. A few things like freedom of religion and freedom of speech."

The woman shifted her body. "But you don't have the right to infringe upon my rights."

"I'm not infringing. You still have the right to remain silent and/or the right to leave," Donald said.

"Donald!" Mrs. Gates said. "Don't be rude."

Donald turned and looked at his mother. "Mama, I'm not being rude. All I want is to be able to praise God for the work I know He's doing in there with my sister and her baby. I want to pray and ask God for His help, His mercy, and His grace. God created us for His glory. He created us to praise Him. You told us that. Since we were little, you've told us not to be ashamed of God, no matter where we may find ourselves. God made a way for me to be able to pray and get my prayers heard, through Jesus, *whenever* and *wherever* I need to. And right now, I feel we need to pray. My sister is in there fighting for her life. Her *life!* Her baby is fighting for its life. We don't have time to be playing around, looking for some conference room just because somebody doesn't want to hear us pray. None of us objected when she was gossiping, talking all loud on her cell phone essentially about nothing! We sat here and had to hear that mess, whether we wanted to hear it or not. She didn't stop and ask if we minded her talking to them. At some point, followers of Jesus are going to have to take a stand and quit letting people continue to push us out."

Donald then bowed his head and began to pray. "Our Father, which art in Heaven. Lord, I know it's been some time since You've heard from me. But Lord, my sister has been a faithful servant. Not perfect by any means, but faithful. And she needs You now."

As Donald prayed, the rest of his family stood, grabbed a family member's hand, and formed a circle. "Lord, I ask You to please place Your arms of protection around her and that little baby. Give them strength. Heal them, right now I pray, Father. Whatever they need right now, Lord, You know. And You're able to do it. Touch them right now. Give us strength, Lord. Have mercy on all of us. Forgive us of our sins. Please hear our cry. Johnnie Mae and I may have had our differences, but I don't want to lose my sister." Donald's voice began to crack and break up. Unable to continue, he stopped speaking.

"Lord, we thank You that You hear us always," Marie said as she picked up where Donald left off when he no longer could go on. "We thank You that You're the ultimate doctor. That You can do what man can't do. That You can go where man can't go. Father, give George . . . Pastor Landris strength, that he may be able to stand—come what may. Help, Lord. Move, Lord. Heal, Lord. Touch, Lord. These and other blessings we ask in Jesus' name. Amen."

When Donald opened his eyes, he saw that the man and the two other women were standing with them. But the woman who hadn't wanted to hear them pray had left.

A few minutes later, Landris opened the door and walked in. He wasn't grinning from ear to ear the way a new and excited father would normally be doing at this time.

"What's wrong?" his mother asked as she rushed to him. "What happened?"

"It's not good," Rachel began to say out loud as she shook her head. "I can tell by the look on his face. It's not good."

Virginia hugged her son as he sat in a chair. "The baby?" she asked.

A momentary smile crossed his face. "A boy," Landris said before he began shaking his head. "He's so small. A fighter for sure, though. But Johnnie Mae . . ." He started to choke up.

"What's wrong with Johnnie Mae?" Mrs. Gates asked as she stepped to him.

Landris looked up at her with tears in his eyes. "She's in SICU," he said. "She's not doing well at all. Dr. Baker says she's extremely critical. She can't promise anything at this juncture. There's nothing more they can do for her. Everything is in God's hands now. Dr. Baker says the next twenty-four hours will really be crucial." He shook his head some more, then allowed his mother to hold his head against her shoulder.

"Is Johnnie Mae conscious?" Rachel asked, her voice trembling as she spoke.

He sat up and shook his head. "No. She didn't even get to see the baby. He's so tiny—three pounds and two ounces. They took him to the neonatal intensive care unit. He's struggling to breathe. They have him hooked up to all these tubes and wires. They say it's not looking good for him, either." Landris sat back against the chair. "I did get to touch him. For one minute, I touched him. For one glorious minute, I held my hand on his tiny body, and I prayed like nobody's business. He was so perfect, this tiny little being—my son. I have a son." He beamed with pride, then a shadow of sadness came. "Johnnie Mae didn't get to see him. Things went haywire. They put me out of the operating room as they worked frantically on her." He looked toward Heaven. "God, she has to pull through. She has to. I realize You're sovereign. But God, please. I know that You didn't bring us this far to leave us."

Chapter 39

Behold, ye trust in lying words, that cannot profit.

Jeremiah 7:8

Montgomery Powell the Second sat in the darkened room with a brandy glass in his hand.

A high-pitched voice broke into the quietness. "My goodness, Montgomery. Why on earth are you sitting here in the dark like this?" The woman turned on a floor lamp.

"Polly Swindle, must you *always* make an entrance when you come into a room?"

"Of course I must always make an entrance. Now, what was so important that you felt you had to summon me here like you did?"

He set the glass on the coffee table. "The box."

"The box?" she asked as she slowly lowered her thin frame down onto the other end of the sofa on which Montgomery was sitting. "What box, Monty?"

"The so-called Wings of Grace box. My sources tell me that you may be in possession of it, as well as a certain Alexandrite necklace."

"Your sources, huh? Well, dearest Montgomery, maybe you should get yourself some new sources." Polly stood up and adjusted her tight-fitting houndstooth crop jacket, then smoothed down the front of her matching A-line skirt.

"Polly, don't play with me. I want the box and everything that was inside of it. As for the Alexandrite necklace, I may allow you to keep that as your reward, provided whatever is inside that box is worth it to me, of course. Now sit down."

She looked at him.

"I said, sit down!"

She quickly sat. "I'm telling you, Monty, it wasn't me."

"Okay, let's start over," Montgomery said. He stood and poured some brandy into another glass. "The box is missing. Lena and Memory are desperately trying to find out what happened to both it *and* the necklace. I know this because I hear that, earlier today, they were questioning the staff at my aunt's home." He handed Polly the glass.

Polly took the brandy, swirled it, sniffed it, then took a polite sip. "Fine as always," she said before setting the glass down on the coffee table. "So you say they're questioning everyone? Have they figured out what might have happened to the things?"

He sat back down. "No. And since I specifically planted you in my aunt's life to find out whatever I needed to know, when I need to know it, then *you*, my dear, need to tell me *something*." Montgomery crossed his legs and began to swing the top one.

Polly picked up her glass, held it up to her face, and swirled it again. "Sarah went to the hospital on Saturday night," Polly said, then took another sip of brandy. "Gayle called me and told me that when they were waiting for the ambulance to arrive. I went to the house and ended up driving Lena's husband to the hospital to meet up with the rest of them. I then brought Lena and her husband back home late that night, and now I'm hearing from you that things are missing from the house. The way you're behaving, they must be quite important—the necklace, I know. But the box sounds like it is as well."

"So what are you telling me?"

"That I don't know anything more than you obviously do," Polly said as she took yet another sip from her glass.

"Pauline," he said, invoking her birth name. "Are you telling me the truth here?"

"Monty, you know me. We've known each other for almost half a decade now. Have I ever lied to you?"

Montgomery stood up. "Well, somebody has to know something." He walked to the window with its drawn, red velvety draperies. "Then who do *you* suspect took them?"

Polly sipped more of her brandy. "You've talked to Gayle, you say?"

"Yes."

"And I gather she told you she didn't take them?"

"That's what she told me when she came by earlier today." He turned and walked back to the sofa. Picking up his brandy glass, he drained it dry, then set it back down.

"And you believe her?"

"I believe her about as much as I believe you," Montgomery said, narrowing his eyes as he gazed at her before he began scanning her body slowly from head to toe.

Polly leaned in seductively, set her empty glass on the table, and smiled. "It sounds to me, Monty, you have serious trust issues. Perhaps you should consider some form of therapy. I know a wonderful doctor, if you're interested."

"Oh, I'm sure you do." He walked over to her and pulled her up to a standing position. "Did you take that necklace and that box?" he asked.

Polly winced. "Montgomery, stop it. You're hurting me."

He pressed in harder. "Did you . . . take . . . those things?"

She tried to pull herself out of his grip. "Stop it! I told you, you're hurting me."

He shook her. "One more time, Polly," he said. "Did you take the Alexandrite necklace and that Wings of Grace box out of Sarah's house?"

"No, I did not take the Alexandrite necklace or the Wings of Grace box *out* of her house! Now let go of me!" Tears made a pool in her eyes as she stared back into his.

Montgomery released her and began to pat and smooth down her shoulders. "Sorry about that. I really didn't mean to hurt you. I spoke with Gayle on her cell before you arrived. When she was here earlier, it was before I knew those things were missing. She said she didn't take them. You say you didn't. What are you two doing there if you can't handle simple tasks?" He went and poured himself some more brandy.

Polly sat down on the sofa and gathered herself. "Okay, I can understand you being upset. But Gayle had plenty of opportunity to get those things for you. She's right there in the house. They trust her explicitly. And she was there on Saturday night when those things went missing. It seems to me, she would be the most likely candidate."

Montgomery stopped and stared at her. "Who said the things went missing Saturday night?"

Polly picked up her clearly empty glass and attempted to drain what amounted to only a drop of brandy.

Montgomery walked over with the decanter and poured a little more brandy in her glass. He put the crystal top back on the decanter. "How did you know those things went missing Saturday?" he asked in a slightly different way this time.

She drank the brandy in two gulps and smiled. "I don't know when they went missing," she said. "I just assumed it was Saturday. It would have been a perfect time with so much happening." She held her glass out to him for a refill. He obliged. "The issue isn't *when* it happened, but who could have taken them. You seem pretty sure Gayle didn't do it. Maybe it was Sarah's cook, Monica, or perhaps the housecleaner, Minnie. Truthfully, I wouldn't put it past that so-called daughter of Sarah's—Memory. We know she stole that necklace once. From her own daughter and granddaughter no less."

"But that just makes no sense. Why steal a necklace you already have in your possession?"

Polly laughed. "Monty, don't you see, darling? You have to think like a criminal. It's the perfect crime with the ideal cover. You take the necklace yourself, act like it was stolen, then sell it. If I were you, I'd have my people check out all the pawn shops and antique jewelry sellers around town." Polly took another sip. "Unless evidence shows up that someone else really might have taken those things, I'd put my money on Memory."

Polly's cell phone began to sing a ringtone by Sting. Looking at the number on the caller ID, she smiled. "It looks like Sarah is calling even as we speak. Excuse me while I take this." Polly answered it, talked for a few minutes, then clicked the phone off. She grinned. "Speak of the devil, and he'll usually appear. That was Memory. Seems Sarah wants to celebrate Christmas early this year. They want me to get my décor people to come to her house and set up Christmas decorations befitting a celebration to top all celebrations. Sarah's planning to have Christmas in June—the twenty-fifth to be exact."

Montgomery snickered. "Christmas in June? Sounds to me like Auntie Sarah may be feeling she doesn't have long for this world. This is perfect! And just think—this will give you even more of a chance to see what else you can find out as you help them plan." He began to rub his hands together. "Now, how marvelous is all of this?" He smiled. "After all these years, things are finally beginning to fall into place. Finally!"

Chapter 40

Hast thou not known? Hast thou not heard, that the everlasting God, the Lord, the Creator of the ends of the earth, fainteth not, neither is weary? There is no searching of His understanding.

Isaiah 40:28

Angel and Brent located Pastor Landris in the hospital waiting room near SICU. Three days had passed since Johnnie Mae had delivered her baby, and she still had not regained consciousness.

"Pastor Landris, you need to get some rest," Angel said after they'd gotten all the pleasantries out of the way and talked general stuff for a few minutes. "Brent and I will stay here until you come back while you go home and get some real rest."

"I'm fine. I want to be here when Johnnie Mae wakes up," Landris said.

Angel quickly glanced at Brent, his cue to feel free to jump right in.

"Listen, Pastor Landris," Brent said, "we're a little concerned about you as well as your health. Your mother is especially concerned. She told Angel you've only gone home to change your clothes, then you're right back here. That's not good, and you know it."

"God is sustaining me. He's renewing me. I'm okay. And I am getting *some* rest."

"Where? In a chair in this room?" Angel asked. "Pastor Landris, we're not saying you shouldn't be here at all. You just need to take better care of yourself, that's all," she said. "You just *have* to."

Landris put his hand in his pants pocket. "My wife is in a coma," he said. "My son is fighting for his life. They need me. They need to know I'm close by. *I* need to be here for them for *me.*"

"But you can't possibly keep this pace up," Brent said. "You're not God, who neither slumbers nor sleeps, nor does He have a need to."

"I know I'm not God," Landris said, frowning at Brent as he took his hand out of his pocket.

Angel stepped a little closer to Brent as she sheepishly looked up at Landris. "Brent didn't intend it the way you're taking it. That's why you need to go home and get some rest. And I mean some good uninterrupted sleep, not just a quick power nap. A person can become edgy when he or she hasn't gotten enough rest. Lack of sleep affects the brain. . . . It affects the way we function. Please, Pastor Landris, all we're asking you to do is to go home and get some rest. That's all. Then you can come back renewed, refreshed, and ready to go another round or two, if you have to."

Landris smiled. "I keep telling you I'm fine. But I appreciate you two for caring about me and my well-being. Johnnie Mae is going to come out of this coma any minute now. I know she is. And I plan on being close by when she does. After this is all over, I can catch all the *z*'s I want. God is *absolutely* sustaining me through this. All of this is merely a trying of my faith. Like a stress test, only we can call it a faith-endurance test."

Angel glanced at Brent before casting her attention back to Landris. "Mrs. Knight called the church yesterday evening. Sherry was out of the office, so they transferred the call to me," Angel said. "She'd heard what was going on, and she asked me to tell you that she's praying for you, Johnnie Mae, and the baby. Also, she'll see you on Saturday."

Landris pressed his hands to his head. "Oh my goodness. Today is Friday, isn't it? Her husband's funeral is tomorrow."

"Yes. That's another reason she called," Angel said. "In light of everything, she wanted you to know that she understands if you're not able to preach Reverend Knight's eulogy."

"But I promised him. I assured her I would do it," Landris said as he glanced at the clock on the wall. The next official visiting time for SICU patients would be in ten minutes. "Please call her and let her know that I will be there as planned."

"Pastor Landris, no disrespect, but we can't even get you to leave here to go home to get some rest. Now, if you won't leave to rest, what makes you think you're going to want to leave tomorrow to preach a funeral?" Brent asked. "And better still, how effective do you really think you're going to be if you're trying to preach, dead on your feet from a lack of real sleep?"

Landris looked at Brent. "I promised Reverend Knight and his wife I would do it, and I intend to keep that promise. The same way I promised the two of you I would perform your marriage ceremony this Sunday. And yes, I plan on keeping my promise on that, too."

Angel looked down at her freshly pedicured sandaled feet, then back up at Landris. "You're not going to perform our ceremony," she said in a low but strong voice.

Landris frowned. "I'm not? And why?" he asked.

"Because there's too much going on in your life at the moment," Brent said.

"So, what are you planning on doing then?" Landris asked. "Who are you going to get to perform your ceremony in my place?"

Brent took Angel by the hand. "Right now, Pastor Landris, Angel and I have decided to focus on what we can do to help you, your family, and the ministry we have committed to."

Landris began to sway slightly, not believing how wonderful they really were. "I appreciate that, but I told you before that I'm fine. I realize there are things that require my attention, and I plan on taking care of them. However, I still maintain that my wife is going to wake up any minute now, and things will be back to normal before we know it. Well, as much as normal can be for us, now that we have a brand-new baby."

"We believe that, too," Angel said, smiling to let him know she was being sincere. "But Brent and I feel there's too much going on for us to only be concerned about ourselves and our own needs. Therefore, we've made the decision to wait until October fifteenth, just as we'd originally planned to do anyway, to get married. In the meantime, we'll be centering a good portion of our attention and energy on what we can do to help you, the church ministry, and Johnnie Mae. I mean, the mail I pick up daily at the post office for you guys is almost an all-day job to go through at this point. And I don't mind."

Landris bowed his head and shook it slowly and reverently. "Thank you," he said. When he looked back up at them, tears filled his eyes. He blinked to force the impending tears back. "Thank you for caring so much. I truly thank God for you . . . both of you. But are you positive about waiting?"

Brent looked lovingly at Angel and smiled. "We're positive. This decision will cause us to have to make a few adjustments in our personal lives, though. But we decided that if we add more of what you normally do to our own duties, we'll be much too busy to even *think* about each other, let alone spend a lot of tempting alone-time together."

"Johnnie Mae really is going to wake up any minute, you know?" Landris said. He was mostly trying to get them not to worry too much.

Angel smiled again. "And when she does, and she goes home, knowing you the way we do, you're still going to be spending a lot of time here," Angel said. "At least you will be until your son is finally released to go home. You'll be right here watching him grow bigger and stronger by the minute."

Landris nodded. He looked at Angel first, then Brent. "You feel I'm not being realistic about this, don't you? You can tell me the truth."

"No, sir," Brent said. "I think you're showing us, by example, the meaning of true faith. You believe, and you're acting like you believe. You want to be here when Johnnie Mae wakes up. You want to be the one who tells her about her new son. Personally, I appreciate you for demonstrating what strong faith looks like. I only pray I will be like that with our family, if and when the time comes," he said, looking adoringly at Angel.

"As you've taught us, there is walking in the flesh, then there's walking in the Spirit," Angel said. "Brent and I know we can choose to either walk in our flesh at this point or walk in the Spirit when it comes to how we feel and act during the times and occasions we're with each other."

"We're choosing, on purpose, to continue to walk in the Spirit," Brent said. "Will that take much prayer?" He laughed. "Oh yes! But people are dealing with a lot these days. If the worst problem Angel and I have right now is that we love each other so much we almost can't stand it, then I think we're doing pretty well here, and we shouldn't complain. With constant prayer, and a determination to keep our eyes on Jesus, I believe our present situation is something we can manage, at least for the next four months."

"Trust me—a man with a ton of experience, especially lately—in certain situations, four months can feel like it's a lifetime. We can still have the ceremony Sunday, now," Landris said. "My being here doesn't mean I'm wholly neglecting my obligations or duties. I'm handling responsibilities and all prior commitments. In fact, there's a nice little chapel here. We can go to it right now, and y'all can tie the knot today if you want. I just know and feel in my heart that by Sunday Johnnie Mae will be up and doing so much better, she'll most likely be figuring out ways to get me to take her to see our son every opportunity she gets. I'm sure she won't mind me missing in action for a little while to perform a marriage ceremony—your marriage ceremony, at that."

Brent smiled. "I know. And should we see we can't handle this like we thought, then we definitely know how to find you. As you can see, we did it today. Besides, how long can it take to say a few vows anyway?"

"I'm serious, Brent . . . Angela," Landris said, calling Angel by the name he usually called her, "you let me know now. And if I need to work a marriage ceremony into my schedule, then I'll do just that."

Landris's cell phone began to vibrate. He pulled his phone out of his pocket and looked at the screen. "Pastor Landris," he said hurriedly. "Yes, Dr. Baker. No, actually, I'm here in the SICU waiting room. Yes, of course. I'll be right there." Pastor Landris clicked off the phone. "That was Johnnie Mae's doctor. She needs to see me right away." He then dashed quickly out of the waiting room.

Chapter 41

Look unto Me, and be ye saved, all the ends of the earth: for I am God, and there is none else.

Isaiah 45:22

Sarah was feeling much better. She was excited about the planned, untraditional Christmas in June. There wasn't a lot of time left to shop before the twenty-fifth arrived. The decorators had done a fantastic job, virtually transforming the mansion into a Christmas winter wonderland. Polly had been to Sarah's house many times, ensuring that things were being handled properly and to her friend's satisfaction. Only after the live fourteen-foot Christmas tree donned presents underneath it was Polly able to get Sarah to talk about anything other than the upcoming celebration.

"So tell me, Sarah," Polly said as they sat leisurely in the parlor admiring the beautifully decorated tree, "what prompted you to want to do this? I mean, what urgency caused you to want to celebrate Christmas in the month of June?"

"I just thought it'd be a grand idea," Sarah said. "This will be my first Christmas with my daughter—my entire family, all together, celebrating it for the first time ever."

"Is that all? There's no other reason you're doing this in June?"

"None, except I just couldn't bear having to wait until

December for Christmas to arrive. It was entirely too far away for me. Besides, this gives me yet another opportunity to spend some quality fun time with my child, grandchild, great-grandchild, and great-great-grandchildren. That's never a bad thing." Sarah smiled just thinking about them.

"Oh, Polly," Sarah bubbled over with renewed excitement, "I am so blessed! I can't explain how wonderful this feels right now. You of all people know how long I've prayed for this to happen. And now it has. My daughter is here with me! We *could* wait until December to celebrate Christmas, but why must we, if we don't have to? Why must we *have* to have specially designated days to spend special moments with the ones we love? Why wait until Mother's Day to let a mother know she is appreciated? I say do it now! Why should Valentine's Day be the day dedicated to show love? What's wrong with now?" Sarah nodded. "I wanted to celebrate Christmas now, so that's what we're going to do. Where in the rule book does it say we *must* wait until December to do it?"

"Nowhere, I suppose. But it is quite out of the ordinary," Polly said in her usual prim and proper way. "*Quite*."

Sarah picked up her teacup and its matching saucer and sipped her green tea. "I'm certain you've figured out by now that *I'm* out of the ordinary. I'll turn ninety years old on October first. Do you have any idea how many people never make it to that age? I've missed seventy Christmases with my daughter—seventy. I know in some folks' eyes, Memory and I may be a tad bit too old to be excited about Christmas. But I've learned to take what I can, when I can, and go with it. We must take the lemons we're given in life and make a to-die-for lemon meringue pie. Christmas is supposed to be about celebrating the greatest gift we, as a people, were ever given. A gift that began our salvation—Jesus' birth. Traditionally when we celebrate Christmas, we give gifts to others. Well, who says we can't celebrate Jesus' birth in June? In fact, what's wrong with Christmas everyday?"

Polly's eyes widened from sheer disbelief. "I certainly *hope* you're not intending on leaving that tree up all year around," she said. "Besides being sociably unacceptable, I hear it's bad luck if a Christmas tree is left up until New Year's day, let alone afterward."

"Forget the tree, okay? And forget superstitions. Anyway, a Christmas tree has nothing to do with Christ, not really."

"People say it represents the hanging of Jesus on the tree," Polly said.

"We won't bother going into a discussion about how pagan practices got mixed in with Christian values, all right? Let's just keep our eyes focused on the fact that, number one, Jesus *was* born; number two, He died on the cross; number three, and most importantly, on the third day He rose; and four, He now sits at the right hand of the Father, making intercessions on our behalf." Sarah blotted her forehead and face with her white handkerchief, then leaned her head back as she gently blotted her neck.

"Are you still hot?" Polly asked, fanning Sarah slightly using her hand.

"Warm, but I'll be all right. It's just part of aging. You'll see as you grow older."

"Sarah, I heard some rumblings around the house about some items they say came up missing a few weeks back," Polly said, trying to work this topic into the conversation.

Sarah sat comfortably and relaxed. "Oh? Now, where did you hear that from?"

Polly stood up and walked over to the tree. "I don't

wish to say," she said. "I don't want to get anyone in trouble. But they say it was a necklace and some sort of special wings box?" Polly looked at Sarah for a response. Sarah remained silent.

Polly moved an angel ornament from one spot to another. She then strolled casually back over to the sofa and stood. "So, did you ever find the items, or do you at least have an idea as to who might have taken them?" Polly continued her probe.

Sarah fanned herself with her handkerchief. "I'm sorry, Polly, but could you go and see what's taking Monica so long to bring out our tray of snacks? She knows I need to eat on a regular schedule."

Polly looked at Sarah and nodded. "Sure. I'll be right back."

When Polly returned, Sarah was still being mesmerized by the beautiful tree.

"That decorating crew did a lovely job, lovely," Sarah said, looking all around.

Polly looked around the entire room as well. "They certainly did. It feels just like Christmas in here. Although I'm not sure I'm in full agreement with you having the fireplace lit at the same time the air conditioner is going full blast. That fire may be what's causing you to be so warm. That and the hot tea you keep consuming."

Sarah laughed. "Oh, I only had them light the fireplace to set the atmosphere. I wanted you to experience the full effect of what it will truly be like the day we celebrate Christmas come June twenty-fifth. And tea contains antioxidants, great healthwise."

Polly sat down next to Sarah. "Sarah, has the doctor told you something that you haven't shared with the rest of us? You know you can always talk to me. So has he?"

Sarah smiled. "You mean besides the fact that I'm

not as young as I used to be? And my best days are most likely behind me?" Sarah sat back, becoming more relaxed.

"Yes, something like that. I'm trying to figure out why you decided it was imperative that you celebrate Christmas right now . . . in June."

Sarah released a sigh. "Polly, the truth is, none of us know how long we have on this earth. I pray I celebrate many, many Christmases . . . many holidays, and, honestly, just plain old regular days with my family . . . with all of you, really. But I also don't want any of us wishing we'd done something that we could have done and didn't." She reached over and patted Polly on her hand. "I want to live the remainder of my life, however long that may be, without any regrets. Do you understand what I'm saying?"

Polly looked at Sarah. She appeared different. There was a glow about her quite unlike anything Polly had ever seen in all her time knowing her. "Sarah, you've always been good to me," Polly said. "And truthfully, you've been a loyal friend. When we first met at church some three years ago, I had no idea how deeply I would come to care for you. You've always treated me like family. Sarah, there's something I need to tell you."

"Sorry, Miss Fleming," Monica said as she brought in a tray of food and set it down on the coffee table. "I apologize for being a bit tardy with your snacks. Alfred, the gardener, cut himself and needed some assistance getting cleaned up. I know how you feel about people who aren't supposed to be inside here roaming free in your house. I had to accompany him to the washroom and wait until he was finished so I could see him out." Monica situated things as needed, which included setting up a tray next to Sarah so she wouldn't have to reach too far to get her food.

"It was a pretty nasty cut," Monica said, continuing

with her story. "I would have gotten Minnie to do it, knowing that you were waiting on this, but she was upstairs working somewhere. Honestly, I didn't think it would take him that long, but as I said, it was pretty nasty, and it took some time to get him fixed back up good."

"Oh dear. So is he all right now?" Sarah asked. "I declare, it seems like every other day that man has something happen to him where he needs some reason to come inside. Just last week, I was sitting outside, getting a little vitamin D via the sun, when I saw him sneak around and go through the kitchen door. I don't think he knew I was out there or that I saw him doing that."

"Oh, that," Monica said. "Well, you see, ma'am, that was kind of my doing. I'd offered him a plate of food. Not one of your good plates, mind you—but the carry-out plates we keep handy for company who want to take food home. Alfred had been so helpful with getting things ready for the people who decorated for Christmas, finding that tree and all. I just wanted to do something special for him. I hope you don't mind."

Sarah continued putting various snacks on her plate. "Of course I don't mind. There's plenty of food here, and if someone doesn't eat it, it's just going to go to waste and end up thrown out anyway." Sarah stopped and shook her head. "I didn't mean to imply that that was the only reason it's okay. We always have more than enough food around here to share, and then some."

"You don't have to explain to me, Miss Fleming," Monica said as she stepped back even farther out of the way. "I understand *exactly* what you mean. You're generous to the bone, with a heart of gold, so no one would ever misunderstand your intentions."

Sarah wanted to put Monica back at ease. "The decorators did a fabulous job with this house for Christmas, don't you think, Monica?"

Monica's eyes lit up. "Oh, Miss Fleming, I was just telling Alfred that very same thing. I had said in the past that it seemed the stores were starting earlier and earlier putting up Christmas decorations. Then you upped and beat them all by doing this in June. Truthfully, I wasn't quite sure how it would feel around here. Some folk might call this crazy, but being here, especially with your whole family expecting to be present, I know it's going to be a special time indeed. And to top it off, you're hiring a caterer so even *I* get to enjoy the festivities, just like I'm part of the family. I got to tell you, that there for me is priceless, Miss Fleming. Priceless, I tell you. I declare, you're the best!"

Polly began to overtly fidget. Monica caught her rolling her eyes a few times.

"Oh, I'm sorry," Monica said. "I'm standing here gabbing away like you two invited me to socialize or something. I didn't mean to hold you up from conversating," Monica said, practically inventing a word. "Conversating"—definition: *talking*.

"You're fine, Monica," Sarah said. "We're just sitting here chewing the fat"—her word for talking—"in awe of this magnificent Christmas tree and other fine decorations."

"Well, if you two need anything else, just yell," Monica said. "I'll be in the kitchen getting dinner ready. I think you're going to like what I'm fixing, Miss Fleming. It's something new, but it involves some of your favorite food items." Monica then left.

Polly couldn't help but notice how content Sarah seemed lately. "Now," she said, but first, clearing her throat, "what were we talking about before we were interrupted?" She was making a big show of how she couldn't recall, when she could. "That's right!" She daintily clapped her hands. "You were about to tell me whether or not you ever found out what happened to the items that were missing. It's my understanding there was some kind of a special box, possibly with important items inside, and a necklace."

"You keep bringing that up," Sarah said. "And you keep saying you heard it from someone here at my house. I'd like to know who you heard it from." Sarah stopped and looked at Polly.

"Now, I told you, Sarah, I don't want to get anyone in any trouble."

"I can assure you, no one here is going to get in trouble," Sarah said, slightly smiling. "So tell me. Where did you hear that those items were missing?" Sarah stopped smiling, her look now somber. "I want to know when, where, and how. And Polly, I want to know now." She sat calmly, sipped some more of her green tea, and waited.

Chapter 42

Then Job arose, and rent his mantle, and shaved his head, and fell down upon the ground, and worshiped.

Job 1:20

Landris walked out of the conference room after speaking with Dr. Baker. Johnnie Mae's vitals were not good at all. Dr. Baker wanted to prepare Landris for the worst. She believed, at this point, it was going to take a miracle for Johnnie Mae to pull through. She told Landris he needed to go home and possibly get some things in order, just in case. When Landris refused to accept her report, she told him to at least go home and get some rest so he'd be refreshed for whatever was to come.

"I insist, Pastor Landris," Dr. Baker said. "You need to get some rest. There's nothing your being here all hours of the day and night can do right now. Go home, get some rest, and come back later. I've given strict instructions that should your wife as much as twitch, the attending nurse is to call both you and me. You'll have time to get here if she wakes up."

"*When* she wakes up," Landris said, correcting her.

Dr. Baker looked at him. "Pastor Landris, you know I believe in God. I *know* God can heal—I've seen it happen. I've also seen people who believed in God with all their hearts, only to find out God's answer was no. Things don't always work out the way we pray and believe it will. It's a part of the circle of life, and the reason there are counselors and support groups for family members to talk to before and afterward. I can call someone who's been through this before to come speak with you, if you like."

"Dr. Baker, my Bible tells me that God's answers are 'yes' and 'amen.' My Bible explains that faith is the substance of things hoped for, the evidence of things not seen. The Word of God is all the counsel and speaking to that I need right now," Landris said. "Listen, I appreciate what you're trying to do here. But I'm not going to allow the devil to sow even one seed of doubt into my mind or find a way to manage to sneak a word of doubt into my confession. The devil *is* defeated. He has no power. Jesus stripped him when He conquered death, hell, and the grave, declaring He had all power. Jesus gave that power to those who confess Him. The Bible states that life and death are in the power of the tongue. Therefore, I'll only say what the Word of God says. I'll only speak life."

"Pastor Landris, you know I respect you *and* your ministry," Dr. Baker said. "But I am a doctor who promised I'd always be up front with my patients and with their families. I'm only telling you the facts about what's happening as I see and have them before me right now."

"And I respect that," Landris said. "But thanks be to God that the facts are not always the truth. The facts may be, from a medical standpoint, my wife is not doing well. But the truth is, by Jesus' stripes, my wife is healed. I don't know how God is going to do what He's going to do, but as long as I have breath in me, I'm going to believe and speak the Word of the Lord. I thank God, who always causes us to triumph."

"I've told you, from a faith standpoint, I'm right there with you," Dr. Baker said. "But medically speaking, I have to say it doesn't look good. It doesn't look good at all. This will definitely be an uphill battle we're fighting."

Landris looked at her. He could see in her eyes, the windows to her soul, she really was pulling for them. "I tell you what, Dr. Baker. I'm going to go home. And I'm going to get before the Lord. I'm going to remind Him of His Word, just like God instructs us to do. Not because He's forgotten, but because He needs to know that *I* know what His Word says. That *I* know when I speak His Word, His Word won't return unto Him void. That *I* understand His Word will accomplish that which He has sent it to accomplish."

Dr. Baker nodded. "Pastor Landris, I pray you're right. But if things don't turn out the way you believe, we both know that God is still on the throne. We also recognize that, on this earth, it really does rain on the just and the unjust."

"I'll continue praying for you, Dr. Baker. All I can tell you is, stand and see the salvation of the Lord. I don't know why my family is going through this. But I know, in the end, this will be used for God's glory. Satan may have meant it for bad, but God is going to use it for good. God will be glorified, regardless of what happens. Now, if it's all right with you, I'd like to go in and see my wife," Landris said.

Dr. Baker took him in to see Johnnie Mae. He prayed for her, laying his hands on her as he prayed fervently. "The prayers of the righteous, avails much," he said softly as he walked out of her room. "The prayers of the righteous, avails much."

Landris then went to see his son. Early on, the staff had told him that parents of babies in NICU were permitted to visit their children at any time, and that a nurse would be with them always. When he arrived at NICU, his baby's doctor was there and wanted to speak privately with him. He informed Landris that his son had suffered a minor setback. They were doing what they could for him. He just wasn't sure whether or not the baby was strong enough to fight his way through this last bout of respiratory complications.

"Of course, had he stayed in his mother's womb even a few days longer, his chances of survival would be much higher," the doctor said. "Right now, we're still looking at a sixty-percent probability that he'll make it. The mortality rate of premature babies has improved much over the past twenty years. It's amazing really," the graying doctor, who looked to be in his early fifties, said. "Modern technology and new medical techniques, the things we now know that weren't known in past years, all of these things are contributing to higher survival rates for preemies," the doctor said. "Just know we're doing everything we can. I'm just not sure whether or not all we can do will be enough to pull your son through. I'm not saying this to be heartless or cruel, but I do like parents of our premature babies to be armed with the facts throughout the process."

The day his son was born, Landris was told that even if his baby did make it, it was possible he might have lasting complications into adulthood. When they'd finished their report to Landris on that first day, Landris had merely responded to them by saying, "Do what you have to do and what you can do, but just know, I speak life over my child, in the name of Jesus, I speak life. And not just life, but life more abundantly. God *can* and *is* able to do what you can't. This I *do* know."

All the doctors associated with his baby's care had tried, both in the beginning and unsuccessfully, to get Landris to see things from a more realistic standpoint. He was told it was great to have faith, but he also needed to deal with reality.

"I hear what you're saying," Landris had said to the

doctor that day. "And no disrespect to you, but I'm going to stand on God's Word. What you're saying to me about my son is not God's best for him. God desires us to have His best, and I declare and decree the Word of the Lord right now over my son. He's healed and he's whole. He *will* live and not die."

"We understand how you feel, Mr. Landris," the baby's attending pediatrician had said. "But we live in a real world, with real issues. At some point, you're going to have to face what *is* and not how you *wish* things to be."

"I beg to differ, Doctor. But at some point, every knee *will* bow, and every tongue *will* confess, that Jesus is Lord. Right now, I'm confessing He is Lord over premature complications. He's Lord over premature death. And I mean that to apply to my wife, whom you have nothing to do with, and my son, who has been placed, at least for a season, in your and this hospital staff's care. Still, my God holds you and the people here, including my son, in His hands. I won't speak anything that doesn't line up with God's Word. I refuse to destroy my son's chances with my mouth."

Now, here Landris was, once again, being given one negative report after another; first, from his wife's doctor, then his baby's. He left the hospital and went home. Princess Rose, who was playing a card-matching game with Landris's mother, ran and greeted him as soon as he walked in the den. "I *miss* you!" Princess Rose said, hugging him tight.

Landris spent time with them, then went upstairs. Closing the bathroom door, he kneeled down in front of the vanity and began to pray like he'd never prayed before.

"I'm not going to ask You why we're going through this, Lord," Landris said. "I'm not. I have to trust You. I don't care what those doctors say. I trust You no matter what problems continue to rear their ugly heads. I pray for all who have been trying to come against us. Forgive them, Lord. I pray for the misguided souls who think they're doing right, when clearly they're marching down the wrong path. Lord, my wife and child are fighting for their lives right now. I don't know anything else to say other than what You've instructed me, in Your Word, to say. I don't know any other way, except Your way. Lord, I've done what You told us we should do during situations like these. I'm leaning completely on You. Please, Jesus, I need You now more than ever. I can't do anything without You. I need You. . . . We need You. Please, hear my cry. These things I pray in Jesus' name, Amen."

Landris stood up. He started unbuttoning his shirt. Frustrated, coupled with exhaustion, he ended up ripping off two buttons when he couldn't get the buttons through the tight buttonholes. He took the shirt off, then placed a towel around his neck and shoulders. Searching for scissors usually kept inside one of the drawers in the bathroom, he found them and stood squarely in front of the vanity mirror. Lifting one strand of dreadlocks, he took the scissors and cut it. He then cut another, and another, until he'd cut off all of his dreadlocks. Landris then walked out of the bathroom to his closet, took a black shirt off the hanger, and put it on. He went downstairs, got into his car without even telling his mother he was gone, and drove off.

"Whoa, man, what happened to you?" his barber, who'd helped him maintain his dreadlocks since he moved back to Birmingham, asked when he walked through the door.

"Reggie," Landris said calmly as he sat in the chair, "shave it off."

Reggie jerked back. "Say what? Look, man, I heard about what's going on with your wife and son. I'm sorry. I know you're under a lot of pressure. I don't think you may be thinking clearly. Maybe you should go home and get a little rest," Reggie said.

"I'm fine, Reggie. Now, please . . . shave it off," Landris said.

Chapter 43

Whereas ye know not what shall be on the morrow. For what is your life? It is even a vapor, that appeareth for a little time, and then vanisheth away.

James 4:14

"What did you do?" Virginia asked her son when Landris walked back in the house. "George, honey, come and sit down."

"Mom, I'm okay," Landris said.

His mother stared at his head as she walked toward him. "I don't think that you are. I think you really need to go upstairs and lie down."

"I told you, I'm okay."

Virginia spoke slowly. "No, George . . . I don't think you are okay. Do you realize you've shaved your head? All of your hair is gone, George. You're . . . bald."

Landris smiled as he rubbed his shaven head, then laughed out loud. "Yeah. Gone. I know."

"So do you want to tell me what made you do that?" Virginia asked, as though she didn't want to talk too fast or too loudly for fear that that might be the thing to send him completely over the edge.

"You know, it's not because I thought my dreads were wrong or against God in any way. There are plenty who have been trying to get me to cut my dreadlocks because they thought it was wrong, or they disagreed with them being on a preacher more than anything." He opened the refrigerator door and grabbed a bottle of water. "But I was praying earlier about everything that's been happening these days."

"I know. I know. It's been hard on everybody," Virginia said, paying close attention to his face to see whether or not she could detect what was really going on with him. "That's what I mean. This is a lot for anyone to handle. Even the strongest person would find something like this difficult to bear."

"Mom, listen to me. I'm fine. I've prayed about what's going on. Now I'm standing on God's Word and His promises. That's all I can do. I didn't shave my head to move God or to make a point or a statement. I didn't shave my head because I felt like I was in sin or in error and that doing this would make things right with God so He could move on my behalf. That's not how God operates. God doesn't look at the outward appearance of man. He looks at our hearts. I shaved my head because I felt the need to take off some dead weight. My hair felt as though it was carrying around in it so much stuff. It's hard to explain, but as soon as I started cutting my dreads off, all of a sudden I started feeling lighter. With each lock I cut, it was as though the things of the past were being cut away as well." Landris ran his hand over his clean-shaven head again.

"Reggie, my barber, cleaned it up for me. So today I start anew," Landris said. "Whatever happened yesterday is gone. Just like my hair—it's gone, all gone."

Virginia began to nod. "I think I understand what you're saying. But you still need to get some rest. When Johnnie Mae wakes up, as soon as she looks at you, she's going to think *you're* the one who needs to be hospitalized. And when the two of you bring that newborn home, believe me, you're going to wish you'd gotten all the sleep you could have."

Landris laughed then kissed his mother on the cheek. "Thanks, Mom. Has anyone told you lately that you're the best?"

"Not in the past"—she looked at her watch—"twenty-four hours. Oh, and before I forget"—she walked over to the counter and tore a sheet of paper out of a pad—"you got three messages while you were out trying to be like Mike."

"Like Mike?"

"Yeah. Michael Jordan. You know, the baldhead thing you've got going there? Which, by the way, let me be the first to tell you, isn't for everyone. Take it from a mother who cares, you need to let at least some of your hair grow back, and I mean quick." Virginia handed him the paper with the three messages on it as she rubbed his head.

Landris looked at the names and numbers. One was from Minister Maxwell, one of the preachers who was taking over things for Landris while he was out of pocket caring for his family; one was from Mrs. Knight; and the last one was from Reverend Walker. Out of all the names listed, Landris was most surprised to see Reverend Walker's. He'd never really talked with him before. In fact, the closest he'd gotten to the man was when Thomas was about to marry Faith, and he and Johnnie Mae had sat outside in the church's parking lot, waiting for his mother to return.

"Did Reverend Walker say anything?" Landris asked with a quizzical look.

"Just that it was urgent he speak to you today." Virginia slid an oblong glass dish into the oven, then wiped her hands with a paper towel. "I'm making Princess Rose macaroni and cheese. She said that's what she wanted for supper tonight. That poor child is missing her mother like crazy." Virginia threw the paper towel in the trash can. "But if you ask me, that Reverend Walker person needs some lessons in manners. Maybe he thought I was your maid or something. But even if that were the case, he needs to learn how to talk to people and not talk down to them. I guess I shouldn't expect any more out of him. At Thomas's wedding, he was planning to keep going forward with the wedding ceremony even though I was stretched out on a church bench." She giggled.

Gathering grapes, Bartlett pears, plums, strawberries, and a handful of blueberries out of the refrigerator into a colander, she walked over to the sink. Running water over them, Virginia transferred the fruit to a bowl. "I'm going down to the game room to play with Princess Rose. But between you and me, the child is driving me crazy with that song, 'Unwritten.' I mean, I like it and all, but she wants to play it over and over again."

Landris laughed as she left. He went and got the cordless phone, then sat down in the den next to the kitchen. Landris decided to call Minister Maxwell first. Minister Maxwell just wanted to check in with him and be sure there wasn't anything he needed from either him or anyone at the church. He brought him up to speed on matters he felt Landris needed to know, without burdening him with the things he didn't. Landris then called Mrs. Knight back. The person who answered said she was gone and wouldn't be back until sometime after seven.

Looking at the third message, Landris dialed the number. He couldn't even *begin* to fathom what Reverend Walker might possibly want with him.

Landris waited for someone to pick up.

"Hello," a deep male voice said.

"This is Pastor Landris calling for Reverend Walker."

"Pastor Landris, thank you for returning my call so quickly. How is your family? Your wife and your new son, specifically?" he asked.

Landris hesitated for a second. He couldn't say they were fine, because, from a realistic standpoint, they were both in critical condition. He didn't know how much Reverend Walker knew already, and for whatever reason, he really didn't want to go into lengthy details regarding the situation. "We believe all is well," Landris said.

"God is able," Reverend Walker said. "And we know that He won't put any more on us than we can bear, that's for sure. If God has brought you to it, somehow He'll bring you through it. That's not a cliché for me. It's a certified fact."

"Absolutely," Landris said as he stood up and began to pace near the fireplace. "I must say, I was surprised to have a message from you. So, to what do I owe the pleasure?" Landris said, deciding to get right to the point.

"Oh, of course. How inconsiderate of me. I know you have a lot going on, with your wife in such bad shape at the moment, and your new baby barely hanging on, a son, right? Have you named him yet?"

"No, we haven't named him as yet. I'm waiting on my wife so we can do that together," Landris said, picking up his bottle of water and taking a swallow from it.

"You probably should go on and do that. Give the baby a name," Reverend Walker said. "I'm sure you want to name him George Jr. or the Second. It's a joy when you produce boys, because you know you have someone to carry on the family name. I have five boys myself—three by my first wife and two by my second. The wife I have now can't seem to birth anything *but* girls, so I now have two little girls. It's okay, though. I have sons to carry on the name, so there's no real pressure on me at this point in my life. I can enjoy my little girls the way a doting father is supposed to. Now, Landris is a pretty unusual name. I know your mother has to be proud that at least one of her children has finally given her her first biological grandchild. Your mother was the one who answered the phone when I called earlier, right? I'm sure she's proud. With Thomas and his condition, I doubt he'll ever have children. How *is* your brother, by the way?"

Landris paused and counted to ten. "Much better, thank you."

"That's good to hear. I really like Thomas. I'm glad he's getting some help. I felt something wasn't right with him when he was here with us, but I try living my life without judging people, at least too harshly, anyway. I'm sure you understand that."

"Listen, Reverend Walker. I can't talk long. I've been at the hospital the past three days and only came home to get a little rest before I go back," Landris said.

"I'm so sorry. Of course. Here I am just going on and on. But I did call for a reason, other than to check on you and your family, of course." Reverend Walker cleared his throat. "I know you're supposed to be preaching Reverend Knight's funeral tomorrow."

"Yes."

"Well, there appears to be a change of plans. I'm sorry, I guess Joyce must not have had a chance to speak with you yet."

"You mean, Mrs. Knight?"

"Yes, Joyce Knight, Poppa Knight's lovely wife. Well, actually his widow now. Anyway, she and I spoke extensively last night, and she now wants *me* to preach Reverend Knight's funeral."

"I don't understand. Reverend Knight asked me, and the last time I spoke with Mrs. Knight, she still wanted me to honor his wishes and do it. So what changed?"

"Pastor Landris, your wife and child are in the hospital fighting for their lives. You don't need this kind of distraction. If I know you the way I *think* I do, it's probably next to impossible to get you to leave that hospital. What if your wife is still in that coma tomorrow? Do you honestly believe you can preach a funeral decently? Poppa Knight has been a great friend to too many people. He deserves the best send-off we can give him, and I intend on doing just that. I'm not implying you won't do a great job, because from what little I've heard of you, they say you're an outstanding teacher of the Word."

Landris began to laugh with disbelief as he sat down, shaking his head.

"Listen, Pastor Landris. Poppa Knight and I were close—closer than most brothers, if you want to get technical. If I may be transparent with you, it's going to be hard, even for me, to stand up there and preach over my dear friend's remains. But I also know I can do all things through Christ, who will give me the strength I need to do it."

"I believe He'll give me strength as well."

"I know that, Pastor Landris. And quite frankly, this is not a contest between you and me. The reality is, your family needs you. There's no reason for you to be worrying about preaching a funeral just because you gave your word to a dying man before you knew what was coming your way. None of us knows what tomorrow will bring. This little time we're here on this earth is like a vapor. One minute you see it, and before you can explain what you saw, it's gone—just like that. That's why, in the book of James, somewhere around the fourth chapter, it tells us we ought to say, 'If the Lord will, we shall live, and do this, or that.' You had no way of knowing this trouble was headed your way. You made a promise you fully intended to keep. God knows your heart. But you need to put your energies toward those who are still on this side of the earth."

"Is that what you told, Mrs. Knight? That she was

being unfair by trying to hold me to a promise I made, that I fully intended to honor?" Landris asked.

"I told Joyce that Poppa Knight was wrong to have asked you in the first place when he'd said I would be doing this if it came to him departing before me. You didn't know him like I knew him. He and I had history together. Lots of it. You knew him when he was a mere shell of his previous robust stature. Now, please don't take this the wrong way, but, Pastor Landris, you cannot do what I'm going to be able to do tomorrow. You just can't. And frankly, your preaching style is not what the people who knew him best are accustomed to. You don't bring enough fire with it, at least not enough for most of our taste."

"Listen," Landris said, "I have a call in to Mrs. Knight already. She called and left me a message earlier. Until I've spoken to her and she tells me otherwise, or unless the Lord says differently, I plan to be standing, at noon come tomorrow, doing what I was asked to do."

"Pastor Landris, I'm going to let you go and get some rest. Clearly, you need some sleep. But allow me to give you a bit of advice before I hang up. You don't *really* want me as an enemy. Trust me, you don't."

"Is that supposed to be a threat?"

"Oh, no. I don't make threats. I make promises. And I promise you, you might want to rethink any idea you may have about crossing me. Greater men than you have tried and failed. But listen, I didn't call you to get into all of this. I'm sure you and I will have our day to really talk. You speak with Joyce. She knows the deal. You see, Poppa Knight is no longer around to flex his muscles against me. People seem to have been under the mistaken impression that I was afraid of him, like he had something on me."

"So did he?"

Reverend Walker laughed. "That's a good one. I respected him, but let's just say that whatever Paul 'Poppa' Knight *may* or may *not* have had on me is safe and securely with him at this point in time. After I say this, I'm really going to let you go. But I once heard someone wisely declare that the only way to keep a secret between three people, is if two of them are dead. I'm not trying to be cold or insensitive, but they also say 'dead men tell no tales.' So whatever Poppa Knight might have known, he kept it to himself all these years, and it looks like he took all of that with him. Now, you take care, and you take care of that family of yours. I'll say a little prayer for all of you. Have a good night," Reverend Walker said, then hung up.

Pastor Landris looked at the phone that now buzzed with only a dial-tone. His mind immediately went to the *Private and Personal* envelope Reverend Knight had given him over a year ago. The envelope he'd been told to keep in a safe place and to open only should Reverend Walker attempt to come against him.

As much as Pastor Landris wanted to open that envelope right now, he knew this was not enough to warrant him learning something, he suspected, ultimately, could have dire consequences for a fellow brethren in the Word.

Chapter 44

The grass withereth, the flower fadeth: but the word of our God shall stand forever.

Isaiah 40:8

Landris spoke with Mrs. Knight over the phone after he woke up from about four hours of sleep. She confirmed what Reverend Walker had said to him earlier.

"Mrs. Knight, I need to ask you something, and I want you to be honest with me."

"Sure, Pastor Landris. What is it?" Mrs. Knight said.

"Is this what you want to do? Would you prefer that Reverend Walker deliver the eulogy for Reverend Knight's funeral instead of me?"

"Honestly, I was in total agreement with what Paul wanted," Mrs. Knight said. "His funeral at the church he'd worked so hard to build, and you preaching his eulogy."

"Then why are you changing things now?"

Mrs. Knight let out a sigh. "Marshall presented a lot of good arguments for why I should allow him to preach it—a few of which I agree with. Truthfully, you really *do* have your hands full with your own family troubles and heartaches. And it *is* wrong of me to insist you do this when there are obviously plenty of others willing and quite capable of carrying on," she said.

"Is that the only reason you're changing it? I really

want to do this, and it's not a problem for me. I've gotten a little rest; I'm ready for another round."

"Pastor Landris, Marshall is not one who is used to being trumped by anyone. It doesn't matter whether it's me, you, or someone else, no one will get in his way. This is not the first time he's reminded me of his position and power. I admit, it's been a long while. When Paul first heard how Marshall was trying to boss and push me around early on in our marriage, he had a nice little *'chat'* with him, as Paul put it. I don't know what all my husband said to him, but whatever it was toned him down in ways I never could have imagined. Every now and then, he would try something again, and Paul would shut him down quickly. I suppose Marshall feels free now to go after any- and everybody he wants, with Paul no longer here to stop him. I don't know."

"Are you telling me Reverend Walker is forcing you to do this?" Landris waited for her answer; she didn't say anything. He then heard sniffling, and he knew she was now crying. "Mrs. Knight, are you all right?"

"Pastor Landris, I don't want any trouble. I just can't handle it on top of everything else I'm dealing with. Please, let it go, okay? You *do* need to concentrate on your own family. In fact, I feel bad taking time away from you right now. Why don't you just focus on your problems and leave me to deal with mine."

"Mrs. Knight, I appreciate you for caring about me and my family. But I also want you to know that I promised Reverend Knight I would look after you for him. If Reverend Walker is trying to intimidate you or is threatening you in any way, I want to know about it. He has no right to do anything like that to you. And I won't stand for it."

"Pastor Landris, what can you do? Marshall Walker is an influential, powerful man of God with a bully pulpit, even more so now that my Paul is gone. That's why it's best you and I just let sleeping dogs lie."

Landris thought again of the envelope. He didn't appreciate Reverend Walker seemingly bullying a woman, an elderly woman at that, who'd just lost her husband.

"Pastor Landris, I'm going to go now. If you find you can come to the funeral tomorrow, I'll be happy to see you. But if your family needs you, then you spend the time with them and don't you feel bad about missing Paul's funeral. I know that's what Paul would have said to you. It's what he would have wanted. You were there for him when he was alive. That's what counts in life. We'll leave Reverend Walker in God's hands. The Lord says vengeance belongs to Him. Marshall's manhandling doesn't bother me. If he wants to preach Paul's eulogy that badly, then he can. And please know that you and your family are definitely in my prayers. God will get the glory in all of this. I know that in my heart. I feel it in my spirit. So don't you get discouraged. God has your back."

"And my front, and my side, my top, and my bottom, too," Landris said. "Mrs. Knight, will you promise me one thing?"

"What's that?"

"If Reverend Walker tries to push you around again, will you let me know?"

She laughed. "You sounded just like Paul when you said that."

"Promise me that you'll let me know," Landris said again.

"If I feel like I really need you when it comes to Marshall, I promise I'll let you know. But in truth, after this funeral is over, I'll probably never have a reason to talk *with* or *to* Marshall again. When your wife wakes up, you tell her what a blessed woman she is. You're a good man, Pastor Landris. And I and my family are proud to know you."

When Landris hung up, he went to the safe in his bedroom and tapped in the four-digit security code. Opening the safe, he moved items around until he found the envelope Reverend Knight had given him. He pulled it out, opened it, and looked inside to see what it contained. Sitting down on the sofa in his room, he examined everything closely.

After he finished, he put everything back in the envelope and clamped it back shut. "Lord, now that's definitely some deep stuff there. I don't know when, if, or how I'm supposed to use a thing like this. I'm really going to need Your guidance on this."

The phone rang. "I got it," he yelled loud enough for his mother to be able to hear him. "Hello," he said.

"Pastor Landris, my name is Nurse Wren, and I'm calling from the hospital. The doctor asked me to call you. We need you to get here as quickly as you can."

"Is this about my wife? Has she awakened?" Landris asked.

"Sir, all I know is that Dr. Freeman asked me to call you and tell you he needed you to come to the hospital as soon as you can. He'll speak with you when you get here."

"Dr. Freeman? But that's not any doctor I'm familiar with. Is this about my son?"

"Sir, just come to NICU and ask any nurse at the desk to page Dr. Freeman upon your arrival. He'll talk with you then."

Landris got off the phone, told his mother he was going back to the hospital without mentioning the call he'd just received, and began to pray as he hurriedly got in his car. "Heavenly Father, I don't know what's going on, but You know. I'm still standing on Your Word, Lord. I'm not going to allow anything to move me off Your

Word. I thank You, in advance, Lord, that my wife is healed. I thank You that my son is healed. You are worthy to be praised. No matter what happens, Lord, I will praise You. I have nowhere else to go *but* You. No one else to turn to *except* You. Please don't ever leave me. Be with me, Lord Jesus. Continue to cover me, I pray."

Chapter 45

Behold, they shall surely gather together, but not by Me: whosoever shall gather together against thee shall fall for thy sake.

Isaiah 54:15

Sarah continued to wait for Polly to speak. Polly fiddled with her hair, then her hands for several minutes. Sarah sat patiently. Polly then glanced down at her watch.

"Will you look at the time?" Polly said, grabbing her purse as she stood up. "I almost forgot; I have an appointment today. I'm supposed to see my therapist at three."

"Sit down," Sarah said sternly, but nicely. "We both know you don't have anywhere you need to be right this minute. Now, Polly, I want to know how you knew about the missing Wings of Grace box and the Alexandrite necklace. And please don't insult my intelligence again by trying to get me to believe that someone here told you and you can't tell me because you think you'll get them in trouble."

"What are you trying to imply?" Polly asked.

"Sit, and I'll tell you what I've learned over this past week."

Polly nervously sat down.

Sarah picked up a petite spinach quiche and bit it. She set the rest back on her plate. "Would you care to tell me how well you know my nephew, Montgomery?"

"Montgomery?"

"Yeah. You know, Montgomery Powell the Second."

"I've met him a few times at various social functions around town. But I don't know if I can answer how well we know each other. That's a relatively broad question."

Sarah began to nod her head slowly. "All right, then. If you like, you can go on to your appointment. There's no real reason for you and I to waste each other's time any longer."

Polly stood up as she watched Sarah. Sarah picked up the rest of her quiche and ate it.

"Sarah," Polly began, "I don't know what you *think* you know, but I believe someone has misinformed you."

"No, Polly. I think someone has misinformed *you.* But if you want to play this little game, then you go right ahead. I just thought the right thing to do was to give you a fair chance to tell your side. However, I can't make you tell the truth if you're bent on keeping up your little charade." Sarah picked up a slice of cucumber and bit it.

"Seriously, Sarah, I don't have a clue what you could be referring to. I mean, I've seen Montgomery. Our paths have crossed. In fact, I admit, I've been to his house a few times, mostly to discuss things regarding you. Truth be told, I didn't appreciate some of the things he's done to you, and I wanted him to know where I stood on the matter."

"Okay, Polly." Sarah picked up another cucumber slice and ate it. "I'll have a check cut tomorrow and put in the mail to you for the work you've done toward this Christmas celebration."

"But I'm not finished," Polly said. "We still have to come up with the menu to give to the caterer we're bringing in. You were going to get that to me by the end of this week, remember?"

"Oh, you're finished." Sarah picked up a broccoli floret, stuck it in her vegetable dip, and ate it. "Trust me, you're finished," she said.

Polly walked closer to Sarah and sat back down next to her. "I don't understand." A worried look came over her face. She covered her mouth. "Okay. Okay. Let's talk about this now. I don't know what all you want to know."

"I want to know why you took those items. I want to know where they are. Then you might want to explain to me how you could come in here, pretend to be my friend, then stab me and my family in the back the way you've done."

"That's not what happened, Sarah. I truly do care about you. I do!"

Sarah wiped her hands on her napkin. "Then *why* did you take those things?"

Polly smiled nervously. "I don't have those things."

"I know," Sarah said.

"Then why are you questioning me?" Polly was starting to break down, shaking slightly. "Why are you acting like this?"

Sarah stood up. "I have such a time with the circulation in my legs these days," she said. "I find when I move around, it really does help." She walked over to the Christmas tree, with the assistance of her walking cane, and gazed up at it. Turning around, she made her way to a straight-back chair and sat down diagonally across from Polly. "Why don't you tell me what really happened that day, dear? Come on, the truth."

"You mean Saturday?" Polly swallowed hard. "The day they say those things likely went missing? Well, let's see. I came by here after Gayle called me and told me you'd been rushed to the hospital. When I arrived, no one was here. Everybody was gone. The house was completely empty."

"That's when you decided to use the key I gave you to get in the house in case something ever happened to me and you had a need to get in? The truth, Polly."

Polly smiled while rocking a little. She nodded. "Yes. But I didn't come in looking for anything in particular. Montgomery had asked me to find out whatever I could on Memory and Lena. What better time to snoop than when I was sure the house was completely empty? But I wasn't planning on giving him anything that would really hurt either of them. Just find enough to make him feel he could continue to trust me."

Polly looked at Sarah, trying to deduce what Sarah was probably thinking now. "I searched the room where Memory was staying," Polly said, continuing with the story. "There really wasn't anything of importance in her room. Then I went to Lena's room, and jackpot! Right there on the bed was a beautiful handcrafted box with the key in the lock. I went over, was about to open the box to see what was inside it, when the necklace laying beside it suddenly caught my eye. I picked it up, not knowing at the time that it was the infamous Alexandrite necklace. I mean, how would I know that? It was my understanding from you that it was missing—taken some years back by Memory from Lena, which had precipitated their falling out." Polly reached down and picked up the glass of iced tea Monica had brought in for her and wet her throat with several swallows.

"Before I got a chance to look in the box," Polly said, setting the glass back down, "I heard someone open the front door and close it."

"Lena's husband, Richard," Sarah said.

"Yes, it was Richard, although I didn't know that at the time. Of course, the last thing I needed was to get caught upstairs snooping with everyone gone. I knew I had to act fast, so I grabbed the box, stuck the necklace inside of it, and as quickly and as quietly as I possibly could, I scurried out of the room. At first, I wasn't sure which way to go. Then it hit me—your room."

Sarah looked puzzled. "My room?"

"Yes, your room. You weren't there, but if I was discovered, I could easily play off my being in there. After all, you'd given me a key to your house. You obviously trusted me and would trust me to get something out of your room if it was needed. You'd gone to the hospital, so I could have easily and plausibly been looking for something for you. I could use our relationship and closeness as a cover if I had to."

"And no one would have been the wiser," Sarah said, shaking her head.

"Exactly." Polly drank some more tea, then politely cleared her voice. "I stayed in your room and waited to see if whoever had come in was planning to come upstairs. When I heard the heavy footsteps on the staircase, I knew I couldn't be caught with that box and necklace still in my possession. So I looked for a good place to hide it until I could come back and retrieve it later." Polly looked at Sarah as she moistened her lips.

"What happened after that?"

"I cracked the door, peeped out of it, and saw it was Richard. He was going into the room I'd just left. I then remembered my car was parked out front, and he most likely saw it when he came home. As soon as he closed the bedroom door, I attempted to sneak down the stairs. Just as I reached the top step, he came back out. I turned in a hurry and pretended I had just made it to the top step and was slightly out of breath. He spoke, and I played it off like I had come in the house a few minutes before him, that I'd been downstairs looking to see if Monica was still around when I heard someone go up the stairs. Thinking it was Gayle, Lena, Memory, or Monica, I'd come up to see."

“Knowing you, you probably then made him believe you were relieved when you saw a man coming out of the door, and it was him instead of some intruder.”

“You know me. I was about to tell him they had taken you to the hospital when Lena called. I could tell she was trying to tell him how to get to the hospital.”

“And that’s when you, being the Good Samaritan that you are, volunteered to drive him to the hospital, further covering you and your actions,” Sarah said.

“That’s not totally true. I volunteered because I was planning to come to the hospital and check on you anyway,” Polly said. “So we left here in my car and went to the hospital to see about you.” Polly pressed her lips tightly together, then relaxed them. “I’m sorry, Sarah,” she said. “I really am.”

Sarah nodded. “Uh-huh. Now, tell me how Montgomery fits into all of this.”

Polly stood up and paced back and forth as she spoke. “Montgomery came to me back in 2001, when you first had him thrown out of this house. Naturally, he was furious with you and everything else that had transpired. He didn’t have an avenue inside here to see what was going on—”

“So he got you to befriend me.”

“Originally, that was my purpose. He asked me to see if I could use some of my Southern charm I was known for and become part of your close inner circle.” Polly walked back over to Sarah and kneeled down in front of her. “But I genuinely did grow to care about you, Sarah. True, it may have begun with him putting me up to it, but you’re a remarkable woman I’ve come to adore over the years. I see you as a true friend.”

Sarah smiled and shook her head. “Unbelievable,” she said. “Unbelievable.”

“Sarah, I haven’t been supplying Montgomery with

much information lately. In fact, he's upset with me right now. He knows the Wings of Grace box is missing, as well as that necklace. But I wasn't the one who told him that. You have to believe me. Someone else on your staff must have leaked that information to him. The part about me having heard it from someone on your staff was true, indirectly anyway. Someone told Montgomery, who told me. But Sarah, Montgomery desperately wants that box, even more than he wants the necklace." Polly sat down on the floor in front of Sarah, which, for an always-prissy Polly, spoke volumes. She took Sarah's hand. "Please forgive me. I've wanted to tell you about this for so long. I just never knew how."

"Of course you did," Sarah said, patting Polly's hand once.

Polly looked up at Sarah with sad eyes. "Tell me, if you will, how did you figure this out?"

"Oh, I didn't," Sarah said.

Polly pulled back. "You didn't?" She got up off the floor, confused now.

"No," Sarah said. "I didn't."

"Then who did?"

"Well, you see, we've been racking our brains about what could have happened. Memory and Lena questioned everyone here but got nowhere. Then today, I started thinking. You were the only one we hadn't questioned, although I really couldn't see how you would have been able to pull anything like that off, if you had. Then I thought about something Richard said about you bringing him to the hospital. He couldn't believe he didn't notice your car outside when he came home from playing golf. But it had to be there, since you were here in the house already. He said you'd come in right before him, but he couldn't understand how you got up the stairs so fast without him hearing you. You're not the quietest, when you walk up steps." Sarah squeezed the arms of the chair.

"I knew I had given you a key to get in," Sarah continued. "But honestly, until just now, I really didn't know you'd done it."

Polly laughed as she began to shake her head. "Wow, you're good."

Sarah looked up at Polly. "Thank you. Now, where are the box and the necklace?"

Polly turned her back to Sarah. "Montgomery asked that same thing last week." She turned around and faced Sarah. "They're upstairs in your room . . . under your bed."

"Is that why you were trying so hard this past week to get in my room? You wanted to get the box and the necklace back," Sarah said in deep thought. "When you brought that empty cardboard box with tissue paper in it to my room the other day and sat it on the floor next to my bed, you intended to get the Wings of Grace box from under my bed and put it in there so you could sneak it out of my room undetected, didn't you?"

Polly flopped down on the sofa. "Yes. You see, after I brought Lena and Richard home from the hospital that night, it dawned on me that the house wouldn't be empty anymore, and I wouldn't be able to get the box out of your room. I needed to get it."

"And what were you planning on doing with the box and the necklace when you got them?" Sarah asked.

"Honestly, Sarah"—Polly smiled—"I really don't know. But Montgomery really wants that box, along with all that it contained inside. So much so, he offered to give me the Alexandrite necklace as a reward for the box, should I happen to get it to him."

"So this past week, your being here on the pretense of helping, while constantly being under foot, was merely a guise . . . a ploy to gain access to my room?" Sarah asked. "And for whom? Montgomery, the man who continued to perpetrate what his father and uncle began some seventy years ago? I shared my heart with you, Polly. You know how hard all of this has been on me just over the years we've known each other." Sarah shook her head slowly. "How could you? How?" She held out her hand. "My key, please."

"I'm sorry, Sarah." Polly opened her purse, took Sarah's house key off her key ring, and placed it in Sarah's hand. "I never used that key to take anything from you."

"Until now." Sarah closed her hand. "I'm sorry as well," Sarah said. "I'll have a check mailed to you tomorrow for services rendered for the Christmas celebration."

"You don't owe me anything. Really you don't. But now that you know everything, can we start over? I'd still like to be friends," Polly said, lowering her head.

"You know, if you hurry, you can probably make that three o'clock appointment you said you had," Sarah said. "Good-bye, Polly." Sarah looked away.

"Sarah, at least say that you forgive me. Please. I need to know you forgive me."

Sarah looked at her. "I forgive you, Polly. Mostly for me . . . but I forgive you."

"Mostly for you? I'm sorry, but I don't understand what you mean by that."

"I forgive you for me," Sarah said. "See, forgiveness is as much for the one who was wronged as it is for the one who did the wrong. I've lost too much in life already to waste time holding on to anything toxic. I forgive you, Polly, because I refuse to allow the negative that comes with unforgiveness to rob me of anything more in my life."

Polly leaned down, tears flowing, and hugged Sarah.

"Thank you," she said. She started to leave. "And for the record, I don't have a three o'clock appointment today."

Sarah smiled as she slowly rose to her feet. "And for the record, I know that. Good-bye, Polly. I do wish you well. Now, please . . . allow me to see you to the door."

Chapter 46

To appoint unto them that mourn in Zion, to give unto them beauty for ashes, the oil of joy for mourning, the garment of praise for the spirit of heaviness; that they might be called trees of righteousness, the planting of the Lord, that He might be glorified.

Isaiah 61:3

When Memory and Lena returned from Christmas shopping later that evening, they were shocked to see Sarah still sitting in the parlor with the Christmas tree. But even more shocking was what was on the coffee table in front of her.

"The Wings of Grace box?" Lena said. "Where did you find it? Who had it?" she asked.

Sarah took the Alexandrite necklace and held it out. "I'm not sure who this goes to now," she said.

Lena and Memory both came closer. Lena looked at Memory. "That's yours," Lena said of the necklace.

"But I gave it back to you," Memory said.

"I know, but I want you to have it. It should have been in your possession to begin with. Grace left it for you, so it belongs to you."

"Then it's mine to give to whomever I want," Memory said, "and I want you to have it. You can give it back to Theresa again, if you like."

"Will somebody just take it?" Sarah said, in a scolding-type voice.

Memory and Lena exchanged looks and laughed. Memory came and got it, then promptly handed it to

Lena. "Please. If you really want to make me happy, you'll take this."

Lena acquiesced and took it.

"Put it on so I can see how it looks on you," Memory said. Lena put it on and stood back, playfully striking poses. "Beautiful," Memory said.

Lena looked at the box. "Grandmother, you haven't said where you found them."

Sarah smiled. "Don't worry about that. I told you both that I still had a few tricks left up my sleeve."

"Have you looked in the box yet?" Lena asked.

Sarah shook her head. "Except to take the necklace out, no, I didn't. For whatever reason, my mother chose to leave the two of you this to view together. I'm a bit tired now. It's been a long and trying day, to say the least. I think it's past time that I go up to my room and retire for the evening."

"I'll help you," Lena said as she started toward Sarah.

"Are you ready to go up now, Miss Fleming?" Gayle asked as she seemingly appeared out of nowhere.

Sarah looked in her direction. "Gayle, dear, as always, your timing is impeccable." Sarah began to stand up. Gayle came over and helped her up the rest of the way. "I think I might be starting to get rusty. That's what happens when you sit for a while." She looked at Memory then Lena as she took a few baby steps forward to get her joints working again. "Let this be a lesson to you all. You need to always keep moving if you don't want to rust up."

Memory laughed. "All right. We'll keep that in mind."

Memory and Lena sat there with the box beside them on the sofa. They quietly waited until they were certain Gayle and Sarah were completely upstairs and they'd heard Sarah's door close.

"Where do you suppose this box came from?" Lena

asked. "I mean, it's been missing now for well over a week. Then, out of nowhere, it suddenly reappears."

"I don't know, but I'm curious as well where she found it. Even more importantly, why wouldn't she tell us any more than she did?"

"Well, the key is still here in the keyhole, just like we left it," Lena said as she examined the box. "Do you think anyone, besides Grandmother taking the necklace out, has been inside of it since we last had it?"

"Who knows? But it appears someone would have had to, since we certainly didn't put the Alexandrite necklace inside of it when we had it. Someone had to open it up to put the necklace in it. And since Sarah's not talking, we may never find out who took it. But I sure would like to know."

Lena ran her hand over the box again. "I just love these boxes," she said. "Shall we?"

"Well, you can have the box when we're finished," Memory said. "It's only fair, especially since I was the one who threw the first one I ever came across in the trash."

"Yeah, but I hear your father made this box with his own two hands. This may be the closest thing you ever come to having something his hands actually touched."

"All the more reason you should keep it. Haven't you figured out yet that I'm not at all the sentimental type?" Memory said. "Now, shall we open this up and check out what's inside before something else happens and stops us again?"

Lena raised the top. The signature carved wings were on the underside of the top. Lena traced the details of the fine craftsmanship with her index finger. "This is so beautiful," she said.

"Yeah, looks like my dad was really talented when it came to stuff like this."

Lena began taking some things out of the box: various papers, a couple of rather unique brooches, two exquisite rings. She then came across a certificate of birth. "Now, this is strange. It's not exactly a birth certificate, but it appears to be something a midwife would give for a child's birth."

"Who is it for?" Memory asked, leaning over to get a better look at it.

Lena handed the frail piece of paper to Memory. "See for yourself."

When Memory looked at it, she saw the child's name, Ransom Powell, although the name Powell had a single line through it, and written above it was the name Perdue. "It looks like my father's birth certificate. But why would his birth certificate be in a box Grace, Sarah's mother, would have? And why would Grace leave it for us to find?"

"I don't know," Lena said.

"The mother's name is scratched out, but it looks like it was someone named Adele Powell," Memory said, holding the paper up close to her eyes so she could get a better look at it. "The father's name is totally scratched out. I can't make out what it was."

"Let me see that again. My glasses are much better than yours," Lena said, holding out her hand. She looked at it. "I can't make it out, either. But why would your father's last name have Powell, then be changed to Perdue? That makes no sense at all."

"I know. Let's see if anything else is in here that might explain things a little better," Memory said. They went through the rest of the things. Other than more jewelry and lots of papers that didn't mean a whole lot to them, there was nothing to help them.

"Well, this other stuff I understand being in here," Lena said. "But I'm lost when it comes to that paper with your father's name on it. There's nothing in here, from what I can see, that explains why Grace felt it necessary to include your father's official birth record in a box left to us. Unless, of course, she merely wanted you to have your father's legal birth record . . . as a keepsake. You know what? We might be too old to do this."

"Didn't you say Grace left a videotape and a journal or something like that along with this box?"

"The tape," Lena said in a tone that clearly indicated Memory was absolutely correct. "I hope I brought it with me." Lena got up and headed out of the parlor to go to her room. "I was in such a hurry to pack and get here. I pray I remembered to bring it, although, if I did, I don't remember exactly where I may have put it when I unpacked."

"I pray you brought it," Memory said as she sat holding the box and the birth record while waiting for Lena to go upstairs to her room and look for the tape.

"Got it," Lena said, triumphantly holding the tape in the air when she came back.

"Now, we need to find a videocassette player in this house," Memory said. "There's definitely not one in here," she said, looking around the room that didn't even have a television.

"Grandmother had one put in the playroom for the children to watch when they come over."

"Let's go," Memory said, hopping up on her feet. "Maybe Grace will open our eyes and tell us something more on the videotape."

They went to the playroom, popped in the videotape, and began watching it.

"I sort of remember her. She was regal-like back then, too," Memory said, seeing the elderly woman on the screen. "She didn't smile much, except on the occasions when she was talking directly to me. Now I know why. I was her granddaughter."

They listened as Grace spoke about various things concerning why she had done what she did, and how much she truly loved Memory in spite of sending her away with Mamie Patterson. How she wished things could have been different. Then they heard it, what they were looking for.

"You may be wondering why Ransom Perdue's birth record is in that box," Grace said. "And why I left that for you two, as opposed to my daughter. Pearl Black, an old friend of the family, brought that to me before she died. I wish she'd given it to me decades ago. Had she, then things for my daughter might have been vastly different. You see, Ransom was born to a woman named Adele Powell. Adele was married to a man named Winston Powell. Adele, incidentally, is the woman my husband was married to prior to me. Adele died right after giving birth to Victor Fleming Jr. Like Pearl, Pearl's mother was a respected midwife. Pearl's mother was there when Adele gave birth to Ransom. The problem was, Adele was a white woman married to a white man. Or so everybody thought. Keep in mind this was in the early nineteen hundreds. Adele was, in actuality, a black woman who had apparently passed for white. She'd married a white man named Winston, and, from what I hear, she'd tried everything to keep from ever having a child with him, claiming she didn't want children. Of course, we now know that her fear really was of having a baby that might come out looking black. Disastrous, when you happen to be married to a racist." Grace took a deep breath and released it.

"Nevertheless, she did get pregnant. And according to Pearl, when it was time for her to have the baby, she made her way to Pearl's mother on some pretense that she was out and about when she went into labor. There is much dispute of that being true. The belief is that she purposely sought out Pearl's mother just in case the baby did come out clearly a black child. Her husband would have most certainly accused her of being with a black man. He never might have guessed it was due to the blood that ran through her veins." Grace took a few seconds to readjust her body before continuing.

"The baby was born. Pearl's mother gave the baby to her and proceeded to fill out the proper paperwork on the newborn as was required by the state. Adele looked at her baby closely, thought the baby had a slight color to him, and asked Pearl's mother honestly what she thought. Pearl's mother concurred that her baby would most certainly darken in a few weeks. He was already dark around the top of his ears. She was told there would be no way of hiding his true color."

Grace uncrossed her legs as she relaxed a little more. "Adele decided to confide in Pearl's mother and asked her if she could possibly find her baby a good home, as there was no way she could take a black child back to her husband's house. No way. From my understanding, especially back during that time, black people were known to take in children that relatives and neighbors didn't want to raise or couldn't take care of. Pearl's mother took the baby and gave him to a friend of hers. People didn't show birth certificates like we do today, so no one ever knew the truth. Ironically, Ransom Perdue grew up being the best of friends with Pearl. Of course, Pearl didn't find out any of this until years after Ransom disappeared. Pearl was a wealth of folks' secrets. Things her mother told her and things she learned firsthand—untold history and knowledge she told me she's written down and documented. Who knows where those documents are, now that she's gone?"

Grace leaned forward. She seemed tired and out of breath now. "I'm going to end this here. But I needed you to know the truth. Montgomery Powell the Second's grandmother was a black woman. Everybody knows how he feels about black people. It wouldn't be impossible to prove this fact about Montgomery's heritage, if needed. Had I been in possession of this information when my stepson, Heath, was alive, I would have used it to get Sarah out of those horrible places and back home where she belonged.

"Sadly, it's too late for me to do anything with it. But Montgomery is as bad as his father was. Should you need leverage on him, I wouldn't hesitate to use this information. And not to sound like I'm chewing bitter grapes, but I don't know if we can really be sure that Adele's son, Heath, was truly even Victor Senior's child. After all, she *was* still married to Winston Powell when she conceived him. Do with this information as you deem necessary, if it's not already too late, and help bring my daughter home where she belongs. Sarah deserves better than she's gotten in life. It's too late for me now. I'm one hundred and two years old now. My time on this earth is at hand. I couldn't save my child, not like I wanted to. I pray, between you two, you can do a better job than I."

The tape went blank.

"Oh my," Lena said. "This is huge."

"I don't get it," Memory said. "This is 2005. Nobody cares about stuff like this anymore. The one-drop rule is a thing of the past. And everybody knows there were some light-skinned black folk who passed for white. I could have passed if I'd ever wanted to. So Montgomery Heath Powell Sr. had a black mother. So what? I had a white mother. So what?"

"You don't understand. For Montgomery Powell the Second, it really is a big deal," Lena said. "You see, the first time I ever met Montgomery, he was acting like the biggest racist. You should have heard him. It was scary, really. He called us all kinds of names. Then Grandmother made a reference to him possibly being a descendant of black people. I don't know if she knew that for a fact or whether she was just bluffing to get him to back down, but it did cause him to get off-balance. Grandmother held up an envelope. She told him she had proof. After everything was over, I questioned her about it. She gave the envelope to me and said that if knowing made that much of a difference to me, I could open the envelope and see for myself what it contained."

"So what did you do with the envelope?" Memory asked.

"I burned it."

"You did what?"

"I burned it," Lena said as she shrugged her shoulders. "I realized it really didn't matter to me. But now this. . . . This is some pretty substantial evidence here."

"So what do we do with it?" Memory asked.

"Grace left this for me and you," Lena said. "It's obvious she still didn't know where her daughter was. I suppose Grace was hoping we might somehow be able to use it to help get Sarah back home where she had failed all of those years."

"I wish Grace had found us. Then we could have all worked together to find Sarah before Grace died. She didn't get to see her daughter for years. It's a generational curse."

"A curse we're breaking now. But Grace likely felt if she wasn't able to help her daughter with all her power and resources, we wouldn't have been able to do much. But why not use this on Montgomery while she was still alive?" Lena asked. "If it could be effective against him, why not use it herself instead of leaving it for us? I don't get it."

"Maybe she did," Memory said. "It's obvious she didn't get this until she was too old and ill to fight anymore. Then you have to know who you can trust, because in the wrong hands, this evidence could have been totally destroyed."

"I do know, before we found Grandmother, Montgomery seemed to have been making plans for *her* to die. I'm not saying he was going to kill her or anything, but he claimed she was ill and near death. I'm sure he was scheming to legally obtain this house. The copy of the deed to this house that was inside the box," Lena said, "wasn't that in Grandmother's name?"

"I believe it was."

Lena pressed the eject button, took out the videotape, and turned off the VCR. "I think we need to talk to Grandmother. It's high time we stop this playing around and start pulling together." They started walking out.

Memory stopped at the doorway. "After you," she said, playfully bowing while allowing Lena to walk past her.

"Thank you, Mother," Lena said.

Memory stood still. She couldn't help but get emotional. After all, this was the first time, since Lena was around six years old, that she'd called her mother.

Chapter 47

Then shalt thou delight thyself in the Lord; and I will cause thee to ride upon the high places of the earth, and feed thee with the heritage of Jacob thy father: for the mouth of the Lord hath spoken it.

Isaiah 58:14

Landris waited for Dr. Freeman at the nurses' station.

"Mr. Landris," a short man with dark brown hair said as he extended his hand to greet him. "I'm Dr. Freeman. Thank you for getting here so quickly."

"Tell me what's going on. I just checked on my son, and he's not in there."

"I'm sorry, Mr. Landris. Did the person who called not tell you *anything*?" Dr. Freeman's beeper went off. His glasses sat close to the end of his nose as he read it.

"No," Landris said. "She just said I needed to get here right away, and you would tell me everything."

"I'm so sorry, Mr. Landris. If you don't mind, can you walk with me?" he said as he started down the hall. "Your son was still having major problems with his breathing. We had what we call an endotracheal tube, ET for short, in his windpipe. This was getting air and oxygen to his lungs at a regulated rate, but something started happening and—"

"Dr. Freeman, is my son okay?" Landris asked in a tone demanding an answer.

"Your son is fine—for now, anyway. I believe we were

able to stabilize him. I sent him down for a few tests. That's why he wasn't in there when you looked in on him."

Landris let out a sigh of relief. "Thank You, Lord," he said, looking upward and lifting his hands in a form of praise.

"I'm sorry if we worried you. I don't like saying this sort of stuff over the phone, because I understand how anxious parents already are. Sometimes things get lost in the translation, and it can create a nightmare of a problem for both the doctor and parents."

"I'd like to see my son. When will he be back? I want to be sure he's okay."

Dr. Freeman nodded. "That was the CNS beeping me to let me know she was on her way back with him now."

Landris had become quite familiar with various medical terms. He knew that CNS stood for clinical nurse specialist. He waited outside NICU for his son's return. When they brought him back, Landris spent thirty minutes with him. Glancing at the clock on the wall, he saw it was seven fifty-five. Eight o'clock was the last official visiting hour of the day for SICU patients. He left his son's side to go be with his wife.

"Johnnie Mae, you need to wake up," he said, letting the rail down, making it easier for him to hold her hand. "We have this beautiful son, and he wants to meet you. He's small, but he's so beautiful. I can't explain how it feels when I look at him. Oh, I know, I'm not supposed to call a boy beautiful. Okay, handsome. He's so handsome. How about that? But he needs you right now. Princess Rose needs you. We all need you.

"Your mother's memory has reverted back. That happened shortly after the baby was born. She did get to see him, and she knew he was your new baby. She also knew you weren't doing well. Something, huh? How she could be so much like her normal self one day, then back to not knowing who anyone is the next. She likes my mother a lot, though. Princess Rose was so happy to be able to spend some time with her, I can't even begin to tell you. Your mother still talks and plays with her, even when she can't remember who she is. I can see it bothers Princess Rose when your mother doesn't recall things. I've had to stop Princess Rose a few times from getting frustrated about it. It's hard to explain something like Alzheimer's to a child. In truth, it's hard for grown folks to understand.

"My mother's been a little tired. She tries to hide it from me, but I can tell. I know it has to do with her heart. That's why she only comes to the hospital once a day. I don't think she's even supposed to be in Alabama, but she had to come see about us. Her doctor wants to perform triple-bypass surgery on her. And Thomas had quit taking his medicine. I didn't tell you before because I didn't want you worrying about it. You were dealing with enough already. I think we convinced him to start back taking his pills. I don't know. I suppose we'll find out soon enough. I wish I knew how to get him to see he can't be playing around with his medication like that. Every time I turn on the news lately, somebody with bipolar disorder is getting killed because they're either not on medication and should be or they were on it and decided to stop taking it. The people who encounter them didn't know why they were acting the way they were and felt threatened. I've got to get through to him that this bipolar disorder is nothing to play Russian roulette with.

"He accuses me of preaching faith and healing but not really believing in it. I don't know, maybe I'm wrong to think medical and Godly healing *can* go hand in hand when needed. Maybe if I had enough faith, you'd be awake by now. Maybe if I had enough faith, our son wouldn't be struggling for his next breath now. They took him for some tests today. He seems okay. I just spent the past half hour with him. Guess what? He grabbed my finger. Well, maybe not *really* grabbed it, more like brushed it when he moved, but it was like he was letting me know that he's determined to hold on. Oh, you're going to be so proud when you wake up and see him. I know you are. He's a fighter, all right. Why won't you open your eyes, Johnnie Mae? I know you can hear me. I know you can." He laid his head down next to her hand, then raised it back up.

"Mrs. Knight is letting Reverend Walker preach Reverend Knight's funeral. I probably wouldn't have minded so much except I believe he bullied her into it. He all but threatened me. I don't know what I've done to make that man have it out for me. Reverend Knight warned me to watch out for him. In fact, he gave me something as leverage against him, should I ever need it. I hadn't planned on ever opening that envelope, but I have to tell you, I did look at it. Reverend Knight was right. If what's in that envelope was ever to come out . . . well, I don't know if the statute of limitations has run out for him to serve jail time for it, but Reverend Walker could definitely be ruined. Then again, in this day and age, who can say how people will really react?

"You're probably wondering what he could have done that could be so bad. How about he raped his twelve-year-old cousin when he was sixteen? Just the thought of that makes me mad. And would you believe he got away with it, too? According to the papers Reverend Knight gave me, when Marshall Walker and Paul Knight were teenagers, supposedly as a prank, they decided to rob Marshall's uncle, who owned one of those mom and pop stores. The family lived above the store. Marshall's young cousin was minding the store that day. I guess Marshall decided, since she was there alone and the opportunity was presenting itself, he'd also take her upstairs and have his way with her as a bonus to the robbery. They'd worn ladies' stockings over their faces as masks when they went in, so his cousin didn't know who he was. Not at first, anyway.

"According to the file, Paul Knight thought Marshall's taking her upstairs was part of the prank. After all, they weren't planning on keeping the money. That's what Marshall had told him prior to them doing it. Marshall just wanted to teach his stingy uncle a lesson. Of course, that wasn't at all what happened. After the incident, the police were called in. Both Marshall and Paul were placed temporarily in juvenile detention while things were being sorted out. A few months following the incident, the store/house burned to the ground. Marshall's uncle and his cousin both perished in the fire, which was ruled accidental due to faulty wiring. Because Marshall Walker and Paul Knight were juveniles at the time of the *alleged* incident, that incidentally was dismissed without prejudice, their records were sealed. Paul Knight kept all of this documented information along with other collaborating and pretty damaging evidence. Information he left to me.

"But enough about that. I'm sure you don't want to hear about all of this junk happening out here in this crazy world we live in. Johnnie Mae, I need you to come out of this. Who else on earth will I have to share my deepest thoughts with? I need you. I love you dearly. I tried to show you how much I loved you before any of this ever happened. But they say you never really know just how much you love a person until that person's no longer around. At least when you or I go out of town, we can pick up the phone and talk. How do I reach you now? So please, Johnnie Mae. Please. Open your eyes. For me, for Princess Rose, for your mother, for our son fighting to make it. He's waiting on a name, and I refuse to name him without you. I have faith you're going to pull through this. So open your eyes. Do you hear me, J. M.? Please . . . open your eyes."

Chapter 48

They shall not labor in vain, nor bring forth for trouble; for they are the seed of the blessed of the Lord, and their offspring with them.

Isaiah 65:23

Lena knocked on the door. "Grandmother, it's me and Memory. Is it okay if we come in?"

"Just a minute," Sarah yelled back. Sarah looked at Gayle. "Not a word to either of them about Montgomery or Polly," she whispered as she leaned forward.

"You know you can trust me," Gayle said in a low tone while continuing to fluff the two pillows she normally placed behind Sarah's back when propping her up. "Are you certain you feel okay? You look a bit flushed. You've been quite a busy little bee today."

"Yes, I feel okay." Sarah yawned as she lay back now. "Maybe I *am* a tad bit sleepy."

"Well, I'll check your blood pressure again as soon as Memory and Lena leave," Gayle said as she finished getting Sarah situated comfortably again. "Then I want you to rest."

"Thanks, Gayle."

Gayle opened the door, letting Memory and Lena in as she headed out.

"Are you gone?" Lena asked Gayle as they literally passed each other in the doorway. "We didn't mean to run you off or anything."

"Oh, you're not running me off. I have a few things

that require my attention," Gayle said as she flashed a smile at Lena. "I'll be back in a little while, Miss Fleming."

Sarah nodded. "I'll be all right."

Gayle left. Memory moved the chair next to the nightstand over to Sarah's bed. Lena went and got the chair usually kept folded in the corner and placed it next to Memory so Sarah could easily see them both at the same time.

"Grandmother, we just went through the Wings of Grace box," Lena said, deciding to get straight to the point. "We then watched the videotape your mother made and left for us, preferably to view together if it was at all possible. Those were her instructions."

"That's right, there *was* a videotape," Sarah said. "I forgot you told me that. I'm sure had she suspected it would be almost four years before that happened, she may not have placed that restriction on it. But knowing my mother, that was her way of ensuring you would find Memory, if you two weren't already in some type of contact." Sarah lay back, relaxing more into the pillow. "Was there anything interesting in the box or on the tape? That's if you can share that information with me. I don't wish to pry into something that may be none of my business, so feel free to tell me if I am."

"Yes, there was something. In fact, there was something of interest to you, I believe," Memory said. "It has to do with Ransom Perdue."

"Ransom Perdue was your father," Sarah said, looking directly at Memory. "I told you about him. Is there something I don't know? Did my mother say what happened to him after he left and never returned?"

"No," Memory said. "But there was something in the box and on the tape that I don't think you knew. We have reason to believe that Ransom Perdue was possibly your stepbrother."

Sarah pressed her body harder into the pillows, as though she needed to be braced. "What? Oh, that's just hogwash!"

Lena looked at Memory, not believing Memory had put it in those terms and blurted it out like that. Although when Lena actually thought about it, that's precisely what it boiled down to. "What she meant to say is, from what appears to be an official record of Ransom's birth, his mother was actually Adele Powell."

"Adele Powell? She was my half-brothers', Heath and Victor Junior's, mother."

"Yes. Adele, your father's wife before he married your mother," Memory said.

"But that can't be," Sarah said. "Ransom was a black man. What are you saying?"

Lena recounted for Sarah everything they'd learned concerning Ransom, his mother, Adele, Pearl's mother's delivery of Ransom, and her secretly finding him a home.

Sarah shook her head. "I'm sure Ransom probably didn't know the truth. That is so sad, so sad. Deception; it's a curse, I tell you. That's what it is—a curse."

"It sounds like Ransom was Adele Powell's son, so that could *technically* make Ransom your stepbrother, although I wouldn't have put it the way Memory did," Lena said, throwing Memory a look of slight reprimand. "I am curious, though," Lena continued, turning her attention back to Sarah. "This has to do with Montgomery the Second. You insinuated on that day we first met that he may have had some black in his blood. Did you know his mother was a black woman passing for a white when you said that?"

Sarah laughed, placing her hand over her heart. "Heavens no," she said.

"Then you were bluffing when you said that to him?" Lena asked.

"I would have made a great poker player, don't you think?" Sarah asked.

"And the envelope you gave me?" Lena asked, referring to the envelope Sarah had held in her hand during her standoff with Montgomery . . . refusing to fold back in October of 2001.

"Oddly enough, I'd picked up that envelope only minutes before I made my way out the door when Johnnie Mae and all y'all came here," Sarah said. "I'd scribbled a note to tell Johnnie Mae what was really going on—the fact that I really was being held against my will. My intent was to slip that envelope to her if anything happened and she was forced to leave me here again."

"So had I opened that envelope instead of burning it . . . ?"

"You burnt it? I never knew that." Sarah laughed. "If you had opened it instead of burning it, you would have found my plea for help. But it worked, didn't it? It flustered Montgomery." Sarah began to chuckle. "And I thought for sure Johnnie Mae's husband was about to give Montgomery a real . . . what do the young folks call it?" She started snapping her fingers to try and help her recall the words. "What do they call it?"

"A beat down," Memory said, familiar with the terminology.

"That's it, a beat down!" Sarah said, continuing to laugh at the thought of it.

"Do you think Montgomery has any idea his grandmother was black?" Memory asked Sarah.

"Probably not," Sarah said. "But Montgomery is the kind who would hate something like that even being out there remotely as a topic of discussion." Sarah coughed a few times. "I believe my nephew is as protective of his so-called pristine reputation as his father was. There's no way Montgomery's white buddies will allow a black man to remain in their exclusive club. I don't care how white he may look on the outside." Sarah began to cough again. She covered her mouth with her hand.

"Are you okay?" Lena asked, getting up quickly and pouring some water, then handing it to her.

Sarah took a few sips. "I'm fine. I suppose I *am* tired, though. I think I'd like to take a little nap. Could you ask Gayle to come up when you go down?" Sarah asked.

"Sure," Lena said, taking the hint that Sarah was ready for them to leave now. She looked over at Memory, who remained sitting. "We're going to go and let you get some rest," Lena said, heading for the door. She was hoping Memory would get the hint this time. Memory continued to sit there. "Oh, Grandmother, before I forget to tell you. Theresa called. They decided they want to celebrate their anniversary on Wednesday, so they're not planning to drive up until Thursday for the celebration on Saturday."

"They should come on up on Tuesday," Sarah said. "They could go out together up here. I could watch the children for them while they're gone. Then they wouldn't have to bother with hiring a babysitter, and *I* would get yet more time to spend with my darling little great-great-grands. Why don't you call Theresa back and tell her that for me?" Sarah took another sip of water, then set the glass on her nightstand.

"That would be too much on you," Lena said. "Those little *darlings*, as you call them, can be a little *handful*. Trust me."

"Personally, I think it's a great idea. I'll be here," Memory said. "Between the two of us, four while Gayle and Monica are still around, we can certainly handle a couple of kids. That way you and Richard could also spend a night out on the town."

"That does sound tempting," Lena said. "It would give

us all a little more time to spend together. And that's always a good thing in my book. Are you two sure about this?" Lena looked from Memory to Sarah for confirmation.

"Absolutely. Call her and see what she says." Sarah closed her eyes. "It will be a joy having my family all here again, under the same roof, this time without any tension or any animosity. My child, grandchild, great-grandchild, and my great-great-grandchildren, five generations, all here together. It will be just as it says in the Bible. They won't labor in vain nor bring forth for trouble because they are the seed of the blessed of the Lord. Yes, I am indeed blessed." Sarah continued talking as her speaking became more and more sluggish, almost as though she was talking in her sleep. "I've got to get someone to talk to the caterer for our Christmas celebration. I'm sure Gayle will help me. I can always count on Gayle. Yeah, I trust Gayle. She's always said . . . I can . . . trust . . . her."

Sarah stopped talking altogether. She'd drifted completely off to sleep. Lena beckoned to Memory for her to get up and leave with her. They stepped out the door and closed it quietly.

"What was she talking about a caterer?" Memory asked when they reached the end of the hall. "Polly's taking care of all of that for her."

"Who knows?" Lena said. "I wouldn't put much stock into what she was mumbling then. She most likely was tired and just talking in her sleep."

"Maybe," Memory said. "Maybe."

Chapter 49

For since the beginning of the world men have not heard, nor perceived by the ear, neither hath the eye seen, O God, beside Thee, what He hath prepared for him that waiteth for Him.

Isaiah 64:4

Landris sat in Johnnie Mae's room. It had been four weeks since she'd had her baby. A baby whose weight was now miraculously up to four pounds and three ounces, but who still didn't have a name donning his incubator-crib other than "Boy Landris." Landris was back at church, preaching on Sundays and doing limited other duties throughout the week. His mother was at his house, helping him take care of Princess Rose, although he'd told her many times she really needed to go home and see her doctor about her heart or at least see a doctor in Birmingham just to make sure she was still doing okay. His mother's presence there seemed enough to satisfy Johnnie Mae's sister-in-law's quest to try and get temporary custody of Princess Rose or cause trouble.

Taking a cue from her son, who was speaking healing scriptures over his wife and child and playing healing tapes in Johnnie Mae's room while he wasn't there, Virginia started listening to tapes on healing. Landris had said this was spiritual warfare, and it was imperative that they fight this war with the right tools. Thomas was out of the halfway-house medical facility, and while he was continuing to grow stronger, fighting to get disability benefits, and find his own place, George had told him he could stay at their house.

Dr. Baker had consulted with other doctors. Landris was told that none of them agreed Johnnie Mae should be kept on life support any longer. After all, it had been a month now. As much as Landris might not want to face the fact, Johnnie Mae appeared all but gone. The majority agreed, with the exception of Dr. Baker and one other colleague, that if Johnnie Mae didn't regain consciousness within the next day, two at the most, realistically, the machine should be disconnected. Certain organs would likely start shutting down soon anyway. There was still the possibility of brain damage, although nothing indicated for sure that that had occurred. They couldn't know for sure *until* she regained consciousness, and it didn't look as though that was going to happen.

Landris listened as doctor after doctor tried to convince him that his wife could likely be in this state for as long as the machines were hooked up to her—months, even years. It was important that he face that fact and make peace with letting *her* go in peace. Turning off the life-support machine wasn't necessarily a death sentence. It was possible she might begin breathing again on her own. It might even jumpstart her system back to recovery. "There are many documented cases where this very thing has happened," one doctor explained.

However, Landris set his face like a flint. There was nothing else to be said if it was contrary to God's Word, as far as he was concerned.

His hair was already growing back. He kept it cut low to his head, definitely a different look on him. He'd been led by the Spirit of God to do a fast—no food or juices, only water to keep him hydrated—while praying for seven days.

The following day, after having heard all the doctor's recommendations, Landris walked in to visit Johnnie Mae on what was the final day of his seven-day fast. Her private room was filled with Rachel and her family, along with Johnnie Mae's mother, who, to Landris, clearly looked as though she didn't have a clue why she'd been dragged in there.

"What's going on?" Landris asked Rachel.

Fighting back her tears, Rachel said, "We came to say our good-byes."

"Good-bye?" Landris asked in sheer astonishment. "Good-bye? Good-bye to whom?"

"I was here yesterday when one of the doctors was here. I asked him point-blank, and he told me the truth, George. They want to take Johnnie Mae off life support tomorrow. I'm sure your insurance provider has long been in agreement with that." Rachel stared hard at him. "You knew about this, and you weren't even planning on saying anything to us? That's low, George Landris. That's low. We deserve to know what's going on. Marie and Donald came by earlier. My brother Christian and his family are planning on being here later this evening. It takes about three hours for him to drive up from Columbus, Georgia. You should have told us what was going on. Johnnie Mae is our sister, my mother's daughter." Rachel started crying. "No matter what *you* believe, we have a right to know the truth."

Mrs. Gates came and patted Rachel on her back. "There, there," she said. "Don't cry. I'm sure whatever it is can't be all *that* bad. It's going to all work out, you just wait and see."

"Listen, Rachel," Landris said, keeping his voice low and even, "we can't go giving up now. We have to believe the Word of the Lord. With long life, God will satisfy her. She will live and not die. That's all God's Word."

"Stop it!" Rachel said. "Just stop it!" She pressed her hands over her ears. "I'm so sick and tired of all you super-religious folks burying your heads in the sand about what God *will* and *won't* do!" She removed her hands from her ears.

"The Bible also says it rains on the just and the unjust," Rachel said. "Plenty of people have prayed for loved ones to live and not die, and do you know what happened to a good number of them?" Rachel stepped away from her mother and children and walked closer to Landris, who was close to the bathroom door. "They died anyway! You've given this your best shot, George. I give you that much. I know Johnnie Mae would be *very* proud of how vigilant you've been throughout all of this." She sighed. "But it's time for you to face some cold, hard facts here. She's gone, George. I wish it was different, but this is real life. And none of us are getting out of here alive. We're all going to die someday. Now is Johnnie Mae's time. We need to say our good-byes, remember the good times and the joys we've shared, and let her go on in peace."

"Rachel, let's not do this in front of Johnnie Mae."

"She can't hear anything, George. She can't hear us! She's all but gone, and you're forcing her to linger here because you don't want to face that truth. If God wanted things to be different, He could have kept her from going through this in the first place. All your praying and believing didn't keep her from getting toxemia. All your praying and believing didn't keep that baby in NICU from being born prematurely. If God loves you so much, then why not just keep you from even having to go through any of this at all? If God cared anything about all of your praying and believing, why hasn't He woken Johnnie Mae up? According to you, God can do anything but fail."

"Excuse me," Mrs. Gates said, "but, little lady, I wouldn't go there if I was you. You don't want to mess with God like that. Trust me, you don't."

"Rachel, I said I don't want to do this in front of Johnnie Mae." Landris spoke through clenched teeth, keeping his voice low. "She *is* going to live and not die! Do you hear me?"

"Says who?" Rachel said.

"Says the scripture I'm standing on."

She laughed cynically as she shook her head. She then spoke softly. "Look at our mother, George." She pointed at Mrs. Gates, who had returned to look out of the window. "Do you know what we've been confessing and believing about her? That she would be healed from this memory robber. That she would return to her old self again. That this is just some mistake, something that can easily be fixed. Look at her!" Rachel said, continuing to point to her mother. "She doesn't even know that's her daughter lying there. But I brought her anyway, and do you know why? Because I felt she needed and had a *right* to be able to say good-bye to her own child—a child she doesn't even remember giving birth to!"

Landris grabbed Rachel by the arm and started pulling her out of the room.

"Let go of me!" she yelled. "Let go! Have you lost your cotton-picking mind? You can't be grabbing on folks like that."

"Stop this!" Landris said after he pulled her outside the room and closed the door.

Rachel snatched her arm out of his grip. "Let me go!" She stood against the wall.

"I'm sorry. I didn't mean to manhandle you. Rachel, look, I know you're upset. But you can't do stuff like that in front of Johnnie Mae *or* your mother." He shook his head. "You can't let your frustrations and your hurt spill out and over to affect others the way you just did in there."

Rachel started crying. Landris gave her a handkerchief and hugged her. "I'm sorry," she said. "I know. I'm just so *mad* right now, I don't know what to do! Why doesn't God hear us? Why does He allow things like this to happen to good people? My sister is a good person. My mother is a good person. My daughter is still on drugs, and I've prayed . . . Lord knows, I've prayed for her. She seems worse off now than before I took the children. I thought at some point she'd hit rock bottom and get some help. I've all but lost her. I'm trying to come to terms with that. My mother, who has served the Lord faithfully, faithfully, do you hear me? Now look what's happened to her. Do you have any idea what it really feels like to have your own mother look at you and ask you who you are or talk to you like you're some stranger she just met on the street? Saying things like she just said to me in there? Then after you tell her who you are she looks at you like *you're* the one who's lost *your* mind? Do you have any idea, George? Do you?"

He stepped back. "I have an idea what it feels like to have the woman you promised to love, honor, and cherish, until death do you part, be lying in a hospital bed with doctors and all their fancy degrees telling you there's no more hope left while you stand in faith, against all hope. I have an idea what it feels like to have your only son be born prematurely with doctors telling you it's a good chance he's not going to make it. And every day, they act like it's a miracle he's still here on *that* day, but they're not sure he'll make it to the next. I know what it feels like to have your brother deal with a mental disorder while accusing you of not having enough faith that God will heal him as he takes himself off his mind-regulating medication, and you're not sure you can get through to him that he can't start playing around with something like that. I know what it feels like to have your own mother being told she needs triple-bypass heart surgery, but she seems determined to put it off while telling you she plans to stand by your side for as long as you need her as you go through some of the darkest hours of your life. While deep in your mind and heart, you're concerned about her heart possibly giving out before she's either healed or had the necessary surgery." He wiped his face with one hand.

"I know what it feels like, Rachel, to pray and expect God to move, only to be told things are still the same, if not worse, the following day. But you have to stand in faith and trust God, because honestly, who else do we have to turn to?" Landris said. "I stretch my hands to God daily. I don't know or have any other help *except* Him. Sure, any of us can throw a temper tantrum like Job did after our interludes of what seem to be unrelenting troubles. The time when Job told God he regretted ever being born.

"We can be upset with God the way the prophet Jeremiah was, despite the fact that God had told him in advance what he could expect to happen. We can refuse to go or do what God has instructed us, the way Jonah did. But trust me. God has a way of getting our attention. Even the apostle Paul experienced some of the same feelings we do. And Jesus, the Son of the living God, prayed and asked God to remove this bitter cup from Him, only to concede seconds later, 'But not my will, but thine be done.' Jesus was on the cross, and during His darkest hour, when it seemed God had turned away from Him completely, Jesus prayed and asked God why had He forsaken Him."

Landris reached out and touched Rachel on her hand. "I know you love your sister. I know you do. I even know that you're mad at God right now for what feels like Him turning a deaf ear to our prayers for her, mine included. But you have to know that God is still in control. He's sovereign, which means He reigns. He has not left us. He didn't leave Jesus, who, by all accounts, appeared defeated when they took Him down from the cross and placed Him in a tomb. It doesn't get any more over than that, but look what God did. Rachel, I don't know how God is going to do what He's going to do. But regardless of *what* happens, God will still get the glory out of it. I refuse to allow Satan to steal God's praises due to Him."

"What are you going to do if Johnnie Mae dies? And there's a great possibility that's about to happen," Rachel said as she wiped her tears with the handkerchief Landris had given her earlier. "God may decide not to save her. What are you going to do then? Will you still be spouting off all this religious stuff? Or will you question your own faith? Will you believe it was your fault because you really didn't have enough faith to move God? Or will you conclude that God really didn't care, and even though He could have raised her up, He chose not to?"

"I'm going to stand, Rachel. That's all God told me to do—stand. In spite of what happens in my life, I'm going to stand and trust God, because God *is* God."

"That's easy to say right now. Johnnie Mae is technically still here with us. I don't think that's what you'll be saying tomorrow or whenever they finally turn that life-giving machine off and her breathing ceases." Rachel dabbed at her now-closed eyes as she continued with sporadic sniffles.

"Let me tell you something," Landris said in voice that emanated peace. "I believe *right now*, when it matters. Faith is now. And that machine in there is not the life giver—God is. I can believe my wife is healed because when Jesus was being beaten, the stripes He endured were *for* our healing. The Bible says, by His stripes we *were* healed. Not that we're going to be—we were. Johnnie Mae is not the sick trying to get healed; she *was* healed by Jesus' stripes over two thousand years ago. It's already done. Now . . . I'm going back in there and lay hands on her and pray and speak the Word only and believe. I believe my wife *will* recover, do you hear me? I know it. And how do I know? By faith. My faith is all the evidence I have to show you, but I believe it's already done. Therefore, I will act like I believe. And if that means putting all the negative people who are hindering God's Word from going forth in that room out, including you and the doctors if I'm forced to, then I'll have all of you put out."

"What?" Rachel asked, jerking back in disbelief as she placed her hand on her hip.

"You heard me. I didn't stutter when I said it. I don't care if they intend to turn the machines off tomorrow or the next day. Right now is an opportunity for God's power to be shown in action. We talk a good talk. But God is looking for faithwalkers. When Jesus went in to heal Jairus's daughter, they laughed Him to scorn. And the Bible says that Jesus put them out. As a follower of Jesus, if I find I have to, I'll start putting folks out or bar them from going in if I feel they're a hindrance for God's healing power to go forth."

Rachel started laughing. "You see, now I know you done lost your mind! That's what happens with you Jesus folks. George, that was Jesus that did that. I know Jesus, and, Pastor Landris, you're no Jesus. These doctors will get a court order on you if they have to. You know they will. That's what that doctor told me yesterday. They will get a court order to have the machines turned off if they feel they need to."

"Rachel, I'm not trying to argue with you right now. And as for that doctor and getting a court order, the Word of God says that no weapon formed against me shall prosper. The point is, Jesus did great works. He said we would do greater works than He did. I believe that, and I intend to operate in it."

"And you're going to look foolish doing it, too."

"Then so be it!" Landris started walking back toward the door. He turned around. "From now on, when you come through this door, you should consider this the no-doubter zone. In other words, if you can't leave your doubts on this side of the door, then don't bother bringing them in there with you."

"You're really crazy, do you know that?" She stepped closer to him.

"So I'm crazy, huh? I've lost my mind? Okay, so we've all but lost Johnnie Mae already, in your eyesight. So tell me, sister-in-law, what do I have to lose if this doesn't work?"

Rachel grabbed him by his upper arm. "George, why don't you go in there and prove *everybody* wrong! Oh, I pray that you do. I pray that God not only hears you, but that He answers your prayer. For my sister's sake, for the sake of all those who want to believe that God not only *can* but *will* move in a mighty way. Go on, George. Prove to *everybody* who may have ever doubted God that we *were* and *are* wrong!"

Landris nodded and smiled at her as he placed a hand on her shoulder and patted it. "So . . . are you coming back in?"

"Sorry, George, I'm going to wait on this side. From what I've been told, beyond that door is the no-doubter zone. But if you don't mind, will you please tell my children and grandchildren to come on out so we can go home, and to bring my mother out with them? And George, when Johnnie Mae awakes, give her a kiss for me, will you?" She nodded, then covered her mouth with her hand as she held in her cry.

Chapter 50

And I have put My words in thy mouth, and I have covered thee in the shadow of Mine hand, that I may plant the heavens, and lay the foundations of the earth, and say unto Zion, Thou art My people.

Isaiah 51:16

It was seven PM, and Landris was alone with Johnnie Mae. He quietly played some of her favorite old-time gospel and contemporary gospel songs while reading scriptures to her from the books of Proverbs, Psalms, and Isaiah. He played a CD he'd recorded on healing and the power of what Jesus has already done for those who believe. Landris took his wife's lifeless hand and prayed with her as fervently and passionately as if she'd been awake and was participating in the prayer with him. He was determined he would continue this vigil through the night. An RN came in from time to time to check on Johnnie Mae.

As the RN was getting ready to leave the room, a little after ten o'clock, she touched Landris on his shoulder. "Pastor Landris, I've never been one to go to church much. But if you don't mind me saying, there's something special about the way you worship and praise God even in the midst of your trials and tribulations that makes me want to know more about Him. Whatever you have, I sure would like some of it."

"God is a person, not an it," Landris said with kind correction. "And He is *truly* worthy to be praised," he said. "When things are going great for us, we should praise Him. When things aren't going so great, we still should praise Him, with our eyes fixed on what He's *going* to do to turn things around. I'm not moved by what I see. For in the natural right now, I'm being told that it looks like there's little hope. I live by faith—faith in who God is and not merely in what He can do. If God never does another thing for me, if God never answers another prayer request, I will still praise Him just for who He is. God is worthy to be praised. Therefore, I praise Him when I'm up, and I praise Him when I'm down."

"You've been told by the doctors that your wife is not doing well," the nurse said, "yet there is such a peace about you. That's the kind of peace I'd like to have. You possess a joy that seems to exude from you . . . like you're expecting something good to happen any minute. I want that kind of joy in my life."

Landris continued to hold Johnnie Mae's hand as he stood and faced the nurse. "Serving the true and living God will have that kind of effect on you. He'll give you a peace that truly does surpass all understanding. I can't explain to you why I'm able to stand in the midst of the storms of life and be at peace, except to tell you that having Jesus onboard makes all the difference in the world. There's something about knowing Jesus is onboard that allows you to sleep like a baby even when the ship is being tossed and driven. When God gives you joy, it's an unspeakable joy, the kind the world can't give and the world has no power to take away—a joy that becomes strength in weakness." He smiled briefly. "I have a question for you. Are you saved?"

She gave him a quick grin. "No, I'm not. I've seen too much hypocrisy in so-called Christians. It's a huge turnoff. I decided a long time ago if that's how being a Christian is, then I didn't care to have any part of it."

"Listen to me. You can't allow other folks to keep you

from receiving salvation. When you face Judgment Day—and you will someday—you're going to have to stand for yourself. You'll be asked why you should be allowed into Heaven. How will you answer that question? Are you going to say you chose not to accept Jesus as your Savior because of how other people, who said they were Christians, acted?" Landris shook his head again. "I'm sorry, but that excuse is not going to fly in Heaven."

"Then what do I say? That none of the Christians I knew and met during my lifetime ever bothered to stop and minister to me? That they saw I wasn't living right but felt it wasn't their job or place to at least tell me about Jesus and His plan for salvation? Pastor Landris, there are plenty of nurses here who profess to be Christians. They make a huge show, carrying and reading their Bibles. But not one of them has ever taken the time to talk to me about Jesus. They talk about their family, their problems—large and small, as though there is no hope. They talk *a lot* about other folks. But not one has bothered to ask me if I'm saved or talk to me about becoming saved the way you are doing now. It's like Jesus is a sort of symbol they use to show how great *they* are, instead of a testament to how great He is. But the way you've been these few times I've seen you since your wife was moved to this floor makes me desperately want what you have. So please tell me, Pastor Landris, what must I do to be saved?"

Landris gently released Johnnie Mae's hand, careful to place it lovingly next to her side. He glanced quickly at the nurse's badge to make sure he had her name correctly. "Jackie," he said, "the Bible says we were all sinners, born into sin because of what the first man, Adam, did. Because of sin, we were separated from God our Father. The Bible declares that the wages of sin is death. But Jesus, God's only begotten Son, the second man, Adam, voluntarily came down to earth to die on the cross to pay for our sins. Mine, yours, my wife's, the world's . . . He died for all our sins. Essentially, Jesus was crucified in our place. Jesus went to hell in our place. And on the third day, God raised Jesus up from the dead. Now, by faith, do you believe this?"

Jackie was crying now. She nodded as she spoke. "Yes," she said. "I believe that."

Landris took her by both hands. "Then I want you to repeat after me. Lord, I'm a sinner. Please come into my heart."

Jackie repeated the words as instructed.

"I confess with my mouth the Lord Jesus Christ. And I believe in my heart that God has raised Him from the dead."

Jackie said those words as she kneeled down on the floor and began to cry even more. She began to thank God for His mercy and His grace as she continued to weep.

"The Bible tells us that if we confess with our mouth the Lord Jesus Christ and believe in our hearts that God has raised Him from the dead we shall be saved. You're saved now because you believe in Jesus and what He did to save you from sin. You're now an heir and a joint-heir with Jesus Christ, my new sister in Christ, and legally part of God's royal family. Jackie, let me be the first to welcome you to the family of God. God is worthy to be praised." Landris released her hands and began giving God a wave offering.

"Thank You, Jesus," Jackie said, crying as she looked upward with her arms extended high. "Thank You for dying for my sins. Oh Lord, I've done so much wrong, but You loved me. Before I ever knew You, You loved me. Thank You for saving me."

"Thank You, Lord," Landris said, praising God along with her. "Oh, we thank You, Lord. I know You and all the Heavenly hosts are rejoicing right now as one more soul has been added to the church—not a building, but the body of Christ. Lord, we thank You for this sister. Touch her right now, in Jesus' name. You know what she's in need of. Pour out a special blessing upon her. Release Your anointing on us. Lord, You're awesome. In the midst of everything that's going on, even now, I feel Your presence in this place. I feel You moving right now. Move, Lord! Heal, Lord! Show Yourself strong, Lord! I bind the works of the devil, right now in Jesus' name. I loose Your angels to perform the Word that You have sent. I speak life! I thank You for healing right now. Thank You, Lord." Landris paced near the bed. "Thank You, Lord. Yes, we praise You. Yes, Lord. Yes, Lord. My soul says yes!"

Landris started jumping up and down. He was trying to keep it quiet since he didn't want to disturb other patients. But it was hard for him to hold his peace. Jackie was jumping up and down, too, praising God. Landris walked over and took Johnnie Mae's hand as he continued his prayer. "Johnnie Mae is already healed, Lord. My wife . . . my helpmeet, bone of my bone and flesh of my flesh . . . by Your stripes, she's already healed, in Jesus' name. In Jesus' name. Now, let Your Word be true and anything that man has declared that is contrary to Your Word, let it fall right now, Lord."

"I feel Your presence," Jackie said, obviously amazed. "He's real. God is real," she said. "I've never felt anything like this before in all of my life." She began waving her hands in the air. "Thank You, Jesus! Thank You for saving me. Little old me! Thank You for loving me so much that You laid Your life down for me! For me. No one has ever loved me like that. I thank You for the work You're doing in this room right now."

Landris kneeled down beside the bed as he continued to hold onto Johnnie Mae's hand. "Lord, Your Word says we will be able to lay hands on the sick, and they *will* recover. Your Word says, when we pray, we should believe that we have received. *When* we pray, that's what Your Word declares. I have prayed, I've delighted myself in You, regardless of what things have looked like. I now believe I *have* received the desires of my heart! I thank You. Thank You, Jesus."

Suddenly, Landris felt a slight squeeze to his hand. He stopped, wondering if it had just been his mind playing tricks on him or merely some type of involuntary movement. He stood and stared at Johnnie Mae, trying to see if what he thought had actually occurred, in fact had. "Look. Did you see that?" Landris asked Jackie. He leaned closer. "Johnnie Mae, open your eyes," he said. "Johnnie Mae, I need you to open your eyes. Come on now. In the name of Jesus, I command you to open your eyes!"

Landris could see it. As he stood there watching her, Johnnie Mae looked like she was definitely struggling to open her eyes.

"We need a doctor here," Landris said, controlling his tone so as not to be too loud, as he glanced at Jackie, who was already on her way out the door. Quickly, his attention returned to Johnnie Mae's face. "Come on, baby. Come on. You can do this. I'm right here. Come on, now. Open your eyes."

Johnnie Mae squeezed his hand a little again. Then, just as a butterfly's wings flutter before the butterfly takes flight and flies away, Johnnie Mae opened her eyes. She looked at him and struggled to reach up, as though she was trying to touch his face. Then, there it was: a tiny smile crossed her face for her beloved.

"Landris," she mouthed his name.

Chapter 51

Even every one that is called by My name: for I have created him for My glory, I have formed him; yea, I have made him.

Isaiah 43:7

Johnnie Mae recovered rapidly following that fateful, faith-full night. It was amazing to all just how quickly. To take some of the miracle buzz making its rounds throughout the hospital away, a few of the doctors who'd declared hope was all but gone reported that it wasn't at all uncommon for someone to come out of coma, even years later, to a full recovery. Johnnie Mae had no damage whatsoever to any part of her body. Her heart was good, her brain was fine, and she hadn't suffered a stroke, which had been a major concern. The next day, she was moved to a different floor.

A nurse stuck her head inside the door of Johnnie Mae's room. "We have a surprise for you," she said as the door opened wider. And there, in a special incubator crib, was Johnnie Mae and Landris's baby boy. Landris, who had opened the door for them, came in behind them.

Seeing her son, Johnnie Mae placed her hands over her mouth and began to cry.

"Oh, please don't cry," the nurse said. "This little fellow has waited a long time, a whole month, to meet you. We even put him in a special little doodad," she said, referring to his blue hooded outfit, "especially for this first meeting."

The nurse gave Johnnie Mae something to sanitize her hands. Then she carefully took the baby out. "Mommy, he's doing so good," the nurse said. "From what I hear from Daddy, the doctors say if the two of you continue improving like you're doing, you both may be going home close to the same time." She placed the baby in Johnnie Mae's awaiting arms.

"Only one thing," the nurse continued as she released him into Johnnie Mae's care, "I believe he *might* be getting a small complex. See, all the other babies have names, and, as you can tell, his placard still says 'Boy Landris.' Now, Mommy, I've been told we've been waiting on you to give this little jewel a name." She looked at Landris and grinned.

Johnnie Mae couldn't take her eyes off her son. "He's beautiful! Oh, Landris, look at him. Isn't he beautiful?"

"Oh, you should have seen him before we started him on that workout routine," Landris said. "The doctors and nurses had their routine for him to do, and I had mine."

"Workout routine?" Johnnie Mae asked, looking to Landris for a better explanation.

"Yeah, workout routine," Landris said. "His faith workouts. He and I have been lifting the Word of God, getting all fit and in shape, like nobody's business. Go ahead—ask him about a scripture. Any scripture. He can probably tell you chapter and verse for some of them." Landris grinned. Seeing his wife and baby son in tandem, he thought how perfect they looked together. He took out his cell phone and, using the camera feature, quickly snapped their picture.

"Landris, don't be doing that," Johnnie Mae said, smoothing down her hair with her hand. "I know I look a hot mess . . . like death warmed-over right now. My hair grew out, while you—on the other hand—went and cut yours completely off. I still can't believe you did that." She looked at his low-cut hairstyle and smiled. "But I like it."

"What did you just say?" the nurse asked Johnnie Mae. "A hot mess? Death warmed-over? I've heard a lot in my day, but I can't say I've ever quite heard it put like *that* before. And if you ask me, I don't see anything wrong with either of your hair. But then again, I'm a red-headed white woman who has trouble deciding whether to part or not to part my hair, and if so, which side, so what do I know?"

"Johnnie Mae, you look beautiful," Landris said, handing his phone to the nurse. "Will you do us the honors of taking our very first family photo, please?" He stepped over next to Johnnie Mae and placed his face against hers. "Say cheese, baby Landris," Landris said.

"Isaiah," Johnnie Mae said.

Landris turned to her. "What?" he said, just as the camera snapped.

"Oh, you moved," the nurse said to Landris. "Now we'll have to take it again." She held the camera up once more. "Okay, ready this time? On the count of three. One, two, three." She snapped it again, then looked at the screen. "Oh, that's a good one!"

"Isaiah," Johnnie Mae said, looking from her son's face to her husband's. "I'd like to name him Isaiah." She then directed her attention exclusively to Landris. "Will you be terribly disappointed . . . I mean, if he's not a junior or the second?"

"Honestly, I'm just grateful to God that Isaiah is finally in his mother's arms."

The nurse handed Landris his phone. She pulled a clipboardlike holder from below the portable crib. "Middle name?" she asked. "Little Isaiah here needs a middle name. If you'll give that to me, then we can finish this form for his birth certificate, you two can sign it, and we can get this baby filed with the State of Alabama and make his name official."

Johnnie Mae looked up at Landris. "Do you have any preferences for a middle name? Any ideas?"

Landris looked at her, then the baby. "You and I were tossing around a few names at one time, remember? I just don't know."

"Well, you can think about it and let us know later," the nurse said. "Someone from the business office usually gets this information. They asked me because they knew I was coming in. Someone can come back and get his middle name later."

"How about Barron Edward?" Landris asked.

"What are you saying? You don't like the name Isaiah?" Johnnie Mae asked.

"No. I mean, no, that's not what I'm saying. Isaiah is a great name. In fact, I've been studying the book of Isaiah these past few weeks. I read passages to you while you were in that coma. What I mean is . . . let's name him Isaiah Barron Edward Landris."

"Four names?" Johnnie Mae said. "Can we do that on a birth certificate?" She looked to the nurse for an answer.

"Sure," the nurse said, looking at the form. "There's nothing that says you can't."

"Isaiah Barron Edward Landris," Johnnie Mae said, repeating it several times. "Oh, I love that! It's so strong." She touched her baby's tiny arm. "What do you think, Isaiah?"

"Well, not that I count, but I love it, too," the nurse said as she wrote it down and handed the board to Landris. "If you two will look that over, be sure everything's correct, then sign it, you'll be all done with giving this precious, precious baby a name that I'm sure all the other babies will be envious of when he returns." She smiled. "Now, don't you go in there telling the other babies I said that, either," she said to Isaiah as she winked. She went over to the wall and pressed the bottle to apply sanitizer to her hands.

"Okay, I have to get little Isaiah back to his temporary place of residence," the nurse said, reaching out for him and taking him out of a reluctant Johnnie Mae's arms. "He's still lifting his weights, as Daddy put it, so he can continue growing better and bigger and stronger. Aren't you, little fellow?" the nurse said in a baby-friendly voice to Isaiah. "We don't want to tire him out too much, especially on his first official day out to see you, now, do we?" she said, again saying that last part using a baby-friendly voice.

Landris and Johnnie Mae signed the form as the nurse carefully placed Isaiah back inside his portable crib. Landris handed the clipboard, with the signed paper, back to the nurse.

"When can I see him again?" Johnnie Mae asked.

"Don't worry," Landris said, "I'll take you in to see him whenever you want. Just as long as you promise me you won't try and overdo things. You're still recovering, you know?"

The nurse pushed Isaiah's crib to the door. "Tell Mommy and Daddy bye-bye," the nurse said as she stood waving. "Say 'Bye-bye, Mommy. . . . Bye-bye, Daddy. I'll see you later,' " she said, mimicking the way Isaiah would probably say it if he could talk.

"See you later, Isaiah," Johnnie Mae said as she blew him butterfly kisses. "Bye-bye. . . . Mommy loves you. Bye." She waved until he was gone. She looked at Landris, rubbed his hair on one side of his head, lovingly caressed his face, then began to cry.

He held her in his arms. "I know, baby. I love you," he said. "Truly, I do."

Chapter 52

Declaring the end from the beginning, and from ancient times the things that are not yet done, saying, My counsel shall stand, and I will do all My pleasure. . . .

Isaiah 46:10

It was the last day of August 2005, and Gayle stood before those in attendance at the reading of Sarah Elaine Fleming's last will and testament to say a few words.

"Miss Fleming asked me, a few months after I came to work for her, if I would consider being the executor of her will," Gayle began. "I told her that I knew nothing about doing anything like that. She assured me that her lawyer"—she nodded to acknowledge Lance Seymour—"would handle all relevant details, and all I would need do was to carry out certain wishes and duties associated with it as requested or required."

Gayle took two steps to her right. "I, like all of you here today, will truly miss Sarah Fleming. Miss Fleming was more than someone I took care of medically, more like a beloved family matriarch than an employer. One of the most joyous occasions I've ever been blessed to have been a part of was this past June when we came together and celebrated Christmas in what some would call out-of-season. As those of us who attended know, it was very much *in* season and very much on time. Who knew that would be her last Christmas celebration? It was indeed Miss Fleming making her exit on her own terms. She almost reached her ninetieth birthday, but that was not to be. She taught us to live in the now and to celebrate each moment as though it were our last. In truth, none of us really know when our last day will be." Gayle nodded as she pursed her lips.

"Most of her wishes are self-explanatory," Gayle said. "I'm sure with some things, you may have questions about why things were done the way they were, or what she may have intended. I'll do my best to answer any questions I'm asked, as best I can. But I can only relay to you what she told me. That being said, I'll turn the actual reading of the will back into the capable hands of her lawyer and good friend, Mr. Lance Seymour."

After the reading was over, Memory sat there utterly stunned. Gayle had been correct about most things not needing to be explained. But there were a few things, not actually regarding the will, she wanted to know for herself.

Memory pulled Gayle off to the side. "May we talk?" she asked.

Gayle smiled. "Sure. Let's go find a room where we can have some privacy."

They went down the hall of Mr. Seymour's place, a once-quaint house now converted into an office building, and found a small room with a couch. Gayle closed the door once they were inside, and they sat down.

Memory bit down on her bottom lip, then pressed her lips together. "My mother was more than generous to me in her will. Frankly, I'm still taken aback by the vastness of her wealth. She was quite charitable to many. Having known her, even for just that short time, I learned the type of person she was. She was truly a remarkable and caring person. I am curious, though, as to how you managed to be chosen as the executor of her will. Listen, I don't know how to say it except to just say it," Memory said.

Memory folded her hands, then placed them in her lap. "Gayle, something, quite frankly, isn't adding up for me about you. You see, twice, once before the Christmas celebration, and then again just before my mother died, I heard you on the phone talking to Montgomery. I know it was him because I overheard you address him by his name both times. I had fully intended to talk with you about that, after the celebration was over, but I wanted to put some distance between such a joyous occasion, and what I knew could potentially turn into an all-out war in the house if things went badly."

Memory looked down at her hands, then back up. "She and I were in her room talking. We were eating chocolate cake. You of all people knew how much she loved chocolate. We were really bonding, having a great time together. She was laughing, then suddenly she got quiet. I thought she'd fallen asleep. Just that fast, she was gone."

Gayle looked at Memory. She tilted her head to the side. "You really *do* favor her. . . . Your mother. You favor her a lot. Especially your eyes. You have her eyes." Gayle smiled. "Memory, there's something I want to tell you. Your mother asked me not to let you or Lena know this originally, but a few days before the Christmas celebration, she said it was okay to tell you anything I felt I needed to. Sarah knew I had talked to Montgomery those days and all the other times before that. In fact, my talking and dealing with him was all her idea."

Memory chuckled. "Gayle, now I *was* born during the day, but let me assure you, it wasn't yesterday. You're going to have to do a lot better than that to pull one over on an old pro like me. Now, it's my understanding that Montgomery, as well as his father before him, did a lot of damage to my mother's life. It was because of their actions that we were both robbed of precious time together. So why would my mother have you talking to the likes of Montgomery at all?"

"It's true, Montgomery did do a lot of damage. Which is why, when I came to work for Sarah, she devised a plan for us to ensure he would never get a foothold or gain that much power over her, her children, or her children's children ever again. Those were her exact words."

"How do I know that you weren't just playing her?" Memory asked. "What if you merely took advantage of an elderly woman like so many others have done in the past? Look, I've done my share of getting-close-and-doing-people-in in my lifetime. I know how this works. This would have been a sweet gig for you—money, power, and wealth, all rolled up into one."

"Memory, your mother trusted me. She trusted me with her life. What you don't know is that the legendary Pearl Black was my grandmother. Her last name was Williams after she married, but most folk still called her Pearl Black. Before my grandmother died, she told me the story of Sarah and her child—that would be you. She'd heard from a woman named Johnnie Mae Landris—I know you're familiar with her—that your mother was possibly still alive. She knew for a fact that unless you'd died after you were with the Pattersons, you were still alive. She told me if there was ever a time where I found I could make things right for Sarah Fleming, she wanted me to do it. I made her a promise that I would. In fact, my grandmother made me promise her two things on that day. So when Sarah needed a home-nurse, I applied for the job. Her lawyer, Mr. Seymour, didn't play when it came to Miss Fleming, especially in the early days when everyone was looking for Montgomery to retaliate in some way. Mr. Seymour and his people did all kinds of background checks on me, both officially and unofficially."

"I'm sorry, but I'm not familiar with Pearl Black. . . ." Memory paused. "Wait a minute. Pearl Black, that was the woman Grace spoke about on the videotape—you mean, that Pearl Black?"

Lena opened the door and stuck her head inside. "I'm sorry. I don't mean to interrupt, but we were worried about you," she said to Memory. "I really wasn't trying to eavesdrop, but did I just hear y'all saying something about Pearl Black?"

"Yes, I just told Memory that Pearl Black was actually my grandmother," Gayle said.

Lena looked shocked. "Pearl Black was your grandmother?"

"Yes. Please come in and sit while I finish the story," Gayle said. "This will save me from having to repeat it to you later, Lena." Gayle scooted over so there would be room for Lena to sit next to Memory.

"As I was telling Memory, Pearl Black was my grandmother," Gayle said, continuing. "I came to work for Miss Fleming at the end of October 2001. And yes, Miss Fleming told me everything, so I know you're familiar with Pearl Black, as well as her significance to your family," Gayle said, addressing Lena at this time.

"I was up front with Miss Fleming from the start about who I was," Gayle said. "Still, Mr. Seymour checked me, and my story about who I was, out thoroughly. As I was just telling Memory, when it came to Miss Fleming, Lance Seymour was always superprotective. I told Miss Fleming all that my grandmother, Pearl, had told me before she died." Gayle then repeated all she'd said that Lena had previously missed.

"Miss Fleming decided to keep who I was a secret from everyone, including her family," Gayle said. "When a man like Montgomery Powell the Second is involved, you can never be too careful."

"I'm sitting here wondering why Grandmother never

told us any of this," Lena said. "She knew I was familiar with Pearl Black. In all these years, she could have mentioned *something* to *me. Something*."

"I can't answer that question, but when Montgomery learned I was employed as Miss Fleming's personal private home-nurse," Gayle said, "as expected, he wasted no time in contacting me and making me a lucrative offer. I listened to what he had to say, then told Miss Fleming everything. She was the one who came up with the plan."

"What plan?" Memory asked.

"That I would keep my identity from everyone including her family and close friends, that I would keep a low profile so as not to draw attention to myself, and that I would not only *talk* to Montgomery but agree to cooperate with him as much as possible. I would essentially be like a double agent."

"So Montgomery wanted you to spy on Grandmother?" Lena asked.

"Yes. He wanted to know everything he could about her intentions, who she talked with, who she visited, who visited her, who she trusted—"

"Who was in her will when it came to her house," Memory said.

"Exactly. Things like that." Gayle stood up and began pacing as she spoke. "Miss Fleming always told me what to tell him. I quickly gained his trust as a reliable informant, just as she'd planned. Even at almost ninety, Miss Fleming was truly a sharp lady, sharper than most that are a third her age."

"So you were the one who told Montgomery about the problems between me, Lena, and Theresa?" Memory asked.

"Yes. I told him about your having taken the Alexandrite necklace from them, which, as it turns out, was like he'd hit the jackpot. He had the necklace, which neither of us knew at the time. He was ecstatic, thinking things were finally 'falling into place perfectly,' as he put it."

" 'Falling into place' because he had been the one to pay the reward for the Alexandrite necklace that caused me to go searching for Lena in order to get it back in the first place," Memory said.

"Yes. But that wasn't part of the plan," Gayle said. "He'd gotten the necklace back before things turned around so badly for him when Miss Fleming returned to the Fleming mansion and took possession of it. Originally, he wanted the necklace because it was part of the family's legacy . . . a family heirloom."

"A family heirloom he obviously didn't have a problem letting go of when it suited his needs," Memory said, referring to how he was willing to trade the necklace for her promise to sell him the house.

"Knowing that the necklace had caused such a rift in your relationship with your child and grandchild fit right into his new plan," Gayle said, standing in front of them. "I'm not implying, by any means, that he shared his thoughts and plans with me. But when things are going well for Montgomery, there's a certain gleam in his eyes, and he *loves* to brag."

"But why would you tell him we were having problems?" Lena asked. "Didn't you know he would use it to try and destroy us if he could?"

Gayle looked more at Lena as she answered her. "My instructions from Miss Fleming were to do whatever it took to make him believe I was on his side. As long as Montgomery trusted me, he would be satisfied with coming to me for information he needed inside the house. That always provided Miss Fleming with a heads-up. I had no way of knowing he had that necklace in his possession to be able to use against you. I could never have guessed that."

"So you were the one who took the necklace and the Wings of Grace box out of Lena's room that night?" Memory asked, sitting back against the couch.

Gayle shook her head. "No, it wasn't me."

"Then who was it, and how did Grandmother get it back?" Lena asked.

"It was her friend Polly. We had suspected Polly might be playing both sides, but we weren't positive how much she was, if she was. Miss Fleming never told me this, but I believe Polly purposely sought her out to befriend her. Although I will say that after Polly spent time with Miss Fleming and got to really know her, she genuinely did care about her. I'm certain that couldn't have done anything except complicate whatever deal she may have had with Montgomery."

"That makes no sense," Memory said. "I don't understand. How could Polly have gotten the necklace and the box? She wasn't anywhere around when it came up missing."

"Polly had a key to the house. Miss Fleming trusted her that much, in spite of her suspicions about her and her loyalty. Miss Fleming learned from Mr. Seymour's people that Polly knew Montgomery well. They happened to roll in the same circles. When Miss Fleming got sick that Saturday and was taken to the hospital, I called Polly to let her know. From what Miss Fleming told me after she learned the truth, Polly came in right before your husband"—Gayle looked at Lena—"came in from playing golf. She saw the necklace and the box on the bed, when she heard someone enter the house. She took the necklace, put it in the box, and left your bedroom. She went to Miss Fleming's bedroom, feeling she'd have an easier time explaining being in there if she got caught."

"I still don't understand. Did she take the box and necklace home? Did she give it to Montgomery?" Memory asked. "What did she do?"

"Fortunately for y'all, she hid it under Miss Fleming's bed with plans to get it later," Gayle said. "And that's where I found them. Actually, it was Miss Fleming who figured all this out and told me where to find them."

"So why didn't she tell us?" Lena asked. "She knew we were trying to find out who took those things. We even questioned you, Gayle."

"Miss Fleming believed deep down Polly was still a good woman. Polly had made a mistake by getting in bed with Montgomery, and I mean that both figuratively and literally. But Miss Fleming cared very much for her. Polly and Miss Fleming had shared lots of great and memorable times together. She was never one to just throw love she had for a person away merely because things had gone badly."

"So that's why she left that brooch to Polly in her will?" Lena said, happy that some things were starting to make a little more sense. "Grandmother took the brooch out and showed it to me right before the Christmas celebration. She told me how much Polly adored it, and just how much it was worth," Lena said. "She was planning on giving it to Polly as a present during our Christmas in June festivity. A festivity Polly was noticeably absent from. Now we know why."

Lance Seymour knocked, then opened the door when he was told to come in. "We were wondering where y'all went. You gals all right in here?" he asked with his deep, pure, unadulterated Southern drawl.

Gayle smiled. "Yes, we're fine."

Lena stood up. "I need to go find Theresa and Richard. I'm sure they're probably wondering if I got lost when I came looking for you. It's getting late. I know everyone's ready to get on home."

Memory nodded as she slowly stood up. Lance and Lena left together. Memory and Gayle stayed behind a few minutes longer.

"I want to thank you for all you did for my mother," Memory said.

"Memory, your mother was truly one in a million," Gayle said. "She loved you more than you'll ever know. I'm going to miss her—truly, I am. But she certainly surprised me leaving me that one hundred thousand dollars in her will. I had no idea she was doing anything like that. No idea. This shows how much executors really know."

"Yes, she was a special woman. I only wish I'd gotten to spend more time with her. That's the tragedy of all of this. But I do love how she put the house in a trust for Theresa's children. Now, that was a real classy move." Memory laughed. "Especially in light of Montgomery's plans to try and get that house. Checkmate!" Memory shook her head as she smiled, looked down, then back up. "So, what are your plans now?"

Gayle shrugged. "I told you earlier how I'd promised my grandmother two things. One, if I ever got the chance to do right by Sarah Fleming, I would. Well, I've accomplished that. Seeing all of you together is such a fantastic feeling. The other thing my grandmother asked me to do was to see if I could locate her oldest daughter, Arletha. I doubt she's still living, but I promised my grandmother I would at least find out what happened to her."

Memory laughed. "That's funny. I met a woman named Arletha a few months back. Arletha Brown is her name. Maybe this woman is the person you're looking for. Arletha is not a common name at all. This woman I met lives in Birmingham, Alabama."

"Interesting. I have a second cousin who moved to Birmingham a few years back. Her name is Angela Gabriel. We call her Angel. She's a member of Pastor Landris's church. You wouldn't happen to know her, would you?"

"No, I can't say our paths have ever crossed," Memory said.

"Angel's mother was Rebecca. She died when Angel was about five years old. My grandmother, Pearl Black, was the one who raised her. Arletha happens to be Rebecca's mother. Until just before my grandmother died, no one—including my grandmother—hardly ever spoke of Arletha or mentioned her name. My grandmother is the reason I ended up moving to Asheville. I came to see her before she died. After she passed away, Angel wanted to pursue a job opportunity in Birmingham. Grandmother's house would have been sitting there empty unless the family decided to rent it out. The thought of strangers in her house, not taking care of it . . . I just couldn't see that. So I bought my grandmother's house and moved in. I'm pretty sure the woman you met can't be my great-aunt," Gayle said as she glanced at her watch, then started for the door. "That would just be *too* easy. Nothing's ever *that* easy."

She and Memory walked out of the door. "Honestly," Gayle said, "I doubt Arletha is even still alive. According to my grandmother, she's been gone for almost fifty years now, by last count. And she never came home to see Grandmother in all of those years. Not once. I can't imagine—I don't care what might have happened—a daughter not *ever* going home to see her mother. Not ever? I do know there was a huge falling out that occurred between them. All Grandmother said was that her daughter was prostituting her body and being loose throughout the neighborhood. She wasn't about to have any daughter of hers acting like a tramp. Not while she was alive and breathing and could do something about it. She told me she even went as far as to disown her. So Arletha left one day, without a word, a good-bye, or anything else. Grandmother said she never heard from her again. She most likely married, so her last name would be different, which always makes a search that much more difficult."

"Well, like I said, Arletha is not a common name. There's no harm in checking out this woman I met. But there's no way the person you just described could be this lady. I rented a room from her for a few weeks. She is super-religious and very judgmental, especially of sinners. But I'll be happy to give you her phone number and address. If it's not her, at least you can scratch her name off your list."

"That sounds great," Gayle said. "Give me her information, and I'll check her out. My cousin, Angel, the one I was just telling you about, is getting married October fifteenth in what my mother claims will be the wedding to top all weddings, at least for our family. I'm going, so I'll be in Birmingham in a few months. Maybe I'll call this woman and see where it leads, although I'm not going to get my hopes up. Still, I promised my grandmother I would try. That's all I can do."

"Maybe you can get your cousin to do some legwork for you since she lives in Birmingham. She could go check out Arletha Brown for you."

"My grandmother specifically asked me not to tell Angel anything unless or until I find Arletha." They reached the lobby area and could see the rest of the family was there waiting for Memory.

Gayle stopped walking so their conversation could remain out of earshot. "As I said, my grandmother or others in the family never spoke of Arletha, so Angel is limited in what she knows. If I bring this up without having found Arletha, it will just open up a can of worms none of us need or want right now. I suppose that's why Grandmother asked me to do this instead of involving Angel. Between me and you . . . my grandmother always favored Angel over all her children, grandchildren, and great-grandchildren. I'm not jealous, though. There's always seemingly a favored one in every family. My grandmother was extremely protective of Angel when she was alive. They were close."

"I understand," Memory said, looking in her pocketbook for a pen and a piece of paper to write down Arletha's phone number and address. She handed the information to Gayle. "In a way, I kind of hope this is what you're looking for. Although I'm not sure that after you meet the Arletha I knew whether you'll believe it to be a blessing or a curse. But at least if this turns out to be her, you would have kept yet another promise to your grandmother."

Gayle took the paper, looked at it, and carefully placed it in the side pocket of her purse.

"If you'll permit me," Memory said, "I'd like to give you a word of advice. This comes from personal experience. I believe it's always better to learn from someone else's bad experiences as opposed to having to always learn from your own. Secrets like these always have a way of coming back to haunt folks. Secrets can rob, and secrets can destroy. If I were you, I'd tell Angel what's going on, even if you never find her grandmother." Memory changed her purse to hang from her other shoulder.

"Personally," Memory continued, "I believe your cousin has a right to know. If I could go back and do things over in my life, there are so many things I would do differently. One thing, I never would have left Mamie Patterson's house the way I did. And I wouldn't have ever taken that necklace from Lena and Theresa. Then I may have learned about Sarah that much earlier, and who knows how much more time she and I might have had together. If only things had been done differently. But you can't go back and change things. So take heed to the counsel of one who knows from firsthand experience. It will be better, for all around, to be up front now. Allow my life to serve you in making a better choice as you proceed."

"I'll take those words under advisement," Gayle said. She and Memory hugged. Then Gayle walked over to the others and said her good-byes to them.

Gayle's job was done. It was now time for her to move on to other things.

Chapter 53

Wherefore comfort one another with these words.

1 Thessalonians 4:18

"In loving memory, the Harris family," the tall, lanky woman said, standing before an overflowing congregation, reading a pledge given, in lieu of flowers, of one thousand dollars toward a newly established scholarship created to bless deserving young people.

Because of her death, people were praying mightily for Pastor Landris. Many speculated as to how he could possibly preach a funeral for one so close and dear to his heart. They'd heard the explanation of why he said he *had* to do it. "It's what she would have wanted," he had said. He was laying aside his own grief and pressing toward the mark of a higher calling in Christ Jesus, just as he'd been anointed and appointed by God to do.

Still, there were plenty that doubted he'd be able to do this without breaking down.

A collective stillness swept over the congregation when he rose to speak. The white casket below was a blanket of beautiful white roses. Landris had truly spared no expense when it came to her. There was nothing more he could do to show his love for her on this side. This time of speaking would be to comfort and minister to those grieving the loss of a loved one or those who would lose a loved one in the future. He needed to tell those who might not know Jesus Christ all about His mercy that endures forever. He wanted to tell them what Jesus has already done to ensure the salvation of those who choose to accept Him as their Lord and Savior.

Landris would never be able to fully explain to anyone exactly why things had happened the way that they had. Yes, she *was* doing well. She had been through a lot, but she had also made it through. In truth, no one expected her to die—not now, anyway. Not when everything was going so wonderfully in her life. It had truly come as a shock.

Isaiah Barron Edward Landris had come home to a grand homecoming. Landris could be thankful and comforted in knowing that she'd at least gotten to spend time with Isaiah before she died. There were still many who questioned why God would allow this to happen. But Landris refused to be dragged into that conversation or speculation. He thanked God for the time she *did* have and for the precious moments she'd gotten to spend with her family prior to this tragedy happening. Landris thanked God for how He had allowed her to see and hold Isaiah. He thanked God for the memories he would forever cherish in his heart of her. Memories he would share with his son one day. Pictures that would forever be embedded, in loving memory, inside of him of her holding Isaiah in her arms . . . flooding his little face with kisses while proudly beaming.

Instead, Landris directed others to begin looking at what they have to be thankful for instead of always focusing on what's lost or what will never be experienced.

"Regardless of what happens," Landris had said, "God is *still* God, and He's *still* worthy to be praised."

He stood before a packed building—a magnificent edifice she'd reverently sat in, in awe of God's power, the day they had officially moved in it as a congregation—now to preach her funeral. There were so many who had come to show their love, support, respect, and to say good-bye. For a brief moment, his eyes rested on Princess Rose as she sat next to Johnnie Mae's mother and his heart couldn't help but go out to her.

"If you will, please open your Bibles to First Thessalonians chapter four, beginning at verse thirteen," Landris said, then waited as the congregation complied. "I want you all to understand that, although we *will* miss her"—he paused, composed himself, and nodded—"and I personally will miss her greatly, this is not a sad occasion. This is a celebration of the life of one who was loved and, to some, adored. This is a celebration for one who has gone home to be with the Lord. We know this is not our home. We didn't come here to stay. We're merely strangers passing through for a few seasons. And although she may have moved out of this earthly vessel, she's not really gone; she simply changed her address. As the apostle Paul so aptly declared, to be absent from the body is to be present with the Lord. She's with the Lord now. In truth, she's in a much better place than even we who remain are, because she *is* with the Lord."

Landris looked down at his Bible. "First Thessalonians four-thirteen says, 'But I would not have you to be ignorant, brethrèn, concerning them which are asleep, that ye sorrow not, even as others which have no hope.' Now, if I didn't read anything more, that Word right there should minister to someone. Our loved ones, who were in the Lord and have gone on, are not dead; they're merely asleep. 'For if we believe that Jesus died and rose again, even so them also which sleep in Jesus will God bring with Him.' Is anybody really seeing what's here? This scripture specifically addresses those who are saved, with salvation being the confession of sins and the belief that Jesus died and rose again. They are the ones who sleep in Jesus—those who are saved. This scripture assures us that God will bring those who are asleep in Jesus with Him. Oh, somebody ought to give God some praise right about now," Landris said.

"Glory! Hallelujah!" people began to cry out along with other words of praise.

"That's right," Landris said. "This is something to be excited about. Verse fifteen goes on to say, 'For this we say unto you by the word of the Lord, that we which are alive and remain unto the coming of the Lord shall not prevent them which are asleep.' Verse sixteen, 'For the Lord himself shall descend from heaven with a shout—'"

"Glory! Hallelujah! Thank You, Jesus," the people said, interrupting him with shouts of praise.

Landris continued. " 'For the Lord Himself shall descend from heaven with a shout, with the voice of the archangel, and with the trump of God: and the dead in Christ shall rise first: Then we which are alive and remain shall be caught up together . . .' " He emphasized the words "caught up" and paused as he raised his fist in the air, fighting hard not to cry. "If we're not asleep, so to speak, and we're here when Jesus comes back, we're going to be *caught up* together with them"—he looked back down at the scripture, blinking back the tears that tried to blur his vision, and continued reading—" 'in the clouds, to meet the Lord in the air: and so shall we ever be with the Lord.'" Landris couldn't hold back. He began jumping up and down. He praised God like he had never praised Him before. He couldn't stop the tears that now freely flowed down his face. "God is good!" he shouted. "God is good! I don't care what's going on in your life, God is *still* good, and He is worthy to be praised! She was saved, and now she's with the Lord! I'm saved! Jesus saved me! Oh, it's *good* to be saved! This is not the end here! When we come to this place in life, this is not the end! God is so good! This is *not* the end of the story!"

The entire congregation was now on its feet, shouting and praising God. They shouted for at least ten minutes.

"If you're here today and you're not saved, or you've backslidden and you want to be restored . . . if you want to get back right with God, then will you come today and give your heart . . . give your life to Jesus? The Bible tells us that Jesus left the riches of Heaven and came down to earth. He walked on this earth, showing us how to live, move, and have our being. He was nailed to a cross, not for anything He'd done. He was crucified for our sins. Our sins. Jesus paid the price for you to have salvation. Freely He has given, freely you can receive. Don't allow the payment Jesus paid for your sins to be in vain. But to receive it, you must come to Him."

Landris stepped up to the edge of the stage. "Whosoever will, won't you come? My intent is not to cause an emotional decision about something this important during a time like this. But I have to put the information out there and give an invitation to come to Jesus because it *is* that important. I want you to meet me in Heaven.

"So every time I get the opportunity, I want to share the message of Jesus so someone who may not know Jesus will be able to hear about Him and accept Him. I'd really love to see everyone here at the gathering that will be in Heaven. And what a day that's going to be. I care about your salvation. God cares, and He doesn't want anyone to perish. There's no reason to. Jesus went to prepare a place for us. And they tell me that the wicked shall cease from troubling there. They say the weary will be at rest. Me, I just want to see Jesus. I want to see Him, face to face. And I won't waste time telling Him what folks did to me down here. He knows, He knows. I just want to walk and talk with Him in Heaven. I want to be in His presence. Do you want to ensure that your name is written in the Book of Life? Then come." Landris spread out his arms as he'd done so many times before.

And people did come. The ushers had them line up in the aisles. After those who were interested were in lines, they were led off to a prayer room to receive salvation or pray for restoration as needed.

The choir began to sing "When We All Get to Heaven."

Landris stepped down and walked over to the casket. "I love you," he whispered, as he kissed two fingers and touched the casket. "See you in Heaven," he said.

The pallbearers came forward to carry the casket out. Landris went to the front row where his family was and hugged his brother, Thomas.

"That was beautiful, George." Thomas gave Landris a long, brotherly embrace. "I don't know how you were able to do that. I know I couldn't have done it. But you did a wonderful job. I know she's looking down, and she is *so* proud of you. I just know that she is."

Landris nodded. He was so full now, he couldn't say anything. He left Thomas and walked over to get the baby. "Come on, Isaiah," he said. "Daddy's got you. Just like God has us safely in His arms, Daddy has you safely in his."

"You did good," Johnnie Mae said as she touched his arm once he had the baby securely on his shoulder. "I know God is pleased. You did what He's called you to do, in season and out of season. Many lives have been changed today. I am so proud of you right now. I know your mother is proud."

Johnnie Mae thought back on all that had happened over the past few months. She'd had a son prematurely. They both had almost died. But against all the odds,

God had brought them through. What a testimony they had to share with the world. Still, she thought of those who had died: Reverend Knight, Sarah Fleming, and now Landris and Thomas's mother, Virginia LeBoeuf. Three people she'd known personally, all within months of each other. She'd often heard her mother say that death seemed to always come in threes. She'd never really taken that statement much to heart. Nonetheless, there was no denying that three people she knew had transitioned. And because they were saved, she could rejoice knowing that they were now . . . present with the Lord.

Landris couldn't help but think about how his mother had come to Birmingham some three months ago expressly to support her family. He thought about how she'd been there when he and Johnnie Mae had needed her the most. How she'd taken care of Princess Rose and was right there when a healthy Isaiah Barron Edward Landris was finally released to come home. *What a day of rejoicing that day was!*

His mother had stayed a month longer, simply because she couldn't pull herself away from her grandchild when he came home. In fact, she was looking for a house to purchase. She was planning to move to Birmingham. She'd assured Landris she would be spoiling Isaiah; she'd already begun making good on her promise.

Then she went back to her own house, opting to have her bypass surgery there if it was still even needed. Landris and Thomas both insisted she could have the surgery in Birmingham, where all of her family already was. Everybody knew that UAB Hospital was world-renown for just that type of surgery. But she opted to go home anyway. She wanted to use the doctor she'd started out with when her heart problem first emerged. All of her records were there. It would just be easier, with less complications, to go home, and if the surgery was still needed, to have it there. Her doctor said she should have the surgery.

So Landris and Johnnie Mae packed up the family, including Thomas, and they went to be there for her the way she'd been there for them. She kept insisting she'd be fine. She had lots of friends and some family around who would gladly come by, check on her, and take care of her if she needed them to. She didn't want them leaving their home to come be with her, not now, not after all they'd been through. "Isaiah just got home. You guys have been through a lot. Spend this time with each other. I'll be back to Birmingham before you know it," Virginia had said.

But Landris wasn't hearing it, and neither was Johnnie Mae. Virginia had been there for them; now it was their turn to be there for her.

Virginia's doctor advised her she should have the surgery even though there were some noticeable improvements in her heart condition. So she consented to the surgery. She went into the operating room and suffered a heart attack during surgery. The doctors tried desperately, thirty minutes or so, to revive her. It was to no avail.

She died on the table.

Johnnie Mae put her arm around Landris as they walked behind the casket and behind Minister Maxwell, who led the recessional out of the church.

When they were about to get into the car to go to the cemetery, Landris leaned over and whispered, "I love you, Johnnie Mae. I really do."

She looked at him, took her thumb, wiped away the tears that rolled down his face, and, with a smile, she said, "I know." She wiped his tears once more, then wiped her own, and said, "I know."

The newest member of Pastor George Landris's church stirs up more troubles than blessings when he decides to rededicate his life to God in . . .

The Truth Is the Light
by Vanessa Davis Griggs

Here's an excerpt from *The Truth Is the Light* . . .

Chapter 1

The stone which the builders refused
is become the head stone of the corner.
—Psalms 118:22

"Crown me!" said the ninety-nine-year-old, dark-chocolate-skinned man, who didn't look a day over seventy. He sat back against the flowery-cushioned chair and folded his arms, all while displaying a playful grin.

"Crown you?" said a thirty-five-year-old with matching skin tone, who resembled a slimmed-down teddy bear. Shaking his head, he mirrored the old man's grin. "*Crown* you?"

"That's what I said. So quit stalling and get to crowning me."

The younger man first started to chuckle before it turned into a refrained laugh. "Gramps, I've told you twice already: we're playing chess, not checkers. The rules are different. There's no crowning a piece when it reaches the other side, not in chess."

"You say that there is my queen, right?" Gramps touched the game piece that represented his queen.

"Yes."

"Well, if there's a queen, then there's *got* to be a king with some real power a lot closer and, frankly, better than this joker here." He touched his king. "So quit bumping your gums and crown me so I can get some real help in protecting my queen." Gramps nodded as he grinned at his favorite grandson, proudly displaying his new set of dentures.

Clarence Walker couldn't do anything but smile and shake his head in both amusement and adoration. "I've told you. Because there's already a king on the board"—he pointed to the king—"we don't crown in chess. Just admit it. You don't really want to learn how to play chess, do you? That's why you're acting this way."

"I tried to tell you from the git-go that I'm a checkers man and strictly a checkers man. When you get my age, it's hard for an old dog to learn new tricks. I know how to fetch. I know how to roll over and even play dead. But all this fancy stuff like walking on your hind legs and twirling around . . . Well, you can take that to some young pup eager to learn. Teach the young pups this stuff. With checkers, I move, I jump, and I get crowned when I reach the other side. Just like Heaven." He pointed his index finger and circled it around the board. "I get enough kings, I set you up, trap you, wipe the board with you, and like normal—game over." Gramps stroked his trimmed white beard.

Gramps was now on a roll. "All this having to remember pawns, knights, rooks, and bishops, which direction each moves in, how many spaces they can move when they move . . . I ain't got time for all of that. Then to have a king that's less powerful than his queen? Check and checkmate? Nope, I can't get with that. You know what your problem is, don't you? You don't like me whuppin' up on you like I normally do. You're trying to find somethin' that'll confuse old Gramps. Now is that check or checkmate?"

"No, Gramps. I'm merely trying to help keep you sharp. That's all. Studies show that when you do something new and different, it exercises your brain. You *do* know that your brain is a muscle, so it needs working out just like the rest of your body does."

"Humph!" Gramps said. "If I was any sharper, merely passing by me too closely would cut you." Gramps sensed his grandson had something more on his mind he wanted to talk about other than chess. Gramps leaned forward and placed his elbows on the table as he put his clasped hands underneath his chin. "Okay, so what's going on with you?"

Clarence sat back and became more serious. "Gramps, I'm getting baptized this coming Sunday night. I gave my life to Christ . . . for real this time. It wasn't just going forward to shake a preacher's hand like when I was twelve and my daddy made me do it to get it over with. Do you think you'd care to come and see me be baptized on Sunday?"

A smile crept over the old man's face as he leaned back against his seat. "So you done finally seen the light, huh?"

"Yeah, Gramps. I've finally seen the light. And I'm not running from the Lord anymore. Something happened to me on Sunday. I can't explain everything about it. But I know that the same man that walked into that building is not the same man that walked out. Something changed on the inside of me; it was an inside job. *I* see a difference."

The old man nodded. "Oh, you preaching to the choir now. I understand exactly how you feel. I ran from the Lord for a long time myself, both physically and figuratively." Gramps readjusted his slender body more comfortably. "I know your mama is happy about all of this. My baby girl has been doing some kind of praying for you, yes she has. And knowing your daddy like I do, I'm sure he acted like the father of the biblical Prodigal Son who finally returned home after wallowing for a time in a pigsty."

"Mom is *too* excited. She kept grabbing my face and pressing it in like she used to when I was a little boy. Like she wanted to be certain that I was really real—that it was actually me she was talking to and not some dream or figment of her imagination. Now Dad, on the other hand, probably would have been happy had I done this at *his* church."

Gramps leaned in. "Hold up there, whippersnapper. You mean to tell me you were somewhere else when this miraculous conversion occurred? You telling me this didn't take place at your daddy's church?"

"No, Gramps. It didn't happen at my daddy's church."

"Well, look out below! I'm sure *that* went over like a boulder falling off a tall building in New York City during lunchtime."

"You know my daddy."

"Yeah. Me, of all people, knows your daddy. Not one of my favorite folks in the world, that's for sure. No need in me trying to pretend he and I are bosom buddies, especially not after the way he treated my daughter. But Clarence, your father did give us you and your older brother, Knowledge. So I don't count him being in her life *all* bad."

Clarence tried to force a smile. "I told him about me being saved and about my scheduled baptism for Sunday. I asked him to come."

Gramps scratched his head. "You don't even have to tell how *that* conversation went. To him, you getting saved—and in another preacher's house at that—had to be the ultimate open-handed slap to his face. In his super-religious eyes, you are officially and publicly humiliating him. And everybody who's anybody knows your father loves the spotlight and equally detests being disgraced—intentional, accidental, or otherwise."

"That's the part of this that I don't understand. The greater point should be that I've repented of my sins and that I'm changing my ways. What difference does it make where it happened and with whom, as long as it happened? Daddy took it like I was deliberately trying to make him look bad . . . like I was purposely trying to embarrass him by getting saved under another pastor's leadership instead of his. But I heard God speak to my heart just as clearly. And in that moment, I knew I had to move right then and there. I realized where I end up spending my eternity depended on my receiving Jesus."

Gramps picked up his bishop's piece off the chess-board and held it up. He began to make air circles with it. "Are you following what God is telling you to do?" he asked.

"Yes, sir."

"Then Clarence Eugene Walker, in the end, that's all that really matters." Gramps set the bishop back in the same spot he'd picked it up from with a deliberate thud. "Marshall Walker ain't got no Heaven nor a Hell to put nobody in. 'Cause the Lord knows, if he had, I'da been in need of an eternal air conditioner ages ago. In fact, on more than a few occasions Marshall has flat-out told me which of the two places I could go, and believe me, it wasn't Heaven. But"—Gramps smiled—"as you can clearly see, I ignored both him and his hearty request. That's what *you* gonna have to do if your father is both-ering you about this. Don't let him get you off track, you hear?" Gramps struggled somewhat as he made his way to his feet with slight assistance from his grandson.

"I'm all right," Gramps said, asserting his indepen-dence to get up without help. "I've told you I can stand up fine. It just takes me a little longer to get my motor started, that's all. Eventually, I get it going, then watch out." He looked at Clarence, now shaking his head and grinning. Gramps nodded. "You can come pick me up Sunday evening," Gramps said as they left the activity room of the nursing home that he, for a year now, had called home. "If the Lord be willing and the creek don't rise, I'll be here waiting on you. There's nothing I'd love more than to see you be baptized." Gramps beamed.

They walked to Gramps's room. Inside, Gramps started grinning like a Cheshire cat as he looked down at Clarence's attaché case. "So, did you bring my stuff? I don't want you conveniently leaving here without giving it to me. I might be old, but as I just told you, my mind is still sharp. I ain't forgot, in case you're counting on me forgetting."

"Gramps, you and I both know I shouldn't be doing this."

"Boy, what did I tell you? I'm grown . . . past grown in case you've failed to notice. Now, did you bring my stuff in that fancy case of yours or not?" Gramps gingerly sat in the tan leather recliner with the built-in massager that his daughter Zenobia had given him Father's Day. He reached over and turned on the blue retro-styled radio, a modern-day replica of a 1950s automobile engine, that sat on his dresser. "Stand by Me" by Ben E. King was playing. Gramps closed his washed-out brown eyes and began to sway as he softly sang—his voice as strong as when he was twenty and just as smooth and calming as milk chocolate. There was no question where Clarence had inherited his singing voice.

"Now that's some real singing right there," Gramps said as the song trailed off. "Ben E. King, Nat King Cole, Otis Redding, Sam Cooke, Mahalia Jackson, Bessie Smith, Josephine Baker, Billie Holiday, Sarah Vaughan, Marvin Gaye, Aretha Franklin, Frankie, Ella, and Lena. And those are just a fraction of some of the greats of my time." Gramps held out a hand to let Clarence know he was still waiting on his "stuff."

Clarence opened his black case. "Gramps, we have some great singers in our time, too. Stevie Wonder,

Michael Jackson, Patti LaBelle, Janet Jackson, Beyoncé, Mariah Carey, Alicia Keys, Vickie Winans, Tramaine Hawkins, goodness! Smokie, Donnie, Kirk, Yolanda, Babyface, Raheem, Whitney, Celine . . . don't get me started." Clarence pulled out a blue, insulated lunchbox. "Then there are groups like Earth, Wind and Fire and En Vogue, who I hear are back." Clarence handed the lunchbox to Gramps. "Here. But I want to go on record that I don't feel right about this. I just want you to know."

Gramps unzipped the lunchbox, looked inside, and began to grin as he pulled out its contents as though the wrong move might cause it to explode. "Ah," he said, placing the still-warm, wax-papered-wrapped item up to his nose. He inhaled slowly and deeply, then exhaled with a sound of delight. The smoky aroma escaped into the room. "Just the way I like it, wax paper and all."

Clarence nodded. "Yeah, three rib bones with extra barbecue sauce, the sweet not vinegar kind, between two slices of white bread, wrapped in your favorite BBQ joint's signature paper." Clarence shook his head. "You *know* you're not supposed to have that."

"Yeah, well, you just make sure you keep your mouth closed about this. Don't tell your mother and we'll be fine. She's the only one trying to keep me from my barbecue rib sandwiches. Like I got these teeth, which incidentally cost a pretty penny, merely for show. Waste not, want not—I'm putting these bad boys to work." He clacked his teeth together. "You're a good grandson, Clarence. You really are. Now sing that song I love."

"You mean the one by Douglas Miller? 'My Soul Has Been Anchored'?"

"Yeah, that's the one." Gramps placed the sandwich on the dresser and handed the now-empty lunchbox back to Clarence.

Clarence put the lunchbox back in his attaché case, then began to sing—holding back his full voice so as not to disturb any neighboring or passing residents of the home.

Gramps closed his eyes briefly as he seemed to take in every note and every word with a metronome-like tick-tock of his head. When Clarence sang the final note, Gramps opened his teary eyes and nodded. "Yes," he said, pumping an open hand upward, "*my* soul's been anchored"—he swung a fisted hand while smiling—"in the Lord!"

Clarence nodded, hugged his grandfather, told him that he loved him, then left.

Chapter 2

If thieves came to thee, if robbers by night, (how art thou cut off!) would they not have stolen till they had enough? if the grape gatherers came to thee, would they not leave some grapes?

—Obadiah 1:5

Twenty-seven-year-old Gabrielle Mercedes and thirty-year-old Zachary Wayne Morgan were at Gabrielle's house in the kitchen cooking fajitas. They'd gone to a highly acclaimed play Sunday night and had a wonderful time. Few Broadway plays made their way to Birmingham, Alabama, whenever those plays happened to travel outside New York. Afterward, Zachary surprised Gabrielle with tickets to "The Color Purple," scheduled for the BJCC Concert Hall in October. Gabrielle couldn't believe she was finally going to get to see this live Broadway hit, after all of these years of wanting to.

The doorbell rang. Gabrielle glanced at the digital clock on the stove. "I wonder who that could be." She lowered the heat on the gas stove to simmer and rinsed her hands at the sink, drying them on the large dish towel she kept draped across the handle of the oven door for just that purpose.

"I got it," Zachary said, turning the heat back to medium as he took over stirring the rectangular-cut strips of marinated steak in the large cast-iron skillet, with plans to add fresh sliced red, yellow, and orange sweet peppers and red onions prior to finishing it, in order to maintain the vegetables' firmness. The doorbell rang again, this time repeatedly.

When Gabrielle saw who was standing there pressing the doorbell, she practically yanked her front door open.

"Well, it took you long enough," Aunt Cee-Cee said as she fanned her face with her right hand and stepped inside. "You must have been in the bathroom or something."

Cecelia Murphy was Gabrielle's aunt on her father's side. She'd taken Gabrielle in—raised her since she was three (close to four) years old after her mother was killed and her father convicted of her murder and sentenced to twenty-five years in prison.

"No. But I *was* busy. I have company in case you didn't notice the car parked outside when you pulled up," Gabrielle said, trying hard not to show her own frustration.

"You mean that black, two thousand and something Lincoln Town Car? I just thought you'd bought yourself another vehicle." Aunt Cee-Cee tilted her head back, nose up. "What's that I smell? Smells like it's coming from the kitchen?" She started walking in the direction of the scent. "It smells like someone's sauteéing onions and peppers."

"We're making fajitas," Gabrielle said, still holding the open door since she hadn't asked her aunt to come in. She was now hurriedly trying to figure out what she needed to do to lure her aunt back toward her and out the door.

"Well, it smells to me like I have fantastic timing," Aunt Cee-Cee said as she continued, undeterred, toward the kitchen. Gabrielle closed the front door and hurried to catch up with her now uninvited, unwelcome, and undeniably unpredictable guest.

"Seriously, Aunt Cee-Cee, this really isn't a good time right now—"

Aunt Cee-Cee stepped into the kitchen and saw Zachary just as he was turning off the stove and lifting up the large cast-iron skillet. He raked a little of the mixture of steak, onions, and colored peppers onto a flat, flour tortilla.

"Well, hello there," Aunt Cee-Cee said as she walked toward Zachary. "Well, well, aren't you something? You must be the Handsome Chef." She let out a slight chuckle. "There's the Iron Chef. So I can only conclude you *have to be* the Handsome Chef who makes house calls." She scanned him from his head to his chest as she smiled.

Zachary looked at Gabrielle, who now stood next to the frumpy-looking visitor.

Zachary set the skillet back down on the stove. "No, but I thank you for the compliment. I'm Gabrielle's friend, Zachary Morgan."

"I'm Cecelia Murphy"—she extended a hand—"Gabrielle's aunt. But everybody calls me Cee-Cee."

Zachary quickly wiped his hand on the towel and shook Aunt Cee-Cee's outstretched hand. "All right then, Cee-Cee. It's a pleasure to meet you."

"Ah, that's what you say now. Give it some time." Aunt Cee-Cee laughed, then hopped up on a bar stool at the kitchen counter. "That sure does look good. I'm *starving*. Gabrielle, why don't you fix me one of those things Zachary's making? Oh, and can you get me something cold to drink? I need to wet my throat." She fanned her face again with her hand. "You wouldn't happen to have a beer or wine cooler around here, would you?"

"No, I wouldn't." Gabrielle's response was stern and cold.

"I would be glad to go and get you something,"

Zachary said, obviously wanting to make a good first, impression. "There's a Quik Mart about five miles from here—"

"You don't have to do that," Gabrielle said before Zachary could finish his sentence. "I have something to drink in the refrigerator. She can drink one of those." Gabrielle turned and looked squarely at Aunt Cee-Cee. "Besides, she'll not be staying long enough for you to go get anything and make it back."

Aunt Cee-Cee glared at Gabrielle only briefly before she broke her stare with a warm (though obviously phony) smile. "Gabrielle's right. I won't be here that long. So"—Aunt Cee-Cee turned her attention back to Zachary—"are the two of you dating?"

Neither Gabrielle nor Zachary answered.

"I said are you two dating?"

"Yes," Zachary said when he realized Gabrielle wasn't planning on answering the question. "But we're actually calling it courting." He couldn't hold back his own blush.

"Courting? Oh, how cute! You don't hear that word much these days. I suppose it's better than wham, bam, thank you, ma'am." Aunt Cee-Cee slid down off the bar stool and sat in a chair at the glass-top kitchen table. She looked at Gabrielle, her way of letting her niece know that she was still waiting on both her food and something to drink.

"Gabrielle is a special woman. We want to do things right," Zachary said. He looked at Gabrielle once more, who still hadn't moved to get her aunt a plate or anything to drink.

"So, Mister Handsome Chef, what do you do for a living?"

"I'm a d—"

"Aunt Cee-Cee, why don't I fix your fajita to go?" Gabrielle promptly went and picked up the plate with the fajita Zachary had already begun making.

Aunt Cee-Cee fastened her gaze on Gabrielle like a laser. "Because I'm not *going* yet. And honestly, the quicker I get something to eat, the quicker I'll get *out* of here. I'm hungry, and I don't care to eat while I drive. Like texting, it's dangerous to drive and eat. In fact, there should be a law against both." Aunt Cee-Cee softened her face with a smile.

After rinsing her hands, Gabrielle hurried to finish rolling the fajita for her aunt.

"Now," Aunt Cee-Cee said, turning her full attention once more toward Zachary. "You were saying. What is it you do for a living? Because I hope you know I wouldn't want my niece, who's like a daughter to me . . . raised her myself, hanging out with no scrub. That's what they call a guy without a job who lives off others, right? A scrub."

Zachary laughed a little. "Well, you know, you could call me a scrub."

Aunt Cee-Cee pulled her body back and placed her right hand over her heart.

"Hold up," Zachary said with a chuckle. "Before you conclude I'm not good enough for your niece, allow me to clarify. I'm a doctor. So technically speaking, in my line of work, I wash my hands a lot, a whole lot, i.e., making me somewhat of a scrub."

"A doctor." Aunt Cee-Cee's words were flirty and sweet. "Oh, my goodness. Mercy me. My Gabrielle is courting a *doctor*, a real doctor. Well, isn't that something." She smiled at Gabrielle before turning back to Zachary. "What type of doctor are you?"

"A burn specialist. I specialize mainly in burn victims, although lately I've been spending my share of time equally in the emergency room when I've been needed."

"A multitasker," Aunt Cee-Cee said. "Gabrielle, why haven't you called and told any of us that you're *courting a doctor*?"

Gabrielle set the plate with the fajita and a can of Pepsi down in front of her aunt. "The last few times I've called, you haven't taken or returned my calls," Gabrielle said.

Aunt Cee-Cee eyed the can. "You got Coca-Cola instead of Pepsi? I prefer Coke."

"All I have is Pepsi. But I can give you water if you'd prefer that. Water is wet." Gabrielle smiled, knowing full well her aunt never drank water, not even with medicine.

"Oh, no. Pepsi is fine. I was just asking. I think somewhere in the Bible it says we don't have because we don't ask." Aunt Cee-Cee picked up her fajita and took a cautious bite. "This is really good," she said. "Handsome Chef, you're a great cook. The meat is so tender and moist and has such a marvelous flavor." She took a bigger bite.

"Actually, Gabrielle did all the work. The tenderness and taste is from the marinade. Lime juice breaks down the meat to make it tender and give it that flavor. She marinated it overnight. I merely stirred and added the vegetables when she went to open the door."

"I'm sure you're giving Gabrielle way too much credit. I'm willing to bet you did a lot more than you're letting on. The peppers and onions are perfect." She took another bite, then opened her can of soda. A hissing sound escaped when the cap popped. "Aren't you two going to eat before it gets cold? It's really delicious." She smacked as she spoke.

Gabrielle was about to say something when Zachary moved over to her, put his arm around her shoulders, and pulled her in close. "We *like* ours cold," he said.

"Suit yourself," Aunt Cee-Cee said. When she finished that one, she asked for another. She chatted on about how terrible things were at their house financially and her not knowing what they were going to do as she woofed down a third fajita. She then asked for yet another one. "Oh, but could you wrap that one up for me as a to-go?" she said. "Those are *so* good." She licked her fingers, then wiped her mouth with a napkin.

Both Gabrielle and Zachary looked at what remained in the skillet. Originally, there had been enough for them to have *at least* two full fajitas each. Aunt Cee-Cee had now eaten three and was asking for one more to take home with her. If they made her the one she was asking for now, there would only be enough left for one of them. Gabrielle made the last two fajitas and gave them both to her aunt.

"Oh, aren't you the sweetest thing!" Aunt Cee-Cee said when Gabrielle handed her the wrapped fajitas. "Would you mind putting them in a bag for me? And if it's not too much to ask, would you put two cans of sodas in the bag as well? Your Uncle Bubba will need something to wash his fajita down with." Aunt Cee-Cee stood up as she waited on Gabrielle to finish.

Gabrielle put the fajitas and drinks in a grocery bag and walked her to the door.

"I'll call you later tonight," Aunt Cee-Cee said. Then she whispered, "Is the doctor spending the night tonight?"

"No, Aunt Cee-Cee. We won't be doing things like that. There'll be none of that."

"You mean he's not spending the night *right* now. But you don't mean you're not planning on doing *anything* with that man until or unless you get married, now, do you?"

"You mean sex before marriage . . . fornicating?"

"Well, you don't have to be so graphic with it. But yes, that's exactly what I mean. Listen, honey, you don't need to let a man like him get away. That's a real catch you have in there." She pointed her head in the direction of the kitchen.

"Aunt Cee-Cee, I'm a Christian now. I told you that. I gave my life to the Lord. God frowns on fornication. Zachary and I agreed we want to do things God's way, and only His way. And that means keeping ourselves pure until we're married to *whom*ever."

Aunt Cee-Cee started laughing. It sounded more like an animal in severe pain than human. "Yeah, well, trust me: I know plenty of Christians, and being a Christian doesn't seem to be stopping most of them from fornicating *or* committing adultery. I'll tell you this: You'd better take care of that man and his needs or he'll find someone who will. Take it from Aunt Cee-Cee. I know how men can be. Sure, in the beginning they'll tell you they're in total agreement about something like being chaste. But men are wired totally different from women. Men don't need as much emotional bonding as we do to move to the next level. That man is tall, light-skinned enough, handsome, can cook, or at least will pick up a spoon and help out, he has a job, *and* he's a doctor to boot. Oh, you'd *better* at least let him sample the cake batter and not have to wait for the baked cake."

"Good night, Aunt Cee-Cee." Gabrielle opened the front door.

"I'm going to call you either later tonight or tomorrow. Better yet, why don't you just call me when you're free so I won't interrupt anything. You'd best heed what I just said. Call me, now. I have something I *desperately* need to talk to you about. It's important, so don't take long in getting back with me. It can't wait any longer than a day."

Gabrielle mustered up one more smile. "Good night," she said.

After Aunt Cee-Cee left, Gabrielle closed the door. She stood there for a few minutes, her forehead resting softly on the door as she quietly listened for her aunt's car to crank. Hearing the car drive away, she exhaled slowly.

"Wow, what a character," Zachary said.

Jarred slightly by Zachary's presence, Gabrielle turned around and forced herself to smile yet again. "Oh, you don't *even* know the *half* of it."

"Just from those thirty-five minutes, I believe I received a pretty good introduction," Zachary said. "So . . . where would you like to go eat?"

Gabrielle put her hands up to her face to compose herself, then took them down. "I'm so sorry. I can't believe she did that. Wait a minute; yes, I can. That's classic Aunt Cee-Cee. And the funny part is, she has no idea that what she just did was totally wrong or completely selfish. No idea at all."

"Oh, she knows," Zachary said. "I get the distinct feeling Aunt Cee-Cee knows *exactly* what she's doing. *Exactly*."

If you enjoyed *If Memory Serves*, don't miss Michelle Stimpson's new book,

LAST TEMPTATION

Coming in November 2010 from Dafina Books

Here's an excerpt . . .

Chapter 1

Quinn's proposal was not a big surprise. Actually, it was one of those "it's about time" moments. We'd been dating for almost eighteen months and that karat was long overdue, in my book. I believe in taking my time, but my body doesn't. Any woman can be celibate when she's single, but throw a six-foot-tall, chocolate-brown brother with a sharp goatee *and* a good job in the mix . . . hmph, a sister is liable to get all shook up. Yes, Quinn was a wonderful man who loved the Lord, loved me, and treated my eight-year-old son, Eric, like his own. The faith was there, the love was there, the Lord was there. But I won't lie—my flesh was so weak for Quinn I thought I was gonna have to go on eBay and find me a chastity belt.

So when he finally popped the question by calling me out and proposing on stage after the local college's production of *A Raisin in the Sun* (which he directed), I breathed a sigh of relief. Finally, the wait was over. A burden had been lifted from my shoulders and a new door had opened in my life.

Don't get me wrong: the single life was good while it lasted. There's nothing like being able to do what you want to do, when you want to do it, how you want to do it. But that gets old after a while—thirty-four years, in my case. I suppose if my best friend, LaShondra, were still single, it wouldn't be so bad. And if Deniessa, my friend and former coworker, hadn't married that good and throwed-off Jamal last year, I would at least have someone to watch *The Best Man* with. Well, now it was my turn to join the ranks of married women and start the next chapter in my life. *Thank You, Lord.*

The first person I called was LaShondra. She and I had been through thick and thin, good and bad, even black and white since she ran off and married a white man. Let me take that back. She didn't "run off," but her husband *is* white and I was not expecting my girl to cross that line. I ain't hatin', though. Stelson is good people. It took some getting used to, but I'm over it now.

I hooked my cell phone up to the Bluetooth and selected her name from the radio display. "Hey, girl," I squealed when she answered the phone, "we've got a wedding on the way!"

LaShondra screamed, "He finally did it?"

"Yes, girl," I said with a big exhale. "We've set a date and everything—the first Saturday in June."

"Congratulations! Ooh—we've got, what, four months to pull this off—in June?" I knew LaShondra was already planning things out in her head. "You told your momma yet? You called the church yet?"

"No, I called you first, girl. You know I have to get your blessing."

"Pulleeze," she laughed, "you know I'm all for it. Quinn is a good man. I've always liked him. He's a Christian, he treats you well, he's good with Eric. What's there to discuss?"

I sighed. "I guess I just had to ask you for the record, so if something goes wrong I can be like, 'You da one who tole me to marry him!'"

"Don't even talk like that, Peaches. What God has

joined together, let no man—or Peaches—put asunder. This is God's doing and you know it. Who else could match you up with the one man in the world who could get past your mouth and your attitude to find the real you?"

"I do not have an attitude!" I screamed. The woman in the next car gave me a confused look. I ignored her.

"Is this Patricia Miller I'm talking to? Oh, wait, I'm sorry. This must be the new and improved Patricia *Robertson*. My bad."

We both laughed at her enunciation of my soon-to-be last name. We ended the conversation with plans to meet Saturday and discuss the happy, snappy wedding. My second call was to my mother, who almost started speaking in tongues. "Oh, my baby! Finally! The Lord blessed you with a husband and Eric with a father!"

"Momma, Eric has a father," I reminded her. Raphael wouldn't win any father of the year awards, but he'd been spending more time with our son and he was finally caught up on child support. I had to give him some kind of credit even though I suspected his fiancée, Cheryl, had shamed him in to doing right by his child.

Next, I called Deniessa. I expected her to be ecstatic, but her response was more dramatic than anything. She busted out crying. I mean, boo-hooing. "Oh, Peaches, I just hope your marriage is a million times better than mine. I want the best for you, girl. Somebody gotta be happy, you know?"

Okay, what am I supposed to say to that—better you sad than me? "Girl, what's *really* going on? Why are you trippin'?"

She pulled in a nasty snot-filled sniff that almost made me disconnect her from my phone. "Go blow your nose!" I said.

"I'm sorry," she apologized. "Marriage is so hard. People just don't understand how hard it can be."

I imagine it *is* hard when you're married to a fool. *Lord, don't let me say that.* I was tired of dealing with Deniessa's drama, but I couldn't say so. After all, I was one of the main ones cheering her down the aisle. Matter of fact, I was cheering everybody down the aisle, hoping to keep the line moving so it would be my turn soon.

I searched my mind for one of those good old standby Christian clichés to soothe her pain. All I could come up with was, "Prayer changes things." I said it in an old, deep, soulful tone—like Sofia in *The Color Purple* would say it—for effect.

Deniessa didn't buy it. "Not if the person you're praying for doesn't *want* to change."

I was not in the mood to go down that road with her. It always led back around to point A: she married someone she had been living with for three years. The only reason he even asked her to marry him was because she gave him an ultimatum. I can't blame Jamal—he knew which side his bread was buttered on. He had to do *something* because it gets cold out there on them streets, I hear.

"Girl, I'll be praying for you. How about me, you, and LaShondra get together this weekend and do one of our girls' movie nights?" I offered. I knew it was a long shot—those two had all but kicked girls' nights to the curb since they jumped the broom.

She sniffed again. "I don't know. I have to see. Jamal is using my car right now."

"Is he working a night shift?" I asked.

"No. He still hasn't found anything yet. But he might need the car Saturday night. I just have to ask."

The words flew straight from my brain out of my mouth before I could catch them. "How you gotta ask to use your own car if he ain't got no job?" I could have bopped myself on the head for fueling the hot mess already flaming in their marriage.

"You tell me." She could only laugh at herself.

I shook my head. "I gotta go, girl. Forgive me for adding my two cents to y'all's business. Let me know if you want to come Saturday night. I'll come pick you up if you need me to. I'm sure LaShondra won't mind taking you home."

"Thank you," she said. "I'll let you know."

I ended the call with Deniessa but continued the conversation with myself and my Father. "Lord, if I *ever* let Quinn use me like that, just take me on home to glory."

I talked myself all the way to Raphael's house to pick up Eric. By the time I got there, I had strengthened my resolve not to lose myself in my husband like I had seen so many married women do in my last, say, fifteen years of marrying off friends and relatives. It's like something clicks in their heads and they lose all sense of identity, all sense of independence, sometimes all sense, *period*.

I had to give it to my girl, LaShondra—she kept moving up in the school district and trying to get where she wanted to be even after she got married. She kept her house, she rents it out. The only thing she didn't keep, which surprised me, was her last name.

"It's not like Smith is a distinctive last name," she had said.

"Neither is Brown! But Smith-Brown—now *that* sounds important."

"Sounds like a law firm," she had giggled.

"Like I said—important. LaShondra Smith-Brown. She don't play. She will sue your behind any day." I'd acted it out as though on a low-budget commercial. She had laughed at me in one of those condescending you-wouldn't-understand-because-you're-not-married laughs. I just rolled my eyes at her. Nonetheless, she dropped the Smith and went straight to Brown. Something I sure wasn't about to do, no matter how plain-Jane Miller is for a last name.

Still high off my list of dos and don'ts, I rang Raphael's doorbell and waited patiently for either Raphael or Cheryl to answer the door of their one-story home in one of the older, more crime-ridden areas of Dallas. I had some reservations about letting Eric spend the weekend with his father in this neighborhood, but once somebody broke into my Mercedes in broad open daylight at my condo, I said whatever. Besides, I figured Eric could use a little "hood" in his life. There's nothing like a good game of baseball in the hood with first base a shoe, second base somebody's car, third base a fire hydrant, and home plate a flattened plastic milk jug, to prove that you can be happy with next to nothing.

Raphael opened the door and Eric squeezed past his father's frame to give me a tight hug. "Hey, son," I said as I rubbed my hand across his head. Apparently, Raphael had taken him to get a haircut—without being asked! That was one for the record books.

"Uh," Raphael asked, "is that a ring on your finger?"

"Yes, it is," I beamed, making note of the mixed expression on Raphael's face. I couldn't tell if he was about to congratulate me or say something sarcastic, so I gave Eric orders to get in the car.

"I'm getting married in June to Quinn. You met him at Eric's school awards ceremony," I reminded him.

Raphael nodded. "Yeah, I remember him. June? Why so soon?" he asked, crossing his arms and looking down from his towering stance. If I could get up on a stool, I might be able to prove he was balding. The hard years of drinking and womanizing had caused him to age quickly. Still, he was good-looking and I truly hoped that our son would grow up to be as handsome as his father.

"Because we're in love," I replied. "And we're not getting any younger."

Then came his true concern. "You're not planning to take my son away from me, are you?"

I rolled my eyes in disbelief. "You know me better than that."

He let his defenses fall to his side along with his arms. Something in me said, "Awww . . . he loves our son. I almost felt sorry for the poor chap (*bless his sorry heart*). But it had taken me eight long years, several hours on hold for the attorney general's office, and countless prayers to get Raphael right where I wanted him and Eric needed him. This was *my* victory, not Raphael's.

"Well, congratulations," he said.

"Thank you."

And loud silence transpired. I gave Raphael a quick smile before saying, "Good-bye."

His lips said, "Good-bye," but I could tell that he wanted to say something more. Finally, he stepped outside of his house, closed the door behind him, and said softly, "Quinn is a lucky man."

You could have bought me for a quarter.

Raphael turned and went back into the house.

"Thank you?" I whispered after he was long gone.

I drove home halfway listening to my son talk about his weekend, and halfway wondering what on earth had gotten into one Mr. Raphael Sadiq Lewis. Well, I suppose I *was* looking extra nice in my form-fitting skinny jeans and my red stretchy button-down blouse. And I had just gotten my short do shampooed and flat-ironed, not to mention my freshly waxed eyebrows. I wasn't much for makeup because my skin turned into a pimple factory with most foundations. My deep brown skin tone held its own and fell into a nice glow after five. It was well after five so I knew I had to be looking good.

Too bad for Raphael. He could have had anything he wanted from me, once upon a time.

I was all Quinn's now.

Chapter 2

I couldn't go anywhere in the building Monday without people congratulating me on the engagement. I must have gotten fifty e-mails from people: Best wishes! God bless your union! All kinds of mess from people who barely spoke to me at work. Who knew that getting engaged would suddenly make me a celebrity at Northcomp?

By ten o'clock, I had to call LaShondra and ask a favor. "Could you please call Stelson and ask him what is the big deal with white people and engagements?"

"It's not a white thing, Peaches. They're just happy for you."

"No, no, no. This is a white thing, I'm telling you. Black folk don't get this excited over an engagement. I'm thirty-four and I've already got a child. I ain't no Cinderella."

"Hmmm," LaShondra thought out loud, "have they been asking to see the ring?"

"Some of them have, but not too many."

"Have they asked to see his picture? You know, when Stelson and I were engaged, people always wanted to see his picture to confirm that I was marrying a white man," she recalled.

"Nobody here thinks I would marry a white man," I replied in straight, loud monotone.

"Anyway!"

That's when I saw it. After wading through the numerous e-mail messages from employees whose names barely rang bells, I finally found the e-mail message from our company's CEO, George Hampton, which explained everything. I read it out loud to LaShondra. "Due to recent spikes in the price of gasoline, a sharp decline in sales, and a less-than-desirable review of productivity, we have determined that Northcomp must make some cutbacks in order to remain a viable competitor for the technological dollar. The personnel office, led by Patricia Miller, in conjunction with our consultants, The Yancey Group, will be working to review assignments, job descriptions, and productivity goals. We anticipate these reviews will result in early retirement offers and reduced demand for human resources. We understand that these changes present a difficult but necessary transition for Northcomp, and we look forward to solutions that are least disruptive for our company and our employees."

"Wow," LaShondra said, "you've got a tough job ahead of you."

"This is crazy!" I hollered.

"What's the problem?" LaShondra asked. I had to forgive her nonprofit world ignorance. Since she was a principal in a public school, her politics were different from mine.

"That man just sent out an e-mail saying that Patricia Miller is going to be firing folks!"

LaShondra whined, "That's not what he said, Peaches."

"He might as well have! Don't you see, LaShondra, he's trying to make me out to be the executioner! He's trying to paint me as the bad guy!"

"The consultants will have input," she tried to reason.

I huffed one good time. "The consultants will be good and gone after the smoke clears. Half these consultant folks don't know what they're doing. They don't know our company—they're just paid to agree with me. This is a corporate nightmare!"

There was a gentle rap on my door and a woman that I remembered vaguely from a past interview stuck her head into my office. "Hold on LaShondra," I said as I acknowledged this unplanned visitor.

"I just wanted to say congratulations—"

"I'm busy right now," I said as I shooed her out with my hand. I just couldn't take the fakeness anymore. The woman's face was suddenly painted with disappointment as she ducked back and closed the door. My blinds were open enough for me to see her stand outside my door for a moment and collect herself. Was she . . . crying? Yes, she was!

"LaShondra," I whispered, "this woman is crying outside of my office."

"What? Why?"

"She's crying because I wouldn't let her come in here and give me her bogus congratulations."

LaShondra fussed, "Maybe she really meant it."

"I'm gonna hang up the phone now, LaShondra. I'll call you later."

"Later, alligator. And stop being so mean."

I buzzed my secretary, Teresa, and told her not to let anyone else in my office for chit-chat purposes. Next, I called George and let him know that I felt—what did I say?—"awkward" about the wording in his e-mail.

George tried to act like he didn't understand my concern. "Patricia, I don't think the message will come across the way you've interpreted it." Yeah, right. Hampton informed me that if we could convince several of the senior employees to take early retirement, we would probably only have to release hourly employees who had been with the company less than two years. "Honestly, this is really more a precautionary measure than anything else."

I still didn't appreciate him making it seem like I was the mad black woman running around with the ax while he was the innocent VP who couldn't be blamed for anyone's demise.

My third call was to the Yancey people to see when they planned to come help me figure out this whole mess. I was on hold so long with their answering service, I swear—there is only one Yancey. There is no group. It's just one old man who probably plays golf with Hampton on Saturday mornings who agreed to put his name on a few forms so that Hampton could go before the board pushing his own recommendations backed by this nitwit nonexistent Yancey Group.

Okay, my attitude was bad that morning. Really bad. So when Quinn called and said he wanted to talk to me over lunch, I was not feeling him. "Baby, I really have a lot going on here today."

"I really need to talk to you," he reiterated. I heard a twang of sincerity in his voice, so I agreed to meet him at the Chili's nearest Northcomp. No matter what he had to say, I didn't have much time to hear it. I needed to get back to work and begin reviewing employees' files as soon as possible.

My man is so sexy in dark colors. He almost made me forget about all my troubles when he walked into the restaurant wearing black slacks and a deep indigo Polo shirt pressed to a "tee." I motioned for Quinn to join me at a small booth and took a moment to appreciate his confident strut. As an experienced man-watcher, I caught the glances of several women in the restaurant as they watched him, too.

He kissed me on the cheek before sitting down across from me. "You look beautiful."

"Thanks, babe. I saw an old lady in red checking you out," I teased him.

He smiled. "Can't do nothin' for her."

"I know that's right," I laughed. I took a glance at my watch and asked, "So what's up?"

He fidgeted for a moment, which was not really in his character. His gaze drifted to the ceramic tiles covering our table. I knew better than to think he'd had second thoughts about his proposal, so I assured him, "Whatever it is, we'll get through it."

"You think we can get through to Philadelphia?" he blurted out.

I squinted my eyes and cocked my head to the side like, What you talkin' 'bout, Willis?"

He continued. "I just got the opportunity of a lifetime, Peaches. They want me to transfer to Philadelphia and head up the marketing department for the Northeast region."

Quinn was all smiles. I was all shocked.

"What do you think, baby? You're always complaining about the Texas heat. Plus, Philly is only a few hours from New York. I could really get into the theaters there, baby. What do you think?"

"Everything is baby, I see," I snapped at him, raising an eyebrow.

"Peaches, I've worked long and hard for this, and I'm really looking forward to starting this new life with you. Just so happens we'll be doing it in Philadelphia, that's all. Oh, and did I mention the raise is all that!"

"Have you looked at the cost of living in Philadelphia versus Dallas?" I really didn't mean to burst his bubble, but how dare he just spring this on me!

"Even with the cost of living increase, it's more than worth it," he tried his best to make it sound appealing.

Philadelphia, Lord? "I don't know, Quinn." I took a sip of the water that seemed to have suddenly appeared at my table. I was so taken aback, I don't even remember a waiter approaching our table. "I can't just up and move to Philadelphia with you."

"You're making it sound like we just met. I'm your fiancé, Peaches, soon to be your husband. And this is a great opportunity for me, you, and Eric. You wouldn't have to work right away. You could take a few years off. Have the baby right away if you want to," he suggested.

Where did that come from? We'd discussed having children and I was all for it, once we had settled into our marriage which, I figured, would be a good three or four years down the line. Quinn was trying to switch up everything at the last minute. "I don't want to be no stay-at-home mom," I retorted. "I like working." Never mind the fact that my job was not the happiest place right now.

Quinn started saying something else about me taking some time off, maybe going back to school, but I wasn't hearing him. My mind was thinking about Eric now. About Raphael. I had all but promised Raphael I wouldn't try to take his son away. Philadelphia was definitely *away*. "I can't go, Quinn."

The vein in Quinn's forehead thickened as he ground his teeth and looked down at the menu. I knew that look all too well. I laughed slightly. "You've already committed to this, haven't you?"

He looked up from the menu for a moment, then back down.

That was all I needed to see. "How can you just unilaterally make a decision about *my* life?"

"It's *our* lives," he stressed. "I've prayed about it and I believe it's the right move for us."

The waiter returned to our table and took our orders. My appetite was gone, but I needed to eat a salad, so I did what was best. Quinn ordered a lunch portion of chicken and pasta combo. He must have lost most of his appetite, too. I stewed over my anger as we waited for our food to arrive. When our plates were set in front of us, Quinn held out his hands in our familiar gesture for prayer. I looked him upside his head and rolled my eyes to a close.

"Lord, we thank You for this food we're about to receive. Thank You for bringing this wonderful woman into my life. Father, guide us in making decisions that glorify You in this marriage and this family. In Jesus' name we pray, amen."

"Amen." The prayer had caused my anger to subside a notch. In my heart, I wanted to do the right thing—whatever that was. "Quinn, I'm not against this promotion for you. And I'm not against moving to Philadelphia, per se. I've worked hard for my position at Northcomp, too, you know." And I still had $13,000 worth of student loans for that MBA to show for it. "And what about Eric? He's really starting to establish a relationship with his father now."

"I'm not trying to come between Eric and Raphael and I'm not trying to undermine your career. Eric is old enough to fly back to Dallas once a month for his weekend with Raphael, and there are plenty of job opportunities in Philadelphia. Doesn't Northcomp have an office there, too?" Apparently, he really had given this a great deal of thought.

"What about my family? My friends? My church?" I rattled off my secondary list of objections.

"Your family and friends will always be here for you. And there are churches in Philadelpha. We won't be the first couple to move after getting married. People do it all the time. I moved throughout most of my childhood because my dad was in the military," he reminded me.

"Okay, I am not a . . . a *globetrotter* like you. I can't—"

"I can't live my life without you," he stopped my heart with those words.

Suddenly, I wasn't sitting across from some man who was trying to run me. I was sitting across from the love of my life. The man who had erased all my doubts and fears about falling in love. The man who had accepted my son as part of the package without hesitation. He was a godsend, no doubt, and I couldn't imagine my life without him, either. Tears filled my eyes as I sat there utterly exposed before Quinn. He was asking a lot of me, but in light of what he had given me, it was nothing.

I knew this.

But I was afraid. I'd seen women lose everything behind a man—jobs, relationships with family members, houses, cars, hair. I would *never* be that stupid.

I set my elbows on the table and pressed my fingers into my forehead. "How soon would we have to move?"

"I think I can hold them off until the wedding, but we'll need to move soon after."

My stomach churned. I just couldn't see myself doing all this for love. "You should have talked to me before you took the offer, Quinn. I hope this is not an indication of how you plan to do things once we get married."

He gave me that one. "You're right. I just didn't think it would be such a big deal for us to get married and move so I can take better care of you and Eric."

Those were fighting words to me. "Then you obviously don't know me."

"Look, maybe I was wrong. Maybe I shouldn't have accepted without discussing it with you. I have one question, though: do you really think it's best for me to stay at my position here in Dallas and pass up this opportunity because you're afraid to trust?" He called me out.

"This is not about trust!" I exclaimed.

"It *is* about trust. But I'm not going to argue with you." He pulled my hands from my head and held them. "I love you, Peaches. I want to marry you. I want to be a second father to Eric and a great father for our future kids." He stopped, licked his lips, then added, "And I can hardly wait to make love to you."

Oh, he almost broke a sistah down with that one. I had to catch the spit from falling off my bottom lip. *Help, Lord!*

He continued, "I want to grow old with you, serve God with you. Peaches, I want to spend the rest of my life with you. All I'm asking is that you let it begin in Philadelphia. We don't have to stay there forever. It's just a stepping stone right now."

I knew in my spirit that I should have kissed my man and said, "Whatever you want, Big Daddy." But I'm sorry. I could not go out like that. I needed Quinn to understand that I was not going to be the type of wife to ask "how high?" when he said "jump." If I started doing it now, I'd have to do it for the next fifty years. I wanted him to sweat it out for a while, for the record. "Let me think about this some more," I finally said.

"Don't *think* about it, *pray* about it," Quinn suggested.